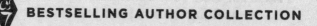
BESTSELLING AUTHOR COLLECTION

In our 2011 Bestselling Author Collection,
Harlequin Books is proud to offer
classic novels from today's superstars
of women's fiction. These authors have
captured the hearts of millions of readers
around the world, and earned their place
on the bestseller lists with every release.

As a bonus, each volume also includes a
full-length novel from a rising star of series
romance. Bestselling authors in their own right,
these talented writers have captured the qualities
Harlequin is famous for—heart-racing passion,
edge-of-your-seat entertainment
and a satisfying happily-ever-after.

Don't miss any of the books in this year's collection!

BESTSELLING AUTHOR COLLECTION

New York Times and *USA TODAY* Bestselling Author

JOAN JOHNSTON

A Wolf in Sheep's Clothing

TORONTO NEW YORK LONDON
AMSTERDAM PARIS SYDNEY HAMBURG
STOCKHOLM ATHENS TOKYO MILAN MADRID
PRAGUE WARSAW BUDAPEST AUCKLAND

Recycling programs
for this product may
not exist in your area.

ISBN-13: 978-0-373-18491-0

A WOLF IN SHEEP'S CLOTHING

Copyright © 2011 by Harlequin Books S.A.

The publisher acknowledges the copyright holders
of the individual works as follows:

A WOLF IN SHEEP'S CLOTHING
Copyright © 1991 by Joan Mertens Johnston

TELL ME YOUR SECRETS...
Copyright © 2006 by Carolyn Hanlon

This edition published by arrangement with Harlequin Books S.A.

For questions and comments about the quality of this book
please contact us at Customer_eCare@Harlequin.ca.

® and TM are trademarks of the publisher. Trademarks indicated with ® are registered in the United States Patent and Trademark Office, the Canadian Trade Marks Office and in other countries.

www.Harlequin.com

Printed in U.S.A.

CONTENTS

A WOLF IN SHEEP'S CLOTHING   7
Joan Johnston

TELL ME YOUR SECRETS...   207
Cara Summers

ACKNOWLEDGMENTS

The Do's and Don'ts for the Western Tenderfoot at the beginning of each chapter come from *The Greenhorn's Guide to the Wooly West* by Gwen Petersen, and are used with permission of the author. I am also indebted to Gwen for the invaluable background information provided in her equally hilarious guide to ranch life, *The Ranch Woman's Manual.* Both books are available from Laffing Cow Press in Cheyenne, Wyoming. I would also like to thank Jim Rolleri of the County Extension Service in Big Timber, Montana, for generously parting with every brochure on sheep ranching he could find in his files. Finally, I would like to thank Jim Overstreet, a banker in Big Timber, Montana, who was kind enough to have lunch with me at The Grand and suggest the sort of financial foibles to which a sheep man can be prone.

A WOLF IN SHEEP'S CLOTHING

New York Times and *USA TODAY* Bestselling Author

Joan Johnston

JOAN JOHNSTON

is a *New York Times* and *USA TODAY* bestselling, award-winning author of forty-nine historical and contemporary novels and novellas. Johnston received a B.A. in theater arts from Jacksonville University, an M.A. in theater from the University of Illinois and graduated with honors from the University of Texas at Austin School of Law. She has been a director of theater, drama critic, college professor and attorney on her way to becoming a full-time author. She lives in Florida and Colorado.

Visit her website at www.joanjohnston.com.

Chapter 1

What do newcomers find abounding in Woolly West towns?
Answer: Quaintness and charm.

Nathan Hazard was mad enough to chew barbed wire. Cyrus Alistair was dead, but even in death the old curmudgeon had managed to thwart Nathan's attempts to buy his land. Cyrus had bequeathed his tiny Montana sheep ranch to a distant relative from Virginia, someone named Harry Alistair. For years that piece of property had been an itch Nathan couldn't scratch—a tiny scrap of Alistair land sitting square in the middle of the

Hazard ranch—the last vestige of a hundred-year-old feud between the Hazards and the Alistairs.

Nathan had just learned from John Wilkinson, the executor of the Alistair estate, that Cyrus's heir hadn't let any grass grow under his feet. Harry Alistair had already arrived in the Boulder River Valley to take possession of Cyrus's ranch. Nathan only hoped the newest hard-nosed, ornery Alistair hadn't gotten too settled in. Because he wasn't staying. Not if Nathan had anything to say about it. Oh, he planned to offer a fair price. He was even willing to be generous if it came to that. But he was going to have that land.

Nathan gunned the engine on his pickup, disdaining the cavernous ruts in the dirt road that led to Cyrus's tiny, weather-beaten log cabin. It was a pretty good bet that once Harry Alistair got a look at the run-down condition of Cyrus's property, the Easterner would see the wisdom of selling. Cyrus's ranch—what there was of it—was falling down. There weren't more than five hundred sheep on the whole place.

Besides, what could a man from Williamsburg, Virginia, know about raising sheep? The greenhorn would probably take one look at the work, and risk, involved in trying to make a go of such a small, dilapidated spread and be glad to have Nathan take it off his hands. Nathan didn't contemplate what he would do if Harry Alistair refused to sell, because he simply wasn't going to take no for an answer.

As he drove up to the cabin, Nathan saw someone bounce up from one of the broken-down sheep pens that surrounded the barn. That had to be Harry Alistair. Nathan couldn't tell what the greenhorn was doing, but from the man's agitated movements it was plain something was wrong. A second later the fellow was racing for the barn. He came out another second later carrying a handful of supplies. Once again he ducked out of sight in the sheep pen.

Nathan sighed in disgust. The newcomer sure hadn't wasted any time getting himself into a pickle. For a moment Nathan considered turning his truck around and driving away. But despite the Hazard-Alistair feud, he couldn't leave without offering a helping hand. There were rules in the West that governed such conduct. A man in trouble wasn't friend or foe; he was merely a man in trouble. As such, he was entitled to whatever assistance Nathan could offer. Once the trouble was past and they were on equal footing again, Nathan could feel free to treat this Alistair as the mortal enemy the century-old feud made him.

Nathan slammed on the brakes and left his truck door hanging open as he raced across the snowy ground toward the sheep pen on foot. The closer Nathan got, the more his brow furrowed. The man had stood up again and put a hand behind his neck to rub the tension there. He was tall, but the body Nathan saw was gangly, the shoulders narrow. The man's face was smooth, unlined. Nathan hadn't been expecting someone so young and...the only word that came to mind was *delicate,* but he shied from thinking it. He watched the greenhorn drop out of sight again. With that graceful downward movement Nathan realized what had caused his confusion. That was no man in Cyrus Alistair's sheep pen—it was a woman!

When Nathan arrived at her side, he saw the problem right away. A sheep was birthing, but the lamb wasn't presenting correctly. The ewe was baaing in distress. The woman had dropped to her knees and was crooning to the animal in a low, raspy voice that sent shivers up Nathan's spine.

The woman was concentrating so hard on what she was doing that she wasn't even aware of Nathan until he asked, "Need some help?"

"What? Oh!" She looked up at him with stricken brown eyes. Her teeth were clenched on her lower lip and her cheeks were pale. He noticed her hand was trembling as she brushed her brown hair out of her eyes with a slender forearm. "Yes. Please. I don't know what to do."

Nathan felt a constriction in his chest at the desperate note in her voice. He had an uncontrollable urge to protect her from the tragic reality she faced. The feeling was unfamiliar, and therefore uncomfortable. He ignored it as best he could and quickly rolled up his sleeves. "Do you have some disinfectant handy?"

"Yes. Here." She poured disinfectant over his hands and arms.

Nathan shook off the excess and knelt beside the ewe. After a quick examination, he said flatly, "This lamb is dead."

"Oh, no! It's all my fault."

"Maybe not," Nathan contradicted. "Can't always save a case of dystocia."

"What?"

"The lamb is out of position. Its head is bent back, not forward along its legs like it ought to be."

"I read in a book what to do for a problem delivery. I just didn't realize..." She reached out a hand to briefly touch the lamb's foot that extended from the ewe. "Will the mother die, too?"

"Not if I can help it," Nathan said grimly. There was a long silence while he used soapy water to help the dead lamb slip free of the womb. Almost immediately contractions began again. "There's another lamb."

"Is it alive?" the woman asked, her voice full of hope.

"Don't know yet." Nathan wanted the lamb to be born alive more than he'd wanted anything in a long time. Which made no sense at all. This was an Alistair sheep.

"Here it comes!" she exclaimed. "Is it all right?"

Nathan waited to see whether the lamb would suck air. When it didn't, he grabbed a nearby gunnysack and rubbed vigorously. The lamb responded by bleating pitifully. And Nathan let out the breath he hadn't known he'd been holding.

"It's alive," she said in a tear-choked voice.

"That it is," Nathan said with satisfaction. He cut the umbilical cord about an inch and a half from the lamb's navel and asked, "Where's the iodine?"

Nathan helped the ewe to her feet while the woman ran to fetch a wide-mouthed jar full of iodine. When she returned he held the lamb up by its front legs and sloshed the jar over the navel cord until it was covered with iodine. He set the lamb back down beside its mother where, after some bumping and searching with its nose, it found a teat and began to nurse.

Nathan glanced at the woman to share the moment, which he found profoundly moving no matter how many times he'd seen it. Once he did, he couldn't take his eyes off her.

She was watching the nursing lamb, and her whole face reflected a kind of joy he had seldom seen and wasn't sure he had ever felt. When the lamb made a loud, slurping sound, a laugh of relief bubbled up from her throat. And she looked up into his eyes and smiled.

He was stunned. Poleaxed. Smitten. In a long-ago time he would have thrown her on his horse and ridden off into the sunset. But this was now, and he was a civilized man. So he simply swallowed hard, gritted his teeth and smiled back.

Her smile revealed a slight space between her front teeth that made her look almost winsome. A dimple appeared in her left cheek when the smile became a grin. Her hair had fallen back over her brows, and it took all his willpower not to brush it back. Her nose was small and tilted up at the end, and he noticed her cheeks, now that they weren't so pale, were covered with a scattering of freckles. Her lips were full, despite the wide smile, and her chin, tilted up toward him, seemed to ask for his touch. He had actually lifted a hand toward her when he realized what he was about to do.

Nathan was confused by the strength of his attraction to the woman. He didn't need—refused to take on—any more obligations in his lifetime. This was a woman who looked in great need of a lot of care and attention. This kind of woman spelled RESPONSIBILITY in capital letters. He shrugged inwardly. He had done his share of taking care of the helpless. He hadn't begrudged the sacrifice, because it had been necessary, but he was definitely gun-shy.

When he chose a woman to share his life, it would be someone who could stand on her own two feet, someone who could be a helpmate and an equal partner. He would never choose someone like the winsome woman kneeling before him, whose glowing brown eyes beseeched him to take her into his arms and comfort her.

Not by a long shot!

Nathan bolted to his feet, abruptly ending the intense feeling of closeness he felt with the woman. "Where the hell is Harry Alistair?" he demanded in a curt voice. "And what the hell are you doing out here trying to handle a complicated lambing all alone?"

His stomach knotted when he saw the hurt look in her eyes at his abrupt tone of voice, but he didn't have a chance even to think about apologizing before a spark of defiance lit up her beautiful brown eyes and she rose to her feet. Her hands balled into fists and found her hipbones. She was tall. Really tall. He stood six foot three and she was staring him practically in the eye.

"You're looking for Harry Alistair?" she asked in a deceptively calm voice.

"I am."

"What for?"

"That's between him and me. Look, do you know where he is or not?"

"I do."

But that was all she said. Nathan was damned if he was going to play games with her. He yanked the worn Stetson off his head, forked an agitated hand through his blond hair and settled the cowboy hat back in place over his brow. He placed his fists on his hips in a powerful masculine version of her pose and grated out, "Well, where the hell is he?"

"*He's* standing right here."

There was a long pause while Nathan registered what she'd said. "*You're* Harry Alistair?"

"Actually, my name is Harriet." She forgave him for his rudeness with one of those engaging smiles and said, "But my friends all call me Harry."

She stuck out her hand for him to shake, and before he could curb his automatic reaction, he had her hand clasped in his. It was soft. Too damn soft for a woman who hoped to survive the hard life of a Montana sheep rancher. He held on to her hand as he examined her—the Harry Alistair he had come to see—more closely.

He was looking for reasons to find fault with her, to prove he couldn't possibly be physically attracted to her, and he found them. She was dressed in a really god-awful outfit: brand-new bibbed overalls, a red-and-black plaid wool shirt, a down vest, galoshes, for heaven's sake, and a Harley's Feed Store baseball cap, which meant she'd already been to Slim Harley's Feed Store in Big Timber. Nathan hadn't realized her hair was so long, but what hadn't escaped to frame her face fell in two childish braids over each shoulder practically to her breasts.

Nothing wrong with them, a voice inside noted.

Nathan forced his eyes back up to her face, which now bore an expression of amusement. A flush crept up his neck. There was no way he could hide it or stop it. His Swedish ancestors had bequeathed him blue eyes and blond hair and skin that got ruddy in the sun but never tanned. Unfortunately his Nordic complexion also displayed his feelings when he most wanted them hidden. He dropped her hand as though it had caught fire.

"We have to talk," he said flatly.

"I'd like that," Harry replied. "After everything we've just been through together, I feel like we're old friends, Mr.— Oh, my," she said with a self-deprecating laugh. "I don't even know your name."

"Nathan Hazard."

"Come on inside, Nathan Hazard, and have a cup of coffee, and we'll talk."

Nathan was pretty sure he could conduct his business right here. After all, how many words did it take to say "I want to buy this place"? Only six. But he was curious to see the inside of Cyrus Alistair's place. He had heard the tiny log cabin called "rustic" by those who had actually been inside, though they were few and far between.

Against his better judgment Nathan said, "Sure. A cup of coffee sounds good."

"I don't have things very organized," Harry apologized.

Nathan soon realized that was an understatement. Harry took him in through the back door, which led to the kitchen. What he saw was *chaos*. What he felt was *disappointment*. Because despite everything he had already seen of her, he'd been holding out hope that he was wrong about Harry Alistair.

The shambles he beheld in the kitchen of the tiny cabin—dishes piled high in the sink, half-empty bottles of formula on the counters, uneaten meals side by side with stacks of books on the table, several bags of garbage in one corner, and a lamb sleeping on a wadded-up blanket in the other—confirmed his worst fears. Harry Alistair needed a caretaker. This wasn't a woman who was ever going to be anyone's equal partner.

Harry had kicked off her galoshes when she came in the door and let them lie where they fell. Her down vest warmed the back of the kitchen chair, and she hooked her Harley's Feed Store cap on a deer antler that graced the dingy, wooden-planked wall.

Poor woman, he thought. She must have given up trying to deal with all the mess and clutter. He hardened himself against feeling sympathy for her.

He was more convinced than ever that he would be doing her a favor by buying Cyrus's place from her.

While he stood staring, Harry grabbed some pottery mugs for the coffee from kitchen cupboards that appeared to be all but bare. He was able to notice that because all the cupboards hung open on dragging hinges. As quickly as she shoved the painted yellow kitchen cupboards closed, they sprang open again. And stayed that way. She turned to him, shrugged and let go with another one of her smiles. He stuck his hands deep into his pockets to keep from reaching out to enfold her in his arms.

Not the woman for me, he said to himself.

The walls and floor of the room consisted of unfinished wooden planks. A step down from "rustic," he thought. More like "primitive." The refrigerator was so old that the top was rounded instead of square. The gas stove was equally ancient, and she had to light the burner with a match.

"Darned thing doesn't work from the pilot," Harry explained as she set a dented metal coffeepot on the burner. "Make yourself at home," she urged, seating herself at the kitchen table.

Nathan set his Stetson on the table and draped his sheepskin coat over the back of one of the three chrome-legged chairs at the Formica table. Then he flattened the torn plastic seat and sat down. The table was cluttered with articles from the internet. One title leaped out at him—"Sheep Raising for Beginners." He didn't have a chance to comment on it before she started talking.

"I'm from Williamsburg, Virginia," she volunteered. "I didn't even know my great-uncle Cyrus. It was really a surprise when Mr. Wilkinson from the bank contacted me. At first I couldn't believe it. Me, inheriting a sheep ranch!

"I suppose the sensible thing would have been to let Mr. Wilkinson sell the place for me. He said there was a buyer anxious to have it. Then I thought about what it would be like to have a place of my very own, far away from—" She jumped up and crossed to the stove to check the coffeepot.

Nathan wanted her to finish that sentence. What, or whom, had she wanted to escape? What, or who, had made her unhappy enough that she had to run all the way to Montana? He fought down the possessive, protective feelings that arose. She didn't belong to him. Never would.

She was talking in breathless, jerky sentences, which was how he knew she was nervous. It was as though she wasn't used to entertaining a man in her kitchen. Maybe she wasn't. He wished he knew for sure.

Not your kind of woman, he repeated to himself.

"Do you have a place around here?" Harry asked.

Nathan cleared his throat and said with a rueful smile, "You could say I have a place that goes all around here."

He watched her brows lower in confusion at his comment. She filled the two coffee mugs to the very brim and brought them carefully to the table.

"Am I supposed to know what that means?" she asked as she seated herself across from him again.

"My sheep ranch surrounds yours." When she still looked confused he continued, "Your property sits square in the center of mine. Your access road to the highway runs straight across my land."

A brilliant smile lit her face, and she cocked her head like a brown sparrow on a budding limb and quipped, "Then we most certainly *are* neighbors, aren't we? I'm so glad you came to see me, Nathan—is it all right if I call you Nathan?—so we can get to know each other. I could really use some advice. You see—"

"Wait a minute," he interrupted.

In the first place it wasn't all right with him if she called him Nathan. It would be much more difficult to be firm with her if they were on a first-name basis. In the second place he hadn't come here to be neighborly; he had come to make an offer on her land. And in the third, and most important place, he had *absolutely no intention of offering her any advice.* And he was going to tell her all those things…just as soon as she stopped smiling so trustingly at him.

"Look, Harry-et," he said, pausing a second between the two syllables, unable to make himself address her by the male nickname. "You probably should have taken the banker's advice. If the rest of this cabin looks as bad as the kitchen, it can't be very comfortable. The buildings and sheds are a disgrace. Your hay fields are fallow. Your access road is a mass of ruts. You'll be lucky to make ends meet let alone earn enough from this sheep ranch you inherited to enjoy any kind of pleasant life. The best advice I can give you is to sell this place to me and go back to Virginia where you belong."

He watched her full lips firm into a flat line and her jaw tauten. Her chin came up pugnaciously. "I'm not selling out."

"Why the hell not?" he retorted in exasperation.

"Because."

He waited for her to explain. But she was keeping her secrets to herself. He was convinced now that she must be running from something… or someone.

"I'm going to make a go of this place. I can do it. I may not be experienced, but I'm intelligent and hardworking and I have all the literature on raising sheep that I could find."

Nathan stuck the article called "Sheep Raising for Beginners" under her nose and said, "None of this 'literature' will compensate for practical experience. Look what happened this afternoon. What would you have done if I hadn't come along?" He had the unpleasant experience of watching her chin drop to her chest and her cheeks flush while her thumb brushed anxiously against the plain pottery mug.

"I would probably have lost both lambs, and the ewe, as well," she admitted in a low voice. She looked up at him, her brown eyes liquid with tears she was trying to blink away. "I owe you my thanks. I don't know how I can ever repay you. I know I have a lot to learn. But—" she leaned forward, and her voice became urgent "—I intend to work as hard as I have to, night and day if necessary, until I succeed."

Nathan was angry and irritated. She wasn't going to succeed; she was going to fail miserably. And unless he could somehow talk her into selling this place to him, he was going to have to stand by and watch it happen. Because he *absolutely, positively,* was *not* going to offer to help. There were no ifs, ands or buts about it. He had been through this before. A small commitment had a way of mushrooming out of control. Start cutting pines and pretty soon you'd created a whole mountain meadow.

"Look, Harry-et," he said, "the reason I came here today is to offer to buy this place from you."

"It's not for sale."

Nathan sighed. She'd said it as if she'd meant it. He had no choice except to try to convince her to change her mind. "Sheep ranching involves a whole lot more than lambing and shearing, Harry-et." He was distracted from his train of thought by the way the flush on her cheeks made her freckles show up. He forced his attention back where it belonged and continued. "For instance, do you have any idea what wool pool you're in?"

She raised a blank face and stared at him.

"Do you even know what a wool pool is?"

She shook her head.

"A wool pool enables small sheepmen like yourself to concentrate small clips of wool into carload lots so that they can get a better price on—" He cut himself off. He was supposed to be proving her ignorance to her, not educating it away. He ignored her increasingly distressed look and asked, "Do you have any idea what's involved with docking and castrating lambs?"

This time she nodded, but the flush on her face deepened.

"What about keeping records? Do you have any accounting experience?"

"A little," she admitted in a quiet voice.

He felt like a desperado in a black hat threatening the schoolmarm, but he told himself it was for her own good in the long run and continued, "Can you figure adjusted weaning weight ratios? Measure ram performance? Calculate shearing dates? Compute feed gain ratios?"

By now she was violently shaking her head. A shiny tear streaked one cheek.

He pushed himself up out of his chair. He braced one callused palm on the table and leaned across to cup her jaw in his other hand and lift her chin. He looked into her eyes, and it took every bit of determination he had not to succumb to the plea he saw there. "I can't teach you to run this ranch. I have a business of my own that needs tending. You can't make it on your own, Harry-et. Sell your land to me."

"No."

"I'll give you a fair—a generous—price. Then you can go home where you belong."

She was out of his grasp and gone before he had time to stop her. She didn't go far, just to the sink, where she stood in front of the stack of dirty dishes and stared out the dirt-clouded window at the ramshackle sheep pens and the derelict barn. "I will succeed. With or without your help."

She sounded so sure of herself, despite the fact that she was doomed to fail. Nathan refused to admire her. He chose to be furious with her instead. In three angry strides he was beside her. "You're as stubborn as every other hard-nosed, ornery Alistair who ever lived on this land!" He snorted in disgust. "I can sure as hell see now why Hazards have been feuding with Alistairs for a hundred years."

She whirled to confront him. "And I can see why Alistairs chose to feud with Hazards," she retorted. "How dare you pretend to be a friend!" She poked him in the chest with a stiff finger. "How dare you sneak in under my guard and pretend to help—"

"I wasn't pretending," he said heatedly, grabbing her wrist to keep her from poking him again. "I *did* help. Admit it."

"Sure. So I'd be grateful. All the time you only wanted to buy my land right out from under me. You are the lowest, meanest—"

He wasn't about to listen to any insults from a greenhorn female. A moment later her arm was twisted up behind her and he had pulled her flush against him. She opened her mouth to lambaste him again and he shut her up the quickest, easiest way he knew. He covered her mouth with his.

Nathan was angry, and he wasn't gentle. That is, until he felt her lips soften under his. It felt like he'd been wanting her for a long time. His mouth moved slowly over hers while his hand cupped her head and kept her still so he could take what he needed. She struggled against his hold, her breasts brushing against his chest, her hips hard against his. That only made him want her more.

It was when he felt her trembling that he came to his senses, mortified at the uncivilized way he'd treated her.

He abruptly released the hand he had twisted behind her back. But instead of coming up to slap him, as he'd expected, her palm reached up to caress his cheek. Her fingertips followed the shape of his cheekbone upward to his temple, where she threaded her fingers into his hair and slowly pulled his head back down.

And she kissed him back.

That was when he realized she was trembling with desire. Not fear. Desire. With both hands free he cupped her buttocks and pulled her hard against him. For every thrust he made, she countered. He was as full and hard as he'd ever been in his life. His tongue ravaged her mouth, and she responded with an ardor that made him hungry for her. He spread urgent kisses across her face and neck, but they didn't satisfy as much as the taste of her, so he sought her mouth again. His tongue found the space between her teeth. And the inside of her lip. And the roof of her mouth. When he mimicked the thrust and parry of lovers, she held his tongue and sucked it until he thought his head was going to explode.

When he slipped his hand over her buttocks and between her legs, she moaned, a sound that came from deep in her throat and spoke of an agony of unappeased passion.

And the lamb in the corner bleated.

Nathan lifted his head and stared at the woman in his arms. Her brown eyes were half-veiled by her lids, and her pupils were dilated. She was breathing as heavily as he was, her lips parted to gasp air. Her knees had already buckled, and his grasp on her was all that kept them both off the floor.

Are you out of your mind?

He tried to step away, but her hand still clutched his hair. He reached up and drew her hand away. She suddenly seemed to realize he had changed his mind and backed up abruptly. Nathan refused to look at her face. He already felt bad enough. He had come within a lamb's tail of making love to Harry-et Alistair. He had made a narrow escape, for which he knew he would later, when his body wasn't so painfully objecting, be glad for.

"I think it's time you left, Mr. Hazard," Harry said in a rigidly controlled voice.

He couldn't leave without trying once more to accomplish what he'd come to do. "Are you sure you won't—"

The change in her demeanor was so sudden that it took him by surprise. Her expression was fierce, determined. "I will not sell this land," she said through clenched teeth. "Now get out of here before—"

"Goodbye, Harry-et. If you have a change of heart, John Wilkinson at the bank knows how to get in touch with me."

He settled his hat on his head and pulled it down with a tug. Then he shrugged broad shoulders into his sheepskin-lined coat. Before he was even out the kitchen door Harry Alistair had already started heating a bottle of formula for the lamb she had snuggled in her arms. It was the first time he'd ever envied one of the fleecy orphans.

The last thing Nathan Hazard wanted to do was leave that room. But he turned resolutely and marched out the door. As he gunned the engine of his truck, he admitted his encounter with Harry-et Alistair had been a very close call.

Not the woman for you, he reminded himself. *Definitely not the woman for you.*

Chapter 2

Are there bachelors in them thar hills?
Answer: Yep.

Once the lamb had been fed and settled back on its pallet, Harry sank into a kitchen chair, put her elbows on the table and let her head drop into her hands. What on earth had she been thinking to let Nathan Hazard kiss her like that! And worse, why had she kissed him back in such a wanton manner? It was perfectly clear now that she hadn't been *thinking* at all; she'd been feeling, and the feelings had been so overwhelming that they hadn't allowed for any kind of rational consideration.

Harry had felt an affinity to the rancher from the instant she'd laid eyes on him. His broad shoulders, his narrow hips, the dusting of fine blond hair on his powerful forearms all appealed to her. His eyes were framed by crow's-feet that gave character to a sharp-boned, perfectly chiseled face. That pair of sapphire-blue eyes, alternately curious and concerned, had stolen her heart.

Harry wasn't surprised that she was attracted to someone more handsome than any man had a right to be. What amazed her was that having known Nathan Hazard for only a matter of hours she would readily have trusted him with her life. That simply wasn't logical. Although, Harry supposed in retrospect, she had probably seen in Nathan Hazard exactly what she wanted to see. She had needed a legendary, bigger-than-life Western hero, someone tall, rugged and handsome to come along and rescue her. And he had obligingly arrived.

And he had been stunning in his splendor, though that had consisted merely of a pair of butter-soft jeans molded to his long legs, Western boots, a dark blue wool shirt topped by a sheepskin-lined denim jacket, and a Stetson he had pulled down so that it left his features shadowed. The shaggy, silver-blond hair that fell a full inch over his collar had made him look untamed, perhaps untamable. Harry remembered wondering what such fine blond hair might feel like. His lower lip was full, and he had a wide, easy smile that pulled one side of his mouth up a little higher than the other. She had also wondered, she realized with chagrin, what it would be like to kiss that mouth. Unbelievably she had actually indulged her fantasies.

Harry wasn't promiscuous. She wasn't even sexually experienced when it came right down to it. So she had absolutely no explanation for what had just happened between her and the Montana sheepman. She only knew she had felt an urgent, uncontrollable need to touch Nathan Hazard, to kiss him and to have him kiss her back. And she hadn't wanted him to stop there. She had wanted him inside her, mated to her.

Her mother and father, not to mention her brother, Charlie, and her eight uncles and their dignified, decorous wives, would have been appalled to think that any Williamsburg Alistair could have behaved in such a provocative manner with a man she had only just met. Harry was a little appalled herself.

But then nothing in Montana was going the way she had planned.

It had seemed like such a good idea, when she had gotten the letter from John Wilkinson, to come to the Boulder River Valley and learn how to run Great-Uncle Cyrus's sheep ranch. She loved animals and she loved being out-of-doors and she loved the mountains—she had heard that southwestern Montana had a lot of beautiful mountains. She'd expected opposition to such a move from her family, so she'd carefully chosen the moment to let them know about her decision.

No Alistair ever argued at the dinner table. So, sitting at the elegant antique table that had been handed down from Alistair to Alistair for generations, she had waited patiently for a break in the dinner conversation and calmly announced, "I've decided to take advantage of my inheritance from Great-Uncle Cyrus. I'll be leaving for Montana at the end of the week."

"But you can't possibly manage a sheep ranch on your own, Harriet," her mother admonished in a cultured voice. "And since you're bound to fail, darling, I can't understand why you would even want to give it a try. Besides," she added, "think of the smell!"

Harry—her mother cringed every time she heard the masculine nickname—had turned her compelling brown eyes to her father, looking for an encouraging word.

"Your mother is right, sweetheart," Terence Waverly Alistair said. "My daughter, a sheep farmer?" His thick white brows lowered until they nearly met at the bridge of his nose. "I'm afraid I can't lend my support to such a move. You haven't succeeded at a single job I've found for you, sweetheart. Not the one as a teller in my bank, not the one as an executive assistant, nor the the one as a medical receptionist. You've gotten yourself fired for ineptness at every single one. It's foolhardy to go so far—Montana is a long way from Virginia, my dear—merely to fail yet again. Besides," he added, "think of the cold!"

Harry turned her solemn gaze toward her older brother, Charles. He had been her champion in the past. He had even unbent so far as to call her Harry when their parents weren't around. Now she needed his support. Wanted his support. Begged with her eyes for his support.

"I'm afraid I have to agree with Mom and Dad, Harriet."

"But, Charles—"

"Let me finish," he said in a determined voice. Harry met her brother's sympathetic gaze as he continued. "You're only setting yourself up for disappointment. You'll be a lot happier if you learn to accept your limitations."

"Meaning?" Harry managed to whisper past the ache in her throat.

"Meaning you just aren't clever enough to pull it off, Harriet. Besides," he added, "think of all that manual labor!"

Harry felt the weight of a lifetime of previous failures in every concerned but discouraging word her family had offered. They didn't believe she could do it. She took a deep breath and let it out.

She could hardly blame them for their opinion of her. To be perfectly honest, she had never given them any reason to think otherwise. So why was she so certain that this time things would be different? Why was she so certain that this time she would succeed? Because she knew something they didn't: *she had done all that failing in the past on purpose.*

Harry was paying now for years of deception. It had started innocently enough when she was a child and her mother had wanted her to take ballet lessons. At six Harry had already towered over her friends. Gawky and gangly, she knew she was never going to make a graceful prima ballerina. One look at her mother's face, however, and Harry had known she couldn't say, "No, thank you. I'd rather be playing basketball."

Instead, she'd simply acquired two left feet. It had worked. Her ballet instructor had quickly labeled her irretrievably clumsy and advised Isabella Alistair that she would only be throwing her money away if Harriet continued in the class. Isabella was forced to admit defeat. Thus, unbeknownst to her parents, Harry had discovered at a very early age a passive way of resisting them.

Over the years Harry had never said no to her parents. It had been easier simply to go along with whatever they had planned. Piano lessons were thwarted with a deaf ear; embroidery had been abandoned as too bloody; and her brief attempt at tennis had resulted in a broken leg.

As she had gotten older, the stakes had gotten higher. She had only barely avoided a plan to send her away to college at Radcliffe by getting entrance exam scores so low that they had astonished the teachers who had watched her get straight A's through high school. She had been elated when her distraught parents had allowed her to enroll at the same local university her friends from high school were attending.

Harry knew she should have made some overt effort to resist each time her father had gotten her one of those awful jobs after graduation, simply stood up to him and said, "No, I'd rather be pursuing a career that I've chosen for myself." But old habits were hard to break. It had been easier to prove herself inept at each and every one.

When her parents chose a husband for her, she'd resorted to even more drastic measures. She'd concealed what looks she had, made a point of reciting her flaws to her suitor and resisted his amorous advances like a starched-up prude. She had led the young man to contemplate life with a plain, clumsy, cold-natured, brown-eyed, brown-haired, freckle-faced failure. He had beat a hasty retreat.

Now a lifetime of purposeful failure had come home to roost. She couldn't very well convince her parents she was ready to let go of the apron strings when she had so carefully convinced them of her inability to succeed at a single thing they had set for her to do. She might have tried to explain to them her failure had only been a childish game that had been carried on too long, but that would mean admitting she'd spent her entire life deceiving them. She couldn't bear to hurt them like that. Anyway, she didn't think they'd believe her if she told them her whole inept life had been a sham.

Now Harry could see, with the clarity of twenty-twenty hindsight, that she'd hurt herself even more than her parents by the choices she'd made. But the method of dealing with her parents' manipulation, which she'd started as a child and continued as a teenager, she'd found impossible to reverse as an adult. Until now. At twenty-six she finally had the perfect opportunity to break the pattern of failure she'd pursued for a lifetime. She only hoped she hadn't waited too long.

Harry was certain she could manage her great-uncle Cyrus's sheep ranch. She was certain she could do anything she set her brilliant mind to do. After all, it had taken brilliance to fail as magnificently, and selectively, as she had all these years. So now, when she was determined to succeed at last, she'd wanted her family's support. It was clear she wasn't going to get it. And she could hardly blame them for it. She was merely reaping what she had so carefully sowed.

Harry had a momentary qualm when she wondered whether they might be right. Maybe she was biting off more than she could chew. After all, what did she know about sheep or sheep ranching? Then her chin tilted up and she clenched her hands in her lap under the table. They were wrong. She wouldn't fail. She could learn what she didn't know. And she would succeed.

Harriet Elizabeth Alistair was convinced in her heart that she wasn't a failure. Surely, once she made up her mind to stop failing, she could. Once she was doing something she had chosen for herself, she was bound to succeed. She would show them all. She wasn't what they thought her— someone who had to be watched and protected from herself and the cold, cruel world around her. Rather, she was a woman with hopes and dreams, none of which she'd been allowed—or rather, allowed herself—to pursue.

Like a pioneer of old, Harry wanted to go west to build a new life. She was prepared for hard work, for frigid winter mornings and searing summer days. She welcomed the opportunity to build her fortune with the sweat of her brow and the labor of her back. Harry couldn't expect her family to understand why she wanted to try to make it on her own in a cold, smelly, faraway place where she would have to indulge in manual labor. She had something to prove to herself. This venture was the Boston Tea Party and the Alamo and Custer's Last Stand all rolled into one. In the short run she might lose a few battles, but she was determined to win the war.

At last Harry broke the awesome silence that had descended on the dinner table. "Nothing you've said has changed my mind," she told her family. "I'll be leaving at the end of the week."

Nothing her family said the following week, and they'd said quite a lot, had dissuaded Harry from the course she'd set for herself. She'd been delighted to find, when she arrived a week later in Big Timber, the town closest to Great-Uncle Cyrus's ranch, that at least she hadn't been deceived about the beauty of the mountains in southwestern Montana. The Crazy Mountains provided a striking vista to the north, while the majestic, snow-capped Absarokas greeted her to the south each morning. But they were the only redeeming feature in an otherwise daunting locale.

The Boulder River Valley was a desolate place in late February. The cottonwoods that lined the Boulder River, which meandered the length of the valley, were stripped bare of leaves. And the grass, what wasn't covered by patches of drifted snow, was a ghastly straw-yellow. All that might have been bearable if only she hadn't found such utter decay when she arrived at Great-Uncle Cyrus's ranch.

Her first look at the property she'd inherited had been quite a shock. Harry had been tempted to turn tail and run back to Williamsburg. But something—perhaps the beauty of the mountains, but more likely the thought of facing her family if she gave up without even trying—had kept her from giving John Wilkinson the word to sell. She would never go home until she could do so with her head held high, the owner and manager of a prosperous sheep ranch.

Harry had discovered dozens of reasons to question her decision ever since she'd moved to Montana, not the least of which was the meeting today with her nearest neighbor. Nathan Hazard hadn't exactly fulfilled her expectations of the typical Western hero. A more provoking, irritating, exasperating man she had never known! Whether he admitted it or not, it had been a pretty sneaky thing to do, helping her so generously with the difficult lambing when he knew all along he was only softening her up so that he could make an offer on her land.

Thoughts of the difficult birthing reminded her that she still had to dispose of the dead lamb. Harry knew she ought to bury it, but the ground was frozen. She couldn't imagine burning it. And she couldn't bear the thought of taking the poor dead lamb somewhere up into the foothills and leaving it among the juniper and jack pine for nature's scavengers to find. None of the articles or books she'd read discussed this particular problem, and she had no internet access to look it up online. Harry knew there must be some procedures the local ranchers followed. Surely they also had deaths at lambing time. But she'd dig a hole in the frozen ground with her fingernails before she asked Nathan Hazard what to do.

For now Harry decided to move the dead lamb behind the barn and cover it with a tarp. As long as the weather stayed cold, the body wouldn't decay. When she could spare the time, she would take a trip into Big Timber and strike up a conversation with Slim Harley at the feed store. Somehow she would casually bring up the subject of dead lambs in the conversation and get the answers she needed. Harry's lips twisted wryly. Western conversations certainly tended to have a grittier tone than those in the East.

Harry couldn't put off what had to be done. She slipped her vest back on, pulled her cap down on her head and stepped back into her galoshes. A quick search turned up some leather work gloves in the drawer beside the sink. A minute later she was headed back out to the sheep pens.

Harry actually shuddered when she picked up the dead lamb. It had stiffened in death. It was also heavier than she'd expected, so she had to hold it close to her chest in order to carry it. Despite everything Harry had read about not getting emotionally involved, she was unable to keep from mourning the animal's death. It seemed like such a waste. Although, if the lamb had lived it would have gone to market, where it would eventually have become lamb chops on some Eastern dinner table.

Maybe she ought to call Nathan Hazard and take him up on his offer, after all.

Before Harry had a chance to indulge her bout of maudlin conjecture she heard another sheep baaing in distress.

Not again!

Harry raced for the sheep pens where she had separated the ewes that were ready to deliver. Instead she discovered a sheep had already given birth to a lamb. While she watched, it birthed a twin. Harry had learned from her extensive reading that her sheep had been genetically bred so they bore twins, thus doubling the lamb crop. But to her it was a unique happening. She stopped and leaned against the pen and smiled with joy at having witnessed such a miraculous event.

Then she realized she had work to do. The cords had to be cut and dipped in iodine. And the ewe and her lambs had to be moved into a jug, a small pen separate from the other sheep, for two or three days until the lambs had bonded with their mothers and gotten a little stronger.

Harry had read that lambing required constant attention from a rancher, but she hadn't understood that to mean she would get no sleep, no respite. For the rest of the night she never had a chance to leave the sheep barn, as the ewes dropped twin lambs that lived or died depending on the whims of fate. The stack under the tarp beside her barn got higher.

If Harry had found a spare second, she would have swallowed her pride and called Nathan Hazard for help. But by the time she got a break near dawn, the worst seemed to be over. Harry had stood midwife to the delivery of forty-seven lambs. Forty-three were still alive.

She dragged herself into the house and only then realized she'd forgotten about the orphan lamb in her kitchen. He was bleating pitifully from hunger. Despite her fatigue, Harry took the time to fix the lamb a bottle. She fell asleep sitting on the wooden-plank floor with her back against the wooden-plank wall, with the hungry lamb in her lap sucking at a nippled Coke bottle full of milk replacer.

That was how Nathan Hazard found her the following morning at dawn.

Nathan had lambing of his own going on, but unlike Harriet Alistair, he had several hired hands to help with the work. When suppertime arrived, he left the sheep barn and came inside to a hot meal that Katoya, the elderly Native American woman who was his housekeeper, had ready and waiting for him.

Katoya had mysteriously arrived on the Hazard doorstep on the day Nathan's mother had died, as though by some prearranged promise, to take her place in the household. Nathan had been sixteen at the time. No explanation had ever been forthcoming as to why the woman had come. And despite Nathan's efforts in later years to ease the older woman's chores, Katoya still worked every day from dawn to dusk with apparent tirelessness, making Nathan's house a home.

As Nathan sat down at the kitchen table, he wondered whether Harriet Alistair had found anything worth eating in her bare cupboards. The fact he should find himself worrying about an Alistair, even if it was a woman, made him frown.

"Were you able to buy the land?" Katoya asked as she poured coffee into his cup.

Nathan had learned better than to try to keep secrets from the old woman. "Harry Alistair wouldn't sell," he admitted brusquely.

The diminutive woman merely nodded. "So the feud will go on." She seated herself in a rocker in the kitchen that was positioned to get the most heat from the old-fashioned woodstove.

Nathan grimaced. "Yeah."

"Is it so important to own the land?"

Nathan turned to face her and saw skin stretched tight with age over high, wide cheekbones and black hair threaded with silver in two braids over her shoulders. He suddenly wondered how old she was. Certainly she had clung to the traditional ways of her tribe. "It must be your cultural background," he said at last, "that taught you not to feel the same need as I do to possess land."

Katoya looked back at him with eyes that were a deep black well of wisdom. "We know what the white man has never learned. You cannot own the land. You can only use it for so long as you walk the earth."

Katoya started the rocker moving, and its creak made a familiar, comforting sound as Nathan ate the hot lamb stew she'd prepared for him.

Nathan had to admit there was a lot to be said for the old woman's argument. Why was he so determined to own that piece of Alistair land? After all, when he was gone, who would know or care? Maybe he could have accepted Katoya's point of view if he hadn't met Harry Alistair first. Now he couldn't leave things the way they stood. That piece of land smack in the middle of his spread had always been a burr under the saddle.

He didn't intend to stop bucking until the situation was remedied.

Nathan refilled his own coffee cup to keep the old woman from having to get up again, then settled down into the kitchen chair with his legs stretched out toward the stove. Because he respected Katoya's advice, Nathan found himself explaining the situation. "The Harry Alistair who inherited the land from Cyrus turned out to be a woman, Harry-et Alistair. She's greener than buffalo grass in spring and doesn't know a thing about sheep that hasn't come from some article or book or internet forum. Harry-et Alistair hasn't got a snowball's chance in hell of making a go of Cyrus's place. But I never saw a woman so determined, so stubborn…."

"You admire her," Katoya said.

"I don't… Yes, I do," he admitted with a disbelieving shake of his head. Nathan kept his face averted as he continued, "But I can't imagine why. She's setting herself up for a fall. I just hate to see her have to take it."

"We always have choices. Is there truly nothing that can be done?"

"Are you suggesting I offer to help her out?" Nathan demanded incredulously. "Because I won't. I'm not going to volunteer a shoulder to cry on, let alone one to carry a yoke. I've learned my lessons well," he said bitterly. "I'm not going to let that woman get under my skin."

"Perhaps it is too late. Perhaps you already care for her. Perhaps you will have no choice in the matter."

Nathan's jaw flexed as he ground his teeth. The old woman was more perceptive than was comfortable. How could he explain to her the feeling of possessiveness, of protectiveness that had arisen the moment he'd seen Harry-et Alistair? He didn't understand it himself. Hell, yes, he already cared about Harry-et Alistair. And that worried the dickens out of him. What if he succumbed to her allure? What if he ended up getting involved with her, deeply, emotionally involved with her, and it turned out she needed more than he could give? He knew what it meant to have someone solely dependent upon him, to have someone rely upon him for everything, and to know that no matter how much he did it wouldn't be enough. Nathan couldn't stand the pain of that kind of relationship again.

"You must face the truth," Katoya said. "What will be must be."

The old woman's philosophy was simple but irrefutable. "All right," Nathan said. "I'll go see her again tomorrow morning. But that doesn't mean I'm going to get involved in her life."

Nathan repeated that litany until he fell asleep,

where he dreamed of a woman with freckles and braids and bibbed overalls who kissed with a passion that had made his pulse race and his body throb. He woke up hard and hungry. He didn't shave, didn't eat, simply pulled on jeans, boots, shirt, hat and coat and slammed out the door.

When he arrived at the Alistair place, it was deathly quiet. There was no smoke coming from the stone chimney, no sounds from the barn, or from the tiny, dilapidated cabin.

Something's wrong.

Nathan thrust the pickup truck door open and hit the ground running for the cabin. His heart was in his throat, his breath hard to catch because his chest was constricted.

Let her be all right, he prayed. *I promise I'll help if only she's all right.*

The kitchen door not only wasn't locked, it wasn't even closed. Nathan shoved it open and roared at the top of his voice, "Harry-et! Are you in here? Harry-et!"

That was when he saw her. She was sitting on the floor in the corner with a lamb clutched to her chest, her eyes wide with terror at the sight of him. He was so relieved, and so angry that she'd frightened him for nothing, that he raced over, grabbed her by the shoulders and hauled her to her feet.

"What the hell do you think you're doing,

leaving the back door standing wide open? You'll catch your death of cold," he yelled, giving her shoulders a shake to make his point. "Of all the stupid, idiotic, greenhorn—"

And then it dawned on him what he was doing, and he let her go as abruptly as he'd grabbed her. She backed up to the wall and stood there, staring at him.

Harry Alistair had a death grip on the lamb in her arms. There were dark circles under her eyes, which were wide and liquid with tears that hadn't yet spilled. Her whole body was trembling with fatigue and the aftereffects of the shaking Nathan had given her. Her mouth was working but the words weren't coming out in much more than a whisper.

Nathan leaned closer to hear what she was trying to say.

"Get out," she rasped. And then, stronger, "Get out of my house."

Nathan felt his heart miss a thump. "I'm sorry. Look, I only came over—"

Her chin came up. "I don't care why you came. I want you to leave. And don't come back."

Nathan's lips pressed flat. *What will be must be.* It was just as well things had turned out this way. It would have been a mistake to try to help her, anyway. But there was a part of him that died inside at the thought of not seeing her again. He wanted her. More than he'd ever wanted a woman in his life. But she was all wrong for him. She needed the kind of caretaking he'd sworn he was through with forever.

It took every bit of grit he had to turn on his booted heel and walk out of the room. And out of her life.

Chapter 3

What is accepted dress-for-success garb for country women?
Answer: Coveralls, scabby work shoes, holey hat and shredded gloves.

I am not a failure. I can do anything I set my mind to do. I will succeed.

Over the next two months there were many times when Harry wanted to give up. Often, it was only the repetition of those three sentences that kept her going. For, no matter how hard she tried, things always went awry. She had been forced to learn some hard lessons and learn them fast.

About a week after the majority of the lambs had been born, most of them got sick. Harry called in the vet, who diagnosed lamb scours and prescribed antibiotics. Despite her efforts, a dozen more lambs died. She stacked them under the tarp beside the barn.

Early on the lambs had to have their tails docked, and the ram lambs, except those valuable enough to be sires, had to be castrated. Several of the older books described cutting off the lamb tails with a knife and searing the stump with a hot iron. Castration was described even more graphically. Faced with such onerous chores, Harry had known she would never make it as a sheep rancher.

At her lowest moment a magazine describing a more manageable technique for docking and castration mysteriously arrived in her mailbox. An "elastrator" and rubber bands were placed on the appropriate extremities, which wasted away and dropped off on their own within two to three weeks. She found the process unpleasant, time-consuming work. But with the information provided in the timely magazine, she'd succeeded when she might have given up.

Unfortunately Harry also lost several ewes during delivery and found herself with more orphan lambs, which she had learned were called bums, that had to be fed with milk replacer. Bottle-feeding lambs turned out to be surprisingly expensive, and she had to dip into the meager financial reserves Cyrus had left in the bank. She would have run out of money except Harley's Feed Store had a sale on milk replacer. That had seemed a little odd to Harry, but a blushing Slim had assured her that he'd ordered too much replacer, and if he didn't sell it cheap, it was just going to sit on the shelf for another year. Cyrus's money had gone further than she'd dared to hope.

It was a month of exhausting days and nights before Harry could wean the lambs off of milk. But she'd made it. She still had money in the bank, and the lambs had all gotten fed. In fact, Harry was still bottle-feeding some that had been born late in the season. She'd forgotten what it was like to get more than four hours of sleep in a row. When there was work to be done, she'd repeat those three pithy sentences. They kept her awake and functioning despite what felt very much like battle fatigue. But then, wasn't she engaged in the greatest battle of her life?

By now even a novice like Harry had figured out that in its best days, Cyrus's sheep ranch had been a marginal proposition. With all the neglect over the years, it took every bit of time and attention she had simply to keep her head above water. But she was still afloat. And paddling for all she was worth. She hadn't failed. Yet. With a lot of hard work, and more than a little luck, she just might surprise everyone and make a go of Cyrus's ranch.

In the brief moments when Harry wasn't taking care of livestock—she had six laying hens, a rooster, a sow with eight piglets and a milk cow, as well as the sheep to attend—she'd thought over her last meeting with Nathan Hazard.

Perhaps if she hadn't been quite so tired the morning he had come to see her, or if he hadn't woken her quite so abruptly or been quite so upset, she might have been able to listen to what he had to say. If he had offered help, she might have accepted. She would never know for sure. Harry hadn't seen hide nor hair of him since.

Nor had anyone else come to visit. She'd made a number of phone calls to John Wilkinson at the bank for advice and had managed to get a few more tidbits of information from Slim every time she made a trip to Harley's Feed Store. But, quite frankly, Harry was beginning to feel the effects of the extreme isolation in which she'd been living for the past two months.

Which was probably why she hadn't argued more when her mother, father and brother had said they were coming out to Montana to visit her. Unfortunately, with the time it had taken her to finish her chores this morning, she only had about fifteen minutes left to put herself together before she had to meet them at The Grand, the bed-and-breakfast in Big Timber where they were staying.

The varnished wooden booths that lined one wall of the luncheon dining room at The Grand had backs high enough to conceal the occupants and give them privacy. Thus, it wasn't until Nathan heard her exuberant greeting that he realized who was soon to occupy the next booth.

"Mom, Dad, Charlie, it's so good to see you!" Harry said.

"I'm sorry I can't say the same, darling," an uppity-sounding woman replied in a dismayed voice. "You look simply awful. What have you done to yourself? And what on earth is that you have on your head?"

Nathan smiled at the thought of Harry-et in her Harley's Feed Store cap.

A young man joined in with, "For Pete's sake, Harriet. Are you really wearing bibbed overalls?"

Nathan grinned. Very likely she was.

Before Harry had a chance to respond, an older man's bass voice contributed, "I knew I should have put my foot down. I didn't think you could manage on your own in this godforsaken place. And from the look of you, I wasn't wrong. When are you coming home?"

Nathan listened for Harry-et's answer to that last question with bated breath.

There was a long pause before she answered, "I am home. And I have no intention of going back to Williamsburg, if that's what you're asking, Dad."

Nathan took advantage of the stunned silence that followed her pronouncement to take a quick swallow of coffee. He knew he ought not to eavesdrop on the Alistairs, but it wasn't as though he'd come here with that thought in mind. He'd been minding his own business when *they'd* interrupted *him*. He signaled Tillie Mae for a refill of his coffee and settled back to relax for a few minutes after lunch as was his custom. He didn't listen, exactly, but he couldn't help but hear what was being said.

"I've been to see John Wilkinson at the bank," her father began. "And he—"

"Dad! You had no right—"

"I have every right," he interrupted. "I'm your father. I—"

"In case you haven't noticed, I'm not a child anymore," Harry interrupted right back. "I can take care of myself."

"Darling," her mother said soothingly, "take a good, close look at yourself. There are dark circles under your eyes, your fingernails are chipped and broken and those awful clothes you're wearing are filthy. All I can conclude is that you're not taking good care of yourself. Your father and I only want the best for you. It hurts us to think of you suffering like this for nothing when in the end you'll only fail."

"I'm *not* suffering," Harry protested. "And I will *not* fail. In fact, I'm doing just fine." That might have been an overstatement, but it was in a good cause.

"Fine?" her father questioned. "You can't possibly know enough about sheep ranching to succeed on your own. Why, even ranchers who know what they're doing sometimes fail."

"Dad…"

Nathan heard the fatigue and frustration in Harry-et's voice. Her father shouldn't be allowed to browbeat her like that. Nathan ignored the Western code that admonished him not to interfere, in favor of the one that said a woman must always be protected. A moment later he was standing beside the next booth.

Harry was explaining, "I know what I'm doing, Dad. I've been reading all the articles I can find about sheep ranching—"

"And she's had help from her neighbors whenever she ran into trouble," Nathan finished. A charming smile lit his face as he tipped his hat to Mrs. Alistair and said, "Howdy, ma'am. I'm Nathan Hazard, a neighbor of your daughter's."

Nathan bypassed Harry's stunned expression and turned an assessing gaze to her father and brother. "I couldn't help overhearing you, sir," he said to Harry's father. "And I just want to say that we've all been keeping an eye on Harry-et to make sure—"

"You've been what?"

Nathan turned to Harry, who'd risen from her seat and was staring at him with her eyes wide and her mouth hanging open in horror.

"I was just saying that we've been keeping a neighborly eye on you." Before Harry could respond he'd turned back to her father and continued, "You see, sir, we have a great deal of respect for women out here, and there isn't a soul in the valley who would stand by if he thought Harry-et was in any real trouble.

"Of course, you're right that she probably won't be able to make a go of Cyrus Alistair's place. But then it's doubtful whether anyone could. That's why I've offered to buy the place from her. And I have every hope that once she's gotten over the silly notion that—"

"Don't say another word!" Harry was so hot she could have melted icicles in January. She hung on to her temper long enough to say, "Mom, Dad, Charles, I hope you'll excuse us. I have a few words to say to Mr. Hazard. Alone."

Harry turned and stalked out to the front lobby of The Grand without waiting to see whether Nathan followed her. After tipping his hat once more to Mrs. Alistair, he did.

Just as Harry turned and opened her mouth to speak, Nathan took her by the elbow and started upstairs with her.

"Where do you think you're going?" Harry snapped, tugging frantically against his hold.

"Upstairs."

"There are *bedrooms* upstairs!"

"Yep. Sarah keeps all the doors open to show off her fancy antiques. We can use one of the rooms for a little privacy." He pulled her into the first open bedroom and shut the door behind them. "Now what's on your mind?"

"What's on my—?" Harry was so furious she was gasping for air. "How dare you drag me up here—"

"We can go back downstairs and argue. That way everyone in the valley will know your business," he said, reaching for the doorknob.

"Wait!" Harry made the mistake of touching his hand and felt an arc of heat run up her arm. She jerked her hand away and took two steps back from him, only to come up against the edge of the ornate brass bed. She stepped forward, only to find herself toe-to-toe with Nathan.

"Hold on a minute," she said, trying desperately to regain the upper hand. "How dare you insinuate to my family that I haven't been making it on my own! I most certainly have!"

Nathan shook his head.

"Don't try to deny it," she retorted. "I haven't seen a soul except Slim Harley for the past two months. Just who, may I ask, has been helping me?"

"Me."

Harry was so stunned that she took a step back. When the backs of her legs hit the bed, she sat down. Her eyes never left Nathan's face, so she saw the flash of guilt in his blue eyes and the tinge of red growing on his cheeks. "You helped me? How?"

Nathan lifted his hat and shoved his fingers through his hair in agitation, then pulled his hat down over his brow again. "Little ways."

"How?"

He cleared his throat and admitted, "Dropped off a magazine once. Broke the ice on your ponds."

That explained some things she'd wondered about. She'd needed the knowledge the magazine had provided, but it wasn't as though he'd come over and helped with the docking and castration of the lambs. And while she'd appreciated having the ice broken on her ponds, she could have done that herself. His interference didn't amount to as much as she'd feared.

"And I talked Slim into putting his milk replacer on sale," he finished.

That was another matter entirely. Without the

sale on milk replacer she'd have run out of money for sure. "You're responsible for that?"

"Wasn't a big deal. He really did order too much."

"Did anybody else get their milk replacer on sale?" she asked in a strained voice.

"No."

Harry's chest hurt. She couldn't breathe. "Why did you bother if you were so certain I'd fail in the end?"

"Thought you'd come to your senses sooner than this," he said gruffly. "Figured there was no sense letting all those lambs starve."

Harry turned to stare out a window draped with antique lace curtains. Her hand gripped the brass bedstead so hard her knuckles were white. "Did it ever occur to you that I'd rather not have your help? Did it ever occur to you that whether I was going to fail or succeed I would rather do it all by myself?"

Nathan didn't know how to answer her. He willed her to look up at him, but he could tell how she felt even without seeing her face. Her pulse pounded in her throat and her jaw worked as she ground her teeth.

To tell the honest truth, he didn't know why he'd interfered in her life. If he'd just left well enough alone, she would probably have quit and gone home a long time ago. Maybe that had something to do with it. Maybe he didn't want her to go away. He still felt the same attraction every time he got anywhere near her. And it was impossible to control his protective instincts whenever she was around. Just look what had happened today.

He reached out to touch her on the shoulder, and she jumped like a scalded cat. Only, when she came up off the bed, she ran right flat into him. Instinctively his arms surrounded her.

The only sound in the room was the two of them breathing. Panting, actually, as though they'd just run a footrace. Nathan didn't dare move, for fear she'd bolt. It felt good holding her. He wanted more. Slowly, ever so slowly, he raised a hand and brushed his knuckles across her cheek. It was so smooth!

She looked up at him then, and he saw her pupils were wide, her eyes dark. Her mouth was slightly open, her lips full. Her eyelids closed as he lowered his mouth to touch hers. He felt the tremor run through her as their lips made contact. Soft. So incredibly soft, and moist.

When he ran his tongue along the edge of her mouth, she groaned. And her mouth opened wider to let him in.

He took his time kissing her, letting his lips learn the touch and taste of her. He felt the tension in her body, felt her resistance even as she succumbed to the desire that flared between them.

Nathan felt the same war within himself that he knew she was fighting. Lord, how he wanted her! He knew he shouldn't be kissing her. But there was something about her, something about the touch and taste of her, that drew him despite his resolve not to become involved.

When he broke the kiss at last, she leaned her forehead against his chest, and all the starch seemed to come out of her. "Why did you do that?" she asked in a whisper.

"I can't explain it myself. I don't want...I don't think we're very well suited to each other." He felt her tense in his arms. "I don't mean to hurt your feelings. I'm only telling you the truth as I see it."

Harry dropped her hands, which she discovered were clutching either side of Nathan's waist, and stepped away from him. She raised her eyes to meet his steady gaze. "I can't disagree with you. I don't think we're well suited, either. I can't explain..." A rueful smile tilted her mouth up on one side. "You're quite good at kissing. You must have had a lot of practice."

Harry didn't realize she was fishing for information until the words were out of her mouth. She wanted to know if she was only one of many.

"I...uh...don't have much time for this sort of thing," he admitted. "Kissing women. A relationship with a woman, I mean."

"Oh?"

"Haven't had time for years," he blurted.

Harry was fascinated by the red patches that began at Nathan's throat and worked their way up. But his admission, however much it embarrassed him, gave Harry a reason for their tremendous attraction to each other. "I think I know why this… thing…is so strong between us," Harry said, as though speaking about it could diffuse its power.

This time Nathan said, "Oh?"

"Yes, you see, I haven't had much time for a relationship with a man. That has to be it, don't you think? We have these normal, primitive urges, and we just naturally—"

"Naturally kiss each other every time we meet?" Nathan said with disbelief.

"Have you got a better explanation?" Harry said. Her fists found her hips in a stance that Nathan recognized all too well.

He shrugged. "I can't explain it at all. All I can say is I don't plan to let this happen again."

"Well, that's good to hear," Harry said. "Now that we have that settled, I'm going back downstairs to inform my family that I'm managing fine *on my own.* And you will not contradict me. Is that clear?"

"Perfectly."

"Let's go, Mr. Hazard." She opened the door, waited for him to leave, then followed him toward the stairs.

"Wait!" He turned and she collided with his chest. His arms folded around her. The desire flared between them faster than they could stop it. Nathan swore under his breath as he steadied Harry and took a step back from her.

"I only wanted to say," he said harshly, "that if you plan to stay in the valley, you'd better get your fallow fields planted with some kind of winter forage."

Harry wrapped her arms around herself as though that would protect her from the feelings roiling inside. "Fine. Is that all?"

He opened his mouth to say something about the stack of dead lambs beside her barn and shut it again. She'd already asked Slim Harley what to do about them. He didn't understand why she hadn't buried them yet, but the closed expression on her face didn't encourage any more advice, let alone the offer of help he'd been about to make. "That's all," he said.

Nathan made his way back downstairs to the bar without once looking at Harry again. As he passed her family, he merely tipped his hat, grim-faced, and resumed his seat in the high-backed booth next to theirs.

Harry made quick work of reassuring her family that she was fine and that she wouldn't be leaving Montana. There was no sound from the next booth.

But Harry knew Nathan was there. And that he was listening.

"We'd like to see where you're living," her brother said. "What's it like?"

"Rustic," Harry said, her smile reappearing for the first time since she'd entered The Grand.

"It sounds charming," her mother said.

"That it is," Harry said, her sense of humor making her smile broaden. "I'm afraid I can't invite you out to visit. It's a little small. And it doesn't have much in the way of amenities."

She heard Nathan snort in the next booth.

"Well, I feel better knowing your neighbors are keeping an eye on you," her father said. "That Hazard fellow seems a nice enough man."

Harry didn't think that deserved further comment, so she remained silent.

"Are you sure you can handle the financial end of things?" her father asked. "Mr. Wilkinson said you've got a big bill due next month for—"

"I can handle things, Dad," Harry said. "Don't worry."

She watched her father gnaw on his lower lip, then pull at the bushy white mustache that covered his upper lip. "All right, Harriet. If you insist on playing this game out to the bitter end, I suppose we have no choice except to go along—for now. But I think I should warn you that if you aren't showing some kind of profit by the fall, I'll have to insist that you forget this foolishness and come home before winter sets in."

Harry was mortified to think that Nathan was hearing her father's ultimatum. She was tempted to let his words go without contesting them. That was the sort of passive resistance she'd resorted to in the past. But the Harry who'd come to Montana had turned over a new leaf. She felt compelled to say, "You're welcome to come and visit in the fall, Dad. I expect you'll be pleasantly surprised at how well I'm doing by then. But don't expect me to leave if I'm not."

Harry allowed her mother to admonish her to take better care of herself before she finally said, "I have to be getting back to the ranch. I've got stock that needs tending."

She rose and hugged her mother, father and brother, wishing things could be different, that she hadn't lived her life by pretending to fail. She would prove she could make it on her own if it was the last thing she did. Harry wished her family a pleasant drive from Big Timber to the airport in Billings, and a safe flight home. "I'll be in touch," she promised.

They would never know the effort it took to summon the confident smile with which she left them. "Things should be less hectic for me later in the summer," she said. "I'll look forward to seeing you then."

She could tell from their anxious faces that they didn't want to leave her in Montana alone. She reassured them the best she could with, "I'm all right, really. A little tired from all the hard work. But I love what I'm doing. It's challenging. And rewarding."

Harry smiled and waved as she left the restaurant. She was out the door before she realized Nathan Hazard had been standing behind her left shoulder the whole time she'd been waving goodbye.

"I'll follow you home," he said.

"Why on earth would you want to do that?"

Nathan looked up at a sky that was dark with storm clouds. "Looks like rain. All those potholes in your road, you could get stuck."

"If I do, Mr. Hazard, I'll dig myself out." Harry indignantly stalked away, but had to yank three or four times on the door to Cyrus's battered pickup before she finally got inside. She spent the entire trip home glaring at Nathan Hazard's pickup in her rearview mirror. He followed her all the way up to the tiny cabin door.

Harry hopped out of the pickup and marched back to Nathan's truck. He had the window down and his elbow stuck out.

"Rain, huh?" Harry said, looking up as the sun peered through the clouds, creating a glare on his windshield.

"Could have."

"Sheep dip," Harry said succinctly. "I've had it with helpful neighbors. From now on I want you to stay off my property. Stay away from me, and don't do me any more favors!"

"All right, Harry-et," he said with a long-suffering sigh. "We'll do it your way. For a while."

"For good!" Harry snapped back.

It was doubtful Nathan heard her, because he'd already turned his pickup around and headed back down the jouncy dirt road.

Harry kicked at a stone and sent it flying across the barren yard. Yes, the work was hard, and yes, she was tired. But she'd loved every minute of the challenge she'd set for herself. Before her talk with Nathan Hazard today she'd indulged fully in the satisfaction of knowing she'd done it all by herself. Damn him! Damn his interference! Damn the man for being such a damn good kisser!

If Nathan Hazard knew what was good for him, he wouldn't show his face around here anytime soon.

Chapter 4

*What do you do when people drop by to visit
and they haven't been invited?
Answer: Serve them coffee.*

Harry was standing in the pigpen, slopping the
hogs and thinking about Nathan, when she spied
a pickup bumping down the dirt road that led to
her place. At first she feared it was her nemesis
and began tensing for another battle with Nathan.
But the battered truck wasn't rusted in the right
places to be Nathan's. After two months of being
left so completely alone, Harry was surprised to
have visitors. She couldn't help wondering who
had come to see her, and why.

The man who stepped out of the driver's side of the beat-up vehicle was a stranger. Harry stood staring as a beautiful woman dressed in form-fitting jeans and a fleece-lined denim jacket shoved open the passenger door of the truck. The couple exchanged a glance that led Harry to believe they must be married, probably some of her neighbors, finally come to call.

The slight blonde woman approached her and said, "Hello, I'm Abigail Dayton. Fish and Wildlife Service."

Harry was dumbfounded. *The woman was a government official!* What on earth was someone from the Fish and Wildlife Service doing here? Her heart caught in her throat, keeping her from responding. Her mind searched furiously for the reason for such a visit. Had she done something wrong? Broken some law? Forgotten to fill out some form? Had she let too many lambs die? Was there a penalty for that?

Harry recognized the instinct to flee and fought it. She had come west to start over, to confront her problems and deal with them. She would have to face this woman and find out what she wanted. Only first she had to get out of the pigpen, which wasn't as easy as it sounded.

Harry finally resorted to climbing over the top of the pen instead of going through the gate, which was wired shut. She heard a rip when her overalls caught on a stray barb but ignored it as she extended her hand to the Fish and Wildlife agent. When the woman didn't take her hand immediately, Harry realized she was still wearing her work gloves, tore them off and tried again. "I'm Harriet Alistair. People mostly call me Harry."

"It's nice to meet you, Harry," Abigail said. She shook Harry's hand once, then let it go.

Harry turned and looked steadily at the tall, dark-haired, gray-eyed man standing beside Abigail Dayton, until he finally held out a callused hand and said, "I'm Luke Granger, your neighbor to the south. Sorry I haven't been over to see you sooner."

Harry was so glad Luke Granger was just a neighbor and not another government official that she smiled, exposing the tiny space between her teeth, and said, "I've been pretty busy myself. It's good to meet you."

So, one agent, one neighbor. Not related. But still no explanation as to why they'd come.

Harry felt a growing discomfort as she watched Luke and Abigail survey her property. It wasn't that they openly displayed disgust or disbelief at what they saw; in fact, they were both careful to keep their expressions neutral. But a tightening of Luke's jaw and a clenching of Abigail's hand made their feelings plain.

Harry wasn't exactly ashamed of her place.

After all, she was hardly responsible for the sad state of repairs. But her stomach turned over when Abigail narrowed her green-eyed gaze on the stack of dead lambs beside the barn that were only partially covered by a black plastic tarp. Harry waited for the official condemnation that was sure to come.

"Have you seen any wolves around here?" Abigail asked.

"Wolves?" That wasn't at all what Harry had been expecting the Fish and Wildlife agent to say. The thought of wolves somewhere on her property was terrifying. "Wolves?" she repeated.

"A renegade timber wolf killed two of Luke's sheep," Abigail continued. "I wondered if you've suffered any wolf depredation on your spread."

"Not that I know of," Harry said. "I didn't even know there were any wolves around here."

"There aren't many," Abigail reassured her. "And there's going to be one less as soon as I can find and capture the renegade that killed Luke's sheep."

Harry watched a strange tension flare between her two visitors at Abigail's pronouncement. Before Harry had time to analyze it further, Abigail asked, "Have you seen any wolf sign at all?"

Harry grimaced and shook her head. "I wouldn't know it if I saw it. But you're welcome to take a look around."

"I think I will if you really don't mind."

Abigail carefully looked the grounds over with Luke by her side. Harry did her best to keep them headed away from the tiny log cabin. She'd already tasted their disapproval once and was reluctant to have them observe the primitive conditions in which she lived. However, before Harry knew it, they were all three standing at her kitchen door. There wasn't much she could do except invite them inside.

Harry felt a flush of embarrassment stain her cheeks when both Luke and Abigail stopped dead just inside the door. The scene that greeted them in the kitchen was pretty much the same one that had greeted Nathan the first time he'd come to visit. Only now there were six lambs sleeping on a blanket wadded in the corner instead of just one. The shambles in Harry's kitchen gave painful evidence of how hard she was struggling to cope with the responsibilities she'd assumed on Cyrus Alistair's death. Harry didn't know what to say. What could she say?

Abigail finally broke the looming silence. "I'd love some coffee. Wouldn't you, Luke?"

Grateful for the simple suggestion, Harry urged her company to seat themselves at the kitchen table. While she made coffee, Harry lectured herself about how it didn't really matter what these people thought. The important thing was that she'd survived the past two months.

Harry poured three cups of coffee and brought them to the table, then seated herself across from Abigail, who was saying something about how wolves weren't really as bad as people thought, and how their reputation had been exaggerated by all those fairy tales featuring a Big Bad Wolf.

Harry wasn't convinced. She took a sip of the hot, bitter coffee and said, "I've been meaning to learn how to use a rifle in case I had trouble with predators, but—"

Abigail leaped up out of her chair in alarm. "You can't *shoot* a timber wolf! They're an endangered species. They're protected!"

"I'm sorry," Harry said. "I didn't know." She shook her head in disgust. "There's just so much I don't know."

Abigail sat back down a little sheepishly. "I'm afraid I tend to get on my high horse whenever the discussion turns to wolves."

Harry ran her fingers aimlessly across the books, magazines and articles that littered the table, shouting her ignorance of sheep ranching to anyone who cared to notice.

"You really shouldn't leave those dead lambs lying around, though," Abigail said. "They're liable to attract predators."

Harry chewed on her lower lip. "I know I'm

supposed to bury them, but I just can't face the thought of doing it."

"I've got some time right now," Luke said. "Why don't you let me help?"

Harry leaned forward to protest. "But I can't pay—"

"Neighbors don't have to pay each other for lending a helping hand," he said brusquely. A moment later he was out the door.

"You know, I bet there's a really nice man behind that stony face he wears," Harry said as she stared after him.

"I wouldn't know," Abigail said. "I only met him this morning."

"Oh, I thought…" Harry didn't finish her thought, discouraged by the shuttered look on Abigail's face. There was something going on between Luke and Abigail, all right. But if they'd just met, the sparks must have been pretty instantaneous. Just like the desire that had flared between her and Nathan. Harry felt an immediate affinity to the other woman. After all, they'd both been attracted to rough-hewn Montana sheepmen.

Abigail rose and took her coffee cup to the sink, and without Harry quite being aware how it happened, Abigail was soon washing the mound of dirty dishes while Harry dried them and put them away. While they worked, they talked, and Harry found herself confiding to Abigail, "Sometimes I wake up in the morning and wonder how long it'll take me to get this place into shape, or if I ever will."

"Why would you want to?" Abigail blurted. "I mean... This place needs a lot of work."

Harry's sense of humor got the better of her, and she grinned. "That's an understatement if I ever heard one. This place is a *wreck*."

"So tell me why you're staying," Abigail urged.

"It's a long story."

"I'd like to hear it."

Harry took a deep breath and let it out. "All right."

It was a tremendous relief to Harry to be able to tell someone—someone who had no reason to be judgmental—how she'd lived her life. Abigail's interested green eyes and sympathetic *oohs* and *aahs* helped Harry relate the various fiascos that littered her past. It wasn't until she started talking about Nathan Hazard that words became really difficult to find.

"At first I was so grateful he was there," Harry said as she explained how Nathan had helped in the birthing of the dead lamb and its twin. "I think that was why I was so angry when it turned out he'd only come because he wanted to buy this place from me.

"I'm determined to manage on my own, but the man keeps popping up when I least expect him.

And somehow, every time we've crossed paths, we end up—"

"End up what?"

"Kissing," Harry admitted. "I know that sounds absurd—"

"Not so absurd as you think," Abigail muttered. "Must be more to these Montana sheepmen than meets the eye," she said with a rueful smile.

"Nathan Hazard is driving me crazy," Harry said. What she didn't add, couldn't find words to explain, was how every time she inevitably ended up in his arms, the fire that rose between them seemed unquenchable. "I wish he'd just leave me alone."

That wasn't precisely true. What she wanted was a different kind of attention from Nathan Hazard than she was getting. Something more personal and less professional. But that was too confusing, and much too complicated, to contemplate.

Harry looked around her and was amazed to discover that while she'd been talking Abigail had continued doing chores around the kitchen. The dishes were washed, the floor was swept, the counters were clear and the things on the table had been separated into neat stacks. Several lambs had woken, and Abigail had matter-of-factly joined Harry on the floor to help her bottle-feed the noisy bums.

"Have you thought about getting a hired hand to help with the heavy work?" Abigail asked.

"Can't afford one," Harry admitted. "Although Mr. Wilkinson at the bank said there's a shepherd who'll keep an eye on my flock once I get it moved onto my federal lease in the mountains for the summer. Anyway, I'm determined to make it on my own."

"That's a laudable goal," Abigail said. "But is it realistic?"

"I thought so," Harry mused. "Since I didn't know a thing about sheep ranching when I arrived in Montana, I've made my share of mistakes. But I'm learning fast."

"You don't have to answer if you don't want to," Abigail said, "but why on earth don't you just sell this place—"

"To Nathan Hazard? Don't get me started again. I'll never sell to that man. Nathan Hazard is the meanest, ugliest son of a—"

Harry never got a chance to finish her sentence because Luke arrived at the door and announced, "I've buried those lambs. Anything else you'd like me to do while I'm here?"

"No thanks," Harry said, scrambling to her feet. "We're about finished here." She put the empty nippled Coke bottle on the kitchen counter and said, "I really appreciate your help, Luke."

"You're welcome, anytime."

It took a moment for Harry to realize that although Luke was speaking to her, his attention was totally absorbed by the woman still sitting on the floor feeding the last ounce of milk replacer to a hungry lamb. From the look on Luke's face it appeared he would gladly take the lamb's place. Harry had wondered why Luke had come visiting with the Fish and Wildlife agent. Now she had her answer.

Harry was envious of what she saw in Luke Granger's eyes. No man had ever looked at her with such raw hunger, such need.

Unless you counted Nathan Hazard.

Harry watched as Abigail raised her eyes to Luke, a beatific smile on her face, watched as the smile faded, watched as Abigail's eyes assumed the wary look of an animal at bay.

Luke's gray eyes took on a feral gleam, and his muscles tensed and coiled in readiness.

The hunter. And the hunted. Harry recognized the relationship because she'd felt it herself. With Nathan Hazard.

An instant later Luke reached out a hand and pulled Abigail to her feet. Harry was uncomfortably aware of the frisson of sexual attraction that arced between them as they touched. She observed their cautious movements as Abigail inched past Luke in the tiny kitchen and joined Harry at the sink.

"I suppose Luke and I should get going," Abigail

said. "We've got a few more ranchers to ask about wolf sightings before the day's done. I've enjoyed getting to know you, Harry. I wish you luck with your ranch."

"Thanks," Harry said with a smile, as she escorted Abigail and Luke back outside. "I need all the luck I can get." She turned to Luke and said, "I hope you'll come back and visit again soon, neighbor."

"Count on it," he replied, tipping his Stetson.

"And I hope you capture that renegade wolf," Harry said to Abigail.

Harry watched as Abigail gave Luke a determined, almost defiant, look and said, "Count on it."

Abigail had trouble getting the passenger door of the pickup open, and Harry was just about to lend a hand when Luke stepped up and yanked it free. Abigail frowned at him and said, "I could have done that."

He shrugged. "Never said you couldn't." But he waited for her to get inside and closed the door snugly behind her before heading around to the driver's side of the truck.

"So long," Harry shouted after them as they drove away. "Careful on that road. It's a little bumpy!" A perfect farewell, Harry thought with an ironic twist of her mouth, seeing as how this had been a day for understatement.

Harry felt sorry to see them leave. She was probably being unnecessarily stubborn about trying to manage all by herself. Nathan Hazard was convinced she couldn't manage on her own. She should probably take advantage of Luke's offer of help and avoid making any more costly mistakes. But the whole purpose of coming to Montana, of putting herself in this isolated position, was to prove that she could do anything she set her mind to do *on her own*. She wasn't the person she'd led her parents to believe she was.

Harry had realized over the past two months that she wanted to prove that fact to herself even more than she wanted to prove it to them.

It would be too easy to stop resisting Nathan Hazard's interference in her business. Harry reminded herself that Nathan didn't really want her to succeed; he wanted Cyrus's land. And he wanted to take care of her, as one would care for someone incapable of taking care of herself. Letting Nathan Hazard into her life right now would be disastrous. Because Harry didn't want any more people taking care of her. She wanted to prove she could take care of herself.

Harry had another motive for wanting to keep Nathan at a distance. Whenever he was around she succumbed to the attraction she felt for him. At a time when she was trying to take control of her life, the feelings she had for Nathan Hazard were uncontrollable. She wanted to touch him and have him touch her, to kiss him and be kissed back with all the passion she felt whenever he held her in his arms, to share with him and to have him share the feelings she was hard put to name, but couldn't deny. Those powerful emotions left her feeling threatened in a way she couldn't explain. It was far better, Harry decided, to keep the man at a distance.

The next time Nathan Hazard came calling, if there was a next time, he wouldn't be welcome.

Harry woke the next day to the clang of metal on metal. She bolted upright in bed, then sat unmoving while she tried to place the sound. She couldn't, and quickly pulled on a heavy flannel robe and stepped into ice-cold slippers as she headed for the window to look outside. Her jaw dropped at what she saw. Nathan Hazard stood bare-chested, wrench in hand, working on the engine of Cyrus's farm tractor.

Her first thought was, *He must be freezing to death!* Then she looked at the angle of the sun and realized it had to be nearly midday and would be much warmer outside than in the cabin, which held the cold. How had she slept so long? The lambs usually woke her at dawn to be fed. She hurried to the kitchen, and they were all there—sleeping peacefully. A quick glance at the kitchen counter revealed several empty nippled Coke bottles. Nathan Hazard had been inside her house this morning. He'd fed her lambs!

Harry felt outraged at Nathan's presumption. And then she had another, even more disturbing thought. Had he come into her bedroom? Had he seen her sleeping? She blushed at the thought of what she must have looked like. She'd worn only a plain white torn T-shirt to sleep in Cyrus's sleigh bed. Harry was disgusted with herself when she realized that what upset her most was the thought that she couldn't have looked very attractive.

It took three shakes of a lamb's tail for Harry to dress in jeans, blue work shirt and boots. She stomped all the way from her kitchen door to the barn, where the tractor stood. Nathan had to hear her coming, but he never moved from his stance, bent over concentrating on some part of the tractor's innards.

"Good morning," she snarled.

Slowly, as though it were the most ordinary thing in the world for him to be working on her tractor, he straightened. "Good afternoon," he corrected.

Harry caught her breath at the sight of him. She didn't see the whole man, just perceptions of him. A bead of sweat slid slowly down the crease in his muscular chest to dampen the waist of his jeans. Only the waist wasn't at his waist. His jeans had slid down over his hips to reveal a navel and a line of downy blond hair that disappeared from sight under the denim. She didn't see any sign of underwear. The placket over the zipper was worn white with age.

When she realized where she was staring, Harry jerked her head up to look at his face and noticed that a stubble of beard shadowed his jaws and chin. Hanks of white-blond hair were tousled over his forehead. And his shockingly bright blue eyes were focused on her as though she were a lamb chop and he were a starving man.

Harry's mouth went dry. She slicked her tongue over her lips and saw the resulting spark of heat in Nathan's gaze. His nostrils flared, and she felt her body tighten with anticipation.

The hunter. Its prey.

Only Harry had no intention of becoming a sacrificial lamb to this particular wolf.

"Don't you know how to knock?" she demanded.

It might have seemed an odd question, but Nathan knew what she was asking. "I did knock. You didn't answer. I was worried, so I came inside."

"And fed my lambs!" Harry said indignantly.

"Yes. I fed them."

"Why didn't you come wake me up?"

Nathan had learned enough about Harry-et Alistair's pride to know he couldn't tell her the truth. She'd looked tired. More than tired, exhausted. He had figured she could use the sleep. So he'd fed her lambs. Was that so bad? Obviously Harry-et thought so.

But her need for sleep wasn't the only reason he hadn't woken her. When Nathan had entered Harry-et's bedroom, she was lying on her side, with one long, bare, elegantly slender leg curled up outside the blankets. The tiny bikini panties she'd been wearing had revealed a great expanse of hip, as well. Her long brown hair was spread across the pillow in abandon. One breast was pushed up by the arm she was lying on, and he'd seen a dark nipple through the thin cotton T-shirt she was wearing.

Not that he'd looked on purpose. Or very long. In fact, once he'd realized the full extent of her dishevelment, he'd backed out of the room so fast he'd almost tripped over her work boots, which lay where they'd fallen when she'd taken them off the previous night.

He'd wanted to wake her more than she'd ever know. He'd wanted to take her in his arms and feel her nipples against his bare chest. He'd wanted to wrap those long, luscious legs around himself and… No, she was damn lucky he hadn't woken her. But he could never tell her that. Instead he said, "Anybody offered me another hour or two of sleep, I'd be grateful."

Harry sputtered, unable to think of an appropriate retort. She *was* grateful for the sleep. She just didn't like the way she'd gotten it. "What are you doing to this tractor?"

"Fixing it."

"I didn't know it was broken."

"Neither did I until I tried starting it up."

"Why would you want to start it up?"

Nathan leaned back over and began tinkering again, so he wouldn't have to look her in the eye when he said, "So I could plow your fallow fields."

"So you could..." Harry was flabbergasted. "I thought you were too busy doing your own work to lend me a hand."

Nathan stood and leaned a hip against the tractor while he wiped his hands on his chambray work shirt. "I had a visit yesterday from a good friend of mine, Luke Granger. He was with an agent of the Fish and Wildlife Service, Abigail—"

"They were here yesterday. So?"

"Luke pointed out to me that I haven't been a very good neighbor."

Harry felt her stomach churn. "What else did he have to say?"

"That was enough, don't you think?"

Harry met Nathan's solemn gaze and found it even more unsettling than the heat that had so recently been there.

Nathan never took his eyes off her when he

added, "I think maybe I've been a little pigheaded about helping you out. On the other hand, Harry-et, I can't help thinking—"

The blaring honk of a truck horn interrupted Nathan. A battered pickup was wending its way up the rutted dirt road.

Harry recognized Luke Granger and Abigail Dayton. "I wonder what they're doing back here today."

"I invited them."

Harry whirled to face Nathan. "You what?"

"I called Luke this morning to see if he could spare a little time to do some repairs around here." He took a look around the dilapidated buildings and added, "There's plenty here for both of us to do."

"You all got together and figured I needed help, so here you are riding to the rescue like cowboys in white hats," Harry said bitterly. "Damn. Oh, damn, damn, damn." Harry fisted her hands and placed them on her hips to keep from hauling off and hitting Nathan. She clamped her teeth tight to keep her chin from quivering. She wanted to scream and rant and rave. And she was more than a little afraid she was going to cry.

Nathan couldn't understand what all the fuss was about. In all the years he'd been offering help to others, the usual response had been a quick and ready acceptance of his assistance. This woman was totally different. She seemed to resent his support. He found her reaction bewildering. And not a little frustrating.

He should have been glad she didn't need his help. He should have been glad she didn't need any caretaking. But he found himself wanting to help, needing to help. Her rejection hurt in ways he wasn't willing to acknowledge.

He turned and began working on the tractor again, keeping his hands busy to keep from grabbing Harry and kissing some sense into her.

"Hello, there," Luke said as he and Abigail approached the other couple.

"Hello," Harry muttered through clenched teeth. Her angry eyes remained on Nathan.

Nathan never looked up. "I ran into a little problem, Luke. The tractor needs some work before I can do anything about those fallow fields."

"Anything I can do?" Luke asked Nathan.

Harry whirled on him and said, "You can turn that truck around and drive right back out of here."

"We just want to help," Abigail said quietly.

"I don't need your charity," Harry cried in an anguished voice. "I don't need—"

Nathan suddenly dropped his wrench on the engine with a clatter and grabbed Harry by the arms, forcing her to face him. "That'll be enough of that!"

"Just who do you think you are?" Harry rasped. "I didn't ask you to come here. I didn't ask you to—"

"I'm doing what a good neighbor should do."

"Right! Where was all this neighborliness when I had lambs dying because I didn't know how to deliver them? Where was all this friendly help when I really needed it?"

"You need it right now," Nathan retorted, his grip tightening. "And I intend to give it to you."

"Over my dead body!" Harry shouted.

"Be reasonable," Nathan said in a voice that was losing its calm. "You need help."

"I don't need it from you," Harry replied stubbornly.

"Maybe you'd let us help," Abigail said, stepping forward to place a comforting hand on Harry's arm.

Harry's shoulders suddenly slumped, all the fight gone out of her. Maybe she should just take their help. Maybe her parents had been right all along. She bit her quivering lower lip and closed her eyes to hold back the threatening tears.

But some spark inside Harry refused to be quenched by the dose of reality she'd just suffered. She could give up and give in, as she had in the past. Or she could fight.

Her shoulders came up again, and when her eyes opened, they focused on Nathan Hazard, flashing with defiance. "I want you off my property, Nathan

Hazard. Now. I…" Her voice caught in an angry sob, but her jaw stiffened. "I have things to do inside. I expect you can see yourself off my land."

Harry turned and marched toward the tiny log house without a single look back to see if he had obeyed her command.

Chapter 5

What do you say when asked, "How's it going?"
Answer: "Oh, could be worse. Could be better."

Nathan spent the rest of the afternoon working outside with Luke, while Abigail worked in and around the barn with a still-seething Harry. Luke and Abigail left just before sundown, knowing Harry's fallow fields were plowed and planted and that the pigpen gate, among other things, had been repaired. Nathan worked another quarter hour before admitting there wasn't enough light to continue. He pulled on the chambray shirt he'd been using for an oil rag and headed toward the only light on in Cyrus's log cabin.

He knocked at Harry's kitchen door, but didn't wait for an answer before he pushed the screen door open and stepped inside. Harry was standing at the sink rinsing out Coke bottles. She turned when she saw him, grabbed a towel from the counter and wiped her hands dry. She stood backed up against the sink, waiting, wary.

"I'm sorry." Nathan hadn't said those two words very often in his lifetime, and they stuck in his craw.

It didn't help when Harry retorted, "You should be!"

"Now look here, Harry-et—"

"No, *you* look here, Nathan," she interrupted. "I thought I'd made it plain to you that I didn't want your help. At least not the way you're offering it. I wouldn't mind so much if you wanted to teach me how to run this place. But you seem bound and determined to treat me like the worst sort of tenderfoot, which I am—a tenderfoot, I mean. But not the worst sort. Oh, this isn't making any sense!"

Harry was so upset that she gulped air, and she trembled as though she had the ague. Nathan took a step toward her, wanting to comfort her, but stopped when she stuck out a flat palm.

"Wait. I'm not finished talking. I don't know how to make it any plainer. I don't want the sort of help you're offering, Nathan."

Nathan opened his mouth to offer her the kind of help she was asking for and snapped it shut. Even if he taught her what she wanted to know, she would be hard-pressed to make a go of this place by herself. And if, by some miracle, she did succeed, he would only be stuck with another Alistair planted square in the middle of Hazard land.

"All right, Harry-et," he said, "I'll stop trying to help."

Her shoulders sagged, and he wasn't sure if she was relieved or disappointed. Neither reaction pleased him. So he said, "I think maybe what we ought to do is call a truce."

"A truce?"

"Yeah. You know, raise the white flag. Stop fighting. Call a halt to hostilities." He tried a smile of encouragement. It wasn't his best, but apparently it was good enough, because she smiled back.

"All right," she agreed. "Shall we shake on it?"

She stuck her hand out and, like a fool, he took it. And suffered the consequences. Touching her was like shooting off fireworks on the Fourth of July. He liked what he felt. Too much. So he dropped her hand and turned to leave.

Before he even got to the door he had turned back—he didn't have the faintest idea why—and caught her looking bereft. The words were out of his mouth before he could stop them. "What would you say to a dinner to celebrate our truce?" She looked doubtfully around her kitchen, and he quickly added, "I meant dinner out."

"A date?"

"Not a date," he quickly reassured her. "Just a dinner between two neighbors who've agreed to make peace."

"All right."

It was the most reluctant acceptance he'd ever heard. Nathan figured he'd better get the plans finalized and get out of here before she changed her mind. "I'll pick you up at eight. Dress up fancy."

"Fancy?"

"Sure. Something soft and ladylike. You have a dress like that, don't you?" He hadn't realized how much he wanted to see her in a dress, so he could admire those long legs of hers again.

"Where is this dinner going to be?" she asked suspiciously.

"Have you ever been to the hot springs at Chico?"

"No. Where is that?"

"About an hour south. Best rack of lamb in two counties." He saw her moue of distress and added, "Or you can have steak if you'd rather."

She smiled, and he felt his heart beat faster at the shy pleasure revealed in the slight curl of her lips.

"All right. I'll be ready," she said.

Nathan left in a hurry before he did something really stupid, like take her in his arms and kiss that wide, soft mouth of hers and run his hands all over her body. He had it bad, all right. The worst. The woman was under his skin and there was no denying it.

Nathan drove home so fast that his head hit the top of the pickup twice on his way down Harry-et's road. He showered and shaved and daubed some manly-smelling, female-alluring scent on himself in record time. He donned a dark, tailored Western suit that hugged him across the shoulders like a second skin and added his best boots and a buff felt cowboy hat.

Nathan wasn't conscious of how carefully he'd dressed until Katoya stopped him at the bottom of the stairs and said, "You are going hunting."

"I'm not exactly dressed for bear."

"Not for bear. For dear. One dear," the old woman clarified with a cackle of glee.

Nathan grimaced. "Is it that obvious?"

"Noticeable, yes. As a wolf among sheep."

He started back up the stairs again. "I'll change."

"It will do no good."

Nathan walked back down to her. "Why not?"

"Even if you change the outer trappings, she will know what you feel."

"How?" he demanded.

"She will see it in your eyes. They shine with excitement. And with hunger."

Nathan looked down at his fisted hands so that his lids would veil what the old woman had seen. "I want her," he said. He looked up, and there was a plea in his eyes he didn't know was there. "I know I'm asking for trouble. She's all wrong for me. But I can't seem to stop myself."

"Maybe you shouldn't try," Katoya said softly. "Maybe it is time you let go of the past."

"Wish I could," he said. "It isn't easy."

"We do the best we can," the older woman said. "Go. Enjoy yourself. What must be will be."

He grabbed the tiny woman and hugged her hard. "You're a wise old woman. I'll do my best to take your advice."

He let her go and hurried out the door, anxious to be on his way. He didn't see the sadness in her eyes as he left or the pain in her step as she headed for the window to watch him drive away in a classic black sports car that spent most of its time in his garage.

For the entire trip to Cyrus's ranch Nathan imagined how wonderful Harry-et would look dressed up. But the reality still exceeded his expectation.

"I can't believe it's you," he said in an awestruck voice when Harry opened the front door to the cabin. She stepped out, rather than inviting him in, and having seen the broken-down couch and chairs from the 1970s that served as living room furniture, Nathan understood why. But he wouldn't let Harry into his car until he'd taken a good look at her.

"Wait. Turn around."

"Do you like it?" she asked anxiously.

How could he describe how beautiful she looked to him? He didn't think he could find the words. "I love it," he managed.

The dress was a vibrant red and made of material that looked soft to the touch. The skirt was full, so it floated around her. The bodice was fitted, crisscrossing in a V over her breasts, so for the first time he could see just how lovely she was. The chiffonlike material fell off her shoulders, leaving them completely bare, but enticed with a hint of cleavage. She'd taken her hair out of the tomboyish braids, and a mass of rich brown curls draped her bare shoulders, begging to be taken up in his hands. She was wearing high heels that lengthened her already-long legs and brought her eyes almost even with his.

He could see how easy it would be to push the material down from her shoulders, leaving her breasts free to touch and taste. How easy it would be to slip his hands under the full skirt and capture her thighs, pulling her close. That thought pushed him over the edge. He felt himself responding to the wanton images that besieged him while she stood there looking lovely and desirable.

"Get in the car," he said in a voice harsh with the need he was struggling to control.

He hates the dress, Harry thought as she obeyed Nathan's curt order. She'd known the red dress was all wrong for her when she'd bought it two years ago. Too bright. Too sexy. Too sensual. Not at all like the Harriet Alistair of Williamsburg, Virginia. But tonight, when she'd looked into her closet, there it was. And it had seemed exactly right for the bold and daring woman who'd moved to Big Timber, Montana. The one who was attracted to Nathan Hazard.

Apparently Nathan didn't agree.

On the other hand, Harry thought Nathan looked wonderful. His Western suit fit him to perfection. The tailoring showed off his broad shoulders and narrow hips, his flat stomach and long legs. Of course, she had never found any fault with the way Nathan looked. Indeed, she'd wanted to touch the rippled chest and belly she'd seen this morning. Would Nathan's skin be soft? Or as hard as the muscles that corded his flesh? Harry had even fantasized what Nathan would look like without a stitch on. But she'd never seen a naked man, and the only images she could conjure were the marble statues of Greek gods she'd seen. And a leaf had always covered the pertinent parts.

Tonight there was a barely leashed power in the way Nathan moved that made Harry want to test the limits of his control. She wanted to touch. She wanted to taste. And she wanted to tempt Nathan to do the same.

Their personal relationship had nothing to do with the land, Harry told herself. It was separate and apart from that. She could desire Nathan without compromising her stand, because they were in the midst of a truce. So when she sat down in Nathan's sports car, she let her skirt slip halfway up her thighs before pulling it back down and leaned toward Nathan so that her breast brushed against his arm.

He inhaled sharply.

Harry looked at him, stunned by the flood of desire in his eyes. And began to reevaluate Nathan's reaction to her red dress.

Nathan didn't leave her in doubt another moment. He leaned over slowly but surely until their mouths were nearly touching and said, "Don't do that again unless you mean it."

Harry shivered and made a little noise in her throat.

Nathan groaned as his lips covered hers and sipped the nectar there. Her mouth was soft and oh, so sweet, and his body tightened like a bowstring with need. His tongue found the edge of her lips and followed it until she opened her mouth and his tongue slipped inside. He mimed the stroke of their two bodies joined and heard her moan. He reached up a hand to cup her breast and felt the weight of it in his hand. His thumb stroked across the tip, and he realized it had already tightened into a tiny nub. His hand followed the shape of her, from her ribs to her waist and down her thigh to the hem of her skirt, where Harry caught his wrist and stopped him.

Abruptly Nathan lifted his mouth from hers. Damn if she didn't have him as hot and bothered as a high school kid! And she'd stopped him as if she were some teenage virgin who'd never done it before. On the other hand, though he felt like a kid, he wasn't one. The small car was damn close for comfort. He could wait. Before the night was through he'd know what it was like to hold her in his arms and feel himself inside her. She wanted it. And so did he.

"All right, Ms. Alistair," he said through gritted teeth. "We'll do this your way."

Nathan started the car, made a spinning turn and, in deference to his delicate suspension, headed at a slow crawl back down the bumpy dirt road toward the main highway and Chico.

Harry was stunned. How had one kiss turned

into so much so fast? She hadn't wanted to stop Nathan. But things were moving too quickly. She didn't want their first time to be in the front seat of a car. They both deserved more than that.

Nathan was on the verge of suggesting they forget dinner and go back to his place. But from the nervous fidgeting Harry was doing, that probably wasn't a good idea. He figured he'd better say something quick before he said what was really on his mind. So he cleared his throat of the last remnants of passion and asked, "What was your life like before you came to Montana?"

"Overprotected."

Nathan glanced briefly at Harry-et to see if she was kidding. She wasn't. "I guess I saw a little of that when your parents were here. They sure don't think you can make a go of Cyrus's ranch, do they?"

"That isn't their fault," Harry said, coming to their defense. "I wasn't exactly what you'd call a roaring success when I lived in Williamsburg."

"What were you, exactly?"

Harry paused for a moment before she admitted, "I had several occupations, but I wasn't interested in any of them. I managed to do poorly at them, so I could get fired."

"Why did you take the jobs in the first place if you weren't interested in them?"

"Because I couldn't say no to my father."

Nathan snorted. "You haven't had any trouble saying no to me."

"I turned over a new leaf when I came to Montana," Harry said with an impish smile. "I made up my mind to do what I wanted to do, my way." Her expression became earnest. "That's why I was so upset by your interference. Don't you see? I wanted to prove to my family, and to myself, that I could succeed at something on my own."

"I'm sorry I butted in," Nathan said curtly.

Harry put a hand on Nathan's arm and felt him tense beneath her fingertips. "How could you know? Now that we've called this truce, things will be better, I'm sure. What about you? Did you always want to be a sheep rancher?"

"No. Actually, I had plans to be an architect once upon a time."

"What happened?"

Nathan glanced at Harry and was surprised by the concerned look on her face. He hardened himself against the growing emotional attachment he felt to her. "Things got in the way."

"What kind of things?"

"Parents."

"You weren't overprotected, too, were you?"

"Not hardly. I was the one who did the protecting in my household."

Harry was stunned by the bitterness in his voice. "I don't understand. Are you saying you took care of your parents? Were they hurt or something?"

"Yes, and yes."

But he didn't say any more. Harry wasn't sure whether to press him for details. His lips had flattened into a grim line, and the memories obviously weren't happy ones. But her curiosity got the better of her and she asked, "Will you tell me about it?"

At first she thought he wasn't going to speak. Then the words started coming, and the bitterness and anger and regret and sadness poured out along with them.

"My mother was an alcoholic," he said. "I didn't know her very well. But I took care of her the best I could. Dumped the bottles when I found them. Cleaned up when I could. Made meals for me and my dad. She didn't eat much. The alcohol finally killed her when I was sixteen.

"It was a relief," he said in a voice that grated with pain. "I was glad she was gone. She was an embarrassment. She was a lush. I hated her." Harry watched him swallow hard and add in a soft voice, "And I loved her so much I would have died in her place."

Harry felt a lump in her own throat and tears burning her eyes. What a heavy burden for a child.

"My father and I missed her when she was gone. Dad wanted me to stay on the ranch—Hazards had been sheep ranchers for a hundred years—but I wanted to be an architect. So I went away to college despite his wishes and learned to design buildings to celebrate the spirit of life.

"The month I graduated my father had an accident. A tractor turned over on him and crippled him. I came home to take over for him. And to take care of him. That was fifteen years ago. He died two years ago an old man. He was fifty-eight."

"Did you ever have the opportunity to design anything?"

"I designed and built the house I live in now. I haven't had time to do more than that."

She could hear the pride in his voice. And the disappointment. "I'm sorry."

"Don't pity me. I've had a good life. Better than most."

"But it wasn't the life you had planned for yourself. What about a wife? Didn't you ever want to marry and have children?"

"I was too busy until two years ago to think about anything but making ends meet," Nathan said. "Since then I've been looking. But I haven't found the right woman yet."

Harry heard Nathan's "yet" loud and clear. Nathan knew her, therefore he must have excluded her from consideration. Which hurt more than she'd expected. "What kind of woman are you looking for?"

Nathan didn't pull any punches. "One who can stand on her own. One who can carry her half of the burden. Ranching's a hard life. I can't afford to marry a woman who can't contribute her share to making things work."

Harry threaded her hands together in her lap. Well, that settled that. She obviously wasn't the kind of woman who could stand on her own two feet. In fact, Nathan had been holding her up for the past two months.

How he must have hated that, Harry thought. He had taken care of her with concern and consideration, but he'd done it because she was someone who was helpless to help herself. Not as though she were an equal. Not as though she were someone who could one day be his partner. How Harry wanted the chance to show Nathan she could manage on her own! Maybe with this truce it would happen. She would continue to learn and grow. As success followed success, he would see her with new eyes. Maybe then…

Harry suddenly realized the implications of what she was thinking. She was thinking of a future that included Nathan Hazard. She pictured little Nathans and Harrys—blue-eyed blondes and brown-eyed brunettes with freckles. Oh, what a lovely picture it was!

However, a look at Nathan's stern visage wasn't encouraging. He was obviously not picturing the same idyllic scene.

In fact, Nathan was picturing something very similar. And calling himself ten times a fool for doing so. How could he even consider a life with Harry-et Alistair. The woman was a disaster waiting for a place to happen. She didn't know the first thing about ranching. She was a tenderfoot. A city girl. She would never be the kind of partner who could pull her own weight.

Fortunately they'd reached the turnoff to the restaurant. The lag in the conversation wasn't as noticeable because Nathan took the opportunity to fill Harry-et in on the history of Chico. The hotel and restaurant were located at the site of a natural hot spring that now fed into a swimming pool that could be seen from the bar. It had become a hangout for all the movie stars who regularly escaped the bright lights and big city for what was still Montana wilderness. The pool was warm enough that it could be used even when the night was cool, as it was this evening.

Nathan and Harry were a little early for their dinner reservations, so Nathan escorted her into the bar where they could watch the swimmers.

"Would you like to take a dip in the pool?" Nathan asked. "They have suits—"

"Not this time," Harry said. "I don't think—" Harry stopped in midsentence, staring, unable to believe her eyes. She pointed toward the sliding glass doors. "Doesn't that man in the pool look a lot like—"

"Luke," Nathan finished for her. "I think you're right. He seems to be with someone. Maybe they'd like to join us for a drink. I'll go see."

Nathan had grasped at the presence of his friend as though it were a lifeline. He'd realized, suddenly and certainly, that it wasn't a good idea to be alone with Harry-et Alistair. The more time he spent with her, the lower his resistance to her. If he wasn't careful, he'd end up letting his heart tell his head what to do. He could use his friend's presence to help him keep his sense of perspective.

Of course, knowing Luke, and seeing how cozy he was with the lady, he knew his friend wasn't going to appreciate the interruption. But, hell, what were friends for?

Thus, a moment later he was standing next to Luke and the woman who had her face hidden against his chest. "Hey, Luke, I thought it was you. Who's that with you?"

After a brief pause, Luke answered, "It's Abby."

Nathan searched his memory for any woman he knew by that name. "Abby?"

"Abigail Dayton," Luke bit out.

"From Fish and Wildlife?" Nathan asked, astonished.

Abigail turned at last to face him. "Luke and I are just relaxing a few tired muscles."

Nathan grinned. "Yeah. Sure."

A female voice from the doorway called, "Nathan?"

The light behind Harry-et made her face nearly invisible in the shadows. At the same time it silhouetted a fantastic figure and a dynamite pair of legs. It irked Nathan that Luke couldn't seem to take his eyes off the woman in the doorway.

"Who's that with you?" Luke asked Nathan.

"Uh…"

"Nathan, is it Luke?" Harry asked. "Oh, hello. It is you. Nathan thought he recognized you."

This time it was Luke who stared, astonished. "Harry? That's Harry?"

Harry grinned. "Sure is. Nathan tried to convince me to take a swim, but I was too chicken. How's the water?" she asked Abigail.

"Marvelous."

"What are you two doing here together?" Luke asked his friend sardonically. "I thought you hated each other's guts."

Nathan stuck a hand in the trouser pocket of his Western suit pants to keep from clapping it over his friend's mouth. "We called a truce. Why don't you two dry off and join us for a drink?" he invited.

Nathan could see Luke wasn't too hot on the idea. But he gave his friend his most beseeching look, and at last Luke said, "Fine."

Luke gave Nathan a penetrating stare, but made no move to leave the pool. Obviously Luke wanted a few more minutes alone with the Fish and Wildlife agent. Nathan turned to Harry-et and suggested, "Why don't we go inside and wait for Luke and Abby."

He took Harry's arm and led her back inside. "You really look beautiful tonight, Harry-et," he said as he seated her at their table.

"Thank you, Nathan." Ever since she'd come outside Nathan had been looking at her a little differently. She'd seen the admiration in Luke's eyes and watched Nathan stiffen. Really, men could be so funny sometimes. There was no reason for Nathan to be jealous. She didn't find Luke's dark, forbidding looks nearly so attractive as she found Nathan's sharp-boned Nordic features.

She was almost amused when Nathan took her hand possessively once he was seated across from her. He held it palm up in his while his fingertips traced her work-roughened palm and the callused pads of her fingertips.

Harry felt goose bumps rise on her arm. She

was all set for a romantic pronouncement when Nathan said, "It's a shame you have to work so hard. A lady like you shouldn't have calluses on her hands."

Harry jerked her hand from his grasp. "I have to work hard."

"No, you don't. Look at you, Harry-et. You spend so much time in the sun your face is as freckled as a six-year-old's."

"Are you finished insulting me?" Harry asked, confused and annoyed by Nathan's behavior.

"I think you ought to sell your place to me and get back to being the beautiful woman—"

Harry's hand came up without her really being aware it had. She slapped Nathan with the full force of the anger and betrayal she was feeling. The noise was lost in the celebration of the busy bar, but it was the only sound Harry heard above the pounding of her heart. "You never wanted a truce at all, did you, Nathan? You just wanted a chance to soften me up and make another plea to buy my land. I can't think of anything lower in this life than a lying, sneaky snake-in-the-grass Hazard!"

"Now just a minute, Harry-et. I—"

She grabbed his keys from the table where he'd set them and stood up. "I'm taking your car. You can pick it up at my place tomorrow. But I don't want to see your sorry face when you do it."

"Be reasonable, Harry-et. How am I supposed to get home?"

"You can ask your friend, Luke, to give you a ride, but I'd be pleased as punch if you have to walk."

"Harry-et—"

"Shut up and listen! You're going to have an Alistair ranching smack in the middle of your land for the rest of your life, Nathan. And you can like or lump it. I don't really care!"

Harry marched out of the bar with her head held high, but she couldn't see a blamed thing through the haze of tears in her eyes. How could she have believed that handsome devil's lies? And worse, oh, far worse, how could she still want a man who only wanted her land?

Nathan stood up to follow her and then sat back down. That woman was so prickly, so short-tempered, and so stubborn—how on earth could he want her the way he did? It was his own fault for provoking her. But he'd been frightened by his possessive feelings when Luke had admired Harry-et. So, perversely, he'd enumerated to her all the reasons why he couldn't possibly be attracted to her and managed to drive her away.

He had to find a way to make peace with the woman. This Hazard-Alistair feud had gone on long enough. There had to be a happy medium somewhere, some middle ground, neither his nor hers, on which they could meet.

Nathan made up his mind to find it.

Chapter 6

How should you behave in a Woolly West bar?
Answer: You don't have to behave in a Woolly
West bar.

Over the next three weeks Nathan thought about all the ways he could end the Hazard-Alistair feud. And kept coming back to the same one: *He could marry Harry-et Alistair.* Of course, that solution raised its own set of problems. Not the least of which was how he was going to convince Harry-et Alistair to marry him.

The way Nathan had it figured, marrying Harry-et would have all kinds of benefits. First of all, once they were married, there wouldn't be any more Alistair land; it would all be Hazard land. Second, the feud would necessarily come to an end, since all future Hazards would also be Alistairs. And third—and Nathan found this argument for marriage both the most and the least compelling—he would have Harry-et Alistair for his wife.

Although Nathan was undeniably attracted to Harry-et, he wasn't convinced she was the right woman for him. Except every time he thought of a lifetime spent without her, it seemed a bleak existence, indeed. So maybe he was going to have to take care of her more than he would have liked. It wasn't something he hadn't done in the past. He could handle it. He'd finally admitted to himself that he was willing to pull ten times the normal load in order to spend his life with Harry-et Alistair.

Only the last time he'd driven onto her place she'd met him at the end of her road with a Winchester. He'd had no choice except to leave. He hadn't figured out a way yet to get past that rifle.

Nathan was sitting at his regular booth at The Grand, aimlessly stirring his chicken noodle soup, when Slim Harley came running in looking for him.

"She's done it now!" Slim said, skidding to a stop at Nathan's booth.

"Done what?"

"Lost Cyrus's ranch for sure," Slim said.

Nathan grabbed Slim by his shirt at the throat. "Lost it how? You didn't call in her bill, did you? I told you I was good for it if you needed the cash."

"Weren't me," Slim said, trying to free Nathan's hold without success. "It's John Wilkinson at the bank. Says he can't loan her any money to pay the lease on her government land. Says she ain't a good credit risk."

"Where is she now?"

"At the bank. I just—" Slim found himself talking to thin air as Nathan shoved past him and took off out the door of The Grand, heading for the bank across the street.

When Nathan entered the bank, he saw Harry-et sitting in front of John Wilkinson's desk. He casually walked over to one of the tellers nearby and started filling out a deposit slip.

"But I've told you I have a trust I can access when I'm thirty," Harry was saying.

"That's still four years off."

Nathan folded the deposit slip in half and stuck it in his back pocket. He meandered over toward John's desk and said, "I couldn't help overhearing. Is there anything I can do to help, Harry-et?"

She glared at him and stared down at her hands,

which were threaded tightly together in the lap of her overalls.

"So, John, what's the problem?" Nathan asked, setting a hip on the corner of the banker's oversize desk.

"Don't expect it's any secret," John said. "Mizz Alistair here doesn't have the cash to renew her government lease. And I don't think I can risk the bank's money making her a loan."

"What if I cosign the note?" Nathan asked.

"No!" Harry said, shooting to her feet to confront Nathan. "I don't want to get the money that way. I'd rather lose the ranch first!"

The banker stroked his whiskered chin with a bony hand. "Well, now, sounds like maybe we could work something out here, Mizz Alistair."

"I meant what I said," Harry declared, her chin tilting up mulishly. "I don't want your money if Nathan Hazard has to cosign the note. I'll go to a bank in Billings or Bozeman. I'll—"

"Now hold on a minute. There's no call to take your business elsewhere." John Wilkinson hadn't become president of the Big Timber First National Bank without being a good judge of human nature. What he had here was a man-woman problem, sure as wolves ate sheep. Only both the man and the woman were powerful prideful. The man wanted to help; the woman wanted to do it on her own.

"I might be willing to make that loan to you,

Mizz Alistair, if Nathan here would agree to advise you on ranch management till your lamb crop got sold in the fall."

Nathan frowned. Teaching ranch management to Harry-et Alistair was a whole other can of worms from cosigning her note.

"Done," Harry said. She ignored Nathan and stuck out her hand to the banker, who shook it vigorously.

"Now wait a minute," Nathan objected. "I never said—"

"Some problem, Nathan?" the banker asked.

Nathan saw the glow of hope in Harry's eyes, and didn't have the heart to put it out. "Aw, hell, I'll do it."

"I'll expect you over later today," Harry said, throwing a quick grin in Nathan's direction. "I have a problem that needs solving right away." She turned to the banker and added, "I'll come in and sign the papers on Monday, John."

Nathan stood with his mouth hanging open as Harry marched by him and out the door.

"That's quite a woman," the banker said as he stared after her.

"You can say that again," Nathan muttered. "She's Trouble with a capital T."

"Never saw trouble you couldn't handle," the banker said with a confident smile. "Anything else you need, Nathan?"

"No thanks, John. I think you've done quite enough for me today."

"We aim to please, Nathan. We aim to please."

Nathan was still half stunned as he walked out of the bank door and headed back to The Grand. He found Slim sitting at his booth, finishing off his chicken noodle soup.

"Didn't know you was coming back, Nathan," Slim said. "I'll have Tillie Mae ladle you up another bowl."

"I'm not hungry."

"What happened?" Slim asked. "Mizz Alistair get her loan?"

"She got it," Nathan snapped. "But it's going to cost me plenty."

"You loan her the money?" Slim asked, confused.

"I loaned her *me.*" Nathan sat down and dropped his head into his hands. "I'm the new manager for Cyrus's ranch."

Word spread fast in the Boulder River Valley, and by suppertime it was generally believed that Nathan Hazard must have lost his mind...or his heart. Nathan was sure it was both.

Of course, on the good side, he had Harry-et Alistair exactly where he wanted her. She would have to see him, whether she wanted to or not. He would have a chance to woo her, to convince her they ought to become man and wife.

Unfortunately, he still had a job to do—making her ranch profitable—which he took seriously. And Harry-et didn't strike him as the sort of woman who was going to take well to the kind of orders he would necessarily have to give.

Meanwhile, Harry was in hog heaven. She had what she'd always wanted—not someone to do it for her, but someone to teach her how to do it herself. Of course, having Nathan Hazard for her ranch manager wasn't a perfect solution. She still had to put up with the man. But once she'd learned what she needed to know, she wouldn't let him set foot on her place again.

Harry was especially glad that she'd secured Nathan's expertise today, because now that she had the funds to pay the lease on her mountain grazing land, she had another problem that needed to be resolved. So when Nathan arrived shortly after dark, Harry greeted him at her kitchen door with a smile of genuine welcome.

"Come in," she said, gesturing Nathan to a seat at the kitchen table. "I've got some coffee and I just baked a batch of cookies for you."

"They smell great," Nathan said, finding himself suddenly sitting at the table with a cup of coffee and a plateful of chocolate chip cookies in front of him.

Harry fussed over him like a mother hen with one chick until he had no choice except to take a sip of coffee. He'd just taken his first bite of cookie, and was feeling pretty good about the way this was turning out, when Harry said, "Now, to get down to business."

With a mouthful of cookie it was difficult to protest.

"The way I see it," Harry began, "I haven't been doing all that badly on my own. All I really need, what I expect from you, is someone I can turn to when I hit a snag."

"Wait a minute," Nathan said through a mouthful of cookie he was trying desperately to swallow. "I think you're underestimating what it takes to run a marginal spread like this in the black."

"I don't think I am," Harry countered. "I'll admit I've made some mistakes, like the one I wanted to see you about tonight." Harry paused and caught her lower lip in her teeth. "I just never thought he'd do such a thing."

"*Who* would do *what* thing?" Nathan demanded.

"My shepherd. I never thought he'd take his wages and go get drunk."

"You paid your shepherd his wages? Before the summer's even begun? Whatever possessed you to do such a thing?"

"He said he needed money for food and supplies," Harry said. "How was I supposed to know—"

"Any idiot could figure out—"

"Maybe an idiot could, but I'm quite intelligent

myself. So it never occurred to me!" Harry finished.

"Aw, hell." Nathan slumped back into the chair he hadn't been aware he'd jumped out of.

Harry remained standing across from him, not relaxing an inch.

"So what do you want me to do?" Nathan asked when he thought he could speak without shouting.

"I want you to go down to Whitey's Bar in Big Timber and get him out, then sober him up so he can go to work for me."

"I don't think this is what John Wilkinson had in mind when he suggested I manage your ranch," Nathan said, rubbing a hand across his forehead.

"I would have gone and done it myself if I'd known you were going to make such a big deal out of it," Harry muttered.

Suddenly Nathan was on his feet again. "You stay out of Whitey's. That's no place for a woman."

"I'm not just a woman. I'm a rancher. And I'll go where I have to go."

"Not to Whitey's, you won't."

"Oh, yeah?" she said. "Who's going to stop me?"

"I am."

Harry found herself in Nathan's grasp so quickly that she didn't have a chance to escape. She stared up into his blue eyes and saw he'd made up his mind she wasn't going anywhere. She hadn't intended to force a confrontation, yet that was exactly what she'd done. She didn't want Nathan doing things *for* her; she wanted him doing things *with* her. So she made herself relax in his hold, and even put her hands on his upper arms and let them rest there.

"All right," she said. "I won't go there alone. But I ought to be perfectly safe if I go there with you."

"Harry-et—"

"Please, Nathan." Nathan's hands had relaxed their hold on her shoulders, and when Harry stepped closer, they curved around her into an embrace. Her hands slid up to his shoulders and behind his neck. He seemed a little unsure of what she intended. Which was understandable, since Harry wasn't sure what she intended herself— other than persuading Nathan to make her a partner rather than a mere petitioner. "I really want to help," she said, her big brown eyes locked on Nathan's.

"But you—"

She put her fingertips on his lips to quiet him, then rested one hand against his chest, so she could feel the heavy beat of his heart, while she let the other drift up to play with the hair at his nape. "This is important to me, Nathan. Let me help."

Harry felt Nathan's body tense beneath her touch, and thought for sure he was going to say no. A second later she was sure he was going to kiss her.

She was wrong on both counts.

Nathan determinedly put his hands back on her shoulders and separated them by a good foot. Then he looked her right in the eye. "Just stay behind me and let me do the talking."

"You've got a deal. When are we going?"

A long-suffering sigh slipped through Nathan's lips. "I suppose there's no time like the present. If we can get your shepherd dried out, we can move those sheep up into the mountains over the weekend."

Whitey's Bar in Big Timber was about what you would expect a Western bar to be: rough, tough and no holds barred. It was a relic from the past, with everything from bat-wing doors to a twenty-foot-long bar with a brass rail at the foot, sawdust on the floor and a well-used spittoon in the corner. The room was packed with people and raucous with the wail of fiddles from a country tune playing on the old jukebox in the corner.

Some serious whiskey-drinking hombres sat at the small wooden tables scattered around the room. Harry was amazed that both cowboys and sheepmen caroused in the same bar, but Nathan explained that they relished the opportunity to argue the merits of their particular calling, with the inevitable brawl allowing them all an opportunity to vent the violence that civilization forced them to keep under control the rest of the time.

"Is there a fight every night?" Harry asked as they edged along the wall of the bar, hunting for her shepherd.

"Every night I've been here," he answered.

Harry gave him a sideways look, wondering how often that was. But her attention was distracted by what was happening on the stairs. Two men were arguing over a woman. Nathan hadn't exactly been honest when he'd said no women ever went to Whitey's. There were women here, all right, but they were working in an age-old profession. Twice in the few minutes they'd been in the bar, Harry had seen a woman head upstairs with a man.

The argument over the female at the foot of the stairs was escalating, and Harry noticed for the first time that one man appeared to be a cowboy, the other a sheepman.

Then she spotted her shepherd. "There he is," she said to Nathan, pointing at a white-bearded old man slumped at a table not too far from the stairs.

Nathan swore under his breath. In order to get to the shepherd, he had to get past the two men at the foot of the stairs. He turned to Harry-et. "Wait for me outside."

Harry started to object, but the fierce look in Nathan's eyes brooked no refusal. Reluctantly she turned and edged back along the wall toward the door. She never made it.

"Why, hello there, little lady. What brings you here tonight?"

The cowboy had put one hand, which held a beer bottle, up along the wall to stop her. When she turned to face him, he braced his palm on the other side of her, effectively trapping her.

"I was just leaving," Harry said, trying to duck under his arm.

He grabbed her sleeve, and she heard a seam rip as he pushed her back against the wall. "Not so fast, darlin'."

Harry's eyes darted toward Nathan. He had just slipped his hands under the drunken shepherd's arms and was lifting him out of his chair. She couldn't bear the thought of shouting for help, drawing the attention of everyone in the bar. So she tried again to handle the cowboy by herself. "Look," she said, "I just came here to find some-one—"

"Hell, little lady, you found me. Here I am."

Before Harry realized what he was going to do, the cowboy had pressed the full length of his body against her to hold her to the wall and sought her mouth with his.

She jerked her face from side to side to avoid his slobbering kisses. "Stop! Don't! I—"

An instant later the cowboy was decorating the

floor and Nathan was standing beside her, eyes dark, nostrils flared, a vision of outrage. "The lady doesn't care for your attentions," he said to the burly cowboy. "I suggest you find someone who does."

The cowboy dragged himself up off the ground, still holding the neck of the beer bottle, which had broken off when he'd fallen. He recognized Nathan for a sheepman, which magnified the insult to his dignity. With all eyes on him there was no way he could back down. "Find your own woman," he blustered. "I saw her first."

"Nathan, please, don't start anything," Harry begged.

Nathan took his eyes off the other man for a second to glance at Harry, and the cowboy charged.

"Nathan!" Harry screamed.

Nathan's hand came up to stop the downward arc of the hand holding the broken bottle, while his fist found the cowboy's gut. The cowboy bent over double, and Nathan straightened him with a fist to the chin. The man crumpled to the floor, out cold.

Nathan looked up to find that pandemonium had broken out in the bar. He grabbed Harry's wrist. "Let's get out of here."

"Not without my shepherd."

"Are you crazy, woman? There's a fight going on."

"I'm not leaving without my shepherd!"

Nathan dodged a flying chair to reach the drunken man he'd left sitting against the wall. He picked the man up, threw him over his shoulder fireman-style and marched back through the melee to Harry. "Are you satisfied?"

Harry grinned. "Now I am."

Nathan grabbed her wrist with his free hand, and glaring at anyone foolish enough to get in his way, was soon standing outside in front of Whitey's. He dumped the shepherd none too gently into the back of his pickup and ordered Harry to get in.

She hurried to obey him.

Nathan took out his fury at Harry-et on the truck, gunning the engine, only to have to slam on the brakes when he caught the red light at the corner. He raced the engine several times and made the tires squeal when he took off as the light turned green.

"Did that bastard hurt you?" he demanded through tight lips.

"I'm all right," Harry said soothingly. "I'm fine, Nathan. Nothing happened."

"You had no business being there in the first place. You should have stayed home."

"I had as much right to be there as you. More right," she argued. "It was my shepherd we went after."

"You and your damned shepherd. The greenest

greenhorn would know not to pay the man in advance. This whole business tonight was your fault."

"I didn't do anything," Harry protested.

"You were there. That was enough. If I hadn't been there—"

"But you were," Harry said. "And you were wonderful."

That shut him up. How could you complain when a woman was calling you wonderful? But if anything had happened to her... Nathan had known his feelings toward Harry-et were possessive, but he hadn't known until tonight that she was *his woman*. Woe be unto the man who harmed the tiniest hair on her head.

Nathan shook his head in disbelief. He hadn't been involved in one of Whitey's barroom brawls since he'd been a very brash young man. If this evening was any indication of what he had in store as the manager of Cyrus's ranch, he had a long, hot summer ahead of him.

As they pulled up in front of Cyrus's cabin, Harry said, "If you'll leave my shepherd in the sheep barn, I'll do what I can to sober him up."

"I'll take him home with me," Nathan countered. "I'm sure my housekeeper has some Native American remedy that'll do the trick. We'll be back here bright and early tomorrow morning. Think you can stay in a Western saddle long enough to help us drive your sheep into the mountains?"

"I rode hunters and jumpers in Virginia."

Nathan shook his head in disgust. "I should have known. All right. I'll be here at dawn. Be ready."

Harry stepped down out of the truck and started toward the house. An instant later she ran back around the truck and gestured for Nathan to open his window.

"I just wanted to thank you again." She leaned over and kissed him flush on the mouth. "You were really wonderful." Then she turned and ran into the cabin.

Nathan waited until he saw the lights go on before he gunned the engine and took off down the rutted road. Before he'd gone very far he reached up to touch his lips where she'd kissed him. There was still a bit of dampness there, and he touched it with his tongue. And tasted her. His lips turned up in a smile.

He felt as if he could move mountains.

He felt as if he could soar in the sky.

He felt like a damn fool in love.

He felt really wonderful.

Chapter 7

When Wade or Clyde or Harley comes
a-courtin', how will you, the greenhorn female
person, recognize a compliment?
Answer: He'll compare your hair to the mane on
his sorrel horse.

Harry had aches where she'd forgotten she had
muscles. She knew how to ride, but that didn't
mean she'd done much riding lately. Her back,
thighs and buttocks could attest to that. But she'd
accomplished what she'd set out that morning to
do. Her flock of sheep had been moved up into
the leased mountain pastures, and the wiry old

shepherd had been settled in his camp with a stern warning to keep a sharp eye out for wolves.

Harry was doing the same thing herself. Actually, she was keeping a sharp eye out for one particular wolf. Nathan Hazard had been acting strangely all day. Silent. Predatory. He hadn't done anything overtly aggressive. In fact, he seemed to be playing some sort of game, stalking her, waiting for the moment when he could make his move. Her nerves were beginning to fray.

After the fracas of the previous evening, Harry hadn't expected Nathan to be enthusiastic about joining her on this mountain pilgrimage. Nor was he. But at least he hadn't said a word about what had happened in Whitey's Bar. Of course, he hadn't said much of anything. Harry had been determined not to provoke him in any way, so she'd kept her aches and pains to herself. Was it any wonder she'd leaped at Nathan's suggestion that they halt their trek halfway down the mountain and take a rest? She had to bite her lip to keep from groaning aloud when she dismounted, but she was so stiff and sore that her knees nearly buckled when she put her weight on them.

Nathan heard Harry-et's gasp and turned to watch her grab the horn of the saddle and hang on for a few moments until her legs were firmly under her. He had to hand it to the woman. She was determined. He couldn't help admiring her gumption. Nathan had suspected for some time that Harry-et was feeling the effects of the long ride. That had suited him just fine. He'd had plans of his own that depended on getting her off that horse while they were still in the mountains. They had reached Nyla's Meadow. The time had come.

He spread a family heirloom quilt in the cool shade of some jack pines and straightened the edges over the layer of rich grass that graced the mountain meadow. At the last moment he rescued a handful of flowers that were about to be crushed, bringing them to Harry-et.

"Here. Thought you might like these."

Harry smiled and reached out a hand for the delicate blossoms. She brought them to her nose and was surprised at the pungent sweetness of the colorful bouquet. "They smell wonderful."

"Thought you also might like to lie down for a while here on Nyla's Meadow," Nathan said nonchalantly, gesturing toward the inviting square of material.

Harry wasted no time sagging down onto the quilt. She groaned again, but it was a sound of satisfaction as she stretched out flat on her back. "You have no idea how good this feels."

He settled himself cross-legged on a corner of the quilt near her head. "Don't guess I do. But if you moan any louder some moose is going to come courting."

Harry laughed. "I'll try to keep it down." She turned on her side and braced her head on her elbow, surveying the grassy, flower-laden clearing among the pines and junipers. "Nyla's Meadow. That sounds so beautiful. Almost poetical. How did this place get its name?"

Nathan's lips twisted wryly. "It's a pretty far-fetched story, but if you'd like to hear it—"

"Yes, I would." Harry tried sitting up, but groaned and lay back down. "Guess I've stiffened up a little." She massaged the nape of her neck. "Make that a lot."

"I'd be glad to give your shoulders a rubdown."

That sounded awfully good to Harry. "Would you?"

"Sure. Turn over on your stomach."

A moment later Nathan was straddling her at the waist and his powerful hands had found the knots in her shoulders and were working magic. "You have no idea how good that feels," she said with another groan of pleasure.

Nathan's lips curled into a satisfied smile. Oh, yes, he did. He longed for the time when there would be nothing between his fingertips and her skin. It seemed like he'd been waiting his whole life for this woman. He didn't plan to wait much longer.

Harry felt the strength in Nathan's hands, yet his touch was a caress. A frisson of excitement ran the length of her spine. She imagined her naked body molded to Nathan's. Joined to Nathan's. Harry closed her eyes against the vivid picture she'd painted. She had no business thinking such thoughts. The sheepman only wanted her land. He'd as much as told her she wasn't the woman for him. Last night certainly couldn't have convinced him she'd be the kind of wife he had in mind. No, the minute she'd learned all she could from him, she intended to bid him a fast farewell.

So why was her body coming alive to his touch? Why did she yearn for his hands to slip around and cup her breasts, to mold her waist and stroke the taut and achy places that had nothing to do with the long ride of the morning? Harry tensed against the unwelcome, uncontrollable sensations deep inside.

"Relax," Nathan murmured as his hands slipped down from her shoulders to the small of her back and began to massage the soreness away.

"Tell me about Nyla's Meadow," Harry said breathlessly.

Nathan's thumbs slowly worked their way up her spine, easing, soothing, relaxing. "Nyla was an Egyptian princess."

Harry lifted herself on her hands and turned to eye Nathan over her shoulder. "What?"

Nathan shoved her back down. "Actually, the princess's name was N-I-L-A, after the Nile River, but somewhere over the years the spelling got changed."

"How did a Montana meadow get named after an Egyptian princess?" Harry asked suspiciously.

"Be quiet and listen and I'll tell you. Long before the first settlers came to the Boulder River Valley, a mountain man named Joshua Simmons arrived here. He'd traveled the world over just for the pleasure of seeing a new horizon, or so the story goes. He'd been to Egypt and China and the South Sea islands. But when he reached Montana, he knew he'd found God's country—limitless blue skies, snowcapped mountains and grassy prairies as far as the eye could see."

"You're making this up, aren't you?" Harry said with a grin.

"Shut up and listen," Nathan insisted. His hands moved down Harry's back to her waist and around to her ribs, where they skimmed the fullness of her breasts at the sides before moving back to her spine.

Harry shivered. She would have asked Nathen to stop what he was doing, but his hands were there and gone before she could speak. The sensations remained. And the ache grew.

"When Joshua reached this meadow, he encountered a Native maiden," Nathan continued. "She appeared as exotic to him, as foreign and mystical, as an Egyptian princess."

"The Princess Nila," Harry murmured sardonically.

"Right. They fell in love at first sight. And made love that same day here on the meadow. When he awoke, the maiden—though she was a maiden no more—was gone. Joshua never learned her name and he never saw her again. But he never forgot her. He named this place Nyla's Meadow after the Egyptian princess she had reminded him of."

Harry shifted abruptly so her buttocks rocked against Nathan. He felt his loins tighten and rose slightly to put some space between the heat of their two bodies.

Oblivious to Nathan's difficulties, Harry rolled over between his legs and scooted far enough away to sit up facing him. He was still straddling her at thigh level.

She pulled the band off one braid and began to unravel it, seemingly unconscious of the effect her action would have on Nathan. "So Nyla's Meadow is a place for falling in love? A place where lovers meet?"

Nathan swallowed hard. "Yes. A place for lovers." He couldn't take his eyes off Harry-et. Her gaze was lambent, her pupils dilated, her lids lowered. She was clearly aroused, yet her mood seemed almost playful, as though she didn't realize the powerful need she'd unleashed within him.

When Harry started to free her other braid, Nathan reached out a hand. "I'll do it."

Her hands dropped onto his thighs. And slid upward.

Nathan hissed in a breath and put his hands over hers to keep them from moving any farther. There was no need for her to actually touch him. The mere thought of her hands on him excited him. He slid her hands back down his thighs, away from the part of him that desperately wanted her touch. When he was relatively sure he'd made his position clear, he let her hands go and reached for the other braid.

Her hair was soft and rippled where the tight braids had left their mark. When both braids were unraveled, he thrust his hands into her rich brown hair and spread the silky mass around her head and shoulders like a nimbus. "You are so beautiful, Harry-et."

Harry hadn't meant to let the game go so far. She hadn't realized just how aroused Nathan was. She hadn't realized how the sight of his desire would increase her own. She wanted to see what would happen next. She wanted to feel what she had always imagined she would feel in a lover's embrace. Her hands once again followed the corded muscles along Nathan's thighs until she reached the part of him that strained against the worn denim. She molded the shape of him with her hands, awed by the heat and hardness of him.

Nathan closed his eyes and bit the inside of his mouth to keep from groaning aloud. The sweetness of it. The agony and the ecstasy of it. "Harry-et," he gasped. "Do you know what you're doing?"

"No," she replied. "But I'm learning fast."

Choked laughter erupted from Nathan's throat. At the same time he grabbed her by her wrists and lowered her to the ground, pinning her hands above either side of her head. He stretched out over the length of her, placing his hips in the cradle of her thighs. "That's what you're doing, lady," he said in a guttural voice, thrusting once with his hips. "I want you, Harry-et."

Harry heard the slight hesitation between the two syllables as he spoke her name that made the word an endearment. He wanted her, but he hadn't spoken of needing, or caring. Maybe that was as it should be. Alistairs and Hazards were never meant to love. History was against it. She wanted him, too. Wasn't that enough?

The decision was made for her when Nathan captured both her wrists in one hand and reached down between the two of them to caress the heart of her with the other. She felt herself arching toward him, toward the new and unbelievable sensations of pleasure.

Nathan caught her cries of ecstasy with his

mouth. His kisses were urgent, needful. He let go of her wrists because he needed his hand to touch her, to caress her. When he did, Harry's fingers thrust into Nathan's hair and tugged to keep him close, so she could kiss him back. Her hands slipped down to caress his chest through his shirt, but the cotton was in her way. She yanked on his shirt and the snaps came free. She quickly helped him peel the shirt down off his shoulders. Just as quickly he freed the buttons of her shirt and stripped it off, along with her bra.

An instant later they paused and stared at each other.

Harry had seen Nathan's muscular chest once before and wanted to touch. Now she indulged that need. Her fingertips traced the crease down the center of his chest to his washboard belly.

Nathan had imagined her naked a dozen, dozen times, but still had failed to see her as beautiful as she was. Her breasts were full and the nipples a rose color that drew his eye, his callused fingers and finally his mouth.

Harry's fingernails drew crescents on Nathan's shoulders as his mouth and tongue suckled her breast. She arched toward him, urging him to take more of her into his mouth. He cupped her breast with his hand and let his mouth surround her, while his teeth and tongue turned her nipple into a hard bud.

Harry moaned. Her body arched into his, her softness seeking his hardness.

"Please." She didn't know what came next. She'd always stopped in the past before she got this far. Only this time she didn't want to stop. She wanted to know how it ended.

"It's all right, sweetheart," he murmured in her ear. "Soon. Soon."

"Now, Nathan. Now."

He sat up and pulled off her boots, then began pulling off his own. They both rid themselves of their jeans in record time. Nathan threw his jeans aside, then went searching for them a moment later. He ransacked the pockets, cursing as he went.

"Did you forget something?" Harry asked.

Nathan grinned as his fisted hand withdrew from his jeans pocket. "Nope."

Suddenly Harry was aware of her nakedness. And Nathan's. He looked awfully big. Not that she had anything to compare him with, but surely that thing was too large to fit...

"What's the matter, Harry-et?" Nathan said as he lay down beside her and pulled her into his embrace.

"Nothing," she mumbled against his chest.

"Having second thoughts?" Nathan held his breath, wondering why he was giving her a chance to back away when he wanted her so much that he was hurting.

Harry had opened her mouth to suggest maybe this wasn't such a good idea when Nathan's lips closed over hers. His tongue traced the edges of her mouth and then slipped inside, warm and wet. Seducing. Entrancing. Changing her mind all over again.

"Hold this for me," he said. "I need both hands free."

"What is it?" she asked through a haze of euphoria.

He quickly removed the foil packet and dropped a condom into her palm.

"Oh. Dear." Harry was unable to keep from blurting something she'd read in a magazine article. "It's Mr. Prophylactic. The guy with the cute little button nose."

Nathan burst out laughing.

Harry blushed a fiery red. Thank goodness Nathan still had his sense of humor. Maybe this wasn't going to be so impossible, after all. Her relief was premature.

"Would you like to put it on me?" he asked.

"I've never done it before," she admitted. "I wouldn't know how. I might do it wrong."

A frown arose between Nathan's brows. He couldn't believe she'd be so irresponsible as not to use some kind of protection in this day and age. As Harry-et's eyes fell, the truth dawned on

Nathan. *She hadn't used protection because she hadn't needed it.*

"How long?" he demanded, grasping her hair and angling her face up toward him.

"What?"

"How long since you've been with a man."

"I haven't ever…that is…this is the first time."

Nathan watched as she lowered her eyes to avoid his gaze, as if she'd committed some kind of crime. Didn't she know what a precious gift she was giving him? Didn't she know how special she'd made him feel? He pulled her into his arms and held her tightly. He had never felt so protective of a woman in his life. Both awed and terrified by the responsibility she'd placed in his hands.

"The first time for a woman…sometimes there's pain," he said, his mouth close to her temple. "I don't want to hurt you, sweetheart."

"You won't," Harry reassured him.

"Darling, sweetheart, I wouldn't mean to, but I'm afraid—"

Harry pushed him far enough away that she could see his face. "You? Afraid? Of what?"

He looked her in the eye. "That it won't be everything you expect. That it won't be perfect."

Harry smiled a beatific smile. "If I'm with you, Nathan, it will be perfect. Trust me."

He eased her back down on the quilt and

lowered himself beside her, giving her a quick, hard hug.

Harry noticed something different about the embrace. Something missing. She chanced a brief glance down at him. "Oh, no," she said, dismayed.

"What's the matter, Harry-et?"

"You're not…well, you're not…anymore," she said, pointing at a no-longer-aroused Nathan.

Nathan chuckled. "You're precious, Harry-et," he said with a quick grin. "One of a kind."

Harry took a swipe at his shoulder with her fist—the same fist that was still holding the condom he'd handed to her. "I don't like being laughed at, Nathan."

He laughed. "I'm not laughing at you." He rolled over onto his back and let his arms flop free, a silly grin on his face.

Harry tackled him.

An instant later she was under him, his body mantling hers. His mouth found hers, and he kissed her with all the passion he felt for her. His hands found her breasts and teased the nipples to a peak. He felt the blood thrumming through the veins in her throat with his mouth. By the time his hand finally slipped between their bodies, she was wet.

And he was hard.

"Oh. It's back," she said.

Nathan grinned. "So it is. Where is Mr. Prophylactic?"

Harry grinned and opened her hand to reveal a slightly squashed condom. "Will it still work?"

"Not unless you put it on."

Her chin slipped down to her chest. She glanced up at him shyly. "Will you help me?"

Nathan helped her place the condom and roll it on until he was fully covered. The way she handled him so carefully, as though he would break, made him feel treasured and very, very special.

"Is that all there is to it?" she asked.

"Pretty simple, huh?"

She caressed him through the sheath. "Can you still feel that?"

Nathan jerked. "Uh-huh."

"Really?" She let her fingers trace the shape of him, encircle him, run down the length of him from base to tip. "You can feel that?"

Nathan inhaled sharply. Slowly he inserted a finger inside her. "Can you feel that?"

Harry gasped. "Uh-huh."

He inserted another finger. "And that?"

Harry tightened her thighs around his hand, reminding Nathan this was new to her. He slowly worked his fingers inside her, stretching her, feeling the tightness and the wetness. He had to be patient. And gentle. And exercise rigid control over a body that ached with wanting her.

"Harry-et," he breathed against her throat. "Touch me."

Harry had been too caught up in her own sensations to think about Nathan's. Until he'd spoken she hadn't been aware that her hands each grasped a handful of quilt. She brought her hands up to grasp his waist instead. Slowly her fingers slipped around to his belly and down to the crease where hip met thigh.

Nathan grunted. The feel of her fingertips on his skin, on his belly, in those other places he hadn't known were so sensitive, was exquisite.

Harry relaxed her thighs, allowing Nathan greater freedom of movement. His mouth found a breast and teased it, then moved down her ribs to her belly, and then lower, where it replaced his hands at the portal she'd guarded against invasion for so many years.

Her hands clutched his hair as she arched up toward the sensations of his mouth on her flesh. "Nathan, please," she cried. She had no idea what it was she needed, but she was desperate.

Nathan's eyes glittered with passion as he rose over her. She expected one quick thrust and was prepared for the pain. Instead she felt the tip of him pushing against her. Just when she started to feel the pain, he distracted her by nipping her breast. Then his mouth found hers and his tongue mimed the action below. Thrusting and withdrawing. Pushing farther each time. Teasing and tempting.

A guttural sound rose in her throat as she surged toward him, urging him inside.

Nathan thrust once more with tongue and hips and filled her full.

Harry tensed with the extraordinary feeling of being joined to Nathan. Her legs captured his hips and held him in thrall. As he withdrew and thrust again, she met his rhythm, feeling the tension build within. His hand came between them to touch her and intensify the need for relief. For release. For something.

Harry was gasping for air, her heart pounding, her pulse racing. "Nathan," she cried. "Please. I ache. Make it stop."

God, he loved her! He wanted to say the words. Here. Now. But once said, they couldn't be taken back. He had no idea how she felt about him. She trusted him, that much was clear. But did her feelings for him run as deep as his for her? She hadn't offered those three words, and there was no way he could ask for them. He could only show her how he felt and trust that it would be enough.

"Come with me, sweetheart. Let yourself fly. It's all right. I'll take care of you."

Harry took him at his word and let herself soar. Nathan joined her in her aerie, two souls surpassing the physical, seeking a world somewhere beyond Nyla's Meadow.

It was long moments later before either of them

touched ground again. Their bodies were slick with sweat, despite the shade in which they lay. Nathan was stretched out beside her with an arm and a leg thrown possessively over her. He couldn't see Harry-et's face, so he wasn't able to judge what she was thinking. But there was a tension in her body that was at odds with the release he'd felt within her just moments before.

"Harry-et? What's wrong?" He must have hurt her. He hadn't meant to, but he had.

She sighed. A huge, deafening sound. Those last few words Nathan had spoken before she'd found ecstasy resounded in her ears: "I'll take care of you." Those words reminded her of why it would be foolish to give her heart to Nathan Hazard. She wanted to stand on her own two feet. He was liable to sweep her off them. She freed herself from his embrace and sat up, pulling her knees to her chest and hugging them with her arms. "This can't happen again, Nathan."

"I'm sorry if I hurt you. I—"

"You didn't hurt me, Nathan. I just don't want to do it…this…with you again."

"It sounds to me like you're sorry it happened the first time," he said angrily, sitting up to face her. "You were willing. Don't try to deny it."

"I'm not denying it. I wanted this as much as you," she admitted. "I'm only saying that it can't happen again."

"Give me one good reason why not," he demanded.

Because I'm in danger of falling in love with you.

Because I'm in danger of losing myself to you.

Because I find you irresistible, even though I know we have no business being together like this.

That was three reasons. None of which she had any intention of mentioning to him. Harry turned away from him and slipped on her bra and panties. She could hear the rustle of clothing behind her as he dressed. The metal rasp of the zipper on his jeans was loud in the silence. She stood and pulled up the zipper on her own jeans before reaching for her boots.

He grabbed the boot out of her hand and shook it, then handed it back to her. "Snakes," he said. "And spiders."

Harry shivered and made sure she dumped the other boot as well before she slipped it on. His warning had been an abrupt reminder that she was a very sore tenderfoot. Harry couldn't very well avoid Nathan until she learned everything from him that she needed to know. She would just have to learn to control the need to touch, and be touched, that arose every time she got near him.

Nathan had no idea what he'd done that was so wrong, but after the most profound lovemaking he'd ever experienced, Harry-et was avoiding him as if he had the measles. She wasn't going to get away with it.

"Harry-et."

"Yes, Nathan?"

"Come here."

"No." Harry turned and marched over to the tree where her horse was tied. She tried to mount, but couldn't raise her leg high enough to reach the stirrup. She laid her face against the saddle and let her shoulders slump.

An instant later Nathan grabbed her by the waist and hoisted her into the saddle. "Move your leg out of the way, tenderfoot," he ordered.

Harry gritted her teeth and did as he ordered, painfully sliding her leg up out of his way as he worked on the saddle.

"Good thing you couldn't reach the stirrup," he snarled. "Damn cinch wasn't tightened. Saddle would have slid around and dumped you flat."

"Stop treating me like I'm helpless," she said. "I can take care of myself."

"I'll believe it when I see it," he retorted.

"I pulled my own weight today. Don't tell me I didn't."

Nathan neither confirmed nor denied her assertion. He tightened the cinch on his own saddle and mounted, then reined his horse to face her. "That story I told you about Nyla's Meadow?"

"Yes?"

"I made it all up."

Harry struggled to keep the disappointment out of her voice. "All of it?"

"Every last word. No one knows how the meadow got its name."

He'd invented a place for falling in love. A place where lovers met. Then brought her here. And made love to her. Now he wanted her to believe it had all been a lie.

"We made love in Nyla's Meadow, Nathan. That was real."

Nathan met her imploring gaze with stony eyes. "We had sex. Damn good sex. But that's all it was." And if she believed that, he had a bog he'd like to sell her for grazing land.

He was waiting for the retort he was sure was on her lips. But she didn't argue, just kicked her horse and loped away from him toward the trail back down the mountain.

"Damn you, Harry-et," he muttered. "Damn you for stealing my heart and leaving *me* feeling helpless."

He kicked his horse and loped down the mountain after her. As he followed her down the mountain, he thought back on the day he'd spent working with Harry-et. Not once had she asked for his help. Not once had she complained. In fact, she'd done extraordinarily well for a tenderfoot. Was it possible that someday Harry-et Alistair could actually stand on her own two feet? He found the idea fascinating, if far-fetched. He stared at the way she rode stiff-backed in the saddle. She had grit, that woman. It sure couldn't hurt to hang around long enough to find out.

Harry's thoughts weren't nearly so sanguine. All day she'd been careful not to let Nathan do too much. If she was going to feel like a success, she had to make it on her own. She had left her family to get away from people ordering her around.

But Nathan had never ordered her to do anything. He'd made suggestions and left the decisions up to her. So maybe she could endure his company a little longer. Maybe she could forget what had happened between them today in Nyla's Meadow and simply take advantage of his expertise.

But it was clear she was going to have to be careful. Give Nathan an inch and he might take an acre. And the man had made no secret of the fact that he wanted the whole damn spread.

Chapter 8

In a small town out West what do you do if you become ill?
Answer: Put on a big pot of coffee, because an hour after you get your prescription from the drugstore, five people will phone with sympathy and two will fetch you a hot dish.

Harry didn't see Nathan for a week, but he called her every day with instructions for some job or other that she had to complete: repairing the henhouse, planting a vegetable garden, spreading manure, harrowing the fields and cleaning the sheep shed. She took great pride in the fact that she managed to accomplish every task alone. Successfully. She knew Nathan had expected her to cave in and ask for help long before now. So when he phoned one evening and told her to clean out all the clogged irrigation channels on her property in preparation for starting the irrigation water through the main ditch, she headed out bright and early the next morning, expecting to get the job done. And failed abysmally.

All Harry could figure was that Nathan had left something out of his instructions. She tried calling him for more directions, but he was out working in his fields and couldn't be reached until noon. She left a message with Nathan's housekeeper for him to call her as soon as he got in.

Nathan did better than that. Shortly after noon he arrived on her kitchen doorstep. "Harry-et, are you in there? Are you all right?"

He didn't wait for her to answer, just shoved the screen door open and stepped inside. When Nathan saw her sitting at the table with a sandwich in her hand, his relief was palpable. His heart had been in his throat ever since he'd read the message Katoya had left him. He'd had visions of Harry-et wounded and bleeding from some farm accident. He was irritated that he cared enough about her to feel so relieved that she wasn't hurt. He forced the emotion he was feeling from his voice and asked, "What was the big emergency?"

"No emergency," Harry answered through a mouthful of peanut butter and jelly. "I just couldn't get the irrigation system to work with the directions you gave me."

"What was wrong with my directions?"

"If I knew that, I wouldn't have called you."

"I'll go take a look."

"I'll come with you." She threw her sandwich down and headed toward him.

Nathan felt his groin tighten at the sight of Harry-et sucking a drop of grape jelly off her finger. "Don't bother. I can do it quicker on my own."

Harry hurried to block his exit from the kitchen. "But if I don't come along, I won't know what I did wrong the next time I have to do it by myself," she pointed out in a deceptively calm voice.

Nathan stared at the jutting chin of the woman standing before him. Stubborn. As a mule. And sexy. Even in bibbed overalls. "All right," he muttered. "But don't get in my way."

When Nathan crossed behind the barn, he saw the backhoe sitting in the middle of her field by the main irrigation ditch. "I didn't know you could manage a backhoe." Handling the heavy farm machinery was how he'd feared she'd hurt herself.

"It wasn't so hard to figure out. I used it to widen the main ditch and clear the larger debris from the irrigation channels. But I still didn't get any water."

She was a remarkable woman, all right. It wasn't the first time he'd had that thought, but Nathan didn't understand why it irritated him so much to admit it now. Could it be that he *wanted* her to need him? *Needed* her to need him? What if she turned out to be really self-sufficient? Where did that leave him? *With an Alistair smack in the middle of his property.* Nathan pursed his lips. The thought didn't irk him near as much as it ought to.

When they arrived at the main ditch, Nathan examined her work. He could find no fault with it. "Did you follow the main ditch all the way across your property?"

"As far as that stand of cottonwoods over there along the river." She didn't add that the thought of snakes hiding in the thick vegetation around the cottonwoods had scared her off.

"Let's go take a look."

Harry was happy to follow him. The way Nathan was stomping around it wasn't likely any snake was going to hang around long enough to take him on.

Harry stayed close behind Nathan and actually bumped into him when he stopped dead and said, "There's your problem."

She leaned around him to see where he was pointing. "That bunch of sticks?"

"Beaver dam. Has to come out of there. It's blocking the flow of water along the main ditch."

"How do I get rid of it?"

Nathan grinned ruefully. "Stick by stick. You'd better head back to the house and get your thigh-high rubber boots."

"Rubber boots? Thigh-high?"

"I take it you don't have any rubber boots," Nathan said flatly.

"Just my galoshes."

He sighed. "They're better than nothing. Go put them on. Get a pair of gloves, too."

"All right. But don't start without me," she warned.

"Wouldn't think of it."

Harry ran all the way to the cabin, stepped into her galoshes and galomphed all the way back to the beaver dam. True to his word, Nathan was sitting on a log that stuck out from the dam, doing nothing more strenuous than chewing on a blade of sweetgrass. But he hadn't been idle in her absence. He was leaning on two shovels, wore thigh-high rubber boots and had a pair of leather gloves stuck in his belt.

"All ready?" he asked.

"Ready."

The beaver dam was several feet long and equally wide and thick, and Harry felt as if she were playing a game of Pick-up Sticks. She never knew whether the twig she pulled would release another twig or tumble a log. Leaves and moss also had to be shoveled away from the elaborate dam. The work was tedious and backbreaking. Toward the end of the afternoon it looked as if they might be able to clear the ditch before the sun went down, if they kept working without a break.

Harry was determined not to quit before Nathan. Sweat soaked her shirt and dripped from her nose and chin. Her face was daubed with mud. Her hands were raw beneath the soaked leather gloves. There were blisters on her heels where the galoshes rubbed as she mucked her way through the mud and slime. It was little consolation to her that Nathan didn't look much better.

He had taken off his shirt, and his skin glistened with sweat. He kept a red scarf in the back pocket of his jeans, and every so often he pulled it out and swiped at his face and neck and chest. Sometimes he missed a spot, and she had the urge to take the kerchief from his hand and do the job for him. But it was as plain as peach pie cooling on a windowsill that Nathan was a heap better at dishing out help than he was at taking it. And though they worked side by side all day, he kept his distance.

Touching might be off-limits, but that didn't mean she couldn't look. Harry was mesmerized by the play of corded muscles under Nathan's skin as he hefted logs and shoveled mud. She turned abruptly when he caught her watching and was thankful for the mud that hid her flush of chagrin.

Nathan hadn't been as unaware of Harry-et as he'd wanted her to think. The outline of her hips appeared in those baggy overalls every time she stretched to reach another part of the dam. He'd even caught a glimpse of her breasts once when she'd bent over to help him free a log. There was nothing the least bit attractive about what she had on. He didn't understand why he couldn't take his eyes off her.

Suddenly, as though they'd opened a lever, the water began to rush past them into the main irrigation ditch and outward along each of the ragged channels that crisscrossed Harry's fields.

"It's clear! We did it," Harry shouted, exuberantly throwing her arms into the air and leaping up and down.

Nathan saw the moment she started to fall. One of her galoshes was stuck in the mud, and when Harry-et started to jump, one foot was held firmly to the ground while the other left it.

Nathan was never quite sure later how it all happened. He made a leap over some debris in an attempt to catch Harry-et before she fell, but tripped as he took off. Thus, when he caught her, they were both on their way down. He twisted his body to take the brunt of the fall, only his boot was caught on something and his ankle twisted instead of coming free. They both hit the ground with a resounding "Ooomph!"

Neither moved for several seconds.

Then Harry untangled herself from the pile of arms and legs and came up on her knees beside Nathan, who still hadn't moved. "Nathan? Are you all right? Say something."

Nathan said a four-letter word.

"Are you hurt?"

Nathan said another four-letter word.

"You *are* hurt," Harry deduced. "Don't move. Let me see if anything's broken."

"My shoulder landed on a rock," he said between clenched teeth as he tried to rise. "Probably just bruised. And my ankle got twisted."

"Don't move," Harry ordered. "Let me check."

"Harry-et, I—" He sucked in a breath of air as he sat up. His right shoulder was more than bruised. Something was broken. "Help me up."

"I don't think—"

"Help…me…up," he said through gritted teeth.

Harry reached an arm around him and tried lifting his right arm to her shoulder. He grunted.

"Try the other side," he told her.

She slipped his other arm over her shoulder and used the strength in her legs to maneuver them both upright.

Nathan tried putting weight on his left leg. It

crumpled under him. "Help me get to that boulder over there."

Harry supported Nathan as best she could, and with a sort of hopping, hobbling movement that left him gasping, they made it. She settled Nathan on the knee-high stone and stood back, facing him with her hands on her hips. "I'll go get the pickup. You need a doctor."

"I'll be fine. Just give me a minute to rest." A moment later he tried to stand on his own. The pain forced him back down.

"Are you going to admit you need some help? Or do I have to leave you sitting here for the next few weeks until somebody notices you're missing?"

"Go get the pickup," he snarled.

"Why thank you, Mr. Hazard, for that most brilliant suggestion. I wish I'd thought of it myself." She sashayed away, hips swaying. Her attempt at nonchalance was a sham. As soon as she was out of sight, she started running and sprinted all the way to her cabin. She tore through the kitchen, hunting for the truck keys, then remembered she'd left them in the ignition. She headed the pickup straight back across the fields, skidding the last ten feet to a stop in front of Nathan.

"You just took out half a field of hay," Nathan said.

"I'm afraid I was in too much of a hurry to notice," she retorted. She forced herself to slow down and be gentle with Nathan as she helped him into the truck, but even so, the tightness of his jaw and his silence attested to his pain.

"Where's the closest hospital?" she demanded as she scooted behind the wheel.

"Take me home."

"Nathan, you need—"

"Take me home. Or let me out and I'll walk there myself."

"You need a doctor."

"I'll call Doc Witley when I get home."

It didn't occur to her to ask whether Doc Witley practiced on humans. It shouldn't have surprised her that he turned out to be the local vet.

Several hired hands came running when Harry drove into Nathan's yard, honking her horn like crazy. They helped her get Nathan upstairs to the loft bedroom of his A-frame home. Harry's mouth kept dropping open as she took in her surroundings. She had never suspected Nathan's home would be so beautiful.

The pine logs of which the house was constructed had been left as natural as the day they were cut. The spacious living room was decorated in pale earth tones. A tan couch and chair faced a central copper-hooded fireplace. Nearby stood an ancient wooden rocker. The living room had a cathedral ceiling, with large windows all around, so that no matter where you looked there was a breathtaking view: the sparkling Boulder River bounded by cottonwoods to the east; the Crazy Mountains to the north; the snowcapped Absarokas to the south; and to the east, pastureland dotted with ewes and their twin lambs.

If this was an example of how Nathan Hazard designed homes, the world had truly lost someone special when he'd given up his dream.

If she'd had any doubt at all about his eye for beauty, the art and artifacts on display in his home laid them fully to rest. Bronze sculptures and oil and watercolor paintings by famous Western artists graced his living room. Harry indulged her curiosity by carefully examining each and every one during the time Doc Witley spent with Nathan.

When the vet finally came downstairs, he found Harry waiting for him.

"How is he?"

"Nothing's broke."

"Thank God."

"Dislocated his shoulder, though. Put that to rights. Couldn't do much with his ankle. Bad sprain. May have cracked the bone. Can't tell without an X-ray and don't think he'll hold still for one. Best medicine for that boy is rest. Keep him off his feet and don't let him use that shoulder for a few weeks. I'll be going now. Have a prize heifer calving over at the Truman place. You mind my words now. Keep that boy down." He gave her a bottle of pills. "Give him a couple of these every four hours if he's in pain."

Harry looked down to find the vet had handed her a bottle of aspirin. She showed him out the door and turned to stare up toward the loft bedroom that could be seen from the living room. Nathan must have heard what the doctor had said. It shouldn't be too hard to get him to cooperate.

Harry looked around and realized Nathan's housekeeper hadn't made an appearance. Maybe Katoya was out shopping. If so, Harry would have to stick around until she got back. Nathan was in no shape to be left alone.

Nathan's bedroom was done in darker colors— rust, burnt sienna and black. The four-poster bed was huge and flanked by a tall, equally old-fashioned piece of furniture that Harry assumed must hold his clothes. The other side of the room was taken up by a rolltop desk. The oak floor was mantled with a bearskin rug. Of course there were windows, wide, clear windows that brought the sky and the mountains inside.

Nathan had pillows piled behind his shoulders and an equally large number under his left foot.

She took a step into his bedroom. "Is there anything I can do for you?"

"Just leave me alone. I'll manage fine."

"Your home is lovely. You show a lot of promise as an architect," she said with a halting smile.

"It turned out all right," he said. "As soon as it was built, I thought of a dozen things I could have done better."

She didn't feel comfortable encroaching farther into his bedroom, so she leaned back against the doorway. "You'll make all those improvements next time."

"A sheepman doesn't have the leisure time to be designing houses," he said brusquely.

"Actually, you're going to have quite a bit of free time over the next couple of weeks," she replied. "The vet gave orders for you to stay in bed. By the way, I haven't seen your housekeeper. Do you expect her back soon?"

"In about a month," Nathan said. "She left right after I got home to visit her granddaughter, Sage Littlewolf, on the reservation up near Great Falls."

"Do you suppose she'd come back if she knew—"

"Yes, she would. Which is why I have no intention of contacting her. There's some problem with her granddaughter that needs settling. She's gone there to settle it. I'll manage."

Harry marched over to stand at Nathan's bedside. "How do you intend to get along without any help?"

"It's not your problem."

"I'm making it my problem."

"Look, Harry-et, I don't need your help—"

"You need help," she interrupted. "You can't walk."

"I'll use crutches."

"With your right arm in a sling?"

"I'll hop."

"What if you fall?"

"I won't."

"But if you do—"

"I'll get back up. I don't need you here, Harry-et. I don't want you here. I don't think I can say it any plainer than that."

"I'm staying. Put that in your pipe and smoke it, Mr. Hazard." Harry turned and headed for the door.

"Harry-et, come back here! Harry-et!"

She kept on marching all the way downstairs until she stood in his immaculate, perfectly antique kitchen, trying to decide what she should make for his supper.

Nathan spent the first few minutes after Harry left the room, proving he could get to the bathroom on his own. With his father's cane in his left hand he was able to hobble a little. But it was an awkward and painful trip, to say the least. He couldn't imagine trying to get up and down the stairs to feed himself. Of course, he could sleep downstairs on the couch, but that would put the closest bathroom too far away for comfort.

By the time Harry showed up with a bowl of

chicken noodle soup on a wicker lap tray, Nathan was willing to concede that he needed someone to bring his meals. But only for a day or so until he could get up and and down stairs more easily.

"All right, Harry-et," he said, "you win. I'll send a man to take care of your place for the next couple of days so you can play nursemaid."

"Thank you for admitting you need help. I, on the other hand, can manage just fine on my own."

"Look, Harry-et, be reasonable. There's no sense exhausting yourself trying to handle two things at once."

"I *like* exhausting myself," Harry said contrarily. "I feel like I've accomplished something. And I'm quite good at managing three or four things at once, if you want to know the truth."

"Stop being stubborn and let me help."

"That's the pot calling the kettle black," she retorted.

"Have it your way, then," he said sullenly.

"Thank you. I will. I'll be back in a little while to collect your soup bowl. Be sure it's empty." She stopped on her way out the door and added, "I'll be sleeping on the couch downstairs. That way you can call if you need me during the night."

Nathan was lying back with his eyes closed when Harry returned for the dinner tray he'd set aside. She sat down carefully beside him on the bed, so as not to wake him. He was breathing evenly, and since she believed him to be asleep, she risked checking his forehead to see if he had a fever. Just as she was brushing a lock of blond hair out of the way, his eyes blinked open. She saw the pain before he thought to hide it from her.

She finished her motion, letting it be the caress it had started out as when she'd thought he was asleep. "I was checking to see if you have a fever."

"I don't."

"You do."

He didn't argue. Which was all the proof she needed that he wasn't a hundred percent. "Doc Witley left some aspirin. He said you might need it for the pain. Do you?"

"No."

She sighed. "I'll leave two on the bedside table with a glass of water, just in case."

He grabbed her wrist as she was rising from the bed to keep her from leaving. "Harry-et."

"What is it, Nathan?"

The words stuck in his throat, but at last he got them out. "Thank you."

"You're welcome, Nathan. I—"

Harry was interrupted by a commotion downstairs. "What on earth—" Someone was coming up, taking the stairs two at a time.

"Hey, Nathan," a masculine voice shouted, "heard you slipped and landed flat on your ass—" Luke stopped abruptly when he saw Harry

Alistair standing beside Nathan. "Sorry about the language, ma'am." He tipped his hat in apology. "Didn't know there was a lady present."

"How on earth did you find out what happened?" Harry asked. "I swear I haven't been near a phone—"

"No phone is as fast as gossip in the West," Luke said with a grin. "I'm here to see if there's anything I can do to help out."

Nathan opened his mouth to respond and then closed it again, staring pointedly at Harry.

"I was just taking this downstairs," she said, grabbing Nathan's dinner tray. "I'll leave you two alone." She hurried from Nathan's bedroom, closing the door behind her.

Luke turned back to Nathan and waggled his eyebrows. "Should have known you wouldn't spend your time in bed all alone."

"Watch what you say, Luke," Nathan warned. "You're talking about a lady."

"So that's the way the wind blows."

"Harry-et is only here as a nurse."

"One of the hired hands could nurse you," Luke pointed out.

"She refuses to leave, so she might as well do some good while she's here," Nathan said defensively.

"Who's going to take care of her place while she's taking care of you?"

Nathan grimaced. "I offered to have one of my hands help her out. She insists on doing everything herself. Look, Luke, I'd appreciate it if you'd look in on her over the next couple of days. Make sure she doesn't overdo it."

"Sure, Nathan. I'd be glad to."

"I'd really appreciate it. You see, Harry-et just doesn't know when to quit."

"Sounds a lot like my Abby."

"Your Abby?"

"Abigail Dayton and I got engaged yesterday."

"I thought you hadn't seen her since she caught that renegade wolf and headed back home to Helena."

"Well, I hadn't. Until yesterday. I figured life is too short to live it without the woman you love. I was already headed over here to give you the big news when I heard about your accident."

Nathan reached out and grasped Luke's hand. "I really envy you. When's the wedding?"

Luke grinned wryly. "As soon as my best man is back on his feet again. You'd better make it quick, because Abby's pregnant."

Harry heard Nathan's whoop at the same time she heard the front door knocker. She didn't know which one to check out first. Since the door was closer, she hurried to open it.

"Hi! I'm Hattie Mumford. You must be Harry Alistair. I'm pleased to meet you. I brought one of my apple spice cakes for Nathan. Thought it might cheer him up. Can I see him?"

The door knocker rattled again.

"Oh, you get the door, dear," Hattie said. "I know the way upstairs."

Harry just barely resisted the urge to race up ahead of Hattie to warn Nathan what was coming. The knocker rapped again. She waited to answer it because Luke was skipping down the stairs.

"Is he all right?" Harry asked anxiously. "I heard him holler."

Luke grinned. "Nathan was just celebrating the news of my engagement and forthcoming marriage to Abigail Dayton."

"You and Abigail?" Harry smiled. "How wonderful. Congratulations!"

"You'd better get that door," Luke said. "I'll just let myself out the back way."

Harry opened the door to a middle-aged couple.

"I'm Babs Sinclair and this is my husband, Harve. We just heard the bad news about Nathan. Thought he might enjoy my macaroni-and-cheese casserole. I'll just take this into the kitchen. Harve, why don't you go up and check on Nathan."

For want of something better to do, Harry followed Babs Sinclair into the kitchen. The woman slipped the casserole into the oven and turned on the heat. Harry didn't have the heart to tell her Nathan had already eaten his supper.

"You better get some coffee on the stove, young'un," Babs said. "If I know my Harve, he'll—"

"Babs," a voice shouted down from the loft, "send some coffee up here, will you?"

The door knocker rapped.

"You better get that, young'un. I'll take care of making the coffee."

For the next three hours neighbors dropped by to leave tokens of their concern for Nathan Hazard. Besides the apple spice cake and the macaroni-and-cheese casserole, Nathan had been gifted with a loaf of homemade bread and a crock of newly made butter, magazines, and a deck of cards. The game of checkers was only on loan and had to be returned once Nathan was well. Harry met more people that evening than in the nearly four months since she'd moved to the Boulder River Valley.

What she hadn't realized until Hattie Mumford mentioned it was that her neighbors had been waiting for her to indicate that she was ready for company. They would never have thought to intrude on her solitude without an invitation. Now that Harry was acquainted with her neighbors, Hattie assured her they would all make it a point to come calling.

Over the next few weeks as she nursed Nathan, Harry was blessed with innumerable visits from the sheep ranchers of Sweet Grass County. They always turned up when she was busy with chores and managed to stay long enough to see them finished. She found herself the recipient of one of Hattie's apple spice cakes. And she thoroughly enjoyed Babs Sinclair's macaroni-and-cheese casserole.

It never occurred to her, not once in all the propitious visits when she'd been exhausted and a neighbor had arrived to provide succor, that while she'd been acting as Nathan's hostess in the kitchen, he'd been upstairs entreating, encouraging and exhorting his friends and neighbors to keep an eye out for her while he was confined to his bed.

So when Harry overheard Hattie and Babs talking about how she was a lucky woman to have Nathan Hazard *taking care of her,* she began asking a few questions.

When Nathan woke up the next morning and stretched with the sunrise, he yelped in surprise at the sight that greeted him at the foot of his bed.

Chapter 9

*How do you know when a handsome Woolly
Westerner is really becoming dead serious
about you?*
*Answer: He invites you to his ranch and shows
you a basket overflowing with three hundred
unmated socks. You realize your own heart is
lost when you begin pairing them.*

Nathan wasn't a good patient. He simply had no
experience in the role. He was used to being the
caretaker. He didn't know how to let somebody
take care of him. Harry bore the brunt of his
irascibility. Well, that wasn't exactly true. Nathan

had more than once provoked an argument and found himself shouting at thin air. Over the three weeks he'd spent recuperating, he'd learned that Harry picked her fights.

So when he woke up to find her standing at the foot of his bed, fists on hips, brown eyes flashing, jaw clamped tight to still a quivering chin, he knew he was in trouble.

"I have tried to be understanding," she said hoarsely. "But this time you've gone too far."

"I haven't left this bed for three weeks," he protested.

"You know what I mean. I found out what you did, Nathan. There's no sense trying to pretend you didn't do it."

Nathan stared at her, completely nonplussed. "If I had the vaguest idea what you're talking about, Harry-et—"

"I'm talking about what you said to Hattie Mumford and Babs and Harve Sinclair and Luke Granger and all the other neighbors who've been showing up at my place over the past three weeks to *help* me. How could you?" she cried. "How could you?"

Harry turned her back on him and walked over to the window to look out at the mountains. "I thought you understood how important it was to me to manage on my own," she said in an agonized voice.

She swiped the tears away, then turned back to face him. "Do you know how many times over the past three weeks I've let you do something for yourself, knowing it was more than you could handle? Sometimes you surprised me and managed on your own. More often you needed my help. But I never offered it until you asked, Nathan. I respected your right to decide for yourself just how much you could handle.

"That's all I ever wanted, Nathan. The same respect I was willing to give to you." Her lips curled as she spit out, "Equal partners. You have no concept of what that means. Until you do, you're going to have a hard time finding a woman to *share* your life."

As she whirled and fled the room, Nathan shouted, "Harry-et! Wait!" He shoved the covers out of the way and hit the floor with both feet.

Harry was halfway down the stairs when she heard him fall. She paused, waiting for the muttered curse that would mean he was all right. When it didn't come, she turned and ran back up the stairs as fast as she could. He was lying facedown on the bearskin rug, his right arm hugged tightly to his body. She fell onto her knees beside him, her hands racing over him, checking the pulse at his throat. "Nathan. Oh, God. Please be all right. I—"

An instant later he grasped her wrist and pulled

her down beside him. A moment after that he had her under him and was using the weight of his body to hold her down. "Stop bucking like that," he rasped. "You're liable to throw my shoulder out again."

"You'll be lucky if that's all the damage I do," she snapped back. She shoved at his chest with both hands and knew she'd hurt him when his lips drew back over his teeth.

"That's it." He caught both of her hands in one of his and clamped them to the floor above her head. With his other hand he captured her chin and made her look at him. "Are you going to listen to me, or not?"

"I don't know anything you could say—"

"Shut up and let me talk!"

She pressed her lips into a flat, uncompromising line and glared at him.

"I want another chance," he began. She opened her mouth, and he silenced her with a hard kiss. "Uh-uh," he said. "Don't interrupt, or I'll have to kiss you again."

She narrowed her eyes but said nothing.

"I've listened to every word you've ever said to me since I met you, but I never really heard what you were saying. Until just now. I'm sorry, Harry-et. You'll never know how sorry. I guess the truth is, I didn't want you to be able to manage on your own."

"Why not?" she cried.

He swallowed hard as he released her hands. "I wanted you to need me." He paused. "I wanted you to love me."

"Oh, Nathan. I do. I—"

He kissed her hard to shut her up so that he could finish, but somehow her lips softened under his. Her tongue found the seam of his lips and slipped inside and searched so gently, so sweetly, that he groaned and returned the favor. It was a long time before he came to his senses.

"So, will you give me another chance?" he asked.

She smiled. "Will you call off your neighbors?"

"Done. I have one more question to ask."

"I'm listening."

"Will you marry me?"

The smile faded from her lips and worry lines furrowed her brow. "I do love you, Nathan, but..."

"But you won't marry me," he finished tersely.

"Not right now. Not yet."

"When?"

"When I've proved I can manage on my own," she said simply. "And when I'm sure you've learned what it means to be an equal partner."

"But—"

She put her fingertips on his lips to silence him. "Let's not talk any more right now, Nathan. There are other things I'd rather be doing with you." She suited deed to word and let her fingers wander over his face in wonder. To the tiny crow's-feet at the corners of his eyes. To the deep slashes on either side of his mouth. To the bristled cheeks that needed shaving.

"Smile for me, Harry-et."

It was harder than she'd thought it would be. She had just turned down a proposal of marriage from a man she loved. Harry told herself she'd done the right thing. If she'd said yes, she would never have known how much she could accomplish by herself. When she sold her lambs in the fall and paid off the bank, then she'd know for sure. Then, if Nathan held to his promise to treat her as an equal, she could marry him. That was certainly something she could smile about.

Nathan watched the smile begin at the corners of her mouth. Then her lower lip rounded and her upper lip curved, revealing the space between her two front teeth that he found so enchanting. He captured her mouth and searched for that enticing space with his tongue, tracing it, and then the roof of her mouth, and the soft underskin of her upper lip. Then his teeth closed gently over her lower lip and nibbled before his tongue sought the honeyed recesses of her mouth once more.

Harry groaned with pleasure. She wasn't an anxious virgin now. She knew what was coming. Her body responded to the memories of Nathan's lovemaking that had never been far from her mind over the past month since they'd made love. But she saw the flash of pain when Nathan tried to raise himself on his arms. And that took away all the pleasure for her.

"Nathan. Stop. I think we should wait until your shoulder's better before—"

He rolled over onto his back and positioned her on his belly, with her legs on either side of him. "There. Now my shoulder will be fine."

"But how…"

His hands cupped her breasts through her shirt, his thumbs teasing the nipples into hard buds. "Use your imagination, sweetheart. Do whatever feels right to you."

Harry smiled. Nathan wasn't wearing a shirt. She took both of his hands and laid them beside him on the bearskin rug. "Don't move. Until I say you can."

Then she leaned over and circled his nipple with her tongue. His gasp widened her grin of delight. Her fingertips traced the faint traces of bruise that were the only remaining signs that he'd dislocated his shoulder. Her lips soothed where her fingers had been. She traced the length of his neck with kisses and nipped the lobe of his ear. Then her tongue traced the rim of his ear, and she whispered two words she'd never thought she'd say out loud to a man. She saw his pulse jump, felt his breath halt. The guttural sound in his throat was raw, filled with need.

His hands clutched her waist and pulled her hard against him, but she sat up abruptly. "You're not playing by the rules, Nathan," she chastised, placing his hands palm down on the floor. "No touching." She smiled a wanton, delicious smile and added, "Yet."

She felt his hardness growing beneath her and rubbed herself against him through his jeans.

"Harry-et," he groaned. "You're killing me. Whatever you do, just don't stop," he rasped.

Harry laughed at his nonsensical request. She reached down and cupped him with her hand, and felt his whole body tighten like a bowstring. Her exploration was gentle but thorough. By the time she was done, Nathan was arched off the floor, his lower lip clenched in his teeth.

"Have I ever told you what a gorgeous man you are, Nathan?"

"No," he gasped.

"You are. These high cheekbones." She kissed each one tenderly. "This stubborn chin." She nipped it with her teeth. "Those blue, blue eyes of yours." She closed them with her fingertips and anointed them with kisses. She moved down his body, her fingertips tracing the ridges and curves of his masculine form, her mouth following to praise without words.

With every caress Harry gave Nathan she felt herself blossom as a woman. She wanted a chance to return the pleasure he'd given her on Nyla's Meadow. She unsnapped his jeans and slowly pulled the zipper down. She started to pull his jeans off, then paused. Her hand slipped into his pockets one by one. Right front. Left front. Right rear. In the left rear pocket she found what she was looking for. "My, my," she said, holding out what she'd found. "Mr. Prophylactic."

"I don't know how that got there," Nathan protested.

"Just thank goodness it was and shut up," Harry said with a laugh. She dropped the condom onto the bearskin nearby and finished dragging Nathan's jeans down, pulling off his briefs along with them, leaving him naked. And aroused.

She couldn't take her eyes off him. She certainly couldn't keep her hands off him. She opened the condom and sheathed him with it, taking her time, arousing him, teasing him, taunting him.

Nathan had reached his limit. He grasped Harry-et's shirt and ripped the buttons free. Her jeans didn't fare much better. He had her naked in under nine seconds and impaled her in ten. She was slick and wet and tight. "You feel so good, Harry-et. Let me love you, sweetheart."

Harry felt languorous. Her body surged against Nathan's. He put a hand between them, increasing the tension she felt as he sought out the source of her desire. When she leaned over, he captured her breast in his mouth and suckled her. Sensations assaulted her: pleasure, desire, and her body's pulsing demand for release.

"Nathan," she gasped.

His mouth found hers as his hands captured her hips. They moved together, man and woman, part and counterpart, equal to equal.

Harry clutched Nathan's waist, arching toward the precipice, reaching for the satisfaction that was just beyond her reach.

Nathan felt her tensing, felt her fight against release. "Let go, sweetheart. It's all right. Soar. Back to Nyla's Meadow, darling. We can go there together."

Then it was too late for words. She was rushing toward satisfaction. Nathan stayed with her, his face taut with the passion raging within him. She cried out, and he thrust again. A harsh sound rose from deep in his throat as he released his seed.

Harry felt the tears coming and was helpless to stop them. They stung her cheeks, hot and wet. Nathan felt them against his face and raised his head in disbelief.

"Harry-et?"

She reached a hand up to brush the golden locks from his brow. "It's all right, Nathan. I just felt so...overwhelmed for a moment."

He pulled her into his arms and held her tightly. "You have to marry me Harry-et. I love you. I want to keep you safe."

Harry buried her face in his shoulder. "I love you, Nathan, but it scares me."

"How so?"

"It's taken me a long time to get the courage to strike out on my own. I've hardly had a chance to try my wings."

"We'll learn to fly together, Harry-et."

What she couldn't explain, what she hardly understood herself, was her fear of surrendering her newfound control over her life. Nathan needed to be needed. She loved him enough to do anything she could to make him happy. That gave him a great deal of power. She simply had to find a way to accept his gestures of loving concern…and still keep the independence she was fighting so hard to achieve.

A knock on the door sent them both scrambling for their clothes.

"That'll be Luke," Nathan said as he yanked on his jeans. "I told him I wanted to talk over the plans for his bachelor party."

"Abigail's likely to be with him," Harry said as she tied her buttonless shirt in a knot. "I wanted to make sure it's all right with her to plan a combination bridal/baby shower."

They finished dressing at almost the same time, then stood grinning at each other.

"Shall we go greet our guests?" Nathan asked.

"I'm ready."

Harry fitted herself against Nathan as he slipped his arm around her shoulder for support. It took them a while to get downstairs, but Nathan had already shouted at Luke to let himself in and make himself at home. Sure enough, when they reached the living room, they found that Abigail was with him. After exchanging greetings, Nathan and Luke settled down in the living room while Harry and Abigail headed for the kitchen.

Luke waited only long enough for the two women to disappear before he asked, "Did you ask her?"

"Yep."

"So?"

"She said she'd think about it."

"For how long?"

Nathan thrust a hand through his hair in frustration. "She didn't give me a definite time-table. But at least until she sells her lambs in the fall."

"Guess that shoots the double wedding," Luke muttered.

"There's no reason why we can't go ahead and plan your wedding to Abby," Nathan said.

"We've got a few months yet before the baby

comes. I'm willing to wait awhile." He grinned. "I've gotten sort of attached to the idea of having a double wedding with my best friend."

Nathan smiled. "What's Abigail going to say about the delay?"

"You won't believe this, but I'm the one in a rush to get married. Abby says she won't love me any less if we never have a ceremony and get a legal piece of paper that proclaims us man and wife."

At that moment Harry was hearing approximately the same speech from Abigail's lips.

"I'm willing to wait to have a ceremony until you and Nathan can stand at the altar with us," Abigail said. "Really, Harry, I can't believe you turned him down!"

"I had no idea you and Luke were thinking about a double wedding with the two of us," Harry said as she measured the coffee into the pot.

"Well, now that you know, why not change your mind and say yes to Nathan?" Abigail said with an impish grin.

Harry pursed her lips. "I'm sorry to throw a screw in the works, but I have some very good reasons for wanting to wait."

"Fear. Fear. And fear," Abigail said.

"Do I hear the voice of experience talking?"

Abigail bowed in recognition of the dubious honor. "But of course. You're speaking to a woman who was afraid to fall in love again. Everyone I had ever cared about had died. I didn't want to face the pain of losing someone else I loved."

"But Luke is perfectly healthy!" Harry exclaimed.

"Reason has very little to do with fear. What is it you're afraid of, Harry?"

Harry poured a cup of coffee and stared into the blackness. "That I'll be swallowed up by marriage to Nathan." She turned and searched out Abigail's green eyes, looking for understanding. "I'm just learning to make demands. With Nathan it's too tempting to simply acquiesce. Does that make any sense?"

"Like I said, there's nothing rational about our fears. I know mine was very real. You just have to figure out a way to overcome it."

"I thought I was taking a big step just coming to Montana," Harry said. "Nathan's proposal strikes me as a pretty big leap into a pretty big pond."

"Come on in," Abigail said with a smile. "The water's fine."

Harry couldn't help smiling back at Abigail. She had come to Montana knowing there were battles to be fought and won. At stake now was a lifetime of happiness with Nathan. All she had to do was find the courage to deal with whatever the future brought.

There was yet another war to be fought, but

on an entirely different field. Harry wanted to convince Nathan it wasn't too late to pursue the dreams he'd given up so long ago. She had already put her battle plan in motion.

While searching for some extra sheets in a linen closet, Harry had discovered Nathan's drafting table. It was in pieces, and she'd spent the past few weeks finding the right place to locate it. She had finally set it up in front of the window that overlooked the majestic, snowcapped Absarokas. Surely such a view would provide the inspiration an aspiring architect needed.

She'd seen Nathan eye the table when they'd come downstairs to greet Luke and Abigail. She knew that as soon as the couple left, she would have some fast talking to do. As Nathan waved a final goodbye to Luke and Abigail, Harry walked into the living room and settled herself in the rocker that Nathan usually claimed.

The instant he closed the front door, Nathan turned to Harry and demanded, "What's that doing in here?"

"I would think that's obvious. It's there so you can use it."

"I've already told you I don't have time for drawing," he said harshly.

"Not drawing, designing," she corrected. Harry watched him limp over to the table. Watched as his hand smoothed lovingly over the wooden surface. *He misses it.* That revelation was enough to convince Harry she should keep pushing. "I couldn't help thinking that all those movie stars moving into Montana are going to be needing spacious, beautiful homes. Someone has to design their mountain sanctuaries. Why not you?"

"I'm a sheep rancher, that's why." He settled into the ladder-back stool she'd found in the tack room in the barn, and shifted the T square up and down along the edge of the drafting table. "Besides, when would I have time to draw?"

"Montana is blessed with a lot of long winter nights," she quipped.

He rose from the table and limped over to stand in front of her. "There are other things I'd rather be doing on a long winter night." He took her hands and pulled her out of the rocker and into his embrace. "Like holding my woman," he murmured in her ear. "Loving her good and hard."

"Sounds marvelous," she said. "Designing beautiful houses. Designing beautiful babies."

"You make it sound simple."

"It can be. Won't you give it a try?"

He hugged her hard. "Don't start me dreaming again, Harry-et. I've spent a long time learning to accept the hand fate has dealt me."

"Maybe it's time to ask for some new cards."

Nathan shook his head. "You never give up, do you? All right, Harry-et. I'll give it a try."

She gave him a quick kiss. "I'm glad."

Nathan had no explanation for why he felt so good. He'd given up all hope of designing significant buildings a long time ago. But mountain sanctuaries for movie stars? It was just whimsical enough to work. He would make sure that the structures fitted in with the environment, that they utilized the shapes and materials appropriate to the wide open Montana spaces. Maybe it wasn't such a crazy idea, after all.

He looked down into Harry-et's glowing brown eyes. He'd never loved anyone as much as he loved her. "Come back upstairs with me," he urged.

"I can't. It's time for me to go home."

"Stay."

"I can't. I'll be in touch, Nathan. Goodbye."

Harry kept her chin up and her shoulders back as she walked out the door. It made no sense to be walking away from the man she loved. Maybe over the next few weeks she could get everything straightened out in her mind. Maybe she could convince herself that nothing mattered as much as loving Nathan. Not even the independence she'd come to Montana to find.

Chapter 10

Where is a Western small-town wedding reception held?
Answer: The church basement if large enough, otherwise the Moose Hall.

Harry found it hard living in her dilapidated cabin again. Of course, her place was tiny and primitive and utterly unlivable in comparison to Nathan's. But she'd coped with those things for months and never minded. Now she couldn't wait to leave Cyrus's cabin each morning. Because it felt empty without Nathan in it.

Harry had spent a lot of time lately thinking

about what was important to her. Nathan headed the list. Independence wasn't even running a close second. Harry was having trouble justifying her continued refusal of the sheepman's wedding proposal. These days Harry was so self-sufficient that it was hard to remember a time when she hadn't taken care of herself. She was starting to feel foolish for insisting that Nathan wait for an answer until she sold her lambs and paid off her loan at the bank.

Everything was clarified rather quickly when she received a call from her father.

"Your mother and I will be coming for a visit in two weeks, Harriet, to check on your progress. While we're there we'd really like to see where you're living."

"My place is too small for company, Dad. I'll meet you at The Grand in Big Timber," Harry countered.

"By the way, how are you, darling?" her mother asked.

"Just fine, Mom. I've had a proposal of marriage," Harry mentioned casually. "From a rancher here."

"Oh, dear. Don't rush into anything, darling," her mother said. "Promise me you won't do anything rash before we get there."

"What did you have in mind, Mom?"

"Just don't get married, dear. Not until your

father and I have a chance to look the young man over."

"Your mother is right, Harriet. Marriage is much too important a step to take without careful consideration."

"I'll keep that in mind, Dad. I've got to go now." She couldn't help adding, "I've got to feed the chickens and slop the hogs."

Harry felt a twinge of conscience when she heard her mother's gasp of dismay. But her father's snort of disgust stiffened her resolve. She was proud of what she'd accomplished since coming to the valley. If her parents couldn't appreciate all she'd done, that was their loss. She wasn't going to apologize for what she'd become. And she sure wasn't going to apologize for the man she'd just decided to marry.

As soon as her parents clicked off, she dialed Nathan's ranch. She heard his phone ring once and quickly hung up. This was too important an announcement to make over the phone. Besides, she hadn't seen Nathan for ten long, lonely days. She wanted to be there to see Nathan's face and share her excitement with him. The pigs and the chickens would have to wait.

Halfway to Nathan's house, Harry realized he would probably be working somewhere on the ranch, out of communication with the house. To her surprise, when she knocked on the door, he answered it.

"What are you doing home?" she asked as he ushered her inside. "You're supposed to be out somewhere counting sheep."

"I'm drawing," he said with a smug smile. "I've been hired to design a house for a celebrity who's moving to Big Timber. Very high muckety-muck. Cost is no object."

She heard the eagerness in his voice. And the pride and satisfaction. "Then I guess I'd better say yes before you get too famous to have anything to do with us small-time sheep ranchers. So, Nathan, the answer is yes."

"What did you say?"

"Yes, I'll marry you."

"Don't play games with me, Harry-et."

"I'm not playing games, Nathan. I said I'll marry you, and I meant it."

A moment later Harry knew why she'd come in person. Nathan dragged her into his arms and hugged her so tightly that she had to beg for air. Then his mouth found hers, and they headed for Nyla's Meadow. When she came to her senses, she was lying under Nathan on the couch and her shirt was unbuttoned all the way to her waist. That didn't do him as much good as it might have, since she was wearing bibbed overalls that got in his way.

Nathan's mouth was nuzzling its way up her neck to her ear when he stopped abruptly. "I don't mean to look a gift horse in the mouth, Harry-et, but what changed your mind?"

"I had a call from my parents. They're coming to visit again."

"And?"

"They wanted to look you over. Like a side of beef. To make sure you were Grade A Prime. I thought that sort of behavior particularly inappropriate for a sheepman. So I've decided to make this decision without them."

"And in spite of them?" Nathan asked somberly. He sat up, pushing Harry-et off him, putting the distance of the couch between them. "I don't want you to marry me to prove a point to your parents. Or to yourself."

"My parents have nothing to do with my decision," Harry protested. "I thought you'd be happy."

"I was. I am. I just don't want you to have regrets later. Once we tie the knot, I expect it to be forever. No backing out. No second thoughts. I want you to be sure you're choosing to be a sheepman's wife—my wife—of your own free will."

Harry felt tears burning behind her eyes and a lump growing in her throat at Nathan's sudden hesitance. "Are you sure you haven't changed your mind?" she accused.

"I was never the one in doubt, Harry-et. I love you. I want to spend my life with you. You're the one who said you didn't want to give up your independence. Do you wonder that I question your sudden about-face?"

"What can I do to prove to you that I'm sincere?"

Nathan took a deep breath. "Introduce me to your parents as your fiancé. Let them get to know me without stuffing me down their throats. Give yourself a chance to react to their reactions. See if you still feel the same way after they've gone. If you want to marry me then, Harry-et, I'll have you at the altar so fast it'll make your head spin."

"It's a deal."

Harry-et held out her hand to seal the bargain and, like a fool, he took it. His reaction was the same today as it had been yesterday, as it would be tomorrow. A bolt of electricity shot up his arm, his heart hammered, his pulse quickened. But instead of letting her go he pulled her into his embrace, holding her close, breathing the scent of her—something stronger than My Sin…more like…Her Sheep. It was the smell of a sheepman's woman. And he loved her for it.

Harry suffered several bouts of ambivalence in the days before her parents were due to arrive.

Maybe she should have pressed Nathan to get married.

Maybe she should have left well enough alone.

Maybe she should have sold her lambs early.

Maybe she should have sold out and gone home long ago.

Harry didn't know why confronting her parents with her decision to marry Nathan should be so difficult. She only knew it was.

She arrived at The Grand on the appointed day with Nathan in tow. "I'll make the introductions," Harry said. "Just let me do the talking."

"It's all right, Harry-et. Relax. Your parents love you."

"I'll try to remember that." And then they were there and she was hugging her mother and then her father and Nathan was shaking their hands. "Where's Charlie?" she asked.

"Your mother and I decided to come alone."

That sounded ominous. "Mom, Dad, this is Nathan Hazard. Nathan, my mother and father."

"It's nice to see you again, Mr. and Mrs. Alistair. Why don't we all go find a booth inside?" Nathan suggested.

Harry let him lead her to a booth and shove her in on one side. He slid in after her while her parents arranged themselves on the other side.

"So, Mr. Hazard—"

"Nathan, please."

"So, Nathan, what's this we hear about you wanting to marry our girl?" Harry's father demanded.

Harry groaned. She felt Nathan's hand grasp her thigh beneath the table. She took heart from his reassurance. Only his hand didn't stay where he'd put it. It crept up her thigh under the skirt she'd worn in hopes of putting her best foot forward with her parents. She grabbed his hand to keep it where it was and tried to pay attention to what Nathan was saying to her father.

"And you'd be amazed at what Harry's done with the place."

"What about that federal lease for grazing land, Harriet? Your banker told me the last time I was here that there wasn't much chance he could make you a loan to cover it."

"We worked it out, Dad," Harry said. "I'll be selling my lambs in a couple of weeks. Barring some sort of catastrophe, I'll make enough money to pay off the bank and have some working capital left over for next year."

"Well. That's a welcome relief, I imagine," Harry's mother said. "Now about this wedding—"

"My mind is made up, Mom. You can't change it. I'm marrying Nathan. I love him. I want to spend my life with him."

"I don't think I've ever heard you speak so forcefully, my dear," her mother said.

"It does appear you're determined to go through with this," her father said.

Harry's hand fisted around her fork. "I am," Harry said. "And I'm staying in Montana. I'm where I belong."

"Well, then, I guess there's nothing left to do except welcome you to the family, young man." Harry's father held out his hand to Nathan, who grinned and let go of Harry's thigh long enough to shake her father's hand.

Harry was stunned at her parents' acquiescence. Was that all it took? Was that all she'd ever needed to do? Had she only needed to speak up for what she wanted all these years to live her life as she'd wanted and not as they'd planned? Maybe it was that simple. But until she'd come to Montana, until she had met and fallen in love with Nathan, Harry hadn't cared enough about anything to fight for it.

She sat up straighter in her seat and slipped her hand under the table to search out interesting parts of Nathan she could surreptitiously caress. His thigh was rock-hard under her hand. So were other parts of him. The smile never left her face during the entire dinner with her parents.

When the meal was over, Harry's mother and father rose to leave. Nathan stayed seated, excusing himself and Harry. "We have a few more things to discuss before we go our separate ways, if you don't mind."

"Not at all," Harry's father said.

Her mother leaned over and whispered in her ear, "Your young man has lovely manners, dear. You must bring him to Williamsburg for a visit sometime soon. And let me know as soon as you set a date for the wedding."

Harry stood and hugged her mother across the table. "To tell you the truth, we'd really like to get married while you're here, so you can come to the wedding. It isn't going to be a large gathering. Just a simple ceremony with me and Nathan…and another bride and groom."

"A double wedding! My goodness. Who's the other happy couple? Have we met them?"

"You will. They're friends of mine and Nathan's," Harry said.

"At least let me help with the reception," her mother said.

"I don't know, Mom. You don't know anyone in town. How can you possibly—"

"Trust me, dear. Just say you'd like my help."

Harry grinned. "All right, Mom. I'll leave the reception in your hands."

Nathan waited only long enough for Harry's parents to leave before he grabbed her by the hand and hauled her out of the booth. "You've got some nerve, young lady," he said as he dragged her up the stairs and closed one of The Grand's bedroom doors behind them.

"What do you mean, Nathan?"

He caught her by the shoulders and inserted his thigh between her legs, pulling her forward so that she was riding him.

Harry gasped.

His mouth came down on hers with all the passion she'd aroused in him when he'd been unable to take her in his arms. "That'll teach you to play games under the table."

"I've learned my lesson, Nathan," she said with a sigh of contentment. "Teach me more."

Nathan reached over and turned the lock on the door. "Your wish is my command."

"Nathan?"

"Yes, Harry-et."

"I love you."

"I love you, too."

They didn't say anything for long moments because their mouths were otherwise pleasantly occupied.

"Nathan?" Harry murmured.

"Yes, Harry-et."

"Where do you suppose my mother will end up having the reception?"

"The Moose Hall," he said as he nuzzled her throat.

Harry laughed. "You're kidding."

"Nope. It's the only place available except for the church basement, and that's too small."

"Too small? How many people are you inviting?"

Nathan smiled and kissed her nose. "You really are a tenderfoot, Harry-et. Everyone in Sweet Grass County, of course."

Harry's eyes widened. "Will they all show up?"

"Enough of them to make your mother's reception a success. Now, if you're through asking questions, I'd like to kiss that mouth of yours."

"Your wish is my command," Harry replied.

Nathan laughed. "Don't overdo it, Harry-et. A simple 'Yes, dear' will do."

"Yes, dear," she answered with an impudent grin.

"You're mine now, Harry-et. Forever and ever."

"Yes, dear."

"We'll live happily ever after. There'll be no more feuding Hazards and Alistairs. Your land is mine, and my land is yours. It's all *ours.*"

"Yes, dear."

"And there'll be lots of little Hazard-Alistairs to carry on after us."

Harry's eyes softened and she surrendered to Nathan's encompassing embrace. "Oh, yes, dear."

* * * * *

To my daughter-in-law-to-be, Gert Fulmer.
Thank you for the love and joy
that you bring to my son, Kevin,
and to our whole family.
(And thanks for being a fan
and enjoying my stories!)

TELL ME YOUR SECRETS...

Cara Summers

Was **CARA SUMMERS** born with the dream of becoming a published romance novelist? No. But now that she is, she still feels her dream has come true. She loves writing for the Harlequin Blaze line because it allows her to create strong, determined women and seriously sexy men who will risk everything to achieve *their* dreams. Cara has written more than thirty-five books for Harlequin Books, and when she isn't working on new stories, she teaches in the Writing Program at Syracuse University and at a community college near her home.

Chapter 1

"I can't make up my mind. Shall I have the scones with clotted cream—and ooooh, look at those strawberries...but the triple-chocolate layer cake is calling my name."

My friend Pepper Rossi was studying the three-tiered dessert caddie the waitress had just delivered as if the fate of the world depended on her decision.

I felt equally serious about the decision that I had made. After plotting and planning for the last three days, I'd come to San Francisco to run it by Pepper.

Nerves knotted in my stomach. But I managed to keep my hand steady as I lifted the silver teapot and filled Pepper's cup and then my own. I'd always run my plans by her when we were roommates in college.

Of course, those days were well behind us now that we were established career women. I had a job as a writer for a successful Los Angeles based soap opera, *Secrets*, and Pepper worked as a P.I. at Rossi Investigations, her brothers' up-and-coming security firm in San Francisco. Recently, she'd met the man of her dreams, Cole Buchanan, an ex-CIA agent who also worked for her brothers. From the glow on her face whenever she mentioned him, it was a match made in heaven.

Even more recently than that, I'd engaged Pepper in her professional capacity to do a job for me. Hiring a P.I. was a first for me. But then life was throwing me one surprise after another lately.

Pepper's hand was still hovering over the dessert caddie. "Take the cake," I urged her. "You know you're not going to be able to resist it." Pepper was a fellow chocoholic.

"You're sure?" she asked.

"If it's as good as it looks, we'll ask the waitress to bring another."

There was a time when indulging in chocolate had gone a long way toward helping me to deal with life's ups and downs. But it had lost some of its therapeutic value since the day five weeks

ago when my whole world had shifted on its axis.
That's when I'd received an anonymous letter telling me that I was adopted.

Up until that moment, I'd led a rather uneventful existence—if you discount the broken collarbone I'd suffered at age eleven when my horse Dandelion's Pride and I had parted company during a jump. I'd believed my parents were John and Marsha Ashby, both successful neurosurgeons in Chicago.

I was sure the letter was a prank, but my curiosity had kicked in and I'd phoned my parents. Mom and Dad had both gotten on the line in one of our typical "conference" calls. As busy and dedicated doctors, they'd always thought it more time efficient if they talked to me together. When I'd told them about the letter, I'd expected them to laugh and deny it, to reassure me that I was indeed their biological daughter and then get back to their busy lives.

But they hadn't laughed and they hadn't denied it. Instead, there'd been this long silence on the other end of the line. With my stomach clenched, I'd pushed for more information, and they'd finally confessed to the fact that they'd adopted me and they gave me the name of the private agency they'd used.

The moment I'd hung up I'd called Pepper and asked her to trace my biological family. A week ago, she'd sent me the information that had given me the first clue to my real past. She hadn't been able to locate my biological mother. Her search had dead-ended when she found the adoption papers for me—and my twin sister, who'd been raised as the only daughter of James and Elizabeth McKenzie on their horse ranch near San Diego.

My first rather giddy reaction when I'd received the news was that this would make a great story line for *Secrets*. Twins separated at birth. My head writer was going to love me. Mallory Carstairs, the bad-girl diva of the show, was currently in a coma, and now she could awake to find she had a twin sister....

Then I'd reined in my overactive imagination for a reality check. I wasn't a character on a soap opera. I was ordinary, nothing-ever-happens-to-me Brooke Ashby.

Except I had a twin sister I'd never met—an heiress who'd been missing for five weeks.

I watched Pepper slice into the chocolate cake. I'd let her enjoy one bite before I told her my plan. My head writer had been thrilled when I'd told her what I was going to do and she'd been more than willing to give me some time off. But I was sure that Pepper wasn't going to be equally happy with me.

I watched with envy as she savored that first bite. Then as she scooped up a second, I took a fortifying sip of tea and said, "I'm going to the McKenzie Ranch and masquerade as my sister."

The cake froze just inches from Pepper's open mouth, before her fork dropped with a clatter. "You're *what?*"

Pepper's voice was loud enough to make the elegantly dressed lady at a nearby table aim a frown in our direction. High tea at the sedate St. Francis Hotel in San Francisco was not the place for loud voices.

I cleared my throat and spoke around the little bubble of panic that had lodged in my throat. "Don't worry. I've plotted it all out. I'm going to the McKenzie Ranch posing as my twin sister, Cameron McKenzie."

"Your *missing* twin sister. Didn't you read the report I sent you? She disappeared five weeks ago. No one knows where she is."

I'd read the report over and over again, trying to glean every detail I could about my newly discovered twin. I tried a confident smile. "If she weren't missing, I wouldn't be able to take her place."

Pepper leaned forward, this time keeping her voice low. "Brooke, you can't be serious about this. Five weeks is a long time. If there was foul play involved in her disappearance, then you could be putting yourself in danger."

Pepper's words had my stomach performing that little "flip" it had been doing ever since I'd first learned that my sister was missing. I set down my teacup. "I knew it. You *do* think something's happened to her, don't you?"

Pepper raised both hands. "I didn't say that. The family hasn't filed a missing persons report. They say she's gone off like this before in a temper or on a whim. They claim not to be concerned."

Wedding jitters was the official story that the family had put out. Always a bit headstrong, Cameron had simply gone away to "settle her nerves" about her upcoming wedding to Sloan Campbell. According to what Pepper had discovered, Sloan Campbell, the orphaned son of a man who'd once run the McKenzie stables, had been raised on the ranch but had left five years earlier to make his own fortune in the world as a horse trainer. He'd been quite successful, too. In May, one of his horses had won the Kentucky Derby. That was where he and Cameron had run into one another again, and it had apparently been love at second sight. One of the press clippings had termed it a "perfect match" for McKenzie Enterprises. Sloan was the expert when it came to horses, and Cameron was proving to be very talented at bringing in new business.

I drew out the report that Pepper had sent me and placed it on the table between us. I had lots of questions about the marriage and about Sloan

Campbell. When someone disappears, it's always the husband or the fiancé who's the prime suspect.

"When Sloan marries Cameron—*if* the wedding actually takes place next month—they jointly inherit both the McKenzie land and the business." The business being a multimillion-dollar horse breeding and training facility that James McKenzie and his father and grandfather before him had established and built. "Why jointly? Why not leave the whole thing to his only daughter?"

"My thought exactly," Pepper said. "So I checked into it and discovered that James McKenzie is a patriarch in the true sense of the word. In spite of the fact that he's survived into the twenty-first century, he has the antiquated idea that a woman can't run the ranch on her own."

I tapped my finger on the report. "My sister sounds pretty competent."

"I agree. But the McKenzies seem to be a stubborn lot, and she hasn't been able to convince her father of that. And there may be more involved from a business standpoint. Bringing back Sloan Campbell was a real coup. After his horse won the Derby, he could have pretty much written his ticket in terms of job offers. But from what I've been able to dig up, he wasn't going to work for anyone else. He was going to use the nest egg he's been saving up for the past few years to buy a ranch and build his own business. That was probably his goal when he left and went out on his own five years ago. I'm figuring a deal where he gets half of the McKenzie Ranch—an already established place—was a powerful lure."

"But even if Cameron only comes into half the estate, there are millions involved and she's missing. Any way you look at it, there's a motive for foul play."

"Which is why I don't want you to go there pretending to be her," Pepper said. "If you're curious, why not just go as yourself?"

"I thought of that. But I'd just be a stranger. They could serve me tea and then brush me off."

Pepper reached over and took my hand in hers. "This is a sister you didn't even know existed until I sent you that report. If you're worried about her, Cole and I can look into this further."

"They don't have to talk to you, either. But if I go there posing as Cameron, there's no way they can brush me off. I'll have a chance to see things and learn things as an insider. And I have a plan all plotted out."

Pepper shook her head. "This isn't a story line for your soap opera. You know you have a tendency to leap into things before you look."

I took another fortifying sip of tea. My parents would have been in full agreement with her. As long as I could remember, I'd been cursed with an *Alice In Wonderland*–like curiosity. It was probably one of the reasons I became a writer. It wasn't that great a leap from wondering what's going to happen next to inventing what's going to happen next.

"I know I can pull it off. I've studied all the photographs you sent me in the file plus a few I've dug up on my own. From what I can see, Cameron and I are identical twins." We both had the same dark red hair. Of course, I wore mine in a braid down my back so I wouldn't have to fuss with it. Cameron, on the other hand, wore hers in one of those chic shoulder-length styles that I'd always admired.

"All I have to do is shorten my hair a bit," I assured Pepper. This was the part of the plan that was clear in my mind. I'd even made an appointment with a hairdresser.

"You're going to need more than a haircut to pull this off."

Exactly. That was why I had come to San Francisco. I was going to need more, and Pepper had the power to provide all of it. I just had to get her on my side. I wasn't worried, not really. Hadn't I been cocaptain of the debate team at the small private college Pepper and I had attended? The only problem was that Pepper had been the other cocaptain and her strength had always been rebuttal.

"I'll need a little help from you, of course. But I know that I can pass for her."

"For how long?" Pepper asked. "A few photos and the information I gave you won't be enough. Someone is bound to figure out you're a phony."

"I told you I have a plan."

"You always do." Pepper's frown deepened. "But sometimes they don't work out."

I could tell she was thinking of the time I had the great idea about slipping away from the dorm and going to a frat party at the neighboring state school. My plan had included donning disguises, climbing out of our dorm window via sheets we had knotted together, and "borrowing" our resident advisor's car. It would have worked if we hadn't had a flat tire and the local sheriff hadn't stopped to help us out.

Pepper squeezed my hand. "Look, I know that this has been a shock to you—first finding out that you're adopted and then learning that you have an identical twin."

This was another reason why I'd driven up to San Francisco to talk to Pepper. Yes, I needed her help, but I also needed someone besides my parents to talk to. Mom and Dad were busy. They'd always been busy. Not that they hadn't loved me and been proud of me. They had. But…

"What can I do to talk you out of this?"

I met her eyes steadily. "You can't. I don't believe that Cameron's disappearance is due to the fact that she needed time away to 'settle her nerves.' I have this feeling that something's wrong and that she needs my help."

Pepper's brows shot up. "A feeling? Are you talking about some special twin ESP?"

"Maybe."

She considered that for a moment and then said, "How does that work when you've never known each other, never even met?"

"How should I know? We came from the same egg, share the same genes. I'm figuring we have to be quite a bit alike." I paused to flip open the file that lay on the table between us. Pepper had been thorough in her research. She'd included pictures and background information on everyone at the McKenzie Ranch. I pulled out a photo that had appeared in the local press announcing the engagement of Cameron McKenzie and Sloan Campbell. "Look at them. They look very happy together."

Pepper rolled her eyes. "They're posing for the press. They probably said 'cheese.'"

"Maybe." But I couldn't believe that what I saw in the photo was faked. It was the only picture that Pepper had included of my sister's fiancé, Sloan Campbell, and the same thing was happening to me that had happened every time I looked at it. I couldn't seem to take my eyes off of his face.

He was dark-haired and tall, nearly a full head and shoulders above Cameron. If she was wearing three-inch heels—and I figured from other photos she was—that meant he was over six feet tall. Even in a tux, it was apparent that his shoulders were broad. There was strength there, and a certain magnetism that would probably be even stronger when it wasn't being filtered through a camera lens. Hollywood and TV producers called it "star quality," and Sloan Campbell had it in spades.

Yet, he wasn't exactly handsome, at least not in a movie star pretty way. In my experience, actors built their muscles and hardened their abs in state-of-the-art health clubs. Sloan Campbell looked as if he kept in shape the old-fashioned way. He might not be movie star handsome, but there was something very compelling about his rugged features, something that made you believe that in a fight, this was the man you'd want on your side.

My instincts also told me that this was a man any red-blooded woman would want in her bed. I blinked as a thought struck me. Was this a man I wanted in my bed? Was that why I was so fascinated by his picture? I could feel heat flood my cheeks. He was my sister's fiancé. And they looked very happy.

"Earth to Brooke."

I dragged my eyes away from the newspaper clipping and met Pepper's again.

"I'm waiting for you to elaborate more on this 'feeling' of yours that your sister isn't a runaway bride."

"Okay." I drew in a deep breath. "From your accounts, Cameron loves the ranch and she holds an important job at McKenzie Enterprises. She gets to travel around the country, entertaining old clients and courting new ones. She's good at what she does, and the business depends on her. The other thing that's clear in your report is that she loves horses. That's one thing I share with her, and I don't think she would run away from her responsibilities. I think she'd handle her cold feet another way. She'd simply break off the engagement."

"Dammit." Pepper leaned back in her chair.

It was my turn to stare. "What's the matter?"

"You're beginning to make sense."

Before I could comment, a waitress appeared at our table.

"Can I get you something else?"

"Two glasses of your best Chardonnay," Pepper said. "I'm going to need more than chocolate to settle my nerves."

As soon as the waitress moved away, she leaned closer. "I've talked about this with Cole, and we tend to agree with you that Cameron wouldn't have run out on the job or the horses for this amount of time."

"Then you can understand why I have to go there."

Pepper grabbed my hand again. "What I see

is a reason why you shouldn't go there. It's too dangerous. If someone else is responsible for your sister's disappearance, he or she is not going to be happy if you show up as Cameron. Plus, we still don't know who sent the anonymous letter—or why."

"You're not going to talk me out of this."

"Yeah," Pepper said as the waitress set down the glasses of wine. "That's why I ordered the drinks."

We reached for the wineglasses together and I raised mine in a toast. "To the best friend ever. Wish me luck?"

She touched her glass to mine and took a long swallow. "I have one more argument."

As cocaptain of the debate team, she'd always had one more argument.

"How in the world are you going to carry this masquerade off? All you know about your sister is in that file. And what about the fiancé? How do you intend to handle him?"

Very carefully, I thought. I had a good idea that Sloan Campbell would be my biggest challenge once I got to the ranch. Once more, I attempted a confident smile. "I've got it covered. I'm going to tell them that five weeks ago I got mugged, and when I woke up in the hospital, I didn't have any ID and couldn't remember who I was. That's why I haven't come back sooner. And that way I won't have to remember a thing about Cameron's past life."

Pepper sighed, then took a good gulp of her wine. "I should have known you'd come up with something. You always do."

I met her eyes steadily. "I have to do this. She's my sister. And I'm going to need your help."

"You bet your life you are." Pepper pulled out a notebook and began scribbling. "The mugging is a good idea. You arrived at the hospital with only the clothes on your back. So there was no way to trace you. We'll need to establish where you've been and what you've been doing for the last five weeks. You're a millionairess. Someone in the family is going to check into everything. And when the press gets hold of the story…"

She paused in her scribbling and tapped her pen on the notebook. "There will have to be a report about the mugging. Here in San Francisco, I think, because Luke has a friend who's a captain in the SFPD. Because of the amnesia, you won't have to explain why you were so far from home."

"I knew you'd know what to do," I said.

Pepper glanced up at me. "If you're determined to do this, I want your ass covered." Then she continued scribbling. "We'll also need a doctor who can verify the memory loss, a place where you've been staying the last few weeks, a job. Maybe when you came to Rossi Investigations to ask for our help, we gave you something temporary. We'll figure it out. Cole's really good at this sort of thing. And what he can't handle, my brother Luke can. He's magic when it comes to hacking into official records and tweaking them a bit."

I smiled at her. "Exactly why I hired your firm to help me find out who I was."

Pepper frowned at me. "And it took us five weeks to do the job?" Then she grinned. "Just kidding. Let them think we're some kind of hick agency. Plus, your mugging took place in San Francisco, and Cameron's disappearance didn't even make the papers around here." Her grin faded. "A definite sign of the power of the family to keep a lid on the story. You're going to have to be very careful."

"I will. Thanks for understanding."

Pepper leaned closer. "I know what it's like to find family that you didn't know existed. But once you get to the ranch, I want you to keep in daily contact with me. Cole has a plane. We can be there in less than an hour."

She set her pen down, and took a sip of her wine. "Once you get to the ranch, what's the rest of your plan?"

"You always ask the tough questions."

Pepper's eyes narrowed. "That's what friends are for."

I shrugged and took a good gulp of wine myself.

"Once I get inside the hacienda, I'm going to play it by ear. I'm sure something will come to me. My best plots always come to me on the fly."

Chapter 2

"We're almost there," Cole Buchanan said as he turned his sporty red convertible onto the winding road that led to the McKenzie Ranch. He and Pepper had decided that Cole should bring me to the ranch, get the lay of the land, and test the atmosphere before he left. He would explain about my memory loss, the investigative work that Rossi Investigations had done to help me find out my true identity, and that way everyone at the ranch would know that there was someone on the outside that I could turn to for help—just in case.

Cole was my driver instead of Pepper because the Rossis had decided he had a bigger intimidation quotient than Pepper did. It was really no contest. At over six feet, with a rangy body that was pretty much all muscle, Cole was not someone you would want to go up against. I'd also learned that he'd done sniper work for the CIA.

The idea that he and Pepper had met, fallen in love and were making a match of it, would never have occurred to me—not even as a remote possibility. But I'd seen them together and they suited each other perfectly. I'd already been thinking of how I could adapt their story for *Secrets*. While looking for her long lost twin, Mallory Carstairs meets and hires an ex-sniper to help her out.

"You can always change your mind."

I jerked my thoughts back to the present.

"You don't have to stay at the ranch," Cole continued. "We can just say that you've hired me to make some inquiries and that you don't feel comfortable staying there until you find out why you ran away."

"No. I'll be fine." The whole idea of my coming to the ranch was to investigate Cameron's disappearance from the inside. "I'm just having a little attack of stage fright."

Truth told, I was having a major attack. Now that I was about to step out onstage, I was suddenly realizing that acting out story lines was a lot different than sitting on the sidelines and writing them. One of the things that I'd discovered in the past few days as I'd been poring over everything I could find about my sister was that we were different in one aspect. She would never have suffered from an attack of cold feet. Cameron had always been in a sort of limelight. Plus, she was confident, outgoing and probably very assertive. I, on the other hand, was a writer. While I experienced life vicariously through the characters I created, she went out there and boldly lived. I envied her that.

"We could also go to plan B and I could stay on as your bodyguard," Cole said.

That, too, was something we'd discussed during the three days I'd spent in the offices of Rossi Investigations while Pepper and Cole established my cover story and drilled into me every fact they'd dug up on the cast of characters at the ranch.

At the end of three days, I knew each one of the players as well as I knew the characters on *Secrets*, maybe even better. But I'd rejected plan B. How was I supposed to find out anything with Rossi Investigation's biggest intimidation factor dogging my every step?

I turned to Cole and put on my most confident smile. "I'm going to be able to do this."

He pulled to a stop in front of an opened wrought iron gate that bore the name McKenzie Ranch. Then he turned to me. "I don't doubt that. Pepper has told me a lot about you. But if you want help, Pepper and I are a phone call away."

I felt tears prick behind my eyes. "Thanks. But I think I have a better chance of learning something if I do this alone. My sister would be able to do this. If I'm anything at all like her, I can, too."

Cole gave me a brief nod, then guided his car through the gate and up the winding driveway. When we rounded the last curve and the hacienda came into view, I gave a little gasp.

The Hacienda Montega was listed in every book that chronicled historic homes in California. In addition to being an excellent example of Spanish architecture, the house had a mysterious and colorful history. I'd done some research on it that went beyond Pepper's report. What I'd discovered was that the mistresses of the hacienda had a tendency to die young. Not even Cameron's father's wives had escaped. James McKenzie's first wife, Sarah, hadn't died, but she'd still been young when she'd run away with Sloan Campbell's father. Of course, I'd tucked that little piece of information away for a possible story line. Then James's second wife, Elizabeth, had passed away shortly after they'd adopted Cameron.

But there was a lighter and even more colorful side to the history, too. Originally built by Don Roberto Montega on the occasion of his marriage to the Spanish Countess Maria Francesca in the eighteenth century, the hacienda had eventually fallen into the hands of a silent film producer who'd only owned it a year before he'd lost both the hacienda and the land to a professional gambler named Silas McKenzie.

And the rest was history, as they say. Silas had married, mended his gambling ways and turned to his first love, raising Thoroughbred horses. From the looks of the hacienda, the stables and the other outbuildings, he must have had a knack for it. James, the current owner of the estate, was his grandson.

All of the pictures I'd seen paled in comparison to what I was looking at now. The main part of the house rose three stories with a bell tower at its center that thrust up another two. The colors were so intense—those golden stones, the reddish-orange tiles on the roof against a bright blue sky. My gaze swept along the arches and stone pillars that framed the courtyard, then rose to the lacy ironwork that fanned each one of the windows on the second and third floors. Flowers bloomed everywhere, crowding the paths bordering the walks, and spilling out of terra-cotta urns.

Beatrice McKenzie Caulfield, the sister of James McKenzie, the aging patriarch, was responsible for the flowers. I ran through the information I knew about her. She was renowned for her gardening skills and was a frequent participant and speaker at garden shows. In addition to that, she'd run the Hacienda Montega for the past twenty-five years since the untimely death of Elizabeth McKenzie. Beatrice was also the mother of Austin Caulfield, Cameron's cousin, who'd taken over her job in her absence.

Cole pulled to a stop in front of the courtyard. Inside, I could see a fountain shooting sparks of light back at the sun.

"It's beautiful," I said.

"That it is," Cole agreed. "Does it trigger any memory?"

I glanced at him in surprise.

"Get used to the question, Brooke. The moment you step out of the car, you're Cameron McKenzie, suffering from amnesia. Are you ready?"

I drew in a deep breath and pushed open the door on my side of the car. "Ready."

My step didn't falter once as we walked up the path past the fountain to the huge wood door of the house. Cole knocked. I counted to ten, and Cole had raised his hand to knock again when the door swung open to reveal a small, brown-skinned woman who was as wide as she was tall. She stared at me for a moment, but even as she tucked the towel she was holding into an apron pocket, her face brightened into a smile that was almost as wide as her girth. "Ms. Cameron, Ms. Cameron, you're safe!" She grabbed my hands, drew me over the threshold and enveloped me in a warm hug.

For a moment, she held me tight and I caught

the scent of vanilla. Then she drew back, studied me at arm's length, then pulled me in for another hug. "They said you'd be back. Mr. James and Mr. Sloan—they weren't worried. But I..."

When she released me, I saw tears in her eyes. This had to be Elena Santoro, the woman who'd been the housekeeper and cook for the McKenzies for more than forty years. According to Pepper's information, much of the job of raising Cameron had fallen on her shoulders after Elizabeth McKenzie had died.

Elena rubbed the heel of her hand against her cheeks. "I was worried. I shouldn't have." For the first time, she seemed to notice Cole at my side.

"Ma'am." He nodded at her and withdrew his license from his pocket. "I'm Cole Buchanan of Rossi Investigations. Ms. McKenzie here was mugged in San Francisco a little over a month ago, all her ID was stolen, and she's been suffering from amnesia ever since. If the rest of the family is home, perhaps you could let them know we're here, and I could explain everything all at once?"

"You were mugged?" She reached out a hand, hesitated and then dropped it. "You've lost your memory?"

"Yes. Hopefully, it's only temporary. But when I woke up in the hospital, I couldn't remember anything—who I was, where I should go...." Seeing the concern in her eyes, I felt a little twinge of guilt, but it didn't seem to be interfering with my ability to lie. "I hired Mr. Buchanan's security firm to help me find out who I was, and they finally did."

"How awful." She did take my hands then and squeezed them briefly.

"The family?" Cole prompted.

"Yes. But only Ms. Beatrice is here. Mr. Sloan went to Kentucky to pick up a horse and Mr. James is in Los Angeles, having his yearly checkup. Mr. James will be back later today, but Mr. Sloan isn't expected back until tomorrow. Mr. Austin is in Saratoga Springs with Ms. Linton at the races. But Ms. Beatrice is in her office. I'll get her."

Elena bustled away down the hall. For the first time I had time to glance around the huge foyer. The hacienda's interior was no less impressive than its exterior. The floor was covered with honey-colored tiles that offered a nice contrast to the gleaming dark wood of a staircase that swept up to a landing, then split off in two directions to the balconied second level. In the center of the foyer stood a round carved oak table, nearly the size of the one I imagined Arthur had gathered his knights around. On top of it stood a huge crystal vase filled with flowers.

Elena led Beatrice McKenzie Caulfield around the side of the table. My first impression was that Beatrice would have made a great snow queen.

Her hair was nearly white, and fell straight and long from a center part almost to her waist. Her eyes were a pale shade of blue, her skin porcelain. Even her clothes were pale. She wore light tan work pants and a shirt in a soft material that seemed to flow as she walked toward us. Her white canvas shoes made no noise as she approached. She was a tall woman, slender, with an ethereal kind of beauty that reminded me of Tennessee Williams's Southern women. Blanche Dubois—but stronger. Colder. I had a feeling that Beatrice would hold her own very well against Stanley Kowalski.

I also had the distinct impression that Beatrice Caulfield had been studying me just as thoroughly as I'd been studying her. When she stopped in front of me, she was the one who broke the silence. "Cameron?"

The word with its question mark came out in a soft voice that somehow matched the rest of her.

"Ma'am." Cole began to tell my story about the accident and my memory loss.

Beatrice interrupted. "Why were you in San Francisco?"

"I don't remember," I said. It was amazing how memory loss came in handy. "Do you have any idea why I might have gone up there?"

She shook her head. "I'm sorry."

Cole continued, telling the part where I came to Rossi Investigations and hired them to find out who I was. He'd nearly finished when a large black cat appeared around the side of the oak table, walked toward us and halted at Elena's feet.

"Hannibal, aren't you happy to see your mistress?" Elena asked.

The cat stayed right where he was, and the look he gave me was not friendly. Did that mean he knew on some cat instinct level that I wasn't Cameron? Here was a complication that I hadn't counted on. Pepper and Cole had warned me there'd be more than one.

Elena scooped Hannibal up and held him out to me.

The cat responded by hissing loudly and taking a swipe at me with his paw.

"Evidently, he's forgotten you already," Beatrice remarked.

"Don't you pay any attention to him, Ms. Cameron," Elena hurried to say. "The two of you were thick as thieves. He just needs some time to get used to you again." She set Hannibal down, and he shot off like a bullet.

I wished that it was as easy to read Beatrice as it was to read the cat. The woman had registered very little emotion at seeing me, but she hadn't shifted her gaze from me once during the time that Cole had talked. I found it impossible to tell from her eyes, but I had a feeling that she didn't harbor any warm feelings for Cameron. Definitely a snow queen, I thought.

Finally, Beatrice turned to Cole. "Would you like something to drink, Mr. Buchanan? Iced tea?"

Cole smiled. "That would be great."

Beatrice had Elena serve us tea on a patio off the kitchen that offered a view of the gardens and the stables in the distance. She was a good hostess and a good listener. By the time we were finished with our drinks, Beatrice knew pretty much everything that had happened to me in the weeks I'd supposedly been missing—everything we wanted her to know.

Finally, she rose. "James will be home late this afternoon. He knew that you'd be back, but I'm sure it will ease his mind to find out that he was right." Then she turned to Cole. "Mr. Buchanan, if you'll leave a card? My brother may wish to speak with you."

Cole took a card out of his pocket and handed it to her.

She turned to me. "Make yourself at home, Cameron. I have work to do in the greenhouse."

I waited until she left before I said to Cole, "Do you think she bought it?"

"I think the jury's out. One of the things that we talked about is that while people may believe you're Cameron, they may suspect you're faking the memory loss. Do you want me to hang around until James gets here?"

"No." I drew in a deep breath and let it out. "I feel like I've been given a little reprieve, not having to explain everything to James and Sloan right away." I was really a bit apprehensive about Sloan and happy that I wouldn't have to face him until the next day. In spite of that I managed a smile for Cole. "I'm going to do a bit of exploring and try to get to know my sister a bit better. I'll be fine. Really."

I walked Cole out to the door and waited until he brought my duffel from the car. In spite of my words, my stomach did a little flip as he pulled away. But in addition to apprehension, I also felt a little thrill of excitement. The adventure was about to begin.

Chapter 3

A half hour later, I was restlessly exploring Cameron's bedroom. Elena had taken me up right after Cole had left, and before I could shut the door, Hannibal had dashed in, leaped onto the bed and enthroned himself on the pillows as if he were staking out a claim.

Before I'd let Elena return to the kitchen, I'd asked her one of the questions that Cole and Pepper and I had decided we needed to know—a question no one had bothered with because Cameron had never been reported missing. Where was each of the cast of characters on the day that Cameron had disappeared? Once I had the information, I was to phone Pepper and then Rossi Investigations could check out the alibis. Since Elena had been able to give such an accurate rundown of everyone's whereabouts when Cole and I had arrived, I'd figured she'd be a good source. And she had been. James and Sloan had been at the ranch that day. Miss Beatrice had been giving a speech at a flower show in San Diego about an hour's drive away. Mr. Austin had been with the Lintons in Las Vegas. There'd been no censure in her tone, but I sensed that Elena didn't entirely approve of Austin's whereabouts.

Thanks to Cole's and Pepper's coaching, I knew who the Lintons were. Marcie Linton was my personal assistant. I'd hired her on about six months ago. Shortly after they'd met, she and Austin had started dating, and they'd since become engaged. Marcie had introduced Austin to her brother, Hal, and the trio had been very close ever since.

Cole had also learned that Hal represented a group of developers who wanted badly to get their hands on a strip of McKenzie land that ran along the Pacific. So far, James had rejected all offers. Evidently, McKenzies didn't part easily with their land.

Once Elena had left, I'd ignored Hannibal, and embarked on the first step in my plan—learning more about my sister. Her bedroom was large and airy with two large floor-to-ceiling windows that opened onto small balconies. In decor the room was feminine—Cameron favored pastels—but it wasn't frilly. The walls were ivory; the rug was an Oriental in muted shades of rose which were picked up in the bedspread and in the upholstered furniture.

In a small alcove, there was a couch—not a love seat, but a full-length couch, one I could imagine stretching out on and reading—or perhaps taking a nap. I tested it, and to my surprise, Hannibal jumped off the bed, ambled over and aimed a glare at me.

In spite of Elena's assurances that cats had short memories and he just needed a little time to get to know his owner again, I couldn't help thinking that Hannibal knew more than he was letting on. "Okay," I said. "Maybe you can sense I'm not Cameron. But I'm trying to find out what happened to her. So we're really on the same side here."

He didn't look convinced.

I didn't have much experience with cats, but I'd handled horses who'd been initially skeptical of my abilities as a rider. The key was never to let them sense your weakness.

I turned to examine the bookcase next to the couch. There, I discovered a variety of books from Shakespeare's Sonnets and well-thumbed copies of classics like *Pride and Prejudice* and *To Kill a*

Mockingbird to a thriller that had recently made the bestseller lists. I'd just read it myself, and I wondered in how many other things my sister's taste and mine might coincide.

From the Queen Anne desk and a delicately hand-carved chair, I assumed she liked antiques. I'd never had the time to hunt for them, but I could appreciate their beauty. On the other side of the couch, I discovered a silly-looking red fox perched on top of an embroidered footstool.

When I picked it up to take a closer look, Hannibal made a growling sound deep in his throat.

I was intimidated enough to put the fox back on the stool, and I turned my attention to the small cabinet. Inside I found a bottle of brandy, a cache of chocolate and a bag of cat tidbits. Had I uncovered the secret to how Cameron and Hannibal had become "thick as thieves"? Selecting one of them, I turned back to the cat.

"Is this what you're hounding me for?"

He moved closer and I gave him the treat. He hadn't been on my list of the players at the hacienda, but if Cameron had kept treats for him right beside her chocolate…

"Look. I'm going to be here for a while, so you'd better get used to me. And I'm not going to steal anything from your mistress. She's my sister."

Hannibal blinked just as if he'd understood what I'd just said.

"We're not enemies. Really. I'm beginning to like her. She has good taste—even in chocolate."

Her cache was made in Switzerland.

Hannibal had no comment. I opened the cabinet, and this time I took out a treat for both of us. As he ate his, I took a bite of chocolate and turned my attention back to the room. Truth told, I not only liked Cameron's taste, I envied it. Since moving to Los Angeles, I'd pretty much buried myself in work, and I hadn't yet taken the time to make my apartment my own.

I investigated Cameron's closet next while Hannibal stood in the doorway to keep watch. What I found was that any possible similarities between my sister and me came to an end when it came to clothes. First off, her closet wasn't a closet. It was a whole room that opened off the larger bed-sitting-room area. My bedroom in my apartment wasn't any larger. One wall housed drawers, cupboards, shoe racks and shelves. Along the other hung Cameron's clothes, neatly arranged and sorted into pants, shirts, jackets, suits and dresses.

If you are what you wear, Cameron McKenzie was a fashion queen. I like clothes, too, but I bought mine off the racks, and Cameron's all came from designer showrooms. No bargains from Wal-Mart here. So far Jimmy Choo shoes were something that I'd only seen on TV shows. My twin owned four pairs. Way to go, Cameron.

Insatiably curious, I'd searched through drawers and found she had a taste for gold, expensive lingerie and short nightgowns. I'd even tested her scent—something exotic and French that probably cost more than what I spent on a month's rent.

But it was the bathroom that gave me the biggest surprise about my sister. The best description I could come up with was that it was like a little slice of paradise. There was a skylight situated so that sun, rain or starlight would be visible from the tub. There were gleaming marble tiles, a shower with frosted glass doors, brass faucets, and enough plants hanging and bursting out of pots to make one think of Eden.

I was aware of all that as I stood in the doorway, but my eyes never left the tub. Surrounding it on a wide ledge were glass bottles in various hues, filled no doubt with scents and oils and creams. And I counted twelve candles. The tub itself sank into the floor and it was big enough for two. I couldn't help wondering if it had ever been used that way. Cameron and Sloan? My sister definitely had a sensuous side.

That shouldn't surprise me. So did I. At least I was pretty sure I did. I just hadn't had much time to indulge it—or perhaps, I hadn't had much of a reason to indulge it. Cameron had her very attractive fiancé.

Turning, I moved back into the bedroom and

began to pace. Bottom line, after an hour in my sister's bedroom, I'd learned she had excellent taste in decor, expensive taste in clothes and the money to indulge it, and a passionate side to her nature— all of which I admired and envied her for.

To top it off, she was going to be heir to half of her father's kingdom—worth millions of dollars.

Compared to hers, my life seemed rather mundane.

But my purpose here wasn't about me, I reminded myself. I was here to learn all I could about Cameron and just why she might have disappeared on that day five weeks ago.

Moving to the window, I focused on what my next move should be. I'd fully expected to spend my first day on the ranch meeting all the major players that I would have to convince that I was Cameron without a memory. With Sloan and James away, I was out of plot line. The view from Cameron's bedroom was the same as the one Beatrice, Cole and I had had on the patio, and my eyes were drawn to the stables. If Sloan had been here, I would have asked him for a tour and perhaps gone for a ride. It had been so long since I'd been on a horse.

But that might not be my best move. I was suffering from memory loss. So it might look strange if I walked down to the stables and asked someone to saddle up a horse. My gaze moved to the hills that bordered the valley the ranch sat in on the east and the west.

But I could ask for a car. After all, I was Cameron McKenzie, home after an absence of five weeks. Memory loss or not, I might be interested in driving around to see if something, anything stirred a memory.

It certainly beat sitting here in Cameron's room with a cat who seemed to value me only for my ability to provide food. Elena would know whom I'd have to speak to. I hurried to the door, opened it, and then glanced back at Hannibal. He was back on the bed, sitting on his throne. "Coming?"

He made no move.

"See you later," I said as I let myself out and shut the door.

Elena had given me the keys to an SUV that was parked right outside the kitchen. It had a McKenzie Ranch logo on the side, and anybody who needed to run an errand could use it. On impulse and out of curiosity, I'd driven up onto the bluff that formed a natural boundary on one side of the valley the ranch lay snuggled in. The road was unpaved and rough in spots. When I'd gone as far as I could with the SUV, I'd parked it and walked another half mile along a path that wove in and out of boulders until I'd reached the top.

All around me as far as I could see, lay the vast

stretch of land that the McKenzies could lay claim to. I knew from the maps that Cole and Pepper had shown me that the shores of the Pacific were blocked by more hills behind me, but the estate extended all the way to the sea. Below me the ground sloped gently before it dropped off sharply into the valley below. Since I have a problem with heights, I was careful not to go near the edge. My view of the hacienda itself was still blocked by some of the boulders that dotted the bluff, so I walked farther along the narrow path to get a better look.

The wind had picked up, and to the west I could see huge dark clouds racing in from the Pacific. Thunder growled in the distance, and lightning split the sky.

Shades of *Wuthering Heights,* I thought. Not a good omen. Then I resolutely turned my back on the approaching storm and walked onward until I had a good view of the flat stretch of land in the little valley below.

From this vantage point, I could see everything that I hadn't been able to see from the patio or Cameron's window. Behind the hacienda there was an Olympic-sized pool and a pool house surrounded by trees and terraced gardens. Fanning off from that I could see orange groves, tennis courts and what must be Beatrice's greenhouses.

If Beatrice was responsible for all of that, my hat was off to her. The stables, along with the training and riding rings and what was probably once the original carriage house, were a short distance away. Here and there, I caught glimpses of a stream twisting like a silver snake in and out among trees which grew thicker in some places than in others.

And this was only the ranch land. The entire McKenzie estate, I reminded myself, included that prime undeveloped real estate along the Pacific Coast. All I could think was *Wow!*

Far below me, a truck pulling a horse trailer drew up in front of the largest of the stable buildings. A second later, two men climbed out and the larger of the two, the driver, went immediately to open the trailer door. Even at this distance, I could tell that the horse he led out by a tether was magnificent. Huge and black, the animal reared up as if he just had to stretch after being cooped up. I grinned, thinking that I'd felt the same way myself just a short time ago.

Then, instead of leading the horse into the stables, I watched the man leap up onto the horse's back and ride him bareback across the nearest field. Admiration and envy streamed through me as rider and horse took the first fence and began to make their way toward the very hills I was perched on.

I let my gaze sweep the estate again as I struggled to identify the other emotions tumbling through me. Excitement and pride that all of this belonged to my twin sister. Reading Pepper's report and studying the photos had whetted my curiosity. Now, seeing the hacienda, the land, from this vantage point was making Cameron even more real to me. But I wanted to know more. I needed to know everything. Obviously, we shared a love of horses, and hers had been easily nurtured here.

Although it had always been a dream of mine, I'd yet to own a horse of my own. My parents had pointed out the difficulties involved with trying to stable and care for one in Chicago. Aside from the expense, would it be fair to the horse? They'd been right, of course. They usually were. And they hadn't stood in the way of riding lessons. Although they hadn't been enthused when I'd wanted to try steeplechasing, they'd come to see me do it. In college I'd been a member of the riding club.

I'd often thought that it must have been hard for them to have a daughter who was so different from them. Oh, they loved me. But there'd always been that sort of bemused expression on their faces when I'd excelled in a field that was so outside of their own areas of interest. They were left brained, and I was right. I found myself wondering if they'd ever regretted not having a child of their own. I also wondered if Cameron had fit in better with her adopted family.

Thunder cracked and lightning split the sky,

but I ignored both. Instead, I continued to think about my twin. Would a love of horses, of riding, be genetic? Wardrobes aside, in what other ways was I like Cameron—or not like her? Would she be able to understand me in a way my parents never had? More than ever, I felt the need to find out.

And soon. The more I saw of the ranch and the kind of life that Cameron had, the more I wondered why she would disappear.

Thunder boomed overhead this time, and the lightning flashed to my left almost simultaneously. I thought I smelled it. Below me, a line of pitch-black shadows raced across the valley reminding me of a shade being drawn down for the night. In the murkier light, the hacienda made me think of Thornfield, Manderley, the Château de Valmy and every other mysterious mansion gracing the pages of those Gothic novels I'd read as a girl. I thought again of the fact that the mistresses of this mansion had seemed to succumb to untimely ends, and a chill skittered its way up my spine.

Ridiculous, I told myself. If I was ever going to pull this impersonation off, I would have to keep a tight rein on my imagination. This was a working horse ranch, not some Gothic mansion plagued by secrets and long-covered-up murders.

On the other hand, my twin sister who stood to inherit at least half of all of this was missing.

People had been killed for much less than this. Another chill moved through me.

Then the sky opened, and rain poured down so thick and fast that I could barely make out the path as I turned and began to wind my way back to the car.

The good news was I was still wearing the jeans, plain T-shirt and sneakers that I'd worn for my ride out to the McKenzie estate. The bad news was that I was soaked to the bone by the time I'd taken three steps and my new "Cameron" hairdo was destroyed. Pushing the sodden mess out of my eyes, I stretched my hands out in front of me like a sleepwalker. The car was too far away to seek shelter there, so I stumbled toward the darker shape of what had to be one of the boulders I'd skirted earlier. Once I reached it, I moved around to the far side and let it block the wind and at least some of the rain. Then I hunkered down to wait out the storm.

I wasn't sure how long I squatted at the side of the boulder—probably not longer than five or ten minutes. The storm ended as quickly as it had begun. The rain stopped first, and gradually the sun began to peek through clouds that were quickly blowing away. As I rose to my feet, I could still hear thunder grumbling in the distance. I'd made my way around the boulder and back onto the path before it finally registered in my mind that the rhythmic pounding I was listening to wasn't just thunder. It was also hoofbeats.

Realization came at the same instant that horse and rider shot around a curve in the path less than fifty yards from where I was standing. My heart lodged in my throat, my body froze, and my imagination took flight. Burned into my mind was the image of horse and man, all muscle and speed, moving in perfect unity—the mythic centaur in the flesh. In that instant, I wasn't sure which animal was more magnificent—man or beast.

Luckily, the man had quick reflexes. He reined the horse in sharply. The animal reared, protesting loudly. It might have been the sound of the horse's distress or perhaps it was the sight of those powerful hooves that jolted me free of the trance I'd been in, but I finally leaped toward the side of the path. I landed hard on the uneven ground, felt my ankle twist and give out just before I crashed into the boulder.

Behind me I heard the struggle between horse and rider, the horse neighing, a deep male voice talking in a soothing tone. Turning, I saw the horse rear again, but the man's hands remained steady on the rope, and he continued to talk in a firm tone.

"Easy, Saturn. Easy, boy."

I suddenly realized that this must be the same man I'd seen take the horse out of the trailer and ride him bareback across the fields. Not only had he kept control of the stallion and saved me from injury, he'd also remained seated. Admiration streamed through me. I had some idea of the skill it was taking to calm the frightened horse.

I was sitting in the shade of the boulder, but the horse and the man were bathed now in sunlight and I was able to take in more details. The man had slid from the horse and stood with his back toward me, talking to the horse and keeping a firm grip on the tether. He and the animal had a lot in common. Both were large and dark and strong—perfectly matched in the struggle that was going on. The man's hair curled around the nape of his neck. He was broad in the shoulders, lean in the hips, and long in the legs. With his jeans and chambray shirt plastered to him like a second skin, I could see the movement of each sculpted muscle as he quieted the horse with patient skill. The horse, still frightened, reared again and pawed the air. The stallion was larger, stronger. But the battle wouldn't be decided on size alone. It would come down to who had the stronger will.

The man let out the rope, then drew it in again, each time getting closer to the horse. The closer he drew, the calmer the horse became. It was like watching a slow, steady dance of seduction. Admiration and something else I was much less familiar with moved through me and settled in a hot little pool in my center. I had the strangest sensation that

I was melting. Then his hands were on the horse, moving gently and firmly over those muscles, while he continued to talk, to croon almost. I had no idea how long I sat there in the shadow of the boulder watching man and horse.

And imagining what it would feel like to have those hands on me.

"Are you all right?" His focus was still on the horse, and since he asked the question in the same tone he'd been using to quiet the animal, it took me a moment to realize that he was speaking to me.

"Yes." My voice was so breathless I didn't recognize it. "I'm fine." To prove it, I dug my fingers into a crevice in the boulder and pulled myself to my feet. I'd totally forgotten about my ankle, and when I put my full weight on it, I sat right back down with a little squeal.

He turned toward me then. "You're hurt. Did one of his hooves…" His voice trailed off and his eyes narrowed. "Cameron? I didn't recognize you at first."

Of course he hadn't. I could understand that. I hadn't recognized him, either. He'd been intent on calming the horse, and I'd been equally intent on him. It was only now as he quickly tethered the horse and strode toward me that I realized this was Sloan Campbell, my sister Cameron's fiancé.

"You could have been killed."

The anger in his voice was clear—even though

it was tightly leashed. And the simple truth of his statement had a chill moving up my spine. He was no less intimidating than when he'd been thundering toward me on the top of the horse. There he'd looked mythical. Now he looked tough, arrogant and furious. He'd evidently spent all of his patience on Saturn.

Why had it taken me so long to realize who he was? I'd certainly spent enough time studying his photos. Perhaps it was because the magnetism I'd sensed in the pictures was even more potent in real life.

"How badly are you hurt?" His tone was sharp with accusation.

"I'm not hurt. The horse didn't touch me. I just twisted my ankle. I—"

He dropped to his knees and focused his attention on my ankle.

"It's swollen," he said. His fingers were as gentle as they'd been on the horse as they moved the wet jeans up my legs. While he probed my ankle, I found myself staring at his hands—the long fingers, the wide palms—and I tried to ignore the warmth that was unfurling in little ribbons up my leg. Other men had touched me, some casually, others intimately, but I'd never felt this kind of intensity before.

Adrenaline. I'd nearly been run down by the horse. That's why I was reacting this way.

"I don't think it's broken." I heard relief in his tone. "Are you hurt anywhere else?" He glanced up at me then.

"No. You handled the horse beautifully. I'm—" Every other word I intended to say slipped out of my mind as I met his penetrating gaze. His eyes… they were dark gray, the color of the kind of fog that could swallow you up and make you lose all sense of direction. I suddenly felt as though I were losing mine.

Then as if he'd satisfied himself that I was all right, he grabbed my shoulders and gave me a quick shake. "Where the hell have you been for the past five weeks?"

Sloan took a deep breath and clamped down hard on the all-too-familiar emotions swirling through him. Anger, annoyance, relief. Those were the standard feelings that Cameron had been able to pull out of him ever since they'd been kids and his job had frequently been to get her out of scrapes.

But not this time. Five weeks ago when she'd first run off, he'd understood her need to get away and think. The truth was, he'd needed some time himself. But as the weeks had rolled by, understanding had turned into annoyance and finally into anger.

"Five weeks is a long time. Couldn't you have at

least called your father to let him know you were safe?"

"I couldn't. I—"

"Couldn't? Or maybe you expected me to come running after you and drag you back here so that you could save face?"

"Save face?"

He barely kept himself from shaking her again. In spite of the fact that James McKenzie had claimed he was confident that Cameron would return when she'd had time to think everything through, the old man had been worried. Hell, he'd begun to worry himself—and now she'd returned, looking so damned innocent. It had been years since Cameron had tried to use that innocent look on him.

That realization was what had him narrowing his eyes and studying her more carefully. There was something about her...something he couldn't quite put his finger on. Her eyes were that same brilliant shade of green, but they seemed different. Darker. And there was something in them right now. Something that he'd never seen before. Arousal?

The sudden response in his gut was also new. He tightened his grip on her arms. "What the hell kind of game are you playing?"

Chapter 4

He thought I was playing a game? I struggled to get my mind around what he'd just said. But as long as I was looking into Sloan Campbell's eyes, my brain felt numb. My body, on the other hand, was far from numb. My senses were operating at full power. Sloan was only touching my shoulders, yet I could feel the pressure of each one of his fingers—hot like a brand on my skin. He was so close that I could catch the scent of rain and horse, so close that I could feel his breath on my lips. So close that if I leaned forward just a bit, I could taste him.

Don't move, I told myself. Don't move. But I was shocked at how hard it was not to.

"Well?" He prodded me with another little shake, and it helped.

"I'm sorry." My voice and my mouth were finally working. Now it was up to my brain. And he was right. I was playing a game, so I'd better make my first move. "I don't remember being Cameron. I am. I must be, but I just don't remember."

"Come again." He dropped his hands then, but I could feel those eyes boring into me while I told him my story—the mugging, the fact that my purse had never been recovered so there'd been no way for the police to identify me. When I told him about waking up in the hospital and not having any idea who I was, I had the distinct impression that he could see right into me, that he knew what I was thinking. A little tendril of fear worked its way up my spine. Sloan Campbell might have a gentle side, but I sensed that this was a man who could be hard when he wanted to be.

"You're saying that you don't remember anything before you were mugged?"

His tone was skeptical, but I'd expected that. I could handle it. After all, how many people encountered a person who'd lost their memory in real life? Mostly, it occurred as a plot device in movies, romance novels, or soap operas. "My doctor assures me it's temporary."

"If you don't remember who you are, how did you get here?"

That explanation I had down pat. I told him how I'd hired Rossi Investigations to find out who I was. "It took them a while because no one ever filed a missing persons report."

"We assumed you'd come back after you'd sorted things out." His tone was neutral. I couldn't tell if he was buying the memory loss or not. I wasn't an actress. I just wrote story lines for professionals who could bring them to life.

Then he was quiet for so long that nerves knotted in my stomach. To fill the void, I said, "I drove one of the SUV's up here to see if getting a bird's-eye view of the ranch would stir up some memories."

"Did it?"

"No."

"Do I look familiar to you?"

I shook my head. "I don't remember you, but I recognize you from the newspaper clippings the P.I.'s gave me. You're Sloan Campbell, Cameron's—my fiancé."

Tilting his head to one side, he continued to study me. "I'm not sure what kind of game you're playing."

The man's eyes were mesmerizing, and for a moment, just one mad moment, I was tempted to confess. Then I thought of Cameron and what I'd come here to do. "That's the second time you've said that. Why are you so sure I'm playing a game?"

He touched me then, just the brush of a finger along my jawline. "Because you're all about games. And you're a sore loser."

"Loser?" I had no idea what he meant. I was finding it very hard to think while he was touching me.

Without warning, Sloan slid his hand to the back of my neck and touched his mouth to mine. I didn't move. I couldn't. The kiss was so soft. He didn't press, didn't demand. He simply tasted very gently. Still a riot of sensations moved through me.

Don't respond, I told myself. But I could feel my lips soften and part. I could feel my whole body melt.

All the time he watched me with those gray, knowing eyes. I had to clench my fingers into my palms to keep from grabbing him. I wanted to use my hands on him, to drag them through his hair, to test the muscles under that shirt. All the while his taste poured into me until I was nearly drunk with it. With him.

When he drew back, I took a minute and prayed that my voice would be steady. Then I said, "What was that for?"

He regarded me for a moment through narrowed eyes. "A welcome back."

But I knew it had been a test. What I wasn't sure of was whether or not I'd passed.

"C'mon." His tone turned brisk as he took my

arm and helped me to my feet. "Let's see if you can walk on that ankle."

I concentrated on doing that. This time I was careful when I put weight on it, but it held. "It'll probably be weak for a few days."

Without comment, he led me over to where Saturn was still munching grass. Then he cupped his hands. "I'll give you a leg up."

I didn't pretend to misunderstand. He intended for me to ride the horse. "I drove up here in an SUV."

"It's your right ankle you twisted. It would probably be better if you didn't drive until it's stronger. I'll send someone up to fetch your car."

Still I hesitated. I had a feeling that as far as Sloan was concerned, this was another test. I just wasn't quite sure what to do to pass it.

"Once he lets off a little steam, Saturn can be a perfect gentleman. If I'd put him in his stall right after taking him out of the trailer, he might have kicked a hole in one of the stable walls. But he'll be fine now."

Turning toward the horse, I raised a hand and ran it down his neck. "Hate to be confined, do you? I can sympathize with that."

To my surprise and delight, Saturn neighed softly and turned his head to nuzzle my shoulder. I laughed as I looked at Sloan. "He's quite a flirt."

Sloan didn't return my smile. Instead, he just

regarded me with an odd expression in his eyes. "You don't usually flirt back."

I had a feeling that I'd failed some sort of test, so I figured I might as well go for broke. Placing my good foot in his cupped hands, I grabbed a handful of Saturn's mane and swung myself up onto his back.

When I looked down at Sloan, he was still studying me. "He likes you, Red."

"Red? Is that what you call me?"

A mocking glint came into Sloan's eyes. "You tell me when you get your memory back."

I met his eyes steadily. I was going to have to learn to hold my own with this man. "You still think I'm playing some kind of game, don't you?"

Without answering, he swung himself up behind me, then reached around me to gather both ends of the rope into his hands. "The jury's out on that one. I'll let you know when I decide. In the meantime, you'll have to tell your story to your father." He raised a hand and pointed to the road that wound its way from the main highway to the ranch. "I believe that's his car right now. If we hurry, we'll reach the ranch about the same time he does."

Sloan urged Saturn down the slope. Then he added, "James McKenzie is not an easy man to fool."

Sloan Campbell wasn't an easy man to fool, either. He loosened the tension on the rope to give

Saturn more freedom to make his way down the slope. He was a man who prided himself on his ability to size up people as well as horseflesh. But "Red"—he'd decided to call her that until he figured out who she was—Red had had him going there for a few moments.

He had to admit that she was a dead ringer for Cameron, but his gut instinct told him that whoever she was, she wasn't Cameron McKenzie. He let his gaze drift to the distinctive red hair, and wondered if hers had come out of a bottle. She had the same slender build, the same surprisingly long legs, considering the fact that she was barely five foot four. In body type and coloring, she could have been Cameron's twin.

Except Cameron didn't have a twin.

Still, whatever annoyance he felt for being taken in by "Red," however temporarily, was more than matched by the admiration he felt for her guts and her creativity. He'd come damned close to buying her memory loss story. He might have if it weren't for her eyes.

He'd seen something when he'd first grabbed her that he'd never seen in Cameron's eyes. Desire. It wasn't something a man could miss, and it had triggered a response in him. The kiss had been a test, and he wasn't pleased by the fact that he'd wanted for a moment to take it beyond a test. What he'd felt when his mouth had pressed against hers had been raw and stunning. And for one brief moment, with her taste pouring into him, he'd wanted to go further. The only reason he hadn't was because he hadn't been sure he could stop himself from taking her right there on the bluff.

No woman had ever pushed him that far that quickly before. Certainly not Cameron. The kiss had been the clincher. The slender woman sitting in front of him was not Cameron McKenzie. But that left the questions—who the hell was she? And where was Cameron?

When Saturn finally reached level ground, Sloan urged him into a trot. His annoyance with himself deepened at the fact that he'd never once questioned that Cameron had run away in a snit five weeks ago. James hadn't questioned it, either. No one had. She hadn't taken her car, but she often used a limo service, claiming that being driven allowed her to get work done.

The night before she'd left, he and Cameron had had words, and she'd threatened to back out of the wedding, and he'd told her to go ahead. Not that he thought she would. Though six years separated them, they'd grown up together, and he knew her very well. She was high-strung, used to getting her own way, and he'd figured she'd stayed away five weeks to figure out a way to come back, go through with the wedding and still save face.

She wasn't going to back out of the wedding. She'd given her word to her father. And while she might be spoiled, Cameron McKenzie never went back on her word. He'd convinced himself that she'd stayed away out of pride.

He'd told "Red" nothing less than the truth. Cameron liked to play games, and she didn't like to lose. Had she found a double and set up this little charade by herself? For what purpose? But if she hadn't set it up, he didn't like the alternative explanations.

His gaze shifted again to the woman sitting in front of him, and his glance fell on the delicate curve of her neck right where it joined her shoulder. Arousal bloomed inside of him again, as raw and primitive as it had been when he'd kissed her.

The attraction he felt for her was going to be a problem. And he'd have to handle it.

Because the alternative was that Red was up to her neck in Cameron's disappearance. A missing heiress and a ringer who was trying to take her place just a month before the wedding? He didn't like that scenario one bit.

And Red might not be in this alone. There were groups of developers who would do a lot to get their hands on that strip of land along the Pacific. Sloan frowned. He liked that scenario even less.

He just had to figure out which way to play it.

To play her. He wouldn't let James or anyone else know his suspicions. No need to worry the old man before he had some evidence or at least a clearer idea of what had happened to Cameron. Besides, he might learn something from letting Red play out her little charade. Give her enough rope and she just might hang herself.

One thing was certain. Until he knew exactly what her game was, he was going to keep her on a very short leash.

Sloan said nothing more on the ride back to the ranch, but I was intensely aware of him behind me on the horse. When we arrived, we rode past the stables and up a path that led to the back of the house. He dismounted, but before I could follow suit, hard hands gripped my waist and the next second I was on the ground. "Be careful when you put weight on that ankle."

He didn't step back right away. He just looked at me as if there was some answer in my eyes that he was determined to extract. If I'd known what it was, I would have given it to him.

By the time he dropped his hands, my knees had gone weak so I was very careful as I followed his advice and tested my ankle gingerly. "It's fine."

"I'm going to leave you in the kitchen with Elena. She'll have an Ace bandage, and you'd better ice it tonight."

I looked at him then, but his expression was unreadable. I wished that I could figure him out. Then maybe I could control my reaction to him. One minute, I was sure he was mocking me or testing me. The next he was kind and thinking of something like an Ace bandage.

Or kissing me. I was trying very hard not to think of that kiss.

An ancient-looking man, who had the slight build of a jockey, and the wrinkled face of Rumplestiltskin had followed us up the path and now took the rope from Sloan.

"Make sure you walk him in one of the rings and cool him down, Gus."

The old man snorted. "You're telling me how to handle a horse? I was working them before you were born."

Sloan laughed as he turned to me. "Ms. Cameron's back, but she doesn't recognize you because she's lost her memory."

Gus shifted his gaze to me and nodded. "Welcome back, Ms. Cameron." His eyes were nearly as penetrating as Sloan's, but I saw a twinkle in them. "Lace Ribbons will be happy to see you. I've seen that she's been exercised regularly while you've been gone." Then with another nod, he turned and led Saturn away.

"He likes me," I said.

The look Sloan gave me was enigmatic. "He's known you since you were able to get down to the stables on your own." Taking my arm, Sloan urged me onto the patio where I'd had tea earlier with Cole and Beatrice and then into the house.

"Now that Gus is spreading the word of your return, I want to be the first to let James know. I'll help him get settled in his rooms, and then I'll send for you. It might be too much of a shock if you just walk in."

"Fine." I watched him head toward the main foyer. That would give me a reprieve—and a little time out of Sloan Campbell's disturbing presence.

As I made my way to the kitchen, I heard Elena welcoming James—my father. I was going to have to start thinking of him that way, I reminded myself.

In the meantime, I really needed to figure Sloan out. The fact that I was attracted to him—and there was no use denying that anymore—meant that I wasn't thinking clearly about him. But I knew enough from creating characters that most people were defined by their motivations—the whys. What were Sloan's? My instinct told me that he was not buying my story entirely. But *why* wasn't he?

Did he have some reason to know for certain that I was not Cameron suffering from amnesia? I stopped short in the middle of the kitchen as I realized one reason he might have for seeing right through my little masquerade. Was Sloan Campbell responsible for my sister's disappearance?

Chapter 5

James McKenzie's rooms were at the back of the house, Elena informed me as she led the way along a corridor. After helping put an Ace bandage on my ankle, she'd taken me to Cameron's room and waited while I changed my clothes and freshened up a bit.

It was my first opportunity to dress in my sister's clothes. Pressed for time, I'd settled on a pair of navy cotton trousers with a white silk blouse and pulled on the closest pair of boots. Luckily, everything had fit. I had stories all ready in case they hadn't. "I lost weight after the accident." Or, "I gained some weight after the accident."

On impulse, I'd grabbed some of Cameron's scent out of a crystal bottle and dabbed it on. It was more exotic than the kind I usually favored, but I'd thought it might help with the cat. And much to my relief and surprise, it had. When I'd stepped out of the closet room, Hannibal hadn't hissed or attacked. He'd simply sent me a bland look from his little "throne."

"See. He's beginning to remember you," Elena had said.

Privately, I figured that Hannibal's more friendly attitude had more to do with his newfound access to cat treats than with memory.

"This is it," Elena announced as she halted in front of the door at the end of the corridor. At her knock, I heard a voice boom, "C'mon in."

When Elena stepped aside, I drew in a deep breath, then, opening the door, I walked in.

And froze. The room was impressive to say the least. It was large, nearly thirty feet long and a good twenty feet wide. Light poured in through three windows that stretched from floor to ceiling and nearly filled the far wall. Each one had a balcony with a lacy wrought iron balustrade, and each was topped with stained glass.

Sloan stood leaning against one of the window frames, his face in the shadows. But I could feel that he was looking at me. James was seated in a thronelike chair to his right. There was a large ornately carved desk in front of him. Through a door to my left, I glimpsed the foot of a bed. The wall to my right was filled with bookshelves. Leather sofas and chairs were clustered on honey-colored wood floors. There was even a game table with a chess set at the ready.

The whole effect was homey and inviting.

"Come closer, gal. I can't see you while you're standing in the shadows."

The deep voice carried the same authority that I'd noticed earlier in Sloan's, and I moved forward, suddenly and overwhelmingly curious to see the man who'd raised my sister. Pepper had shown me a photo, but as I drew closer, I saw that it hadn't done him justice.

James McKenzie was as impressive as the room. He was a large bear of a man, and in spite of the fact that arthritis had largely confined him to his wheelchair, his complexion was still ruddy, and he was strikingly handsome. Though his hair was streaked with white, I could tell that it had been red at one time. But it was his eyes that held my attention. In the short time that I'd been standing there, I knew that I had been quickly and thoroughly summed up. That ability to cut through everything and see right to the core was another thing that he shared with Sloan, I thought.

Did that mean he was going to be just as suspicious of me as Sloan was?

"Surprised that I'm still alive, are ya?"

"No. I mean…I don't…"

"Remember anything," he finished for me. "Sloan filled me in on your mugging. It's the only reason that I'm not giving you a dressing-down for putting us through all this worry."

I glanced at Sloan, but with the light shining through the windows behind him, I still couldn't see his expression.

When I looked back, James was still studying me with an almost hungry look in his eyes. And I thought I saw a trace of sadness, too. Or regret? Wasn't he happy that I was back?

James rose from his chair and extended his arms. "Come give me a hug, gal. I've missed them. And you."

I moved around the desk and walked into James's outstretched arms. "Welcome home. It's good to have you here."

The words and the fierceness of his hug warmed me. My parents had never been much for showing affection in a physical way, and I found myself envying my sister. On impulse, I wrapped my arms around James and held tight for a moment. "I'm really glad to be here." And I was.

When he finally drew back, James studied me for a minute. "You don't remember anything?"

I shook my head. "I'm sorry. I don't even remember how I ended up in San Francisco."

He released me and eased back down in his chair. "You seen anything yet that triggers a memory?"

"No. I went through my room and my clothes, and I rode up into the hills to get a view of the whole ranch, but it was like I'd never seen any of it before."

"Good. Keep at it," James said. "The sooner we get you back to normal the better. I've discussed it with Sloan, and I'm going to contact the rest of the family and summon them here for a dinner party tonight to welcome you home. Your cousin Austin's in Saratoga Springs, but he's got the jet. You up to it?"

"Sure." My stomach lurched a bit, but what else could I say?

Sloan circled the desk so that he stood with me in front of it. "James's theory is that seeing one or more of them may help you remember. I'm more of the opinion that meeting them all en masse might cause you to run away again." The two men exchanged a look that held both understanding and humor.

He loves the old man, I thought. It was then that I realized that Sloan had come here to pave the way for me, not out of kindness to me, but because he truly loved James. My admiration for him moved up a notch.

"Don't let Sloan sour you against your kinfolk,"

James said with a grin. "We'll let them do that all on their own."

Sloan laughed then, and the rich sound filled the air. I found myself smiling at him, and he smiled back. There was no mockery in his eyes this time. But I could see something else, something more intimate and it had something hot spreading through me. The heat kicked up several degrees when he lifted a hand and with one finger traced a little half circle under my eye. "You're tired, Red. You'd better rest so that you're up to handling them and dealing with their questions."

I couldn't move. I was sure my legs had turned to water. He'd barely touched me, but I felt it clear down to my toes.

He dropped his hand abruptly and turned to James. "I have to get back to work." Without another word, he strode to the door and opened it.

I stared after him, finally accepting what I had tried to deny before. I was attracted to Sloan Campbell. Big-time. I'd been attracted from the moment I'd first seen his picture, and it had only increased when we'd met face-to-face on the bluff and he'd kissed me. I could no longer blame it on adrenaline. It was lust.

My stomach knotted. I'd come here to learn all I could about my sister, to find a clue to her whereabouts—not to fall in lust with her fiancé. And I couldn't yet dismiss the possibility that he might have had something to do with her disappearance. These were the kind of plot complications that would be great for *Secrets*. But they should not be happening to nothing-ever-happens-to-me Brooke Ashby.

At the door, Sloan turned back and looked at me. I realized something else. He knew exactly what effect he was having on me.

What in the world had I gotten myself into?

"Take a nap," he said in that authoritative way he had.

"You'll be here for dinner," James said to him.

"I wouldn't miss it."

When Sloan closed the door, I turned to face James and there was a moment of awkward silence between us.

"He's a good man," James finally said.

"Yes." So far, I could agree with that assessment.

"He'll make you a good husband."

I didn't have an answer ready for that. But I sensed that Cameron and he had had this conversation before. "Do you have any idea why I ran away?"

James watched for a moment. "Everyone figured it was bridal jitters."

I studied him right back. He was a man who was used to getting what he wanted. "And I'm the type of coward who would have run away?"

"No." I saw a flash of something in his eyes.

Pride? "But you're headstrong and you have a temper. You and Sloan had a little argument the day before you disappeared."

"About what?"

James shrugged. "You'll have to ask him."

"So I ran away to punish him?" I could understand that my sister, the woman that I was coming to know, might have done that.

"You ran away to think," James corrected. "From the time you were a little girl, you liked to get away from everything and think."

Something moved through me. I'd always done the same thing. Wasn't that one of the reasons I'd borrowed the SUV and driven up into the hills? "So you weren't surprised when I just disappeared?"

"No. I knew you'd eventually get it all figured out and then you'd come home. And I was right." He smiled at me. "Marriage is a big step. But it's always better when there's love and at least a bit of chemistry involved, right?"

I nodded, not sure where he was going.

"You and Sloan have the chemistry. The love will follow. Now go on and get out of here, gal." He waved his hands at me. "I'm an old man and I need a nap before the festivities begin."

My thoughts and emotions were still spinning as I left James's suite and hurried back to Cameron's room. I'd better keep reminding myself of that—Cameron's room, Cameron's family, Cameron's fiancé.

But when I reached the room, I found Hannibal still reclining on the pillows at the head of the bed. The look he gave me was not friendly. I wasn't in the mood for a turf war, so I went to the cabinet and got us both a treat. It wasn't enough to lure him off the pillows, but he didn't give me any grief when I stretched out well away from him on the foot of the bed and bit into chocolate.

For a while, I closed my eyes and let my thoughts spin in my head. This was a technique I often used when I was working on story lines. Complications were great when I was developing ideas for a plot, but they were trickier to handle in real life.

What I'd learned so far about my sister and her disappearance confirmed what had been in Pepper's report. Cameron was a bit headstrong and spoiled, so no one had been very alarmed when she'd disappeared. James thought her sudden flight might have been triggered by a lover's quarrel. I made a mental note to find out what she and Sloan had quarreled about.

Though he hadn't said it outright, James had hinted that Cameron and Sloan were not in love, but had a chemistry between them. I could relate to that. My reaction to Sloan Campbell was pure chemistry.

But he was my sister's fiancé, her future husband. *Big* complication! If Mallory Carstairs were faced with the problem, I knew exactly what the "bad girl" diva would do. She'd jump his bones.

Hannibal made a growl-like noise from the head of the bed. When I opened my eyes to check on him, he growled again. Could he read my mind?

I made a second trip to the cabinet and got more treats.

"Don't worry," I told him as I tossed one at him. "I'm not Mallory Carstairs." No matter that I'd like to have her guts. My sister had disappeared, and I'd come here, impersonating her, to find out what had happened to her. If my plan was going to have any chance of success, my best strategy would be to steer clear of Sloan Campbell.

Plopping myself once more at the foot of the bed, I let chocolate melt on my tongue. The problem was he might know more than anyone else about what had happened to Cameron. So I was caught between a rock and a hard place. I was going to have to handle Sloan Campbell very carefully—and at the same time keep my hands off of him.

This time, the sound Hannibal made sounded suspiciously like a snort.

Chapter 6

When I approached the door of the main parlor that evening, I felt a little like Cinderella arriving late at the ball. She too must have feared that she'd be exposed for the imposter she was when she'd first entered that ballroom.

I'd slept for two hours. I might have been out even longer except that Hannibal had decided to nudge me awake—and off the bed. I couldn't help thinking that he knew I didn't belong in Cameron's bed. I'd bribed him with another treat and that had settled him as I'd raced around dressing for dinner.

I'd chosen the first dress I'd looked at—a simple black sheath that fit as if it had been made for me. I'd recognized the designer label, and realized that my twin had probably spent more on that one outfit than I would spend on clothes for the next year. The strappy sandals I'd settled on would have taken care of my budget for the year after that. But when I stood in front of the mirror and saw myself, I'd definitely envied Cameron. And I had felt different somehow. More like Cameron?

The memory of that feeling gave me the courage to step into the parlor. The room was large, just short of cavernous. In the wall across from me four sets of French doors stood open to showcase a breathtaking view of the gardens. The scent of flowers mingled with burning candles, and there was music, soft strings beneath the clink of glasses and the buzz of conversation.

Paintings were scattered over ivory-colored walls—scenes of the ranch, I decided. The style was simple and compelling, and the artist had captured the beauty of the land. I wondered who had painted them. Suddenly, I became aware that one by one conversations had halted, and everyone had turned to stare at me.

A little bubble of panic moved through me as I scanned the faces. People were clustered in groups down the length of the room, and there were more than I'd anticipated. Definitely more than family.

"Cameron, there you are. Come in. Come in." James's voice boomed down the length of the room. He was seated in a wheelchair tonight but even framed by the huge fireplace that filled one wall of the room, he managed to look larger than life. "Sloan, fix your fiancée a drink."

Sloan appeared at my side, causing me to wonder if he'd stationed himself near the entrance for just that reason. He wore an open-collar shirt and lightweight blazer with jeans and boots.

"What would you like to drink, Red?" he asked as he led me to the drink cart.

"Wine. White," I replied.

"White wine?" Sloan asked.

Nerves knotted in my stomach as I glanced at him. "Yes. Do I usually drink something different?"

"No. You even have a favorite vineyard." He lifted a bottle, and I recognized the label. It was a wine I'd bought for special occasions. Once again, I felt something move through me at the thought that Cameron and I appreciated the same kind of wines.

"Does it stir any memories?" Sloan asked.

"No." He was testing me again, I realized. And since it was impossible to read his expression, I had no idea whether I'd passed or failed. Maybe it didn't matter. This whole masquerade was turning out to be much trickier than I'd anticipated. When Sloan handed the glass to me, I had to stop myself from drinking it all at once.

"Who are all these people?"

"A mix of business associates and family. James has told them about your temporary memory loss. They're a tough crowd, but they won't bite you. At least not in front of James." He spoke in a low tone only I could hear.

"I'll have something to look forward to then," I murmured.

When he chuckled, I felt some of my tension ease. And in spite of my earlier resolve that I should steer clear of Sloan, I was grateful for his presence at my side as he urged me toward the first group of people.

I recognized the man from the photos Pepper had included in her report even as Sloan said, "This is your cousin, Austin, and his fiancée, Marcie Linton."

They made a striking couple, I thought. The tall blond Austin was the perfect foil for the petite and perky brunette. In stature and appearance, Austin took after his mother with his fair complexion, finely chiseled features and pale blue eyes. He looked like a cross between a Viking and a surfer.

According to Pepper, he had the reputation of a playboy and he gambled. In response to Sloan's introduction, he raised his glass in a toast. "Long time, no see, cousin. Congratulations. Uncle James has killed the fatted calf for you."

Marcie Linton sent him a quick frown. Austin

didn't look overly happy to see me. Recalling Pepper's report, I thought I knew why. In my absence, he'd stepped into my shoes, and he probably wasn't too keen on stepping back out of them.

In response to Marcie's frown, he merely shrugged and took another sip of his drink. Marcie Linton was small, and she was even prettier than she'd been in her photos. Her slender body was encased in an ivory-colored linen dress, the perfect contrast to the jet-black hair that fell straight from a center part to below her shoulders and set off her delicate bone structure and porcelain-fair skin. Pepper had said that Cameron had hired her on as her personal assistant, and that when she and Austin had met, it had been love at first sight.

Giving up on Austin, Marcie sent me an apologetic smile and took my free hand in hers. "Don't pay Austin any heed. In your absence, your father has asked him to fill in for you, and he's done quite well. One of our new clients is here tonight—the Radcliffs." She gestured toward the far end of the room where James was seated in his wheelchair. "Austin signed them last week. I've assured him that you'll continue to need his help, at least until you're up to speed. Perhaps you could even put in a good word with your father."

"Sis, this isn't the time to talk business." I turned to face the man who'd joined us. His resemblance to Marcie was striking. He was taller, but under six feet. His features were more chiseled, the line of his chin stronger. His photos hadn't done him justice, either. In person, Hal Linton reminded me of George Clooney, one cool charmer. I must have been staring because I didn't realize that he'd taken my hand from Marcie's until he raised it to his lips. "Welcome home, Cameron."

Sloan's grip on my elbow tightened fractionally. "This is Marcie's brother, Hal."

"I've missed you," Hal said as he finally released my hand.

The use of the singular pronoun had me wondering. I could sense undercurrents. Sloan was annoyed and Hal was aware of it. Did the two men have some history? Had Hal used the singular— "*I've* missed you"—just to tick Sloan off, or did his use of it mean that he'd had some sort of relationship with Cameron?

Or was my imagination merely running wild again?

"I think we'd better talk to James," Sloan said and drew me away.

As we started down the length of the room, I said to Sloan in a low voice, "I thought my father said he was inviting the family. Who are all these people?"

When he replied, Sloan's voice was barely audible. "The older couple at the drink cart are the Lakewoods. They've done business with James ever since he took over the place from his father. The woman next to them is their daughter Rachel who is concerned about who will run the place after James. The Bolands haven't arrived yet. They have similar concerns and James will hold dinner for them."

I wanted to ask why James had invited these business associates, but Sloan continued, "The younger couple standing near your father are Jane and Sandy Radcliff."

I studied them. They must have been in their midthirties. "They breed horses in Texas, and thanks to you, they're interested in having us train three of their new colts. In your absence, Austin has done the paperwork, but you're responsible for bringing them on board." So Marcie hadn't told me the whole truth.

"Then I'm good at what I do?"

He glanced down at me. "You have a knack with people, and you have a lot of plans for expanding McKenzie Enterprises. The older man standing behind James's wheelchair is Doc Carter. He's widowed now, and he has a house within walking distance on the estate. He's been the family doctor ever since I can remember."

Doc Carter hadn't been in Pepper's report so I studied him now. He was medium height with a portly build and he wore wire-framed glasses. His mustache and the hair he had left were white.

And when he threw back his head and laughed at something James said, he reminded me a bit of Santa Claus.

"James trusts him implicitly," Sloan was saying.

Who wouldn't trust Santa Claus, I thought.

"He and your mother traveled the year she was carrying you, and they took Doc Carter and his wife along. Lucky thing because you arrived a month early, and he had to make all the arrangements in a hospital in Switzerland."

As Sloan's words sank in, I very nearly stumbled. "I was born in Switzerland?"

"Yes. You were about a month old when they brought you back."

My head was spinning. Was it possible that Cameron had been passed off as James's biological daughter? Didn't anyone here know that Cameron was adopted? Then I did stumble.

"Are you all right?" Sloan asked.

"Yes," I lied. My mind had jumped ahead to another explanation. What if Cameron hadn't been adopted? What if she and I were both James McKenzie's daughters—only I had been given up for adoption?

And that was ridiculous. My imagination really did run wild at times. Pepper had discovered adoption papers for both of us. Still…it would make a great story line for *Secrets*.

But this new information did leave open the

possibility that no one besides James knew that Cameron was adopted.

"The woman to James's left is—"

"Is my aunt Beatrice," I finished for him. The Snow Queen. "I met her when I arrived this morning."

Tonight, she wore a powdery-blue dress, outdated in its design. The filmy material flowed around her and I was once more reminded of a Tennessee Williams heroine—fragile, lovely, but clinging to a bygone day. But when she took my hand, I discovered her grip was surprisingly hard, and I recalled my earlier impression that she had strength that didn't appear on the surface.

"Welcome back, Cameron." Beatrice's voice was as ethereal as her appearance, and once more I couldn't read anything in her expression.

"Isn't it about time you paid your old father some attention, gal?" When I turned, James took my free hand and tugged it. With a smile, I leaned down and kissed his cheek.

"James has told us what happened to you," Jane Radcliff said. "It must have been horrible to wake up in a strange place and not know who you are."

I met her eyes and smiled. Of all the strangers I'd met since I'd walked into the room, I sensed that she was sincere.

"Odd to think that you don't remember us," her

husband, Sandy, said. "You're the reason that we decided to join forces with McKenzie Enterprises."

"She'll be up to speed in no time," James assured them.

"It's a miracle that she's back with us," Doc Carter commented. "Memory loss, even the kind that's caused by sudden trauma, can last for a long time. You look none the worse for wear," Doc Carter said. "But James wants me to see you tomorrow and check you out for myself."

I opened my mouth to protest, but Doc Carter continued. "It'll set James's mind at ease."

"Fine," I reluctantly agreed.

"The Bolands are late as usual," James said. "Sloan, while we're waiting, why don't you take Cameron for a stroll in the gardens? Maybe something there will trigger a memory."

I glanced at Sloan. "I'm sure he'd rather stay here."

"Nonsense," James declared. "He's wanted to get you alone since he brought you here. Beatrice and I can hold down the fort until dinner is served. Go." He shooed us with his hands. "You've been away from each other for over a month. You need some time alone together."

Chapter 7

Sloan took my hand and led me through the nearest set of French doors. Once we'd crossed the terrace and started down the short flight of stairs to the garden, I asked, "Does my father always order people around like that?"

"Yeah."

I shot him a sideways glance. "You don't impress me as a man who's easily ordered around."

"I learned a long time ago to pick and choose my battles with James." When we reached the bottom of the steps, he guided me along a flagstone path which wound its way through a garden that had been laid out with meticulous care. Flowers of every color and size bordered the path, and their scents floated on the early-evening air.

"There are times when I go to the mat with him."

"Who wins?"

After a moment, he said, "Usually, I do. James is a smart man. He knows that when we disagree, there's a good reason, and he listens to what I have to say."

"Did he and Cameron butt heads often?"

He glanced at me then, and I could have sworn that there was a mocking glint in his eye.

"What?"

"It's odd hearing you refer to yourself in the third person."

He was sharp. I'd have to remember that. "I feel strange when I try to think of myself as Cameron McKenzie. It's going to take some getting used to."

Sloan steered me toward a wrought iron bench at the edge of the path. "We'll take a longer stroll another night when your ankle's had time to heal."

I started to protest, but he merely said, "Sit."

"You're as bad as my father is."

"Thanks. I'll take that as a compliment." He smiled as he sat down beside me, and I found myself wanting to smile back. Though I wouldn't call him charming, I was discovering that Sloan Campbell could be very disarming.

"Thank you for your help back there. It was... kind of you to fill me in on everyone."

"No problem."

I was very aware of the fact that Sloan had placed his arm along the back of the bench and that we were sitting close enough so that I could feel the heat of his body. As much to distract myself from that as out of curiosity, I asked, "Why was Dad so anxious to get us out of there?"

"The way I see it he's trying to accomplish three things at once. First, he's aware that tonight is a strain for you—meeting all these people that you don't remember."

His tone was neutral and he didn't look at me, but I sensed that he wasn't quite buying that yet.

"He's also showing the family and a select group of business associates that everything is back to normal on the McKenzie Ranch. Cameron has returned, and the engagement is right back on track."

"*The* engagement? You mean ours?" I could hear a thread of panic in my voice.

Sloan shifted that intent gaze of his to mine and studied me for a moment. "Yes, our engagement. James's health has deteriorated in the past year. His heart attack last winter gave everyone a scare, and his arthritis is causing him to use his wheelchair more frequently."

"But the engagement is not back on track. Not really. I don't remember you."

"Enter Doc Carter. He's here tonight to assure everyone that he's going to work with you on recovering your memory. I imagine James will be emphasizing that while we're out here. By morning, the Lakewoods and the Bolands will be spreading the word to others."

I thought about it for a minute. "You said Dad was trying to accomplish three things at once. He doesn't want the evening to be too stressful for me, and he wants to reassure business associates. What's the third reason?"

"I suspect he's doing a bit of matchmaking."

I frowned at him. "Hasn't he already done that? We're engaged."

"But you don't remember me. James is providing us, not too subtly, with an opportunity to get reacquainted, Red. He's a master at manipulating people."

I was once more aware of how close we were on the bench. I could smell him above the scent of the flowers—soap and sun and something more elemental and very male.

I had to clear my throat. "And you're willing to go along with that even though you don't trust me?"

He raised his hand and touched the ends of my hair. "I told you the jury's still out on the trust issue. Has anyone ever told you that you have honest eyes?"

"No." I barely got the word out. Every cell in my body was aware of his fingers as he tucked the strand of hair he held behind my ear. He was so close now that I could see his eyes were darker. They didn't remind me so much of fog as of the kind of dark-colored smoke that shoots up from a fire, and I found myself wondering what it would be like if he really touched me. I imagined the brush of those fingertips and the press of that hard palm against my shoulder, my arms, my...

I managed to clamp down on the images moving through my mind, but I couldn't prevent the arousal that started deep and spread as quickly as the ripples a stone would cause when it was tossed into a pond.

I drew in a deep breath and let it out, wishing I could just as easily get rid of the heat that was flooding through me. I reminded myself of my mission. James might have had his agenda for sending Sloan and me into the garden, but he'd also given me an opportunity that I couldn't afford to ignore. "Why did I run away?"

Sloan studied me for a minute.

"Or why do you think I ran away?"

"The usual reason. You needed time to think."

"About what? Was I having second thoughts about the wedding?"

"Perhaps."

I couldn't read anything in his expression. He was still playing with the ends of my hair.

"Were you worried that I'd change my mind?"

"No. The whole wedding thing was your idea. You proposed to me."

That was news. "Dad said we argued the night before I went away. What about?"

Once again, he hesitated for just a beat. "If I told you, you'd only have my version. I think you should wait until you get your memory back."

Once again, I caught something in his eyes—just a hint of mockery. "You don't think I really lost my memory, do you?"

"The thought has crossed my mind that you're faking it." He hadn't dropped his hand from my hair, and he seemed to be even closer. I had to struggle to keep my voice steady. "Why do you think that Cameron—that I would come back here faking memory loss?"

"It all goes back to why you ran away in the first place. As I said, my best guess was that you were having second thoughts about the wedding. You needed some time alone to think, so you took off. The memory loss story gives you a chance to come back without having to admit that you ran away. You always hated to admit you were wrong, or worse still, make a fool of yourself."

The fact that he could believe my sister capable

of such duplicity intrigued me. Might I have tried the same kind of masquerade in her situation? Then it occurred to me. Wasn't the impersonation I was engaged in just as daring? Perhaps Cameron and I weren't as different as I'd originally thought.

"Would I really do something like that?"

"Oh, yes. You like to play games, and you always like to win."

As he continued to play with the ends of my hair, I realized that the bigger question was why would any woman be having second thoughts about marrying a man like Sloan Campbell? Or was I just blinded by the fact that I was so attracted to him?

"You know me very well then?"

"I've known you pretty much all your life. I was born and raised here. My mother died when I was a baby. My father had the same job that I do now—he was James's right-hand man running the stables and training horses. They were best friends until my father ran away with James's first wife, Sarah."

Pepper had written briefly about this story in her report, but it was different hearing it from Sloan. I found my heart going out to the little boy. I reached out and took his hand. "How old were you?"

"Two. But you needn't feel sorry for me. James never harbored any resentment against me. He took me in and raised me as if I were his own. He remarried two years later, and you were born two years after that."

I did the math quickly in my head. Sloan was about six years older than I was. That made him thirty-one.

"What happened? Did your father ever contact you?"

Sloan shook his head. "James hired a P.I. to trace them, but he wasn't successful. My guess is that he wasn't much interested in tracking them down. I hired a P.I. five years ago to look into it, but the trail was cold by then."

I continued to study him. There was so much I wanted to know. I wanted to ask him why he'd left the ranch five years ago, but I wouldn't have any way of knowing about that. The memory loss thing was tricky—especially with someone who thought I might be faking it.

"Penny for your thoughts," Sloan said.

When I didn't immediately answer, he ran the pad of his thumb over my bottom lip. "I'll share mine for free. I've been thinking of how soft your mouth is."

His gesture and the words had my mouth trembling, and I felt a flare of something deep inside me that was raw and stunning. He was going to kiss me.

I should have said something. There were so

many reasons for not kissing Sloan again, I could have made a list. But right now I couldn't seem to summon up even one reason, not while his breath whispered over my skin, not while those dark eyes were looking into mine.

The alarm bells ringing in my mind warned me to move away, but my body was no longer taking orders from my brain. Or perhaps my brain was no longer capable of giving any intelligent kind of orders. Bottom line, I wanted Sloan to kiss me again.

But he wasn't moving. He was waiting for me.

Just one more time, I told myself. Didn't I have a right to know if it would be as intense an experience as the first time? My curiosity would be satisfied and then I would move on. That was the problem with forbidden fruit—one taste was just never enough. I leaned forward.

The first brush of his lips against mine was light, exactly as it had been before. And not exactly what I wanted. Still, I felt the soft caress right down to my toes. All of my senses were immediately heightened. I felt the firmness of his hand, those strong fingers moving up and down on the nape of my neck while his thumb rested at the hollow of my throat. A mix of anticipation and longing moved through me. I could hear my pulse hammer, feel it beat in a frantic rhythm against his thumb.

His mouth brushed over my lips, slowly, as if

he wanted to commit them to memory. The movement was so lazy, so mesmerizing. I'd never been so aware of a man before, never experienced this kind of intensity in a man's touch. I wanted to simply melt into him.

As if he could read my mind, he put his arm around me and drew me close until every hard angle and plane of his body was pressed against mine. Then I *was* melting. I felt parts of myself slipping away. I tried to say his name, but all I heard was a sound, part sigh, part moan. He took my bottom lip between his teeth and bit it sharply, then used his tongue to soothe the ache. Explosions of pleasure shot through me, as he drew my lip into his mouth and sucked hard on it. Desire twisted tight in my center.

My fingers dug into his shoulders, and as if he were waiting for that particular response, Sloan finally pressed his mouth fully to mine. I knew the sensation of instant fire—I couldn't tell whether it came from me or him or both of us. But in that moment it was clear this man could make me want more, demand more than I ever had before.

My tongue met his, seeking, searching. His mouth was…paradise. The rich, dark taste of him was so enticing, so absorbing, I could have explored it forever. Jolts of hot pleasure coursed through me, and I needed more. I felt his muscles so hard beneath my palms, and the sound he made deep in his throat told me he was feeling at least something of what I was. I pressed myself against him, felt his arms tighten around me.

Passion had never tasted this ripe, this dark before.

Desire had never been so sharp, so overpowering that it hurt.

I was so caught up in it, so lost in the moment and in the man that I wasn't even aware when we were interrupted.

I just knew that Sloan drew away, and I nearly shivered at the abrupt loss of heat. He didn't release his grip on me. If he had, I think I would have slid right off the bench. Instead, he settled my head against his shoulder, holding me as he spoke to whomever was standing behind me on the path.

"We'll be right in."

I heard the words, but it took my mind a few beats before I could make meaning out of them. We were being called into dinner. I had to get it together. More than that, I had to face Sloan. Gathering all my strength, I lifted my head from his shoulder and drew away.

I met his eyes, and he met mine. Neither of us spoke for a moment, and I wished that I could tell what he was thinking. What does one say to a man who's just turned you into a puddle of lust? I was a writer. I should have had lots of words and phrases at my command, but what popped out of my mouth surprised me. "I can't imagine why I would have run away from you."

The look he gave me was enigmatic. "You don't know me yet."

A short distance away, a shadow silently moved among other shadows in the garden, watching as the man and woman rose and moved back toward the patio.

She was back. Just thinking the words had the anger building. It wasn't fair. It wasn't right. Everything had been going so smoothly. She'd been eliminated. Finally, justice had been accomplished.

But she was back. Fury erupted. Then ruthlessly the emotion was shoved down. Anger never solved anything. That had been a lesson learned at an early age.

Anger never changed what was. It wouldn't change the fact that she'd returned. Speculating on how was a waste of time. The plan had been perfect.... But the only thing that mattered now was a new plan.

All that mattered was that she had to be eliminated...again. This time there would be no mistake. And then everything would be perfect.

Chapter 8

I barely bit back a sigh as two servants carried in yet another set of platters from the kitchen. The dining room was every bit as cavernous as the main parlor had been. Three crystal chandeliers hung from the ceiling, and we sat at a huge oak table that looked as if it had been used by Don Roberto Montega, the man who'd built the hacienda. There were small vases of flowers at intervals along the table.

Instead of four or five courses, Elena and another woman had carried in platters heaped with rare roast beef, chicken in a delicate lemon caper sauce and bowls of salads, grilled vegetables and warm bread. I'd eaten in self-defense because I couldn't very well talk when my mouth was full, could I? Beatrice, who sat to my left, for the most part ignored me and played the gracious hostess, making sure that the meal unfolded smoothly.

Austin was drinking quite a bit. He would have had even more if Beatrice hadn't signaled one of the servants to stop refilling his wineglass. She'd done it in such a subtle and smooth way that I assumed it was something she'd had to do frequently in the past. My cousin still wasn't trying to hide the fact that he resented my presence, and he hadn't said a word to me all during dinner. Marcie tried to compensate for his behavior by inviting me to go riding with them the following afternoon. She and Austin were sure that I would want to reacquaint myself with my horse, Lace Ribbons.

Because I felt a bit sorry for her, I might have agreed anyway, but Doc Carter said, "I think that would be a good idea, Cameron. You love riding. The more you familiarize yourself with Cameron's routines, the quicker your memory might come back."

"Fine." I aimed a smile in Marcie's direction. But I couldn't help feeling that I was being maneuvered by her just as surely as James had maneuvered me earlier. I promised myself that I would get away from all of them in the morning and do a little exploring on my own.

Then because I had Dr. Carter's attention for the moment, I said, "I'm trying to get a feel for what my last day here was like—I mean before I left. Do you remember seeing me that day? Did we talk?"

Dr. Carter studied me for a moment. "That's good. I think it might be a very good idea to try and put together that day."

"Did you see me? Were you here that day?"

He shook his head. "If I remember correctly, it was a Monday, and I spent the day in my backyard working on my putting. Since I retired, I had a putting green put in, and if the weather permits, I'm out there every day. Golf has become my obsession since my wife passed away. But I did walk over here in the late afternoon to check on James, of course. And we had our usual chess game." He smiled at me. "And if I played the way I usually do, I probably lost. Does that help at all?"

"No." I could give Pepper the information, but if Doc Carter lived alone, it meant that he didn't have an alibi. Not that I could believe that Santa Claus could have had something to do with my sister's disappearance.

He patted my hand. "Patience. Your memory will return when you least expect it."

Sloan. The moment that Doc Carter turned

away, I cut a piece of roast beef off and pushed it around my plate. The evening would have been stressful enough anyway, but my reaction to Sloan's kiss had made it even more so because I couldn't put it out of my mind.

I shouldn't have allowed it to happen. I could have prevented it. But all the should-haves and could-haves didn't change the fact that I hadn't followed my plan to steer clear of Sloan Campbell. Now I was in trouble, and I had a hunch that it was going to get worse.

The good news was that he'd been seated at the far end of the table from me with James, the Bolands and the Radcliffs. I understood the strategy of the arrangement. Sloan was able to finally spend some time with clients, and I was isolated from them, surrounded by family and projecting an image of normalcy.

But that hadn't made it any easier to digest my food. I sliced off another piece of roast beef and rearranged its position on my plate.

The dining room walls were an ochre color and paintings by the same artist whose work had been displayed in the main parlor also hung here. There was something about the stark simplicity of them that appealed to me.

"Do you know who the artist is?" I asked Doc Carter.

He gave me a searching look. Of all the people

in my immediate vicinity, I liked him the best. There was an easy geniality about him, a kindness in his eyes, and not once during the meal had he pressed me about my memory loss, other than to suggest I go riding with Marcie and Austin.

"Do they look at all familiar?" he asked.

I shook my head. "I assume they're scenes of the ranch."

"They are. Your mother painted all of them," he said.

My mother. He had to be talking about James's second wife, Elizabeth. My gaze returned to the painting that hung on the wall above Beatrice's head. It was a landscape that must have been painted from one of the bluffs where I'd stood earlier in the day to get my bird's-eye view of the hacienda.

I recalled my earlier suspicion that James had passed Cameron off as his biological daughter. Had my sister been kept just as ignorant of her real background as I had been? The possibility stirred something inside of me. Did we have more in common than I'd thought?

I turned to Doc Carter intending to find out more information about my mother, but he was talking to Jane Radcliff.

"Elizabeth was a very talented painter."

I turned to Beatrice. It was the first she'd spoken to me since we'd sat down at the table. Not that she'd spoken much more to Marcie and Austin. She was a quiet, self-contained woman.

"Did she ever sell any of them?" I asked.

"If she hadn't passed away, Elizabeth would have had a show in a gallery in San Francisco," Beatrice said. "It was all arranged, but after her death, James canceled the show. He couldn't bear to part with any of her work."

"What did she…my mother die of?" I asked.

There was a beat of silence, then Beatrice replied, her voice even softer, "After she and James returned from Europe with you, she began to have frequent bouts of illness and depression. Each one left her weaker than the last. The doctors couldn't seem to find anything wrong with her."

"It sounds like postpartum depression." We'd just run a story line on *Secrets* in which one of the lead ingenues had nearly killed her child. "It could have been treated."

"It was. Doc Carter tried everything," Beatrice assured me. "Your father spared no expense, and for a while, the drugs seemed to work. She even began painting again."

Whatever else she might have told me was forestalled by James, who tapped on his wineglass until he had everyone's attention. "We'll have coffee and after-dinner drinks in the parlor. I have an important announcement to make."

I rose and followed the procession that was

making its way back to the parlor. But as soon as I stepped into the hallway, Hal Linton, who hadn't spoken a word to me during dinner, took my hand and turned me around to face him.

"I have to speak with you in private," he said.

I'd thought that Beatrice was behind us, but over Hal's shoulder, I saw that she was headed down the hallway in the opposite direction. A quick glance over my own shoulder told me that Austin and Marcie had already entered the parlor leaving Hal and me alone.

As Hal drew me into an alcove, I had the distinct impression that I had been manipulated again. And I was getting tired of it.

Hal raised my hand and pressed his lips to it. "I've missed you. When can I see you?"

I tried to draw my hand away, but he tightened his grip. "You're seeing me right now."

He studied me intently. "I need to see you alone. You can't have forgotten what happened between us the night before you left."

The implication of what he was saying had my head spinning. What had been my sister's relationship with this man?

"I've been so worried about you. When you disappeared so abruptly, I thought he'd gone into a jealous rage and done something to you."

A sliver of ice worked its way up my spine.

This time I managed to get my hand free. "What are you talking about?"

"Sloan. He's incredibly possessive of you, and he discovered us in the garden that night. We were kissing, and he demanded that you go with him. Everyone knew that you quarreled. And he has a terrible temper." He had his hands on my shoulders and was drawing me closer. "Do you know what it's been like for me, worrying about you for weeks? And then tonight, seeing you come into the parlor, sitting across from you at the table and not being able to touch you. Please—"

"No." I put my hands on Hal's chest and gave him a shove that sent him back against the wall of the alcove.

Behind me came Sloan's even tone. "James is waiting for you, Cameron."

My legs felt like rubber as I turned and walked out of the alcove.

"Can you explain what just happened back there?" I asked Sloan softly as we walked side-by-side down the hall.

"Looked pretty obvious to me," Sloan said. "Old Hal made a pass and you nixed it."

What was obvious to me was that Sloan didn't seem to care a bit. There hadn't been a trace of anger or annoyance in either his actions or his voice. Didn't he care if someone made a pass at his fiancée? How could he have kissed me as he had in the garden and then been so cool when he'd found me extricating myself from another man's arms?

And I couldn't forget what Hal had said. His version of the argument that Sloan and Cameron had had on the night before she disappeared differed from James's version. And Sloan had refused to talk about it at all.

When I entered the parlor, James was sitting near the fireplace, pouring champagne into flutes and the bartender was passing them out to the guests. He'd said he had an announcement to make. Had he and Sloan closed some kind of important deal over dinner?

Sloan took two glasses from the tray he was offered and handed one to me.

"I mentioned an announcement," James said, "and I don't think it should come as a surprise to anyone. My daughter's disappearance was a harsh reminder of how little time there is and how quickly it passes. As a result, I've decided that her wedding to Sloan, which would have taken place in September, will take place here on Friday evening."

Friday was the day after tomorrow. I nearly dropped the glass of champagne I was holding. I would have if Sloan hadn't reached out and steadied my hand. "He can't mean that," I said.

"He means it all right," Sloan confirmed in a

low tone. "He's a sneaky, manipulating bastard, and it's just like him to pull something like this."

"I don't have the patience to wait any longer," James continued. "And I don't think Sloan does, either. Since I've known all of you from the start of McKenzie Enterprises, you're invited. The ceremony will be at five in the chapel, and we'll have a small celebration afterward." Then he raised his glass in the air. "To the happy couple."

"If you don't do something," I said in an undertone to Sloan, "I will."

"Be my guest."

I had the distinct and annoying suspicion that Sloan was enjoying this. That only increased my determination.

I strode forward until I was standing directly in front of James, who was flanked on one side by Beatrice and on the other by Doc Carter. I kept my eyes on James. "I can't do this. I don't remember Sloan. I need more time."

James took my hand and squeezed it. "Humor an old man, Cammy. Doc Carter is convinced that all you need is a bit more time. Everyone here will help you to get your memory back by Friday. Sloan will see that you get a grand tour of the estate first thing tomorrow. You'll see. You'll be back to normal in no time."

I turned back to Sloan, still hoping that he'd join me in protest, but he seemed perfectly okay with the announcement. In fact from the look he gave me, I was sure he'd been anticipating it. I couldn't believe that he was letting James do this.

James squeezed my hand again and drew me down closer. "Please. You and Sloan were meant for each other. Trust me and do this for me. The future of the McKenzie Ranch depends on you."

Sloan was right. James was a manipulative and wily old man, and he'd staged this on purpose in front of clients. In fact, I was sure that's why the Bolands and the Lakewoods and the Radcliffs had been invited. I could have put up a bigger fight if there'd just been the family. And I would have, I told myself.

"Cammy?" James said.

"Yes. Okay." I told myself I had two days to talk James or Sloan or both of them out of this. In a soap opera story line that was plenty of time. And I was good at inventing new plot twists. If all else failed I could just say no when I was at the altar. I couldn't be forced to marry anyone. Could I?

"To the bride and groom and to the future of McKenzie Enterprises."

"Hear, hear!"

As we all raised our glasses and sipped champagne, I scanned the faces of Cameron's family. From what I could see, only James seemed happy with the surprise announcement.

"To the bride," Sloan said, slipping his hand into mine.

As everyone drank again, I turned to find both amusement and challenge in his eyes. I promised myself that I was going to figure him out.

If it killed me?

Chapter 9

The moment he got back to the carriage house, Sloan slipped out of his jacket and pulled off his boots. Then he grabbed a beer out of the refrigerator and walked out onto the deck that offered a view of both the stables and the hacienda. Settling himself in a cushioned chair, he propped his feet up on the railing and took a long swallow of beer.

Taking a half hour to sit down, put his feet up and review the events of the day was a habit he'd developed in his late teens—minus the beer, of course. Sometimes he turned some music on, but tonight he wanted the quiet. He had a lot to sort through. And it all centered on Red.

He'd called her that at first because he wasn't going to call her Cameron. And he had figured it might annoy her or at the very least throw her a bit off balance. But the name seemed to somehow fit her.

And he'd kissed her again. The kiss hadn't been a test this time. He wasn't a man who felt there was anything to be gained by lying to himself. He'd kissed her again because he wanted to. And because he hadn't been able to resist finding out if she'd have the same effect she'd had on him the first time.

And now he knew. He wanted Red with an intensity that he'd never felt for any other woman.

It hadn't done much good telling himself that she might be a lying little, fortune-hunting imposter. The fact remained that he wanted more from her than a kiss. And there was no use lecturing himself that he shouldn't take more. No use at all pretending that he wouldn't take more. Because he would.

Hell, he nearly had.

His gaze dropped to the garden below. He thought he could make out the bench where they'd kissed just a few hours ago. If someone hadn't interrupted them, he would have made love to her right there. He was skilled enough, and she'd been aroused enough. It would have been wild, and crazy...and very dangerous. Everything else aside, he certainly hadn't gone to James's little dinner party with condoms at the ready. He hadn't been tempted to run a risk like that since he was a teenager in the grip of almost-terminal hormones.

Red could certainly push his buttons all right. And why not? Any man would be tempted by the passion that was simmering just below the surface. One taste of her and all he could think of was having her beneath him, of losing himself inside of her.

That didn't bother him as much as the fact that when he'd seen her in Hal Linton's arms, jealousy had sliced through him right to the bone. He hadn't felt that when he'd seen Hal kissing Cameron in the garden five weeks ago.

Sloan took another swallow of beer. The other thing worrying him was that he was coming to like Red. He thought of the way she'd marched across the parlor to face down James. Even in his wheelchair, the old man had been able to glower at her at eye level. David taking on Goliath, he thought with a smile. And there was that shove she'd given Linton. It had sent him tumbling back against the wall.

Not only was he beginning to like her, he was also more and more intrigued by her. She was dead set against marrying him. Before the party broke up, she'd taken him aside to try and talk him into persuading James to postpone the wedding. His gaze shifted to the hacienda and the light he could see in James's suite. She was there with him now, trying to plead her case.

Why? If she was the fortune hunter he suspected her of being, why wasn't she happy about the wedding? She had to figure that in two days, James would sign his new will and she'd be a millionairess.

And just what kind of a game was James playing? Had he moved up the wedding because of what he'd said in the parlor or was he involved in something deeper?

He couldn't help wondering what part Cameron might be playing in all of this. Leaning his head back against the chair, Sloan closed his eyes and tried to sort through what he knew and what he didn't.

Fact number one, Cameron had disappeared five weeks ago, and everyone including himself had believed that she'd taken off because she was having second thoughts about the wedding.

He knew for a fact that she had been. Right after he'd caught her kissing Hal Linton in the gardens, they'd argued. He'd told her that it wasn't the kind of behavior he would accept after they were married, and she'd blown up, told him she'd act whatever way she pleased. She'd threatened to call the wedding off, and he'd told her to go ahead.

But there hadn't been any real passion in the

fight. Cameron had been angry, but not at him. She'd been angry with her father, angry that he wouldn't leave the land to her because she was a woman. As a result, their quarrel was more like an argument he would have had with Cameron years ago—the kind that a brother and sister might have.

And that was the crux of the problem. As the wedding date drew closer, both of them were realizing what they would be giving up if they went through with the marriage.

They'd have the land, and he had no doubt that they'd eventually have children. But there would never be anything between them but the kind of love that exists between siblings or good friends.

Opening his eyes, Sloan looked at the hacienda and the stables beyond drenched in moonlight. What he and Cameron shared was a passion for this land, but not for each other. That was why Cameron had asked him to marry her. He wasn't sure whether it had been entirely her idea or if James had proposed it. But he knew why Cameron had gone along with it. She'd been scared when James had had the heart attack. She'd been angry then, too, because James was not going to leave the estate entirely in the hands of a woman. In the will he'd made out after the heart attack, he'd left it to a board of directors he'd personally selected. The board would make all the business decisions.

Cameron would be provided for, but she'd have little control in the daily running of the ranch.

Sloan rubbed a hand over his face. The old man knew how to push the right buttons to get what he wanted. If Cameron was a game player, she'd come by it honestly. Wasn't that why he'd left five years ago—because he'd wanted to decide on his own what he wanted in life? He hadn't wanted to spend his life working for James McKenzie. He'd wanted to run his own ranch.

The proposition that Cameron had made to him at the Derby would allow him to do just that. They would be equal partners. He would be in charge of the horses and the ranch. She would be in charge of client relations and recruiting new business. They'd both have what they wanted. All they had to do was get married.

He swept his gaze over the estate again, lingering first on the stables and then on the hacienda itself. This was what he'd always wanted, from the time he was a kid. He'd accepted Cameron's proposal because of this.

And she wasn't the only one who'd been having second thoughts five weeks ago. He had been, too, and he'd secretly relieved that she'd taken off and given them both a little time to think.

That brought up fact number two. Red's appearance raised the question of whether or not Cameron's disappearance was voluntary or if someone else had played a hand in it. To answer that question he was going to have to spend a lot of time with the woman he was calling Red.

And that was going to lead to…having her. He was not going to fool himself about that. In spite of those honest eyes, she was a liar and possibly a fortune hunter. Worst-case scenario, she might be a pawn in some deeper game that James McKenzie was playing. But even that possibility was not going to make a difference.

Realizing that his thoughts had come full circle, Sloan reached down for his bottle and discovered that it was empty. He took his feet off the railing, but he didn't go into the house for a very long time.

When I finally let myself into Cameron's room, my stomach was in knots, I had a headache pounding behind my eyes and I very badly wanted to kick something. The room was dark except for the moonlight pouring through the balconied windows on either side of the bed. I moved to one of the tables and flipped on a lamp.

Hannibal was sprawled across my pillows glaring at me through narrowed eyes.

I fisted my hands on my hips. "You don't want to mess with me. I've had a very bad night."

The cat's expression didn't change. He didn't even blink.

"Okay," I said. "You don't like me and I don't

like you. But I need some sleep, and I intend to sleep in this bed—not curled up on the foot like a…like a…" Cat, I finished silently.

It occurred to me then that I was taking out my frustration on the poor cat when what I really wanted to do was strangle Sloan.

With a frustrated sigh, I strode to the cabinet and got out treats for both of us. Luckily my sister kept a generous supply. After tossing a couple of cat tidbits at Hannibal, I walked to the window and took a bite of chocolate. I'd learned after the guests had left that Sloan didn't live in the main house. He lived in the carriage house beyond the stables. I could just make it out in the moonlight.

I'd never met a man like him before. Not that I hadn't had to deal with some difficult men in my life. Male soap stars whose careers can depend on what twist a story line takes are not the easiest people to deal with. But at least their ego-driven motivations were always clear. Sloan Campbell's were a mystery to me.

He hadn't seemed at all upset when he'd found me with Hal Linton. What had his relationship with my sister been? Was their marriage strictly a business arrangement? Or was it one of those "modern" deals where, after the knot was tied, the two individuals went their separate ways? Sloan hadn't impressed me as that kind of a man. And I hoped that my sister wasn't that kind of a woman.

I turned back to Hannibal. "Maybe I'm just too much of a romantic. And I'm not rich." My parents had been able to raise me in a very comfortable house, provide me with a good education, private schools and nice vacations. But they weren't rich, rich. Cameron was. I'd already discovered that there was a world of difference between the contents of my closet and hers. And Sloan Campbell would be rich when he married her and James deeded the estate and the business to the two of them.

I knew enough, had lived long enough to know that the rich *were* different. I turned back to look out over the gardens and the stables. Maybe inheriting a place like this was motive enough to settle for an arranged marriage. Perhaps in Cameron's shoes, I would have agreed to it. I now knew from experience how persuasive James could be.

But Sloan? Somehow, I couldn't picture him allowing anyone to push him into something like that. Not even for money. Unless he was doing it for James. James McKenzie had raised him, and I could see that Sloan loved him like a father.

I frowned and pressed my hands against the headache that was beginning to drum at my temples. Even if Sloan had originally agreed to the marriage out of love for James, that didn't explain why he was agreeing to the rushed wedding now.

Hadn't the man told me that he picked his battles

with James, and that when he went to the mat, he usually was able to make the old man see reason? So why had he allowed us to be manipulated into this wedding on Friday?

He couldn't possibly want it any more than I did. Good heavens, the man thought I'd run away and now was faking amnesia just to save face. Agreeing to the marriage in the first place was one thing. But why in the world would he want to go through with it when Cameron was so clearly ambivalent? His acquiescence contradicted everything that my instincts told me about the man.

Unless my instincts were being clouded by the fact that he attracted me so strongly and on such an elemental level. Or unless there were facts that I didn't know.

Turning, I walked to the bed. I needed to sleep on it. I found that sleeping on problems—knots that I couldn't untie in a plot—often solved them. Hopefully, my unconscious mind would sort through everything, and in the morning I would have a fresh perspective.

Hannibal was still sitting on his throne of pillows at the head of the bed.

"Okay," I muttered to him. "I'll share, but I'm not sleeping at the foot of the bed. You're going to have to move over."

After shooting me a bland look, he began to lazily clean one of his paws. Hoping it wasn't a threat to scratch me, I circled around the bed. It was only then that I noticed my duffel bag. I'd brought it up when Elena had first taken me to the room. It was sitting on the bench at the foot of the bed, but I was sure that I'd left it in Cameron's closet. I was equally sure that the zipper had been closed, and it was open now.

I reached in and pulled out my wallet. A quick check assured me that my money was still there. But the bills had been pulled out and stuffed back in carelessly. The few clothes that I'd brought had been rifled through.

Ice formed a hard little ball in my stomach as I sank down onto the bench. Someone had come into my room and searched my duffel bag and wallet, and they didn't care if I found out. Somehow that frightened me more than the fact that someone had searched my things.

Who?

The answer to that was anyone could have done it sometime during the evening with the possible exception of James. After everyone else had left, he'd asked me to accompany him to his suite. I'd gone because I'd thought I might be able to reason with him and get him to change his mind about the wedding on Friday. But he'd looked tired when we reached his room. And fragile. For the first time I'd realized that the evening had been as much of a strain for him as it had been for me.

I frowned down at the wallet that I was still holding so tightly that my fingers had begun to ache. Even Sloan would have had an opportunity to come up here and search through my things before he'd returned to the carriage house.

Deliberately, I willed my hands to relax and set the wallet down on the bench beside me. Why was it that my mind constantly circled back to Sloan Campbell? He'd been the one person to express openly his doubts about my being Cameron.

But that wasn't the only reason I couldn't stop thinking about him. The man had a grip on me, mind and body, that I'd never experienced before. If I wasn't careful, he might turn into an obsession.

I forced myself to think about what had happened as if it were a plot line I was developing. Character—who could have done this? And then motivation—why? Why usually pointed to who.

Anyone could have slipped in here. Austin, for example. He didn't like me and had made no effort to hide it. Plus, my return meant that he had to step down from a job that he might have grown attached to. I knew from Pepper's report that Austin was only a year older than Cameron, so they'd grown up in the same house together. Had they always been in competition with one another? That might explain why he hadn't bothered to hide his animosity toward me from James.

In spite of his mother's intervention, Austin had

been drinking pretty heavily at dinner. That might explain why he'd been so careless about looking through my things. Or he may have wanted me to know that he'd searched them.

Then there were the Lintons—Marcie and Hal. What was their stake in all of this? Marcie had been friendly enough, but if she hadn't lied about who had signed the Radcliffs as clients, she'd certainly stretched the truth. Hal had been a bit too friendly, and it was clear from what Cole and Pepper had found out that he had an agenda. The land developers he represented wanted that strip of McKenzie land along the Pacific. Romancing the heiress apparent could be his way of furthering that agenda.

And I couldn't shake the thought that Austin and Marcie had helped Hal Linton get me alone after dinner. It had been too neat a maneuver to have been an accident.

Marcie was engaged to Austin. Had Hal made a move on my sister with the hope that if he could prevent the marriage, then James might decide to leave the estate to Austin…? I was going to have to find out more about Cameron's relationship with Hal. Did he have his sights set on becoming Mr. Cameron McKenzie or was he playing a deeper game?

Any one of the possible scenarios I'd just cooked up would work beautifully in *Secrets*, but in real life…?

Rising, I started to pace back and forth at the foot of the bed. I needed to find out more about these people. And I could do that. I was a writer, and I knew how to do research. First thing in the morning I'd call Pepper and give her the information I'd gotten from Elena so she could check out alibis, and I'd ask her to check out the Lintons more thoroughly. And I'd talk again to Elena. Servants knew a lot about the families they served, and she might have more objective insights than I was likely to get anywhere else.

Who else could I interview? Doc Carter. He was going to drop by tomorrow after lunch to see me, and I'd use my time with him to gather more information. And then I'd go riding with Marcie and Austin and gather more data from the "horse's mouth" so to speak.

I jumped at the sound of my cell phone, then grinned. It had to be Pepper. Was this ESP or what? She was the only one who had the number for my new cell. I pulled it out of the duffel and pressed the button to take the incoming call.

The voice was soft and tinny sounding.

"You should never have come back. You weren't supposed to come back. Ever. Leave now or you'll share the fate of the other mistresses of the Hacienda Montega."

I wasn't aware of it when my knees gave out. The next thing I knew I was sitting on the floor staring down at the cell phone in my hand. There was a lump blocking my throat, I was shivering, and even my brain cells seemed numb.

In spite of that, questions filtered through. What had been the fate of the mistresses of this house? And had my sister already shared it?

Chapter 10

"Good morning."

I had to swallow disappointment when I saw Marcie Linton at the foot of the stairs. I smiled and said, "You're an early riser."

"Not usually. But I was hoping to get a chance to talk to you...alone."

"Sure," I said. I had to admire her strategy. I'd gotten up at six-thirty and managed a quick shower and an even quicker phone call to Pepper in the hopes of doing the same thing with Elena.

"We usually have breakfast in here." Marcie led me down a short hallway.

There was an energy about the petite brunette that I admired. But I didn't quite trust her. Of course, my perspective on her could have been tainted by the fact that she reminded me of the ingenue on *Secrets* who had put Mallory Carstairs in the coma. But Cameron had hired her, I reminded myself.

"You'll be my new best friend if you can find me coffee," I said.

Marcie laughed. "It's Elena that's your new best friend then. She keeps fresh coffee in the breakfast room all morning. There's also tea because that's what Beatrice prefers."

"You seem familiar with the routine."

She glanced over her shoulder at me. "Austin and I have been spending more time here since you...went away."

We stepped into a bright sunny space with terrace doors that opened out to the gardens and the pool. The room was considerably smaller than the formal parlor and dining room that I'd been in last night, but the dark oak buffet and table, though they were built on a large scale, fit easily into the room. Unable to resist, I ran my hand over the intricate carving on the buffet. "It's beautiful."

"These pieces were shipped over from Spain as part of the Countess Montega's dowry," Marcie explained as she selected a mug from the buffet, filled it and handed it to me.

I took my first sip and waited for that first jolt of caffeine to spread through my system. My night's sleep—what there'd been of it—had been plagued by strange dreams and turf battles with Hannibal. The cat had actually nudged me right onto the floor at one point.

"Much of the original furniture and all of the art was sold off at one time or another over the years," Marcie continued, "but the larger-scale pieces were either too hard to remove or less marketable at the time. Silas McKenzie was lucky in that respect."

She was not only at home here, I thought, but she was also very much up to speed on the history of the house. I sipped more coffee. She was being very nice to me, but I didn't doubt for a minute that she had an agenda. Charming or at least disarming me had to be at the top of her list.

"What would you like for breakfast? I can highly recommend Elena's huevos rancheros."

"That's fine," I said.

"Good. I'll be right back." She disappeared through a swinging door.

Alone for the moment, I admired the roses that filled a large cut crystal vase. Everywhere I went in this house, there seemed to be flowers. Beatrice's doing. Then I stepped out onto the sunlit terrace. I hadn't been out of the house since Sloan had brought me back here the day before—except for that short stroll in the garden last night. And I wasn't going to think about that. Or about the kiss.

Pushing the thought and the temptation away,

I crossed slowly to the edge of the terrace. The early-morning sun was already warm, and the air carried the scent of mown grass, flowers and horses. A far cry from the scents I was used to as a city girl.

From the terrace, I had a view of one of the riding rings, and I spotted Sloan immediately. He was already at work with one of the horses. Saturn.

He turned at almost the same instant that I saw him. I could have sworn that my heart stuttered. He was at least three football fields away, and still, something not unlike a little electric shock moved through me. Then my heart stuttered again when he leaped onto the horse, urged him to take the fence and rode toward me.

I walked down the steps of the terrace and on one of the paths to meet him. It wasn't wise. This was not someone I should be having these feelings for. But I couldn't seem to help myself. As he grew closer, I once again marveled at the beauty of the way man and horse moved together as one.

Sloan was wearing sunglasses, so I couldn't see his eyes until he dismounted and lifted them to rest on the top of his head. It was against all logic, but I was ridiculously happy just to see him again. So I smiled.

He put a finger under my chin tilting it up. Then he just studied me for a minute. Once again, I felt the intensity of his touch right down to my toes.

"You didn't sleep well last night, Red," he said.

"Did the bags under my eyes give me away?"

The corners of his mouth twitched. "You might say that. If you want to postpone the grand tour I'm supposed to give you, we can do it tomorrow."

"No. I want to see the ranch." That was the truth, but not the whole truth. The whole truth was that I felt safer now that he was here than I had since I'd gotten that phone call last night. I knew it was probably a mistake, a big one, but I couldn't seem to help myself. I wanted very much to trust Sloan Campbell.

Saturn whinnied and pushed his nose into my shoulder. Sloan grabbed my arm to steady me. Then Saturn nudged me again, harder.

Laughing, I patted the horse's neck. "What's the matter, you beauty?"

"Looks like he wants his share of attention," Sloan said.

As I continued to stroke the horse, I said on impulse, "I'd love to ride him. May I?"

Sloan's eyes narrowed. "Don't let his looks fool you. He can be difficult to control."

"That would be the challenge, wouldn't it? My…" I caught myself just in time. I'd been about to tell Sloan about Dandelion's Pride, one of the horses that I'd ridden in several shows.

"You were saying?" Sloan asked.

"Nothing." I didn't meet his eyes as I came up

with a lie. "For a moment there, I thought I remembered something."

"If you want to ride Saturn, it'll have to be in a few days. I want to give him a chance to get used to his surroundings. Then you can give him a try."

"Thanks." I was ridiculously pleased that he'd agreed to let me ride the horse.

"Sloan."

We turned to see Beatrice hurrying down the terrace steps. She was back in light-colored trousers and a shirt that flowed around her as she moved. "James wants to see you. He saw you riding this way from his window and sent me down to fetch you."

There was an urgency in her voice that caused me to ask, "Is something wrong?" I recalled how tired he'd looked when I'd left his room the night before.

Beatrice turned to me. "He had a restless night. He always does when he overexerts and goes off of his diet."

Her voice was mild and there was nothing in her tone or her eyes to indicate that she was accusing me. Still, I felt the tug of guilt.

"He'll be fine. He's calling me up there to yell at me over something or other." Sloan tied Saturn to a post on the balustrade of the terrace. At Beatrice's pointed look, he pulled his cell phone out of his pocket. "I'll have one of the stable hands come up and fetch him."

Then in a quick movement that took me by surprise, he cupped the back of my neck with his free hand and lowered his mouth to mine. The contact was brief, hard and possessive, and it was enough to bring back all the sensations of both kisses we'd shared the day before. My insides heated and began to melt. I wasn't even aware I'd grabbed handfuls of his shirt until he drew away.

I had enough wits left to recognize satisfaction on his face before he said, "I'll pick you up at ten for the tour."

As he strode up the steps and disappeared into the house, I found myself both envious and a bit annoyed that he could walk. I wasn't at all certain that I could.

Something drew my eyes to one of the balconies that graced the second- and third-story bedrooms, and I saw that Austin was standing almost directly overhead. Our gazes held for a moment and I thought I saw a look of pure hatred before he turned abruptly and disappeared into his room. I couldn't help wondering if Sloan had known he was there when he kissed me.

"I thought you might like me to show you around the house so that you'll be familiar with it," Beatrice said.

I turned to find that she was regarding me with

the most intent expression I'd yet seen on her face. "I'd like that very much. If you're sure you have the time."

"I'll make the time. I enjoy showing off the hacienda." She glanced down at the slim gold watch on her wrist and when her gaze returned to mine, her eyes were once more unreadable. "I have something to attend to in the greenhouse, but it should only take me twenty minutes or so."

"I'll meet you here."

Without another word, she turned and walked away down the path.

"Breakfast is about to be served," Marcie called from the terrace doors.

As I joined her, I wondered if she, too, had seen Sloan kiss me. Had he done it for our multiple audiences? And I couldn't help but wonder if that was the way he'd kissed my sister. More guilt tugged at me. I was sinking deeper and deeper and I was beginning to wonder how in the world I was going to get out.

"This has got to be difficult for you," Marcie said as we sat down at the table. "Not remembering anything."

Understatement of the year was my first thought. "Yes, it is. Would you mind telling me how I came to hire you?"

If the question surprised her, she covered beautifully. "I met you at a fund-raiser about six months ago. I was working for the woman who was cochair of the event. You mentioned to her that you were looking for an assistant, so I sent you a résumé. We met for lunch—I guess it was my interview, because you hired me over dessert."

"And what is it I hired you to do?" I asked.

She smiled. "I'm supposed to keep you organized. I also handle correspondence, keep track of your calendar and generally serve as your gal Friday."

"Are you good at it?"

She met my gaze steadily. "Yes, I am."

I really wanted to believe her. After all, my sister had hired her. And if I hadn't known about her brother's connection to those land developers, I might have.

She picked up her mug, then set it down. "I know that you have a crowded schedule today, so I'll get right to the point. I want to apologize for Austin's behavior last night." Marcie ran her finger around the rim of her mug. "You have no way of knowing this, but he's not usually like that."

"You mean he's not usually rude?"

"No." The corners of her mouth lifted in a wry smile. "He can be extremely charming when he wants to. But he's different when he drinks. He doesn't usually drink that much," she hurried to assure me. "Well, not anymore. He used to. But he's changed. This is difficult to explain. Your father has never given him the kind of responsibility that Austin wanted and thought he deserved. When Sloan left five years ago, Austin thought that at last James would turn to him, but instead, he started giving more responsibility to you. These last few weeks while you've been away, his uncle has finally given him the chance to prove his worth to McKenzie Enterprises. And he's done well. The surprise of seeing you last night made him think it would all slip away from him again. He's very embarrassed about his behavior."

I was pleased when Elena appeared with our breakfasts because I wasn't sure how to reply to what Marcie had said. It certainly confirmed what I'd been thinking the night before. Austin wasn't happy to have me back at the hacienda, and he could have been the one to rifle through my bag. He could have discovered my cell phone number simply by turning it off and then turning it on again, then made the threatening call later.

And if he was truly as sorry for his behavior as Marcie was professing, why wasn't he here in person to make his apology?

Marcie waited until Elena had returned to the kitchen before she said as if she'd read my mind, "Austin would be here himself, but he has a bit of a hangover."

I avoided making a comment by sampling the eggs and I immediately envied my sister for having a cook like Elena. Back in L.A., breakfast was something I ate on the fly—a granola bar if I'd remembered to grocery shop or a muffin out of a vending machine at work. With coffee—lots of it. I took another sip from my mug, trying to decide how to frame the question. Finally, I asked, "Why is it that my father waited until I disappeared to give Austin the kind of job he wants?"

Marcie set her fork down. "Austin has never been able to compete with you or Sloan. He doesn't have a natural love of horses the way that you and Sloan do. In college, he decided to rebel and he picked up the reputation of being a bit of a playboy. But that's not who he is, not really. And he's really good at the PR end of the business. I'm hoping that you'll give him a chance to continue to prove that. He'll be an asset to McKenzie Enterprises."

"Unless he's drinking too much to keep his mind on business," I said.

She leaned toward me. "He won't. If you'll just give him a chance to prove himself. That's one of the reasons I asked you to come riding with us this afternoon. I hope that Austin's behavior last night won't make you change your mind. It will give you a chance to get to know him a little better. And we can show you the ranch."

The idea of being alone and away from the ranch with two people who had motive and opportunity to search my duffel and make the threatening phone call I'd received should have made me wary.

But Marcie looked so sincere, so desperate, and I had to add in the fact that Cameron must have trusted her. But what finally decided me was that my inner Alice wanted to know more about both of them. "Of course, I'll go with you. How about we meet at the stables at three o'clock?"

"Thank you." She reached out and took my hand. "Thank you so much."

Her relief was palpable, and I suddenly realized that Marcie Linton was either in love with Austin or she was a good enough actress to audition for a part on *Secrets*.

Chapter 11

"This is the ballroom." Beatrice led the way into one more cavernous room. The walls were a rich ochre color, and the deep red velvet drapes were pulled back from the floor-to-ceiling windows. Five crystal chandeliers, even larger than the ones in the dining room, hung from the ceiling. There were two large fireplaces, one at either end of the room, and the honey-colored oak floors were unmarred by carpets.

"Lovely," I murmured. It was a word that I'd repeated often during my tour. As I'd followed Beatrice down long hallways and through a myriad of salons, parlors and bedroom suites, I couldn't help but imagine what it must have been like grow-ing up in a place like this. Hide-and-seek games could have gone on forever. And Cameron would have had two siblings to play with—Austin and Sloan. So far my absolute favorite space had been the library with its floor-to-ceiling shelves filled with books. One wall, nearly all glass, had let the garden in. To me it was paradise. I could have lingered there all day, but Beatrice allowed no loitering. She was on a schedule. She reminded me a lot of my resident advisor in college, the one Pepper and I had "borrowed" a car from. I won-dered not for the first time how she and James could be brother and sister. He was so outgoing, and she was so contained.

"Countess Montega had her wedding celebra-tion here, and since then it's been a tradition that all the hacienda's brides hold their receptions here. Except for you." The tone held just a hint of cen-sure. "Because of the small group of people who will be there, your father wants to use the parlor and the dining room. We'll have dancing on the terrace."

Feeling guilty, I said, "I'm sorry that Dad is rushing this wedding. It's got to be a lot of work for you, but I couldn't talk him out of it."

Her brows shot up. "From the time you were born, you've always been able to wrap your father around your little finger."

"Not about this. I couldn't. I thought that I might be able to reason with him last night after everyone had left, but he looked so frail. I didn't have the heart."

I thought I saw a flicker of surprise in her eyes.

"If he would just wait, we could keep the tradition intact." She sighed. "But I couldn't talk him out of it, either."

I wondered if that's what she'd been doing in his bedroom this morning before she came to fetch Sloan. As we walked along, I asked, "What can I do to help?"

She turned in surprise. "Why, nothing. You've always allowed me to make those kinds of decisions, said you were too busy to run the house. Are you going to want to change that arrangement after your wedding?"

"No. No, of course not."

Without further comment, Beatrice gestured toward the wall to our right. "The portraits of all the hacienda's brides are on the walls. This first one is of the Countess Montega."

What I saw was a small, dark-haired woman with very sad eyes. For some reason, my heart went out to her. "She looks so unhappy."

"She was," Beatrice said. "There are copies of her diaries in the library. It was an arranged marriage, and she was ill on the voyage over here. According to the story that's been handed down, Don

Roberto Montega was anxious to have an heir, and she was able to produce one within the first year, but she never recovered her health. His second wife lasted longer—five years." She pointed to another portrait of a tall, more amply proportioned woman. "She gave him three more sons before she died of a fever."

There were two other Montega brides, all in black, neither of them smiling. According to Beatrice, they'd both died young, too.

A chill moved through me as I studied the portrait of the woman Beatrice had pointed out as the last of the Montega brides. I'd read about them when I'd done my research on the hacienda, but it was different standing there and seeing how young they really were. "The mistresses of this house don't seem to have very good luck."

Beatrice gestured to the next portrait. "This one did."

It was a picture of a laughing green-eyed woman with red hair. The emerald-green dress dipped low in the front and the skirt fell in overlapping ruffles to the floor. She was a bright relief after her more somberly dressed predecessors. "Who is this one?"

"That is my great-great-grandmother. The story goes that Silas McKenzie rescued her out of a brothel and made her his bride."

I grinned, thoroughly intrigued. This was a

piece of information that neither Pepper nor I had come across. "It sounds very romantic."

"To some it might sound that way."

I got the distinct impression that Beatrice wasn't among them. I wondered how I might work it into a story line. "I understand that Silas was a bit of a rogue himself."

For the first time, I saw just the hint of a smile curve Beatrice's lips. "True. I suppose you might say that they were well suited. And she *was* a fine gardener."

Ah, a saving grace, I thought.

"She produced three sons before she died. The hacienda brides usually have a knack for producing heirs."

And for dying young.

"Except for your father's brides," Beatrice said as she led the way to the next picture. "Neither of them gave him a son."

I glanced up to see a painting of a fragile-looking beauty with long blond hair and blue eyes. She wore a long-sleeved dress that matched the color of her eyes, and the cat on her lap was either Hannibal or one of his more recent ancestors.

"That's Sarah McKenzie."

Once again I marveled at how little in the way of feelings Beatrice allowed into her voice. This was the woman who'd deserted Beatrice's brother for Sloan's father. I stepped forward to study the portrait more closely. She was lovely with a kind of ethereal beauty that men might easily covet. "It must have been very hard for Dad when she ran away with Sloan's father."

Once again Beatrice's gaze grew intent. "How did you know that, or are you beginning to remember?"

"Sloan told me the story," I explained. Thank heaven he had. I was going to have to be careful to remember what I'd been told since my arrival and what I knew from Pepper's report.

"It was a scandal at the time. A McKenzie running away with a stable manager."

I heard just a hint of distaste in her voice.

"I imagine it must have been a blow to Dad both in a business and personal sense, losing both a stable manager and a wife."

"The business never faltered. My husband took over as manager of the stables. And James is very resilient. He married again in less than two years."

This time I was almost sure that I heard a note of disapproval in her voice. She led the way to the next portrait. "This is Elizabeth, your mother."

I simply stared at the portrait. I couldn't even put a word to what I was feeling. All I could think of was that the woman staring down at me could have been my sister. My heart had leaped to my throat and it beat there, fast and hard. Many of Elizabeth McKenzie's features were ones I saw in the mirror every day—the nose, the pointed chin, even the shape of the eyes. Hers were a darker shade and more hazel than green. Her hair was different, too, a dark blond, and she wore it in a long braid that fell over her shoulder.

Questions flooded my mind. Could this be my biological mother? How else could Cameron and I look so much like her? But if that were true, how could Cameron and I have been put up for adoption? Pepper had found adoption records for both of us. And someone else knew about those papers—the someone who'd sent me that anonymous letter.

Questions—too many of them were swirling around in my mind. And as usual, I was jumping to too many conclusions. I struggled to rein my imagination in.

"Do you remember her?"

Beatrice's calm voice helped me to get a grip. I couldn't ask any of my questions right now. Not until I knew more. Not until I figured out what had happened to make Cameron run away.

I turned to her. "No. I can see the resemblance, and I know that she must be my mother. But I don't remember her at all. How did she die? You never got to tell me last night."

"Come," Beatrice said. "I'll show you."

She led the way out of the ballroom and down the corridor to a wide oak door. "Your father keeps it locked," she explained as she drew an iron key out of her pocket and inserted it into the lock. "No one is supposed to come up here, but I do every once in a while. I used to love this place as a girl."

The door creaked on its hinges and Beatrice had to put her back into it to get it open. In front of us was a wooden staircase that curved upward hugging the stone wall and hanging next to us was a thick rope. With a sinking stomach, I realized that we were going to climb into the bell tower.

I didn't like heights. Two or three stories—like the balcony in Cameron's room—was fine. But put me on a terrace or a balcony or, heaven forbid, a rooftop that was more than four or five stories above terra firma, and I froze. My parents took me to Europe when I was fourteen, and I couldn't even kiss the Blarney Stone. I'd nearly had a panic attack when we went to the top of the Eiffel Tower.

I told myself that the bell tower was only five stories as we rounded the first curve and continued upward. The stairs were flanked by the stone wall on one side and a railing on the other. Following Beatrice, I stayed near the wall and kept my hand on it for support. My palms were slick with sweat. My breath was coming shorter now, and it didn't have anything to do with the fact that I was climbing stairs.

We reached the tower room much too quickly for my liking. It was small, not more than eight feet square. The bell was overhead, and the walls on each side were only waist high. Beatrice crossed to the wall that overlooked the front of the hacienda. "Isn't the view beautiful?"

"Yes." I was sure it was, but my eyes were shut. I couldn't bring myself to look yet. A cold sweat had formed on my forehead. Taking a deep breath, I placed my hand on the iron railing that ran along the top of the wall on all sides. Opening my eyes, I kept them downcast as I felt my way along. Then I raised my gaze to the bluffs that I'd stood on only yesterday. Of course, there I'd been careful to stay back from the edge. I'd be all right as long as I didn't glance down, I told myself.

Out of the corner of my eye, I could see the riding ring where Sloan was working Saturn. Knowing that he was there steadied me a bit.

"I've missed the bells," Beatrice said. "When I was a girl, they were rung for the Angelus at 6:00 a.m. and 6:00 p.m. every day."

"Is the bell broken?" I asked. I wasn't looking at the bluffs anymore, but at Sloan and the horse.

"No. But the tower has a bad history, I'm afraid. The first Countess Montega threw herself from this very spot."

My vision blurred, and I blinked my eyes to clear it.

"After her son was born, she fell into a habit of

walking in her sleep. The official story goes that she wandered up here one night and fell."

I couldn't keep myself from picturing it in my mind—that tiny woman I'd seen in the portrait, climbing the stairs in her sleep, walking out into the tower and falling...falling....

A wave of dizziness moved through me. I gripped the railing with both hands now, and my vision blurred again. I could imagine how easily someone could fall over it.

"Of course, that was the story that they gave the priest," Beatrice continued. "If she'd committed suicide, she couldn't have been buried in the church. Her husband and son would never have been able to eventually rest beside her."

"You think she committed suicide?" I asked. I made the mistake of shifting my gaze to her, and another wave of dizziness washed over me.

"You saw her portrait—those sad eyes. I've read some of the entries in her diary. I think she was homesick for Spain, and I think she was unhappy in her marriage. One night she wandered up here, and it would be so easy to just lean over the edge and let yourself fall. Don't you think?"

I didn't want to think about it. I shifted my gaze back to Sloan and drew in a deep breath.

"Then everything would be all right," Beatrice continued. "The loneliness and pain would be ended."

Her tone was matter-of-fact, but her words effectively formed the image in my mind again. I took several quick steps back from the wall.

Beatrice reached out and grabbed my hand. The strength of her grip surprised me. "Be careful. The back wall is just behind you."

I turned to see that I was only a foot away from it. My head was spinning fast now. "I…I need to get out of here."

"Heights bother you? I had no idea," Beatrice said as she led me to the stairs.

"Yes." I slapped my hand against the stone wall to steady myself.

"Sit down," Beatrice instructed, "and put your head between your knees."

I did as she said, and after a moment the dizzy feeling subsided. When I raised my head, I found she was sitting next to me.

"I didn't realize you were afraid of heights. If I'd realized it, I wouldn't have brought you up here."

She sounded worried and sincere. It was the most emotion I'd ever heard in her voice. "I thought that if I brought you here, you might remember something."

"What would I remember? You said that the tower has been closed off for almost twenty-five years. So I could never have been up here before."

Beatrice's gaze became intent again as she studied me. "I thought you might recall the story. Your mother followed in the first bride, the Contessa's footsteps. She threw herself off of the tower. That's why your father locked the doors and forbade the ringing of the bells."

My mind filled again with the horrible image of someone falling to the ground below. My voice sounded hoarse to me when I said, "How old was I?"

"Just a baby." She laid her hand over mine, and without thinking, I gripped hers tightly.

For a moment, I concentrated on gathering myself. It wasn't just the vertigo that was affecting me. I was still struggling to absorb the suspicion that had formed in my mind when I'd looked at Elizabeth McKenzie's portrait—that I might be her biological daughter. I had to moisten my lips to ask, "Could you please tell me what you know?"

"It happened a few months after your father and mother brought you back from Europe," Beatrice replied.

"Why?"

"Why did she do it?" Beatrice's tone was musing now. "I don't suppose we'll ever know for sure. Doc Carter might give you more of an insight. Elizabeth never quite recovered from her pregnancy with you. She didn't want to have children. She had her art. She told me once that she hadn't even wanted a husband, but she'd fallen in love with James. And my brother can be very persuasive."

Tell me about it, I thought. Beatrice wasn't looking at me. She was looking straight ahead at the stone walls of the tower as she continued, "She agreed to have a child for James, and he's always blamed himself for her death."

I thought of how the story paralleled in a way my own adoption. My mother hadn't wanted to take a break from her medical training to carry a child. "Why didn't they just adopt?"

The look Beatrice gave me suggested that the answer was obvious. "Your father wanted an heir, someone with McKenzie blood." Then she slipped her hand from mine, glanced down at her watch, and rose. "It's nearly nine-thirty. You'll want to change for your tour with Sloan."

I looked at my jeans. My elegant sister would probably not wear these even to ride around the ranch.

"We'll go down slowly. I'll lead the way, and you stay right behind me. If you get dizzy, we'll sit and rest."

As we descended the stairs, my mind continued to spin. But this time it was with questions. My inner Alice was now on full alert.

What had caused Elizabeth to commit suicide? And could her tragedy somehow be connected to her daughter's disappearance?

Chapter 12

The moment I entered my room, I raced for my cell phone to see if Pepper had called back. But I hadn't taken it with me—I'd barely wanted to touch it since that threatening call had come in last night. I hadn't recharged it, either, so I held my breath as I checked to see if the battery had worn down. It hadn't.

I sank onto the bed, and Hannibal voiced his disapproval. I turned to find him still on his self-claimed throne. He really gave added meaning to the phrase "squatter's rights."

"Don't you have to eat or pee or something?"

His only reply was a bland and superior stare.

And no wonder. Of course, he didn't have to go anywhere to eat when I was providing a seemingly endless supply of cat tidbits. I rose and got him a few more from the cabinet. And I bet he had his own secret methods for exiting and entering Cameron's room when I wasn't there. He hadn't moved from his position during the night—not even when I'd climbed in and stolen one of the pillows for myself.

"Look," I said as he disposed of the cat treats. "I know this is hard for you. But we have a common goal. You want Cameron back and so do I. You might think about cooperating a bit."

He seemed to be listening; at least he wasn't licking his claws or hissing or making any other threatening gesture. Satisfied for the moment, I turned my attention back to the phone and saw I had a message. I held my breath while I retrieved it, but it was Pepper's voice with one word. "Call."

I punched her number into my phone, then held my breath again and prayed that she'd pick up.

She did on the second ring. "Brooke?"

"Yes."

"I've got an update. It looks like Austin and both Lintons were indeed in Las Vegas. At least, their credit cards were. Cole is checking it out further as we speak."

"Marcie Linton told me that Austin had reformed."

"As of five weeks ago, he hadn't. He dropped close to ten thousand as far as Cole can tell. Tomorrow, Cole's going to San Diego to check on the flower show that Beatrice was presenting at. Are you all right?"

"I'm fine." I'd had a little argument with myself about just how much I was going to tell her and I'd decided on as little as possible—and certainly not about the phone call. I didn't want her rushing out here with Cole. Not yet anyway. "But I think I may know who my mother is."

There was a beat of silence on the other end of the line. "Wait."

I could picture her grabbing her notebook, then turning to a fresh page.

"Okay, who?"

"Elizabeth McKenzie."

"James's second wife?" Pepper asked. I heard a little plop. Had she dropped her pencil?

"It shocked me, too. And I could be wrong. But I've seen her portrait and I look like her. The story they're telling here is that Cameron was born in Switzerland. I thought at first the trip might have been made to hide the fact that Cameron was adopted. But since I saw Elizabeth's portrait, I think the trip to Switzerland was for something else."

"To cover up that two little girls were born and only one was brought home?"

"Maybe." My stomach clenched. I was finding it hard to accept the fact that we were talking about me. The little girl that wasn't brought home.

"But why?" Pepper's tone was thoughtful and I could hear the tapping of a pencil. "I found adoption papers for both you and Cameron in the records of a private adoption agency here in the States and no clue as to the mother."

"Which effectively stopped you from checking further," I pointed out.

"Yes, it did."

I heard a trace of annoyance in her voice.

"A Doctor Carter went on the trip with James and Elizabeth."

"Hmmmmm," Pepper said. "I'll bet the good doctor is in this up to his ears."

"That would be my guess. He's a close family friend who appears to be very kind and concerned. I can't imagine him having anything to do with Cameron's disappearance, but I'm thinking he might have sent me the letter. And he doesn't have an alibi for the day of Cameron's disappearance. He claims he was home using this putting green he has in his backyard."

"I'll get my brother Luke to let his fingers do the walking on his computer keyboard. He'll check out your good doctor and if there are any records anywhere, he's the best bet we have of getting to them."

Just talking to Pepper was settling my nerves a bit. There were answers to the questions that were whirling in my mind, and we'd get them.

"I'm liking less and less the fact that you're there alone," Pepper said. "Why don't I join you? You can say that you need the comfort of having a friend from your present close at hand while you're exploring your past. Something like that."

"No." I'd anticipated that Pepper would suggest something like this, so I was prepared. "I need you to find out more information for me. See what else you can find on Hal Linton, too. He made a move on me last night."

"Really?"

"I'd like to know what his relationship with Cameron was before she disappeared. In your report, you said they met through Austin and Marcie. If they were having an affair, someone in Linton's business circle might have been aware of it."

"I'm on it. Anything else?"

On impulse, I said, "Check into Beatrice's husband. He ran the ranch for a while after Sloan's father ran away with Sarah McKenzie. But he's not here anymore, and no one talks about him. I don't even know his first name."

"I'll get it." I could hear Pepper scribbling. "Cole thinks I made a mistake, that I should have talked you out of this masquerade—which is a dangerous plan. His words."

I drew in a deep breath. "Well, the good news is I'm going to be leaving here by Friday evening."

"That is good news," Pepper agreed. Then after a beat, she said, the frown clear in her tone, "That's tomorrow. It's not that I'm not happy about it, but why do you have to get out of there so soon?"

I cleared my throat. "Because James has decided to move up the wedding. Tomorrow night Sloan and Cameron are going to be tying the knot in a small, private ceremony in the hacienda's chapel."

"Wait. Time-out. He wants you to marry Sloan Campbell tomorrow?"

"That's right. But don't worry. That's not going to happen."

"Liar."

"I'm not kidding."

"I know you, Brooke. If you haven't found what happened to your sister by tomorrow, you won't leave."

"That's why I'm calling you. I need anything you can find out ASAP."

"I don't like this."

"Gotta go. Sloan is giving me a tour of the ranch to see if he can stir up any memories. Find out what you can."

"Brooke—"

"I'll check in with you later today so that you'll

know I'm all right. Bye." I disconnected the call and frowned. She'd worry about me now. I couldn't help that. I was worried myself. But at least Pepper didn't know about the threatening phone call. And after a morning with Marcie and Beatrice, I wasn't one step closer to finding out who'd made it.

"Hey, Red?"

It was Sloan's voice. I hurried to the window and saw him standing in the garden below me. Once again, I felt a rush of pleasure just seeing him. Not good, I thought.

"Beatrice told me you were in your room. I'm running a little late, and I have to stop at the stables."

I glanced at my watch. "You said ten. I still have to change my clothes."

"When you're changed, come over to the carriage house. It'll save us some time."

"Sure."

With a little salute, Sloan turned and walked away. I kept my eyes on him as he strode down the same path he'd ridden on earlier with Saturn. He didn't look as though he was hurrying, but those long legs of his really ate up the ground.

And he belonged to my sister. I should write that on the palm of my hand the way I used to write reminders when I was in junior high.

The brush of something against my leg made me jump. Glancing down, I saw that it was Hannibal, and my heart returned to its usual place in my body. The cat flicked me a look and then rubbed against me again.

"Are you trying to suggest a truce, or are you warning me off Cameron's fiancé?"

Hannibal made a soft purring sound in his throat that I wasn't quite able to interpret. "I was just lecturing myself about the same thing. I'm going to have a talk with Sloan while we're taking our tour." And I was also going to find out why he hadn't tried to talk James out of moving the wedding up.

I'd tell him that I didn't want him to kiss me again. Which was a big fat lie. And he'd know it because so far my response to his kisses on a scale of one to ten could be measured at about a thirty.

Hannibal purred again. Did I actually hear a note of skepticism, or was I just projecting?

"I'll explain that I need time to get used to him again." Hopefully, that would work. But my eyes shifted back to Sloan. Who was I kidding? If I got any more used to him, I'd be in his bed. One more day, I reminded myself. Surely, I could keep from jumping his bones for that long.

"It isn't as though I don't have other things to occupy my time." Like finding out what had happened to my sister. And getting to the bottom of why I looked so much like Elizabeth McKenzie. I glanced at my cell phone. Not to mention, avoiding the fate of the previous mistresses of the Hacienda Montega.

"My plate's full," I assured Hannibal. And myself.

After taking one last look at Sloan, I turned and strode into the closet. Out of the corner of my eye, I saw Hannibal leap onto the bed, but he didn't go back to stake his claim on the pillows. Instead, he made a circle, then sat near the side where he could watch me select an outfit to wear.

Quickly, I located a pair of riding breeches and boots, but I couldn't decide on a blouse. Cameron seemed to have a weakness for silk, and I was torn between the peach, ivory or pale blue one. I held each in front of me. Hannibal growled at the blue one.

As I stripped off my jeans and T-shirt and dressed in Cameron's clothes, I couldn't help smiling at the idea that I was taking fashion advice from a cat. I wondered if this was something that he and Cameron did on a daily basis. I wanted to think that it was, that there was a softer side to the picture of my sister that everyone else was painting.

When I was done, I turned in a full circle for Hannibal's benefit. He made no further noise, nor did he make any threatening gestures. I decided to take his lack of reaction for approval, and I felt a little closer to my sister as I left the room.

***

The carriage house had been built of the same colored stone as the hacienda, making me assume that it dated back to the same era. At one time, it had been used to store horse-drawn carriages. The lower floor had been renovated and now offered the modern convenience of automatic sliding doors.

It seemed a little far from the main house to use as a garage. Curious, I peeked through one of the glass windows and discovered there were indeed cars inside. The rugged truck that I'd seen Sloan use the day before along with its trailer, a black SUV with the logo of the ranch on it, and a sporty little red convertible that only seated two. It was built for speed, and it was exactly the kind of car that I hoped to own one day.

Was it Sloan's? Or perhaps it was Cameron's.

At the side of the building, I found a set of iron stairs to the second floor. On my way up I reviewed in my mind what I was going to tell Sloan—that I needed time to get to know him better and it would be better if he didn't kiss me again.

That at least wasn't a lie. It would be a lie if I told him I didn't *want* him to kiss me again. I knocked on the screen door.

After waiting a bit, I knocked again. When there was still no response, I allowed my inner Alice to open the door and walk into a spacious kitchen that was neat as a pin. Two arches in the wall to my right allowed access to other rooms. Through the far one came the sound of running water and a man singing.

I moved to the closest arch and spotted a large flat-screen TV, what looked to be a state-of-the-art entertainment center, and two large speakers. Boy toys. There was a comfortable-looking leather couch, and an oak coffee table with a paperback book lying open facedown to mark the page. There were more books in built-in glass-doored book-cases that flanked the fireplace.

My gaze shifted to the art on the walls, and moving closer, I saw that each piece held four photos that had been clustered in the center, then matted and framed. In one group, I saw a man who resembled Sloan standing next to a horse with a baby in his arms. The same man was captured in other poses, two with James. Sloan's father?

In another, there was a cluster with James and an older boy. He looked to be five or six in one, a teenager in another, and in the others he was a man—Sloan Campbell. It was like having a family album on the walls. Except there were two families and the mother was missing in each set of photos.

Cameron and he had that in common—a mother they'd never known. In spite of that loss, I envied Sloan in a way. My own family was not the type to take photos. There were no albums, no framed pictures on the walls. The ones I had were some that friends like Pepper had snapped and given to me. I glanced around the room and realized that there were no pictures of Cameron—not as a little girl and not as a woman. I found that odd.

Slowly but surely, I was learning about Sloan Campbell. He was a man who worked hard, was good at what he did, and who liked a comfortable, quiet place to come home to at night. I suppose that didn't make him much different from a lot of men. Or women. I liked to come home to a quiet space myself.

My sister, on the other hand, evidently liked to go out, to meet clients for dinner and drinks—if I could make judgments by her wardrobe and what others had told me.

The singing had stopped, but I could still hear water running as I returned to the kitchen. I knew I was pushing it but I quietly opened the two cupboards that framed the sink. Dishes were stacked in neat piles, mugs arranged in rows. One drawer contained towels, the other a minimal selection of flatware. Then I just had to open Sloan's refrigerator. You could tell a lot from a person's refrigerator. I'd once had Mallory Carstairs take an inventory of the contents of her current lover's fridge and decide to break off the affair. He had been planning to kill her and the telltale mushrooms were right there on the bottom shelf.

There were no mushrooms in Sloan's fridge. In fact there wasn't much in the way of food at all. He kept it stocked with bottled water and beer. The top shelf held a bottle of white wine—the same Chardonnay that he'd claimed was Cameron's favorite. Behind it was a paper bag. Opening it, I saw it contained cheese—three kinds—and a bag of plump green grapes.

"Hungry, Red?"

I dropped the bag and whirled around to face Sloan. "I—"

For the life of me I couldn't get another word out. He was standing in the archway wearing only a pair of jeans, bare-chested and barefoot. I could see that his skin was still a bit damp from his shower. Heat flooded through me. I tried to tell myself that it was from embarrassment because he'd caught me snooping, but that was a lie. It was Sloan who was making my body burn and my mouth water. Oh, I was hungry all right. Only it wasn't for food. I wanted a taste of Sloan Campbell.

Chapter 13

"Hungry, Red?" He definitely was, Sloan thought as she jumped and whirled to face him. He'd been watching her for some time as she'd poked through his cupboards and studied the contents of his refrigerator as if there was some secret there she was determined to discover. Her concentration had been total. He'd seen the same intentness the evening before when he'd been introducing her to family and guests, and he couldn't help wondering if she would bring that same concentration to the task of making love to a man. To him.

He'd spent a sleepless night trying to talk himself out of what he was going to do. He'd even tried to sell himself on the idea that if he could have her just once, he could get her out of his system. He hadn't been successful at either endeavor.

He wanted her. She wanted him. That was the one truth between them. He was going to start there, and see where it would lead. And for the first time in his life Sloan was going to damn the consequences. But he'd wanted to choose the time and the place. And he had. He'd chosen the perfect spot, and he'd planned to take her there.

He studied her now as she stood silently regarding him. She was wearing Cameron's clothes, well-tailored riding breeches and one of the silk blouses Cameron always favored. He even caught a hint of the scent that Cameron always wore. But it wasn't Cameron's eyes he was looking into. Her eyes had never held that combination of heat and promise and innocence. He wasn't sure which pulled at him more or which caused the desire building inside of him to turn so quickly into a burning ache.

What he was sure of was that his plans had changed. The time and the place was now.

"I thought we'd take the wine and grapes with us," Sloan said as he walked toward her. "There's a place I'm going to show you, your favorite place on the ranch, and I thought we'd have a picnic. But we could enjoy them now. If you think you can't wait."

* * *

"Wait…" My voice was working. Now all I needed was some more words. Thoughts would be good, too. They'd drained out of my mind the moment I saw him standing there. Now that he'd moved closer, I could feel his heat and the sensation was only heightened by the coolness of the open refrigerator at my back. I felt trapped between ice and fire. I took a breath and drew in his scent—soap and something uniquely male, something that was Sloan Campbell. It made my mouth water.

I had to say something. Anything. "I…was just…snooping. I'm sorry. I once read that you can learn a lot about a person from what he or she keeps in their refrigerator. And so I thought I would take a look and—" Now I was babbling. I bit down on my lip because if I kept it up, I might give myself away.

"What did you learn about me?" He took a step closer.

"I…" Just as quickly as it had come, the power to form words and string them into sentences deserted me again. When Sloan touched my arm, I jolted.

"Easy," he said in the same kind of tone I'd heard him use on Saturn. "I just want to shut the refrigerator door."

Keeping his hand on my arm, he picked up the bag, replaced it on the shelf and closed the door.

When he finally turned back to me, I found myself pinned against the counter.

"So what did you learn about me?"

I cleared my throat. "You don't cook much here."

"Thanks to Elena, I don't have to. She spoils me. Is that all you learned?"

"You like to read." I thought of the photos in the living room. "I think that family is important to you. I looked in the other room. I was curious, and when you didn't answer my knock, I just—"

"You don't have to apologize. Given the chance, I'd love to search the place where you've been staying for the last five weeks. I'm curious about you, too."

It was a mistake to keep looking into his eyes. The heat there was even more intense than what I was already feeling. He rubbed his thumb over my bottom lip, and I heard my breath catch.

"You're so responsive." He lifted his other hand to cup the back of my neck.

I knew what Sloan was going to do. He was going to kiss me. So I raised a hand and pressed it against his chest. Big mistake. His skin felt like warm velvet stretched over steel. The hand at my neck was hard, too. Heat rocketed through me from both contact points.

"I want to kiss you."

"No." I don't know how in the world I got the word out. It was such a lie that I marveled lightning didn't strike me dead. Never had my mind and body been so diametrically opposed.

"Why not?"

Desperately, I tried to remember my sister and what I'd come here to do. I moistened my lips. "That's what I came to talk to you about."

"About kissing?" He rubbed the pad of his thumb over my bottom lip again.

"No. About *not* kissing. I know that you probably were curious on the bluff and again last night in the garden, and then this morning you kissed me again to make a point to Marcie and Hal and Beatrice. I understand that. But I don't want you to kiss me anymore."

"Liar."

Okay. So I desperately wanted him to kiss me again. And wanted to kiss him back. And more.

"You're wrong about why I kissed you." His thumb began a gentle stroking up and down the back of my neck. Any minute I was going to evaporate into steam.

"Each time I kissed you it was because I wanted to. Because I couldn't help myself."

"Really?" He didn't look entirely happy about that. Still, at his admission, a mix of pleasure and astonishment flooded through me. The fact that he could be feeling the same kind of attraction, the same level of lust that I was feeling made my knees go even weaker.

"In a minute, if you don't let me go, I won't be able to help myself, either," I said.

"You can't say something like that to me and expect me not to act on it."

I could have moved then. I didn't.

He did. His mouth covered mine, and there was nothing of the gentle exploration that he'd used in the garden the night before. Today his lips were hard, his tongue and teeth demanding. Little explosions of pleasure shot through me, making my hunger build with a speed I'd never experienced before. My tongue met his, tangling and caressing. I tasted the hot, minty flavor of his toothpaste and something darker that reminded me of chocolate, only better.

When he bit my bottom lip, pleasure sharpened. I wrapped my arms around him, flattened my palms against that hard smooth skin and tried to absorb him. When hard hands cupped my bottom, I scooted up to wrap my legs around his hips. Through layers of clothes, I felt the rigid length of his penis pressed against my center, and I rubbed myself against it.

With a groan, he eased me onto the edge of the counter and broke off the kiss. For a moment, we were both oxygen starved and breathing hard. He drew away, just a little. But he didn't release me entirely. He left one hand on my side, his thumb stroking my nipple. The palm of his other hand lay heavily on my thigh, and that thumb was moving up and down between my legs, teasing, promising. The friction at both contact points had me quivering with need.

Sloan's eyes were narrowed, and his voice was husky when he spoke. "If you want me to stop, say so now."

He was giving me a choice. But with his hands on me, I couldn't seem to say a thing. All I wanted was him, hot and hard inside of me. I couldn't think of anything else.

"If you don't say something, I'm going to take it as a yes."

My inner Alice was shouting yes. My saner self, the part that always reminded me of the trouble I usually got into when I gave in to impulse, remained silent.

Still he hesitated as if he needed some sign from me. "Yes or no?"

This was wrong. It had to be. But I didn't care. I'd never felt this way before. Maybe I never would again. "Yes."

It was triumph now that I saw in his eyes. Then he lifted me off the counter and carried me through the archway and into the bedroom. He laid me on the bed, and then he positioned himself on top of me. My legs parted for him, and once he'd settled between them, he rocked against me. I arched up or tried to. But I was trapped beneath him. His legs were hard between mine, and I could feel the hardest part of him—a solid ridge of granite—pressing against me through way too many layers of clothes.

Then he levered himself off me, and settling himself beside me, he took my wrists in one hand and pinned them above my head.

I started to protest, but he countered by kissing me again. My head began to spin. He still held my hands above my head, and with his foot, he'd pinned one of my ankles to the bed. With his free hand he began to unbutton my blouse, slowly, tantalizingly. Each sensation was so intense—the heat of his body beside me, the dark, rich taste of him and the slow movement of those fingers as they released one button after another. Each time they slipped beneath the silk and brushed my skin I trembled. All the while he feasted on my mouth, exploring every part of it in slow strokes of his tongue as if there was some flavor there he hadn't yet sampled.

Sloan tugged the blouse free of my slacks and pushed it aside. Then he raised his head and looked down at what he'd uncovered. "Pretty," he murmured in a husky voice as he ran the palm of his hand over my breast. Through my thin bra of silk and lace, I felt the heat of his touch like a little electric shock. I did my best to arch into his palm.

"I've been wanting to touch you, really touch you." He paused to move his hand lower until it rested flat on my stomach. "Ever since you appeared out of nowhere on that bluff." He undid the button of my riding pants and drew the zipper down slowly. The sound it made as it opened was incredibly erotic.

"Your skin is so soft. Like rainwater." He pressed his hand against my stomach and lowering his head, he covered my breast with his mouth. Ever so slowly, he began to stroke my nipple with his tongue. The moist heat of his mouth combined with the friction of the silk against my skin had me trying to arch upward, reaching for more....

I whimpered something, and as if he had been waiting for that sound, he moved his hand lower on my stomach, sliding his fingers beneath my panties and then between my legs until he reached the spot that felt so empty. I stopped breathing then, trapped between exquisite pleasure and the painful ache that was building inside of me.

I tried to move and found that I was trapped physically, too. My hands were still pinned above my head, my foot still held captive by his. All I could manage to do was wiggle my hips, but it wasn't enough.

"Please." My voice was barely a thread of

sound, and just as I thought I might die of wanting, he drew my nipple into his mouth, sucking it hard at the same moment that he pushed two fingers into me.

"Sloan," I cried out.

He drew his fingers out and pushed them in, drew out, pushed in, matching the rhythm of his hand to the movement of his mouth as he suckled at my breast. I was burning, melting, searching….

And then suddenly he withdrew from me. The sense of loss was so acute that for a moment, I couldn't say anything. Even though he'd released my hands and my foot, I couldn't move. I watched him rise from the bed and begin to take off his jeans. My gaze followed the dark denim as it slid down those long muscled legs. Beneath them he wore white Jockey briefs, and I could see the evidence of his arousal pushing at the fabric. When the underwear followed the path of the jeans, I finally saw what I'd only felt before. My mouth went dry as dust. He was so big—not just where my eyes were currently glued, but all over. His chest was wide, the bronze skin sprinkled with dark hair, and he had the shoulders of a linebacker. I had never wanted anyone the way I wanted him.

"Hurry," I said. At least that's what I tried to say. The sound that came out was more like a moan.

And he didn't hurry at all. At least not to the bed. Instead, he moved to the bedside table, opened the drawer and took out a condom. I'd thought the sound of my zipper opening was erotic, but the rip of that foil packet topped it. When he'd fully sheathed himself, I sat up and said, "Hurry."

He didn't move. He simply stood there, looking down at me. My skin had chilled when he'd moved away so abruptly, but now it began to heat again.

"You have too many clothes on," he said.

Glancing down, I realized that I was still mostly clothed. I'd been so mesmerized watching him strip that I'd completely forgotten.

"Take them off for me." His voice was husky, but I found the thread of command in his voice arousing. And he was driving me mad. He'd been teasing and tormenting me, taking me right to the brink and then withdrawing. Maybe it was time I gave as good as I was getting.

Raising my eyes to meet his, I deliberately started with my boots. I dropped one and then the other over the side of the bed. I took my socks off next, drawing out the process as long as I could. His eyes narrowed and I could hear the harsh sound of his breathing in the room. I turned my attention to my bra next. It was a good thing that he'd unbuttoned my blouse because my fingers were growing numb. Then lying back down, I lifted my hips off of the bed and began to wiggle out of my riding breeches.

I'd only managed to get them halfway down my

legs when he joined me on the bed and dragged them off the rest of the way. Then Sloan knelt between my legs and tore away the lace that still separated us. Power streamed through me as he gripped my hips and positioned himself over me. But then once again, he paused.

I wrapped arms and legs around him. "Dammit, Sloan. Do it."

He framed my face with his hands. "Do what?"

"Come inside me. I want you inside right now."

He drove into me, and I went off like a rocket. The orgasm ripped through me so fast and so hard that I think I lost consciousness for a moment. The next thing I knew, my arms had dropped away from him and so had my legs. They felt like limp noodles. But Sloan was still on top of me, still filling me.

I opened my eyes to find him regarding me in that intent way he had. I read triumph and satisfaction in his eyes. And something. A question?

He withdrew and pushed into me again. To my astonishment my knees came up and my arms wrapped themselves around him.

"Hold on," he said in a hoarse voice. "It's going to be a rough ride."

It was. And incredibly I was ready for it. As he drove into me again and again, each stroke built in speed and intensity. My world narrowed to this man, the heat and hardness of his body, his hands, and the movement of him inside of me. I felt another climax building, more slowly this time, but as we raced toward it together, I felt parts of myself slipping away.

"Come with me." His voice was harsh in my ear. "Now."

I had no choice. When the first wild spasm tore through me, I cried out. But it didn't end there. He showed me more, driving me up again until I knew only that searing heat. And him. His voice joined mine as I gave myself to him and we flew over that last peak together.

Sloan came back to awareness slowly. He couldn't think. All he knew were sensations. His face was buried in Red's hair, his body pressing hers into the mattress. His heart was racing, his breath coming in gasps.

And he was trembling. That was a first. A little sliver of fear moved through him. What in the world was she doing to him? Still dazed, he raised his head and studied her. Her eyes were half-closed, her skin still flushed from passion.

He'd wondered where it would lead when he made love to her. But he hadn't expected this…this loss of self. How could he? How could a man anticipate something he'd never experienced before? Something he was already wanting to experience again.

Incredibly, he felt a fresh wave of desire ripple through him. How could she do this to him—this woman who looked so much like Cameron. But who wasn't Cameron.

"Who the hell are you?"

Chapter 14

"Who the hell are you?"

The question, especially the not-so-friendly tone of it, blew some of the fuzz out of my brain. I opened my mouth, not at all sure what was going to come out, but Sloan pressed a finger against my lips to silence me.

"Don't even think of lying, Red. I know that you're not Cameron McKenzie."

Okay, the jig was up. There was always the possibility that someone would see through my impersonation. But I couldn't think of a worse spot to be in—lying naked beneath the man who'd just unmasked me. Worse than that, I was lying naked beneath a man I'd just had mind-blowing sex with. A man that I incredibly wanted again, so my brain was still deep in the fuzzy zone. Otherwise, I might have thought up something. Anything.

"What's your name?"

"Brooke Ashby."

"Brooke Ashby." He said the name as if he were testing it on his tongue. "I can check it out."

"Yes, you can." Temper began to flare inside of me. "And you can get off me."

He rubbed his thumbs over my cheekbones, and something else began to fire up inside of me.

"I'm not moving until you tell me what game you're playing, Brooke Ashby."

"Game?"

"You come here with an amnesia story and pass yourself off as Cameron McKenzie. Several scenarios have occurred to me. In one of them, I figure you came across a picture of Cameron, were struck by the resemblance, and decided that impersonating her was the ticket to getting your hands on her inheritance."

I stared at him. Had seducing me been just part of his plan to unmask me? Well, I didn't like his tactics. Or rather I'd liked them too much.

"Get off me!" I shoved hard against his shoulders, but I might as well have been trying to move one of those boulders on the bluff. "What kind of man are you? You thought that I would do something like that and…and yet you made love to me?"

"Yeah. And I want to again."

I felt the truth of what he was saying inside me. And I felt my body's reaction. There was a part of me that was angry, but there was also a part of me that was almost weeping to have him moving in me again. Since I wasn't having much luck controlling how my body was responding, I concentrated on keeping my brain unfuzzed. "That's not going to happen."

"Yeah, it is." As if to prove his point, he surged forward, and we both felt the way my body reacted. Heard the way my breath caught in my throat.

Sloan withdrew. "We'll get to that in a minute. First, I want the truth about what you're doing here."

"I'll need to breathe. And I'll be able to think more clearly if you get off of me."

"Fair enough." He rolled to my side, but he kept an arm around my waist and one leg over mine. "But you're not getting out of this bed until you answer my questions."

My mind raced for a moment trying to decide just what to tell him. But he hadn't moved far enough away for me to completely get the static out of my brain.

Finally, I did what I usually do when my back is

against the wall. I went with impulse. Not that following my impulses always got me out of scrapes. Case in point—giving in to my impulse to make love with Sloan Campbell. But I wanted to tell someone, and since Sloan already knew that I was an imposter, he was the most likely candidate and perhaps he could be useful. "If I tell you, will you help me find out what happened to Cameron?"

His gaze remained steady on mine. "Then she didn't send you here?"

"No. Why would you think that? Oh. The face-saving thing again? She sends me here to seduce you. Then she has a good reason not to go through with the wedding." I stared at him. It would make a great story line for Mallory Carstairs on *Secrets*. But... "Would Cameron actually do something like that?"

"She has a lot of her father in her. She likes to play games."

Evidently, the big difference between Cameron and me was that I could dream up plot lines, but she could really carry them out.

"Did James have a hand in your coming here?" Sloan asked.

"No. And you haven't answered my question. If I tell you, will you help me find out what's happened to Cameron?"

"Why do you think something's happened to her?"

"Because I'm her twin, and I can feel it."

Surprise flickered over his face. "Her twin?" He frowned. "I don't think so. Cameron doesn't have a twin sister."

"I didn't think I had one, either, until five weeks ago. That's when I received an anonymous letter telling me that I was adopted."

I found that telling him about the letter was like pulling my finger out of a dike. Everything else came pouring out with it. I told him about talking to my parents and how they'd confirmed I was adopted and that my whole life had been a lie. I told him about hiring Pepper and what she'd discovered and my decision to come to the ranch to find out what I could about Cameron.

Spilling all the beans probably wasn't my wisest strategy, but Sloan was a good listener. He didn't interrupt, didn't react in a judgmental way. And it was helping, I found, to put everything I'd discovered so far into words.

I also became aware that lying there in his bed and revealing all my secrets to him was almost as intimate as making love with him had been. For a while after I was finally finished, he didn't say a word. My insides twisted into knots. What must he think of me? I claimed that I'd come to the ranch to find out what had happened to my newly discovered sister, and as part of my little adventure, I'd agreed to marry him on Friday and then I'd slept with him. Looking at it from an objective point of view, his scenario about my coming here seemed a lot more feasible than the truth.

But when he finally spoke, all Sloan said was, "So you're telling me that you believe Cameron and you are twin sisters, separated at birth and both put up for adoption."

"Yes. Except Cameron wasn't adopted, was she?"

He was looking at me in that intent way he had. "No. At least not that I'm aware of."

"Beatrice gave me a tour of the ballroom this morning, and I saw Elizabeth McKenzie. I could be her daughter. Cameron and I could both be her daughters."

"You're implying that Elizabeth had twins and she and James gave one of you up? I can't see James doing that."

I was having trouble with that, too. "And it doesn't explain my friend Pepper's discovery of Cameron's adoption records. She's checking into it again. But that's not what's important right now. What's important is to find Cameron. I have a really bad feeling—I've had it ever since I found out that she was missing—that something horrible has happened to her. She didn't just go off in a snit like everyone seems to think. What did the two of you argue about?"

"I caught her kissing Hal Linton in the garden. After I sent him off, I reminded her that part of our agreement was that although our marriage was partly a business arrangement, we would be monogamous. She lost her temper then. But I don't think what I said was the only thing that set her off. Something else was bothering her. Anyway, she said she was going to call off the wedding. And I told her to go ahead. I knew that once she thought it over, she'd back down. Cameron never accepts criticism well. When she went missing, none of us were worried about her. It's not unusual for her to disappear like that."

"But five weeks? You think she needs that much time to figure out whether or not she wants to go through with the wedding?"

"It's possible that she's decided to call it off. She doesn't like to back down once she's given her word. So she may be figuring out how to persuade her father to side with her on this."

He didn't sound angry or upset that Cameron might be deciding to call off the wedding. I tried not to read too much into that because whatever the truth was surrounding Cameron and Sloan's marriage, it didn't change the fact that I'd just made love with my sister's fiancé. Or the fact that I wanted to do it again. I was all too aware of the strength and the heat of his arm lying across my stomach.

As if he were reading my mind, Sloan slid his hand up to cup my breast, and my nipples—traitors that I'd already found them to be—hardened.

"Don't," I said. But my voice didn't sound convincing even to me. In spite of the satisfaction I'd experienced only a short time before, my body was already heating, yearning.

"Why not?"

I nearly cried out in protest when he removed his hand and levered himself into a sitting position.

"Because…"

My voice trailed off when I saw that instead of leaving, he was taking off the condom and replacing it with another.

I just lay there mesmerized, watching him do it. I couldn't think of my sister or the wedding or anything but making love to Sloan again. When I finally raised a hand, it wasn't to push him away. Oh no. Instead, I ran my fingers over the long hard length of him, and I wished I'd thought to do it before he'd slipped the latex on.

The sound he made deep in his throat echoed what I was feeling almost perfectly. He moved quickly then, first lifting away my hand and then finding a place for himself between my legs.

Exhibiting my usual total lack of control where he was concerned, I immediately wrapped arms and legs around him and arched upward.

But he didn't fill me. Instead, he said, "You haven't yet asked how I knew that you weren't Cameron."

I hadn't. It was a sure sign of how far gone I was that my inner Alice hadn't kicked in on that little issue. "How?"

He leaned down to brush his mouth over mine. "Your reaction to Saturn was a clue. At the Derby, Cameron was afraid of him. He didn't take to her, either." He paused to trail a line of kisses along my jaw.

When his teeth nipped my earlobe, pleasure fizzed through me. "But that wasn't it."

His voice was a husky whisper in my ear, and I could feel him against me right where I needed him. But it wasn't enough. He wasn't letting me move, and I wasn't sure I could speak.

"It was when I kissed you the first time on the bluff, I knew that you weren't Cameron, and in the garden last night, I confirmed it. You see, I never kissed Cameron quite that way before, and I never wanted to do this to her."

He entered me in one fast plunge, filling me so completely I cried out.

"I don't want to stop doing this to you, Brooke." He withdrew and pushed into me again. And again. True to his word, he didn't stop for a very long time.

When I could finally breathe and think again, I found that Sloan and I were lying side-by-side, tucked together like spoons, and as much as I knew I should, I didn't want to move. This was why forbidden fruit was forbidden, I reminded myself— the addiction factor.

"We'll have to tell James," Sloan finally said.

"No." I wiggled around to face him. "We can't. Not yet. If we do, I'll have to stop impersonating Cameron, and having amnesia gives me the perfect excuse to ask a lot of questions."

He studied me. "Questions about what?"

"About who was around on the day Cameron disappeared." I swallowed hard. "And about who might benefit if she doesn't come back."

"Because you have a 'feeling' she was the victim of foul play?"

He was frowning, and I could still hear skepticism in his tone. So I drew in a deep breath and told him about the anonymous phone call I'd received.

When I was finished, he continued to study me with that I-can-see-right-through-you look of his.

"Cameron is an heiress," I said. "You were

quick enough to jump to the conclusion that I came here masquerading as her to get her money. What happens if she never comes back and your marriage can't take place? What will James do with the estate then?"

"I don't know. But I imagine he'll do a variation of what he intended to do before Cameron and I agreed to marry. In his current will he leaves Cameron the estate and the land, but all of the decisions about running the ranch and the business, including any sale of the land, is placed under the control of a board of directors, a group hand-picked by James. He's been pretty closemouthed about whom he's selected, but my guess is that Doc Carter would be on it, perhaps Rachel Lakewood and Jack Boland. They are all close friends of James and very like-minded. James would like to have control of this place even from the grave."

"But he was going to give that up and turn the place over to you and Cameron if you marry because…?"

Sloan gave me a wry smile. "My guess is that Cameron gave him an offer he couldn't refuse. She'd marry someone he'd approve of with the ability to run the ranch just as well as his hand-selected board, and he'd have at least the hope of grandchildren. That's just a guess on my part, but she'd know what kind of a carrot to dangle in front of her father. Of course, it could have been that the marriage part was James's idea. A carrot he dangled in front of Cameron's nose—marry someone I approve of and I'll leave you both everything."

"And Cameron chose you?"

"Perhaps. It could have been James's idea. He didn't want me to leave five years ago, and he knows how much I love this place. He also knew what to dangle in front of me to get me to come back."

I swallowed hard again. I didn't like putting my growing suspicion into words. "And if something has happened to Cameron, who would James leave the place to then? Beatrice and Austin with the board making all the decisions?"

"Probably. I hadn't given it any thought." His frown deepened. "But that would be a good guess, and I don't like where this is going."

"I don't, either. Who might know James's backup plan? Who would he confide in?"

"Doc Carter," Sloan said without hesitation. "He and James have been close since they were kids. James trusts him."

"Promise me you won't tell anyone yet who I really am, not until we know more about what might have happened to Cameron."

"And if something has happened to Cameron, your impersonation of her puts you in danger. I don't—"

I stopped him by putting my fingers against his lips. "Just until tomorrow. I'll have to let James know who I really am before the wedding."

For a moment, he hesitated. "On one condition."

"What?"

"We'll ask questions together. I don't want you wandering off with any of them alone. Whoever went through your things and left that message on your cell phone was at the hacienda last night."

"I agree and I promise."

He drew me into his arms and just held me. "Don't forget that there's at least one other person who hasn't been fooled by you."

"The person who sent me the anonymous letter." In spite of the warmth of Sloan's body, I felt a little chill move through me.

"Yeah," Sloan said. "Someone is playing a very deep game here. The question is who?"

Soon. Soon. Soon. The shadow waited in the shade of the trees, repeating the word over and over again until it became a chant. A promise. A prayer.

The mistakes of the past could be corrected. One could always achieve what one wanted with patience. And persistence. One didn't have to be second best. That perception could be corrected—with time.

She would be here very soon. She always came

here. So predictable. That's what had made it so easy the last time.

And there would be no mistakes this time. Rage rose like a bitter-tasting bile and was quickly repressed. There was no need for anger or self-recrimination. Never again. Not when a mistake could be so easily remedied.

The shadow ran a hand over the weapon. The gun, a sleek Winchester, would ensure that this time the end would be final.

Soon.

Chapter 15

"We're taking a tour of the ranch in that?" I'd stopped short the moment I saw the shiny red plane on a short runway behind the stables.

"Yeah. Isn't she a honey?"

To me, the plane looked small, very small, like a shiny red kid's toy. And it had propellers. Sloan strode quickly toward it, and I had to double my pace to keep up. I glanced down at my breeches. "I thought we'd be riding."

Sloan climbed up on one of the wings, and held out a hand to me. "It's a big ranch, and believe me, this little beauty will be a lot easier on your seat than if we did the tour on horseback."

I let him help me up and I took a skeptical look into the tiny cockpit. "Where will the pilot sit?"

He laughed then. "I'm the pilot."

I turned to stare at him. "You fly?"

"James taught me when I was in my teens. Want to see my license?"

I could see the excitement in his eyes, and I realized that the little red plane was a toy. Sloan's toy.

"Don't tell me you have a secret fear of flying."

"Of course not." But I preferred my planes to be jumbo jets. Or at least jumbo period.

He opened the door, and I climbed over the pilot's seat and into the passenger's. "You're the one who insisted that we take the tour."

He had me there. I'd convinced him that if we didn't, someone might suspect something. And James wouldn't be pleased if Sloan didn't show me the ranch. There were bound to be questions, and since I'd already blown my cover with Sloan, I wanted to make sure that I didn't do the same with anyone else.

I buckled myself in, then gripped the edge of my seat hard.

"You are afraid of flying," Sloan said, and this time I heard the concern in his voice.

"No. Really. I have a slight aversion to heights, but it's never affected me in a plane. And I do want to see the ranch."

He sent me a smile as he turned on the engine. "I'll try not to fly too high. Just relax."

Whatever anxiety I'd been experiencing faded as the nose of the plane rose into the bright late-morning sky. The only clouds I could see were far away in the direction of the Pacific. So I wasn't prepared when a tricky patch of crosscurrents sent the little plane rocking. My heart shot to my throat and I dug my fingers into the edge of my seat.

"Easy," Sloan said. "I've got it handled."

I could see that he did, and I gradually blew out the breath I was holding.

I glanced at him. He was comfortable at the controls. It occurred to me then that he was a man who would be competent at any job he took on. I thought of the way he'd calmed Saturn on the bluff when we'd first met. Even if he didn't come out on top in a fight or a competition, he wouldn't stay down long. Hadn't that competence and determination been a big part of what had attracted me to him from the get-go?

I forced my hands to release their grip on the seat. "I'm sorry that I'm such a coward."

The look he shot me held surprise. "You're not. Coming here to take your sister's place because you're sure that something's happened to her—that takes a kind of courage that few people would have."

His compliment warmed me and had my heart

doing a little flutter. No, I thought. I was not going to go there. Heart flutters were out. It was bad enough that I had this uncontrollable chemistry with a man who belonged to my sister. I was not going to even think of letting my heart get in the mix.

Sloan leveled off the plane and banked it to the right into a circle. "If you can manage to look down, you'll treat yourself to the best view there is of the hacienda."

I made myself glance down and discovered he was right. We were directly over it, and I could see the tower reaching toward us. The sun turned the water falling from the fountain into what looked like different-colored gems. The lush green of the gardens in stark contrast to the mostly arid land surrounding the ranch gave the hacienda a fairy-tale appearance.

It was hard in the bright sunlight to believe that there were secrets here, but I knew there were. "It's a beautiful place to have such a sad history."

"How so?" Sloan asked.

"The mistresses of the Hacienda Montega don't have a very good survival rate. Beatrice took me to view the portraits in the ballroom. Only one of those women made it to her fortieth year."

"I've never given it much thought," Sloan said. "But you're right."

"I wonder if there's a curse?"

Sloan glanced at me. "Do you believe that?"

"No." But it would make a good story line. "Perhaps not a curse, but there's an interesting pattern…."

He banked the plane again and set a course for what I thought was the Pacific. As we headed over the first hills, we hit a bit of turbulence, but this time I didn't go into white-knuckle mode. It was clear that Sloan knew what he was doing. True to his word, he flew low. At times, I could even see individual cars moving along a stretch of highway. The terrain below was marked by little valleys here and there, and vast stretches of land that had been unmarred as yet by civilization.

"This property must be worth millions," I said.

"The latest offer James received for the area along the coast was a cool quarter of a billion, but they would have been willing to go higher."

I stared at him. "Why doesn't he sell?"

"Because he loves this place, and he doesn't want to see it turned into a vacation destination with malls, gas stations, golf courses and a string of high-rise hotels along the coast. I'm quoting him directly on that."

I could almost hear James saying it.

The coast came up fast, and Sloan took the plane out over the ocean before he turned and followed the coastline. What I saw beneath me was rugged, pristine and beautiful. High cliffs bordered the

Pacific, and we were flying low enough to see the power of the water as it crashed into the shore.

Out of curiosity, I asked, "What about you and Cameron? Will you respect James's wishes?"

"I would never sell." He hesitated for a moment. Then he continued. "I think I can say the same for Cameron. But she's gotten very friendly with Hal Linton, and he's connected to a group of buyers who are very interested in acquiring the property we're flying over right now."

"How long has he known her?"

"Six months or so. Since shortly after she hired Marcie." Sloan glanced at me. "Cameron isn't a fool. She wouldn't be taken in by Hal. She knew what he was about. James made sure she did."

I kept my own counsel. Of course, he might be a very good actor, but I wasn't so sure that Hal's interest in Cameron was purely monetary. But then, Marcie had almost convinced me that her interest in Austin was sincere. I couldn't discount the possibility that the brother and sister were very accomplished actors. "If James knows that Hal Linton represents a buyer, why does he allow him to be a guest at the hacienda?"

Sloan smiled then. "He likes to keep his enemies in his sights."

It was my turn to laugh then, and to my surprise, Sloan reached out and took my hand. "You have a nice laugh. I'd like to hear it more often."

My heart did that little flutter thing again. I was barely able to register it before the plane took a sudden and violent bump that had me grabbing for a handhold.

"What was that?"

Sloan didn't answer. But I got a clue when the glass in the door to my right shattered. Someone was shooting at us.

"Get down!" Sloan shouted, unnecessarily. I'd already ducked my head as close to my knees as I could.

The plane was dropping like a rock toward the ocean and so was my stomach. Sloan swore under his breath as he struggled to get the nose back up. The swearing part wasn't good. But he was, I tried to tell myself.

"Look toward the cliffs," Sloan said in that terse tone of command that was becoming familiar to me.

Lifting my head, I did what he asked.

"Tell me what you see."

I was ready to say "the cliffs," but then I saw the dark-colored vehicle as it sped away from a spot on the cliffs behind us. "An SUV, I think. It's driving away."

What I also saw were dark plumes of smoke spiraling away behind us. When I summoned up the courage to look down, I saw that we were close, very close to the ocean. Another few yards and we were going to hit.

"Hold on," Sloan said. Sweat stood out on his forehead as he struggled with the stick in front of him, pulling it hard. The strong winds blowing in from the sea at this level had the plane pitching first one way and then the next. At one point, I was sure that I saw the spray from a wave hit the windshield.

Then suddenly, miraculously, the nose of the plane began to rise again, higher and higher. I held my breath, praying as Sloan fiddled with the controls and coaxed the plane up to the level of the cliffs. The engine coughed and sputtered. For a moment, I was sure we were going to take that long fall to the water below. Then land was coming up to meet us.

The wheels hit the ground with a vicious, teeth-jarring thud. The plane shook, shuddered, teetered to one side, and then skidded in the direction of the cliff. I held my breath. Sloan's hands remained steady as he fought to regain control. The engine sputtered one more time, went silent, and we rolled to a stop with only a few feet to spare.

I barely had time to let out the breath I was holding before we were engulfed in thick, black smoke. I tried not to breathe it in, but I must have failed because I heard myself coughing.

I felt Sloan's hands as he unstrapped me from the seat, but I could barely see him.

"C'mon." His voice was a terse command in my ear as he grabbed my hand and the backpack he'd stored behind the seat. We scrambled across the wing, jumped and hit the ground running. I didn't look back until Sloan finally stopped. The little red plane was totally engulfed in the smoke, but I didn't see any flames.

Gripping my shoulder, Sloan turned me to face him. "Are you all right? Did one of the bullets hit you?" He swore, pulled out a hankie and began to dab at my cheekbone. "You're bleeding."

"Glass," I said, remembering that the window had shattered. "I'm fine." Even as I said it, my knees went weak and a mix of shock and disbelief settled into a knot in my stomach. "Someone shot at us."

"Yeah." Sloan pulled me hard against his chest and just held me there. "You're sure it was an SUV you saw?"

"Yes." I thought about the one that I'd seen in the garage and the other that I'd driven up to the bluff the day before. Either could have been the one that I'd spotted.

He didn't say anything, but I knew that we were thinking the same thing. Sloan's arms tightened around me. For a few moments I let myself rest against him. Just until the fear subsided and I got my breath back. The steady beat of his heart soothed me, and the warmth of his body melted away the sudden chill that had engulfed me.

There was none of the heat that I'd experienced before in his arms, nothing of that all-consuming passion. Instead, I just felt as if I'd come home. Not good. Because Sloan Campbell would never be home to me. He could never be mine.

When I drew back, he regarded me steadily for a moment, then leaned down and pressed his lips gently against the scratch on my cheek. This time my heart didn't just flutter. It turned a full somersault.

Drawing back, he said, "You're right. Someone wanted Cameron out of the way."

The knots in my stomach tightened. This was one argument I would have preferred to lose.

"They want you out of the way, too." Sloan's tone was grim.

"Who?" Now that I'd finally convinced him that Cameron hadn't just taken off in a snit, I wanted his opinion. He knew these people far better than I did.

"Anyone who was at that dinner party last night and who heard James announce that I would give you a tour."

"But they wouldn't have necessarily known that you would take the plane, would they?"

"They wouldn't have to know how I'd bring you

here. All they had to know was that we'd come to this spot, and it wouldn't take a rocket scientist to figure that out. Anyone who knows Cameron knows that this is her favorite place on the whole ranch. Ever since she was a little girl, she's come here. She calls it her 'gathering place.' If any place would jar her memory, this one would."

Curious, I turned to study the area, careful to keep my eyes off of the still-burning plane. We were standing near the edge of a forest that covered this portion of the ranch. The view was spectacular—lush green trees, sheer cliffs and the power of the Pacific in front of me stretching all the way to the horizon. I could see why Cameron would fall in love with this place. I could also see that it would make the perfect spot for an ambush.

"Did you come here with her?" I asked.

Sloan glanced at me. "No. She never wanted anyone with her when she came here. But I flew James out here the day after she disappeared. He was sure that she came here the morning after I argued with her."

He lifted a hand and pointed to a gap in the trees. "There's an old logging road that leads up here. It's rutted, but Cameron drove her car up here frequently."

"So someone hid in the trees and just waited for us. Someone driving an SUV."

"That doesn't narrow it down much. The ranch

owns two. Austin has his own, and Doc Carter drives one, too."

Much as I tried to block it, another thought slipped into my mind. If Cameron had indeed come up here on the day she disappeared, someone could have been waiting for her, too. I knew that Sloan was thinking the same thing when his arm tightened around me.

"I'm calling the police," he said. "The car you saw may have left tracks, and they may be able to find a bullet."

Chapter 16

The edge of the cliff was long and rocky. Since we had half an hour to kill until the police would arrive, Sloan had suggested we walk along it to get away from the still-smoking plane. He'd also called Gus at the stables and asked him to come out and pick us up. At my curious glance, he'd explained that though James had given him a place to live after his father had left, it was Gus and Elena who'd raised him. And right now, Gus was the only person he trusted.

The breeze coming in off the water carried a fresh, salty scent, and below us I could see water hurl itself against the rocks and rise in a misty spray that now and then would split into the colors of a rainbow. My nerves were gradually settling and my mind was clearing. No wonder my sister loved this place. I would be hard-pressed to find such a solitary and peaceful spot in the madness that was L.A.

I might have been able to appreciate the spot and the view even more if most of my mind hadn't been preoccupied with trying to figure out who had shot at us. I agreed with Sloan that anyone at the ranch who knew Cameron would have known Sloan would bring me here today. Somehow, we had to find a way to narrow the list of suspects—fast.

Ahead I saw a large flat rock. When we reached it, Sloan urged me to sit down and then sat next to me. "Cameron always said that she was going to build a house right here on this spot one day. The slope of the cliff isn't as steep here, and she had plans for building stairs down to the ocean."

My throat tightened at his use of the past tense. Somehow, now that I'd convinced him that something might have happened to Cameron, the possibility was becoming more real to me. I reached for his hand. Swallowing hard, I said, "I don't want her to be...I don't want something to have happened to her. We don't know that something has."

He gave my hand a squeeze. "You're right." Then in what I was sure was an effort to change the subject, he pulled the bottle of Chardonnay, cheese and grapes out of the backpack. As he quickly and efficiently removed the cork, he suggested, "Why don't we eat while we discuss what we're going to do when we get back to the ranch."

In a matter of moments, I had a plastic glass in my hand, and a small picnic was spread out on the rock. I took a quick sip of the wine to brace myself for the upcoming battle. I was betting that Sloan would want me to stop pretending that I was Cameron, and I didn't want to. Not yet. Drawing in a deep breath, I said, "You're going to want to tell James who I really am, and I want to wait."

"I think we should wait, too."

As I stared at him in surprise, he continued, "Anything we tell him right now will only upset him. And as you just pointed out, we don't really know anything definite about what might have happened to Cameron yet."

It was one of the arguments I'd intended to use on him, and I found it both odd and comforting that our minds would be so in tune. "The first thing we should do is to narrow the list of suspects. Whoever took that shot at us had access to an SUV and would have been absent from the house for at least an hour."

"Gus might be able to help with that. He keeps a pretty good eye on the comings and goings of the McKenzies and their houseguests."

I took a bite of cheese and glanced around the area again.

"Whoever shot at us would have to be very good with a gun. Does that eliminate anyone?"

Sloan thought for a minute. "I'm not sure about the Lintons, but hunting has traditionally been a favorite McKenzie sport. James used to take Cameron, Austin and me with him when we were younger. Doc Carter hunts, too, and I'm pretty sure that Beatrice can handle a gun."

"I'll ask my friend Pepper to check out the Lintons and see if they have any expertise with guns. They do seem to have a motive for wanting Cameron out of the way. Austin might inherit and be more amenable to selling the land."

"They'd still have to convince whomever James appointed to his board."

"But they might have a better chance of doing that with Austin. He'd probably be on their side. At least that's the way I'd see it if I were writing it."

"If you were writing it?"

"That's what I do for a living. I live in L.A. and I write plots for a soap opera, *Secrets*."

"No kidding." He poured more wine into my glass. "Tell me more about Brooke Ashby."

For another quarter of an hour, I did just that. Soon Sloan knew as much about me as anyone did—except for perhaps Pepper and my parents.

The man was so easy to talk to, he'd have made a great cop or P.I. Suspects would probably line up to spill their guts to him.

The man had gotten to me. Not good, I told myself. He wasn't mine. He couldn't be mine.

But when I finished my life story, he said, "You're full of surprises, Brooke Ashby." Then he leaned over and took my mouth with his.

He might not be mine, but I definitely wanted to be his. Not good at all.

The kiss might have turned into something else, if we hadn't been interrupted by the sound of a truck rattling up the road. A second later, it broke through the woods and rolled toward us.

"Our ride." Sloan rose from the rock and walked toward it while I started packing up the picnic. By the time I finished, Gus had climbed out of the truck and was deep in conversation with Sloan. They started walking along the cliff to take a closer look at the plane. A few moments later, a state trooper's car appeared, and two officers joined Gus and Sloan at the plane.

I took a moment to move closer to the edge of the cliff. The breeze was steady and sweet. I'd always loved to be near the water. Going to the beach—even when it was one of the crowded ones on Lake Michigan or near L.A.—had always had a calming effect on me. I could see why my sister loved this place and why she'd planned to build a house here one day.

And this side of her, the part that would want to use this place as a retreat, seemed to contradict the spoiled and headstrong socialite that others had described to me. Oddly enough, I could relate to both sides of her. I might not be a socialite, but I'd left the Midwest and taken a job in Tinseltown. And we shared the need to get away from it all. When I was younger, it was riding that had helped me do that. Now I tried to hike on the weekends.

I felt as though I was gradually coming to know Cameron, and I was even starting to miss her. I wanted her to be alive. A little band tightened around my heart. Then I moved to the edge of the cliff, and my mind began to weave a story. If she'd come here on the day she disappeared, she might have been standing right where I was standing now. Sloan had said that she'd threatened to call the wedding off—a threat he hadn't taken too seriously. But I couldn't help wondering if Cameron had indeed had second thoughts about settling for a marriage that was primarily a business arrangement.

I could see why she might be torn. Her father had had a heart attack, and he was refusing to leave her everything outright. Looking around, I wondered what I might be willing to sacrifice to keep the land and to ensure that a place like this would remain as pristine as it was today.

I could picture the scene in my mind as if it were one I had written for *Secrets*. Cameron had come here alone to think it through. The sound of the surf was louder here, the wind stronger. If someone had come up behind her, would she have heard them?

Another thought occurred to me. If someone from the ranch had followed her, they wouldn't have had to sneak up, would they? If she hadn't been expecting it, it wouldn't have taken much in the way of force to make her lose her balance....

I couldn't help myself. I risked a quick look down. Just before my head began to spin and I had to raise my eyes, I thought I saw the glint of something. Directly in front of me, a seagull circled lazily on a current of air.

"Show-off," I muttered. Closing my eyes, I drew in a deep breath. Then I dropped to my knees, took a firm grip on the rocks that formed the cliff's edge and looked down again. There was definitely something on a ledge about twenty feet down, something that was reflecting sunlight.

I glanced back over my shoulder and I saw that Sloan and Gus were still in conference with the police at the plane. I dropped my gaze to the ledge, willing my eyes not to stray to the ocean below. There were all sorts of rocks and crevices to provide a handhold or foothold. And there was more of a slope to the cliff face than what I'd seen when Sloan had been flying alongside it. A talented engineer could probably find a way of attaching a set of stairs that would allow access to the beach below.

Once again, I measured the distance to the ledge and gauged the risk. I'd had to climb some pretty steep hills when I was hiking in the Hollywood Hills. This wouldn't be too much different.

Yeah, right, said a little voice in my head. I frowned, finding it interesting that my saner voice was piping up again now that Sloan Campbell wasn't around. But my inner Alice hadn't deserted me. *I could make it down there,* she was assuring me. *I just shouldn't look down.*

Without another thought, I turned, swung my legs over the edge of the cliff and felt for the first crevice with my foot. It wasn't as bad as I thought it would be. I just kept my eyes straight ahead, reminded myself that I was doing this for my long-lost twin, and climbed slowly down. Once I was on the ledge, it was a bit trickier. To minimize the problem if I had a dizzy spell, I dropped to my hands and knees.

It was then that I saw a larger crevice formed where the ledge met the cliff wall. It was large enough that I could have fit right into it. Instead, I crawled to the far end of the ledge where I'd seen the shiny object. It was a gold locket, and I thought I recognized it. I'd seen Elizabeth McKenzie wearing it in her portrait—and in the photo that Pepper had given me of Cameron.

Fear crept into me and settled in a cold, hard ball in my stomach as two scenarios played themselves out in my mind like little film clips. In one, the locket was ripped off as Cameron struggled with her attacker. In the next, she was standing at the edge of the cliff, fingering the locket as she tried to figure out what to do, and she'd torn the locket away herself when she'd been pushed. In both images, I could picture Cameron falling and striking the rocks below.

A wave of dizziness struck me with such force that my stomach pitched, and I nearly lost the little picnic lunch that I'd just enjoyed. I flattened myself on the ledge and ordered myself to breathe. I gripped the locket tightly in my hand as if by doing so I could hold on to my sister, and gradually the images faded.

The instant the dizziness eased, I knew that I had to get off the ledge. And I couldn't afford to think about it. After tucking the locket into my pocket, I inched my way back to where I'd landed. Then I drew in a deep breath and, using the crevices in the cliff wall for support, I rose to my feet and began the climb upward.

It wasn't as easy as the trip down. The wind

seemed to have picked up a bit. I thought that I could hear someone calling my name. One hand-hold, one foothold at a time, I told myself. It was one thing not to look down, but it was another much harder thing not to picture the distance to the rock ledge in my mind. My heart was beating fast when my hand finally clamped down on the rocks that bordered the cliff.

I felt one swift wave of relief followed by a spurt of pure panic when the rock beneath my left foot crumbled. As I dug the fingers of both hands into the cliff, I pictured rocks plummeting through the air and smacking into the foamy sea below. All the weight of my body was on my weak ankle. A wave of dizziness hit me, and for a moment I felt myself teeter. I was going to fall.

A hand grabbed my wrist. A second later another hand joined the first and I felt myself being hauled upward. The moment that my feet were on solid ground, Sloan's hands gripped my shoulders and he gave me a hard shake.

I opened my eyes to see fear in his.

"Are you all right? What happened? Did you fall?"

"No. I climbed down because I saw something."

He gave me another shake and fury joined the fear in his eyes.

"I found something." Reaching into my pocket,

I pulled out the locket. "It was on the ledge. It's hers, isn't it?"

Sloan took the locket. "Yes. She wore this every day."

"Someone pushed her. It must have torn off in the struggle. I—"

I couldn't go on. There was something in my throat that stopped me. A sob. I didn't realize it, but I must have been crying because Sloan pulled me abruptly against his chest and just held me close. I might have been able to pull myself together if he hadn't done that. I'd been so certain that Cameron was alive—I still wanted to believe that she was. I wanted to be able to get to know her, to love her. And then I thought of Sloan and I held on to him even tighter and wept for both our loss.

It was more than an hour later before we got back to the ranch. The troopers had found some tire tracks and they'd remained at the scene to make plaster casts.

Sloan was angry with me. On the ride back to the hacienda, he barely said a word to me. At least Gus hadn't overheard my outburst about Cameron. He'd still been inspecting the damage to the plane when Sloan had realized I was missing and the older man had stayed with the troopers.

Once I'd recovered from my weep-athon, I'd

tried to convince myself that the two scenes I'd pictured so vividly in my mind could be worst-case scenarios. Finding the locket on the cliff didn't necessarily mean that Cameron had fallen over. There could be other explanations.

Along with my inner Alice, I also had an inner Little Mary Sunshine. I didn't want to give up on Cameron yet.

But it wasn't looking good.

Now that I'd gotten a bit of a grip on myself, I was willing to concede that Sloan might have a reason to be upset with me. I'd taken a risk climbing down to the ledge. But I'd found Cameron's locket. That had to count for something. We now had proof that Cameron had been to the cliff, and that something had happened to make her drop it.

When Gus finally pulled his truck to a stop at the stables, Sloan told me to go up to the main house. He'd be up as soon as he and Gus made arrangements for the plane. Then they disappeared into Sloan's office. I didn't much like being dismissed as if I were a disobedient child. Still, I started to do just what he'd said—partly because I'd been raised to be a "good girl." One of the reasons I was growing to like Cameron was because I sensed that she had a little more of the "bad girl" in her than I did.

Then there was the fact that the day had been an eventful one. I'd had mind-blowing sex, nearly lost my life in a plane crash, faced my biggest fear by climbing down to that ledge, and then indulged in a crying jag.

Okay, so it was only twenty feet to the cliff. I'd still done it. And I'd found Cameron's locket. Going up to the hacienda would give me some time to figure out what it meant.

Or I could battle Hannibal over who the bed really belonged to and take a nap.

Both of those options disappeared the instant I saw Marcie, Austin and Hal coming out of one of the stable doors.

"There you are," Marcie called. "I told Austin you hadn't forgotten we were going riding."

Truth be told, I had. Completely. I tried to glance at my watch unobtrusively, and found that it was a little after three. Time flies when you're being shot down out of the sky.

"We had your horse saddled for you," Marcie added.

I thought of the promise I'd made to Sloan that I wouldn't go off with any one of them alone. But this was a group. Surely, there was safety in numbers. Besides, time was of the essence, and if I went with them, I might be able to find out more about Cameron's disappearance.

Hal and Austin each led a saddled horse, and Marcie was leading two. Doc Carter and Beatrice brought up the rear of the little parade, sans horses.

"You haven't changed your mind, have you?" Marcie asked.

I hesitated for one more instant. But when the horse neighed softly and pushed her nose into my shoulder, I was immediately won over. Hadn't I been longing for a ride ever since I'd first stood on that bluff and seen the horses?

"Of course, I haven't changed my mind." I smiled at Marcie and took the reins she held out to me. Then I turned to Beatrice and Doc Carter. "Will you be joining us?"

Doc Carter chuckled. "Not today. Austin and Marcie wanted us to see the horses that the Radcliffs are turning over to us. You young ones go off and enjoy yourselves." He took my hand and patted it. "Perhaps we can get together when you get back."

"Sure."

"See you then."

Hal and Austin were already seated by the time I put my foot in the stirrup and mounted my horse. She was a beauty and as I leaned over to pat her neck, I asked Marcie, "What's her name?"

"Oh, sorry. I keep forgetting about the amnesia. Her name is Lace Ribbons. You call her Lacey."

I patted her neck. "You're a beauty, Lacey." And she was. She was black as pitch with not a brown hair on her. And she had a dainty air about her. I thought of Saturn and felt that they might make a perfect match.

"You've had her since she was a two-year-old. You never ride any other mount," Marcie said.

Austin and Hal were leading the way out of the stable yard, and we fell in behind them.

"Why don't I ride any other horse?" I asked.

Marcie glanced at me. "I never thought much about it. But you confessed to me once that you'd been thrown off a horse as a child, and you'd been careful about your mounts ever since. Lace Ribbons has perfect manners."

I didn't doubt that she did. But I was thinking of Saturn.

I saw that Austin and Hal were leading us toward the area of the ranch behind the hacienda and its gardens. I searched the map I'd made in my mind on the bluff the day before and recalled that a stream, bordered by woods, wound its way through this part of the property.

Sure enough, Austin urged his horse into a trot and started toward the stream. It had been so long since I'd ridden that I was yearning for a fast run. I was about to say so to Marcie when she moved her horse forward and Austin fell back.

I bit back a sigh and managed a smile for my "cousin." I had a hunch that the Lintons and Austin had an agenda that didn't include the gallop I was longing for.

"I want to apologize for my behavior last night," he said as soon as he drew alongside me.

To my surprise, I heard a note of sincerity in his tone and read it in his expression. "No apology needed. I'm sure that my sudden return must have been a…" I paused to search for the right word. "…a bit of a shock to you."

Austin met my eyes steadily. "I'm happy to know that you're all right. It's just…"

"That you've been doing very well in the business and you think now that I'm back, that will change."

"I know it will." There was anger in his tone. His jaw tensed, and his knuckles whitened on the hand holding the reins. "Everything will go back to the way it was."

Austin's horse, sensing the anger, moved restlessly beneath him, and I became aware suddenly of the fact that my cousin and I were virtually alone. We'd ridden more deeply into the woods and we were going even more slowly now, following the winding path of the stream. Marcie and Hal had moved ahead and trees blocked them from my sight.

"Why don't you tell me why you think everything will change now," I said.

"Because Uncle James doesn't trust me. Now that you're back and you're marrying Sloan, I'll go back to babysitting a desk. He's never given me the kind of chance I deserve."

He sounded a bit like a whining child. "Why not?"

"Because my father had a gambling problem and embezzled hundreds of thousands of dollars while he was running the ranch. No one suspected anything until he died of a heart attack on one of those riverboat gambling cruises."

I made a mental note to tell Pepper that the mystery of Beatrice's disappearing husband had been solved. "That doesn't have anything to do with you."

"It shouldn't. But Uncle James is big on bloodlines. You're his blood. And he figures I've inherited my father's bad genes. Add that to the fact that I've never been able to compete with you and Sloan. I have as much McKenzie blood in me as you do, but I'm not good enough to be trusted with any responsibility."

I studied him for a moment, putting what he'd just told me together with what Marcie had said and with what Pepper had written in her report. "I've been told that you like gambling better than you like to work."

Color flushed Austin's face. Once again, I saw his knuckles whiten. Clearly, my cousin had anger management issues. "I've made mistakes. I know that. While I was in college, I figured if everyone thought I was like my father, I might as well live up to the name. But things have changed since I met Marcie. I've changed, and I've made a fresh start. I know I didn't make a good impression last night, but that was…not me."

"Marcie says that you haven't had that much to drink in a long time."

He met my eyes. "My reformation began when you hired her six months ago. She's made me see things differently because she sees me differently. No one has ever believed in me the way Marcie does. She's helped me to change."

He was in love with her. I could see it in his eyes, hear it in his voice. Did he have any idea that Marcie's interest in reforming him might be motivated by the possibility of his coming into a great deal of money and land? And if Marcie was so intent on helping Austin change his ways, why had she been with him in Vegas on the very day that Cameron had disappeared?

"Look. I've done a good job in the last month. You can even ask Uncle James about that. All I want is the chance to continue."

In spite of the questions and suspicions spinning around in my head, I really wanted to believe Austin. There was the possibility that he'd been taken in by the Lintons and that he was just a pawn in a bigger game the sister and brother were playing. But there was also the possibility that Austin was his father's son and was trying to con me. In my mind, I could picture the story line going either way. And if Austin *was* trying to con me, my best bet was to let him think he'd been successful.

"I don't see that as a problem," I said.

A mixture of relief and hope washed over his face. "You'll give me a chance then?"

I reached out and covered his hand with mine. "Of course, I will."

"Thanks, Cam." He looked so pleased as he leaned over to brush a kiss on my cheek that I felt a twinge of guilt. "I won't disappoint you."

What was he going to think when he found out who I really was and that my assurances meant squat?

As Austin urged his horse forward to join Marcie again, my cell phone rang. I dug it out of my pocket and checked the caller ID. Pepper. I reined in Lace Ribbons. "What have you got?"

"Hello to you, too," Pepper said with a laugh.

"I'm out riding the range," I explained. Well, not really, I thought as I glanced around. As we'd followed the stream, it had widened and the forest had dropped back a bit from the bank. There was still plenty of room for the horses, but trees effectively hemmed us in from the open country.

"You have company I take it, so I'll be brief. Cole checked in Las Vegas, and Austin and Marcie were both seen in a restaurant and at the gaming tables. One of the croupiers remembers that Austin lost about ten thousand dollars. However, no one was able to verify that Hal was with them."

"Interesting," I said. It meant that Austin hadn't been quite truthful about his reformation. He'd been gambling on the day that Cameron had disappeared. It also meant that Hal didn't have an alibi for that day. Ahead of me Austin and Marcie urged their horses into a trot and disappeared around a bend. Hal turned his horse around and headed toward me.

"Beatrice was indeed at the flower show in San Diego," Pepper said. "Several people saw her there. She gave a speech at the luncheon."

So that left Sloan, James, Doc Carter and Hal Linton without alibis. "Any chance you could find out if either of the Lintons have any expertise with guns?" I asked in a low voice as Hal slowly but surely closed the distance between us. Through the trees to my right, I saw that Marcie and Austin had veered off from the path we'd been following and were probably headed out of the woods.

"Sure, but I don't like the sound of that."

What I didn't like was the fact that I'd once more been outmaneuvered by the Lintons. Unless I wanted to turn tail and run back the way we'd come, I was now alone in an isolated area with a man who had no alibi for the day my sister had disappeared. A man who might have a very good reason for wanting her to disappear.

Chapter 17

"I'm sorry for last night," Hal said as he reined to a stop directly in front of me.

No, I decided. I was not going to turn around and run. Mallory Carstairs certainly wouldn't and I didn't think Cameron would, either. Besides, this was my chance to learn more about the man my sister had kissed in the garden the night before she'd gone missing. "This seems to be my day for getting apologies."

He had the grace to wince a bit. "Austin and I both behaved poorly last night."

I couldn't help but wonder if behaving badly was an aberration for Hal Linton, too. I thought it might be. The man had all the marks of one smooth operator. He reminded me a bit of a character on *Secrets* who managed to always come out on top.

Studying Hal, I tried to see him as Cameron might have seen him. With that dark hair, tanned skin and good bones, he was handsome in a pretty way that Sloan wasn't. Hal's features were smooth while Sloan's were rugged. Hal was sleekly groomed, his hair neatly trimmed. Sloan looked as if he was long overdue to see his barber. I remembered how it had felt to run my hands through that hair and of how messed up it had looked when we'd just finished making love. Heat crept into my cheeks.

Hal dismounted and held up his hand. "Why don't we rest the horses and walk for a bit?"

I hesitated, looking to my right, but Marcie and Austin had completely disappeared.

"Please," he said. "This is a place that we came to more than once. Doc Carter thought it might help you remember."

Curious now, I held out my hand and dismounted. Hal's palm was soft and smooth with none of the calluses that were on Sloan's. He was a more sophisticated dresser, too. Last night, he'd worn Armani, and I knew that the golf shirt and riding breeches he wore today had designer labels. There was a sheen of money and sophistication here. This was a man who'd court a woman carefully with flowers, champagne, elegant restaurants. As a lover, he'd be both smooth and skilled.

If Sloan wanted a woman, I didn't think he'd bother with all that. In fact, he hadn't. In my mind, I pictured him standing in the archway to his kitchen and the way he'd looked at me when he'd closed the distance between us. He'd had me right then. But later, he'd provided the romance. I thought of our picnic on that flat rock in Cameron's favorite place.

"Cameron?"

"What?" Dragging my thoughts back, I turned to see Hal looking at me in an odd sort of way.

"Are you all right? Are you remembering something? Do you want me to take you back to the ranch?"

"I'm fine," I said. At least I would be if I could stop thinking about Sloan Campbell. I'd been away from him for—what?—twenty minutes, but I couldn't get him out of my mind. Ridiculous. I should be thinking of finding out what this man might know about my sister's disappearance. "What did you just say?"

"Does this bring back any memories?" He gestured to the space around us, and for the first time I took it in. We'd walked into a little clearing. The stream widened a bit here, and wildflowers grew along its border. Their scent filled the air, and there was a place just ahead of us where a cluster of trees offered complete privacy. "It's lovely."

"But you don't remember anything?"

I met his eyes and saw that he was studying me very intently. "I don't remember ever being here before."

There was a tightening in his jaw that I didn't like. So there was temper beneath that smooth-as-silk facade. While I found it interesting, I didn't much like the fact that I'd let myself be manipulated into being alone with him. He was even carrying my horse's reins.

Drawing in a deep breath, he said, "I don't want to pressure you. Doc Carter said that's the worst thing I could do."

"What exactly do you want, Hal?"

"I want you to remember what we meant to each other, what we were before you went away."

To my surprise, it wasn't just temper I saw, but pain and perhaps regret. Had Hal Linton actually been in love with Cameron? Had she been in love with him? Was that what she had gone to the cliffs to think about? I wanted to know.

"What exactly were we to each other?" I asked.

Hal looked at me for a moment. "Do you know how hard it is for me to see you standing there, to hear you say that you can't remember me? We were…friends. I wanted more. You didn't. But that was going to change."

"Why?"

"Because you were having second thoughts about marrying Sloan."

"I told you that?"

"Yes. Several times. You told me that the night before you disappeared, the night that your fiancé eavesdropped on us and caught us kissing in the garden."

Something knotted in my stomach.

He gripped my shoulders. His hands might have been smooth, but they were strong. I felt a skip of panic.

"You're in danger. I sensed it that night. I should have done something. If I had..." He broke off, releasing me as if he'd just realized he'd grabbed hold of me. He ran a hand through his hair. "Sorry. I promised myself that I wouldn't touch you."

He turned and paced a few steps away, as if he had to keep his distance if he was going to keep his promise. "I'm going to tell you something that I didn't tell you before you left. When I ran into you at the Derby, it wasn't by accident. I was hired by the group of investors who have approached your father with an offer to buy this place. My job was to make contact with you, to get close to you. Hell, I was supposed to use any means I could—including seduction—to convince you to persuade your father to sell the place."

"The surprise announcement of my engagement to Sloan must have thrown a spanner into the works."

Through the tan I could see a flush stain his cheeks.

"I'm not proud now of what I had planned to do. At the time, when my associates proposed the job, it seemed easy enough. It paid well, and I found you attractive. That was the kind of man I was before I met you. Everything changed then. The last six months we've had fun together. You're different than other women for me. We'd become friends. You confided in me. And I fell in love with you."

I didn't say anything. I couldn't speak for Cameron. And I wasn't quite sure that he was telling the truth. He looked sincere enough, but the man had to be an accomplished liar to have gotten where he was in life.

"I won't tell you that you felt the same way," Hal said.

I raised my brows. "Isn't that exactly what you tried to do last night?"

His face reddened even more. "I was worried about you. You have amnesia, for God's sake. I wanted to give you some reason for not being swept up in James's plans again. Believe the worst about me. But I want you to know that you were having second thoughts about your upcoming marriage on the night before you disappeared."

He took a step toward me, but kept his hands at his sides. "Don't marry him, Cameron. For your own sake, wait at least until you get your memory back and can remember why it was that you felt you had to run away from here."

Once again, I couldn't think of anything to say. Everything he said made sense, and his account of what had happened in the garden matched Sloan's. Was he confessing all this because he was concerned about my safety? Or was he doing it on purpose to confuse me?

Marcie, Austin and Hal all seemed perfectly fooled by my impersonation. They believed that I was Cameron McKenzie suffering from amnesia. The person who'd been suspicious of me from the get-go was Sloan. Was that because he knew what had really happened to Cameron?

No. I didn't believe that. He'd been in that plane with me. Both of us could have been killed. My head began to spin, and I pressed a hand to my temple. Not because I was suspicious of Sloan, I wasn't. It had just been an eventful day. I'd been shot down in a plane, nearly toppled off a cliff.

"Something is wrong." Hal took my arm. "I'll take you back to Doc Carter."

"No. I'm fine. I—" I broke off when I heard hoofbeats approaching, and I knew before I turned that it would be Sloan and Saturn. I could feel the anger radiating off him in waves as he reined in Saturn and dismounted. But his voice was controlled and it was Hal he addressed when he reached us.

"Your sister and Austin are waiting for you. James sent me to bring Cameron back. He needs to see her."

Sloan's tone was even, pleasant almost, but it was clear that Hal was being dismissed.

Hal turned to me, a worried expression on his face. "I'll stay if you like."

"No." I didn't glance at Sloan. I knew he'd have that mocking look in his eyes. "I have something that I want to talk to Sloan about before we go back."

Hal's expression changed, lightened. "Good. That's good." He gave Sloan a nod before he mounted his horse. "See you in a bit then."

Sloan waited until Hal was out of sight and ear-shot before he turned to me and even then he kept his voice low. "You promised that you wouldn't go off alone with any of them."

"I didn't go off alone. There were four of us." Okay, technically, I knew I was on shaky ground.

"I only counted two when I got here." His voice might have been under control, but there was anger in his eyes and in the way he grabbed my arm to lead me toward the horses. "C'mon."

"Wait just a minute." I dug in my heels. Maybe it was the culmination of the dramatic events of the day, or maybe it was because I felt I was being lectured like a child, but my own temper rose to meet his. "I came here to try to find out what happened to my sister. I can't do that if I'm confined to the house. Austin, Marcie and Hal all have reasons to want Cameron to disappear."

"Which is exactly why it was reckless and stupid of you to go off riding with them."

"Stupid?" I used my free hand to poke him in the chest.

"Yes, stupid."

I poked him again. "Stupid was sitting around for five weeks without even wondering if something had happened to Cameron."

I saw in his eyes that my comment had struck home.

"Okay—you've got a point. But you've convinced me that Cameron is at the very least in trouble. And so are you. The plane nearly crashed. You nearly fell off that cliff. I came close to losing you twice, and then I learn you've gone off riding with three of the people who might have been responsible for Cameron's disappearance!" Sloan grabbed my shoulders and gave me a shake. "Which is why you're going to go back to the house and stay put until we figure out who's behind all this."

He'd raised his voice, so I did, too. "Until we figure this out, *we* includes me. I'm not going to cower in my room. I came here to find my sister, and you're not going to stop me!"

His eyes were bright angry slits. "You're just like her—stubborn, unreasonable—"

"I'm not Cameron."

He gave me another shake. "No, you're not. She could never push me this far. No one could. No one but you."

His mouth crushed down on mine, and in one fluid move I was beneath him on the ground. Passion erupted with such force, such speed. Was this what had been simmering inside of him since he'd pulled me to safety off that ledge? Was this what had been simmering inside of me?

Those hands could be so gentle. This time they weren't. This time he was relentless. Those hard, callused fingers ran over my skin in that meticulous way he had, scraping, setting new fires and fueling the ones that were already burning.

This is what I'd been craving—the fury, the fire, the freedom. I yanked at his shirt, pulling it free of his jeans and ran my hands up his back, exploring the steely strength of those muscles.

Roughly, he bit my bottom lip and more flames shot to life inside of me. I could feel everything— the hard ground beneath my back, the sharp press of pebbles through the thin silk of my blouse. With each breath, I drew in the scent of wildflowers, horses and Sloan. I saw the play of light and shadow over my closed eyelids.

And his taste—I couldn't seem to get enough of the endless flavors that I found each time he kissed me. There was always something new, some elusive nuance that I hadn't sampled before. This time I tasted anger, but there was also desire—hot, dark, restless. And addicting.

My whole world narrowed to this moment, to him, to us and what we could bring each other.

He rolled over suddenly so that I was straddling him and he began to work on my clothes, pulling the buttons loose. I heard the erotic sound of silk tearing as I struggled with his belt. Once I yanked his shirt up, he rose to help me pull it off. We discarded clothes, hands grasping, groping, fumbling, growing more and more desperate.

Free at last, he rolled me beneath him again and took his hands on another lethal journey. I thought he'd shown me everything before, but he unveiled more secrets as he began to use his mouth on me.

Each one of my muscles melted, my bones liquefied, and one shudder after another racked my body as Sloan took his lips and teeth on a journey down my torso, my stomach and inner thigh and finally up again. He was taking things from me, things I'd never get back, and I only wanted to give him more.

My fingers were digging into his shoulders,

my voice crying out his name when he finally put his mouth to my center. The climax slammed into me, a hard, bare-fisted punch that sent me flying higher and higher into a spiral that it seemed I might never come out of. I was still shuddering when he rose over me to sheathe himself in the condom.

I should have been sated, but I wanted more.

He positioned himself between my legs, then framed my face with his hands. "I want you."

"Take me," I said.

He thrust into me, quick and hard, and then we began to move piston quick. With each second, with each thrust, there was more and more plea-sure, seemingly endless until we shot headlong over that final airless peak—and shattered.

Afterward, we lay together on the ground. Some-how, I'd ended up sprawled across his chest with no clear memory of how I'd gotten there. My head rested on his shoulder, my hand on his chest. I could feel his heart beat fast and steady beneath my hand, hear the sound of his breathing in my ear. Above that came the sound of the stream, the rustle of leaves. Inexplicably, I felt at home.

And I shouldn't. I couldn't. Still, I let myself drift, savoring the feeling. When I finally stirred, I felt his arms tighten around me for a second before he let me raise my head and meet his eyes.

"Who won?" I asked.

Sloan's lips curved in one of those rare smiles as he pulled some twigs out of my hair. "The fight? I did."

My eyes narrowed. "In your dreams. Want to go another round?"

He laughed and I felt my heart do that little flutter thing again. It was happening more frequently, and I was going to have to think about it. Just not now.

"I'm not sure I'm up to it," he said as he sat up and settled me more comfortably on his lap. Then his expression sobered and something like regret slid into his eyes. Lifting a hand, he tucked my hair behind my ears. "What am I going to do with you, Brooke Ashby?"

He was talking about more than settling our argument, but I pretended that was what he'd meant. "How about a compromise? You want me to stay in my room, and I need to keep investigating what happened to Cameron. I've already made people uncomfortable."

The sound he made was close to a snort. "You've done more than that. Someone shot our plane down. And the minute I turn my back, the Lintons and Austin have spirited you away. I want to call off your whole masquerade."

I drew in a deep breath and marshaled all the arguments I could think of. "Just give me until tomorrow night. As long as everyone thinks I'm Cameron, we have a better chance of learning something."

"And you have a better chance of getting hurt."

I turned and met his eyes steadily. "If it turns out that I'm James's biological daughter, I might be in just as much danger as Cameron was."

For a moment, Sloan's arms tightened around me. Then they relaxed. "I wish to hell that I didn't agree with you."

Pushing my advantage, I said, "How about we work together until we figure it out? I won't spend another minute out of your sight."

He considered that for a minute. "I took you up in the plane and nearly got us both killed."

"We weren't killed thanks to you."

He was on the brink of agreeing with me, so I summoned up all my debate skills. "Even if you lock me in my room, I'll find a way to get out. I'm only on the second floor. I've had experience tying bedsheets together and rappelling down walls."

He studied me. "For a woman who's afraid of heights, you've picked up some interesting skills."

I nearly had him. "You were right earlier. I am stubborn. I'm not going to give up on this, and two heads are better than one." I gave him a quick kiss. "It means that we'd spend more time together, and I'd owe you big-time."

The corners of his mouth curved. "Are we talking about sexual favors?"

I smiled at him. "I certainly hope so."

Sloan framed my face with his hands and ran his thumbs gently over my cheekbones. "Okay, but I want your word that you won't go off on your own again."

"You've got it. And I want yours that we share all information. Like what you were doing in your office with Gus while I was riding out here with the Lintons and Austin."

"I told Gus and he'll tell Elena who you really are, and I brought Gus up to speed on what we now believe about Cameron's disappearance." He pressed his fingers to my lips. "I told you before that I trust Gus, and we can trust Elena, too. They'll watch our backs."

"Okay. I guess we could use that."

"Gus is checking into who might have used that SUV this morning, and he'll keep tabs on comings and goings. Elena can be our eyes and ears in the house. What did you learn from the Lintons and Austin?"

"Not much. They're either totally innocent or they're accomplished liars."

I filled him in on the update Pepper had given me on the alibis, as well as what I'd discovered during the ride. "Austin sounds like he really wants a chance to prove that he's not his father's son.

And Hal—I hate to say it—but he's got me almost believing that he really fell for Cameron."

"That might explain why she was kissing him in the garden," he said. "But both Austin and Hal have every reason in the world to lie to you. And Hal doesn't have an alibi for the day Cameron disappeared. They could be working together."

I smiled ruefully. "There's that, of course."

"You have a soft heart, Brooke Ashby."

"Did Cameron?" I asked, suddenly hungry to know more about my twin.

Sloan thought for a moment. "She had a tougher outer shell than you. And she wasn't above running a few cons herself. She had a lot of James in her."

As we talked about Cameron in the past tense again, I felt my throat tightening. "In spite of everything we've learned today, I can't think of Cameron as being dead. I've had this feeling all along that she's in trouble, and that I had to do something about it—fast. But I never had the feeling that she was dead."

Sloan tipped my chin up so that our eyes met. "We'll find out."

The words and his simple faith in them cheered me. "And isn't it convenient that we have all the prime suspects gathered together in one house— just like in an Agatha Christie novel?" Another thought struck me. "And we owe that to James. The wily old fox."

"What do you mean?" Sloan asked.

"Scheduling the wedding for tomorrow was a perfect excuse to keep everyone here. If he hadn't done that, Marcie and Hal and Austin would have gone right back to Saratoga Springs. The races and the parties have another week to run."

"Yeah, you're right. I've been wondering just what James's role is in all of this."

"You're not thinking he was involved in Cameron's disappearance?"

"No. But it's just like him to find a way to keep everyone here and try to stir something up. You're like him in that way."

That surprised me. "I am?"

His brows shot up. "You came here masquerading as your sister with a story of memory loss. I'd call that a sure-fire recipe for stirring things up. And you've succeeded."

With that he shifted me to the ground, rose to his feet and held out a hand.

I found myself reluctant to take it. Once we were back at the hacienda, I'd have to start thinking again and planning. Who should I talk to? What kinds of questions should I ask? And I'd have to think about Sloan. What we had was temporary, I wasn't going to lie to myself about that. And I could feel the minutes I had with him ticking away.

"C'mon," Sloan said. "We can rinse off in the stream before we ride back."

The moment I was on my feet, he scooped me up in his arms, carried me into the stream, and when the water reached his waist, abruptly let me go. Then to top it off, he placed a hand on my head and shoved me under.

I was sputtering when I finally surfaced. And Sloan was laughing. It took me two tries to get my feet under me, and he rewarded me by cupping water in both hands and throwing it in my face. I choked, lost my footing and went under again. When I came up, I saw that he'd gone into fresh gales of laughter.

My heart did more than a flutter this time. It went into a full-fledged somersault. I pressed my hand against my chest. This serious, enigmatic man I'd been fascinated with from the first time I'd seen his picture had just dropped me in a stream and purposely dunked me.

It was while I was watching him, his head thrown back, the sound of his laugh filling the air around us, that I admitted to myself what I'd been trying to deny since the first time I'd looked into his eyes. I could fall in love with Sloan Campbell.

A mix of panic and joy swirled through me. Talk about complications. I had no idea how to plot my way out of this. And since I didn't want to think about it and was barely ready to accept it, I decided that I could at least get even with him. Drawing in a deep breath, I slipped under the water, then pushed off in his direction. Circling around, I came up behind him, grabbed one of his feet and yanked it hard. Looking up through the water, I saw his arms flail and then he pitched forward like a felled tree.

Of course, my revenge would have been more perfect if I could have escaped unscathed. But he twisted, grabbed my waist and pulled me close. In the wavering shafts of light piercing the gray water, he looked like some kind of sea god, and I wanted him as fiercely as I had such a short time before.

As if he'd read my mind, he kissed me. Sensations shot through me—the chill of the water, the heat of his mouth and hands. The hardness of his fingers at my waist, the soft, thorough movement of his tongue on mine.

Suddenly we were shooting upward. Sloan dragged his mouth from mine, and we both drew in huge gulps of air.

"We could have drowned."

"We might yet," he said as he lifted me and positioned my legs around him. "I want you." Suiting actions to words, he pushed into me. But it wasn't far enough. I tightened my legs around him and tried to wiggle closer.

"Hold on tight."

I thought then that he was going to move to the bank of the stream, but instead, he withdrew and pushed in again, withdrew and pushed in again, teasing me. When he withdrew the third time, he paused. "I don't have a condom."

"I'm on the pill."

His gaze narrowed. "Are you involved with someone back in L.A.?"

"No. I like to be prepared."

"Good." He thrust into me this time all the way. "That's good."

I couldn't have agreed more. Then we both began to move. The water was working against us, slowing us down, keeping the ultimate pleasure just out of reach until I thought I would simply go mad.

"Now." Sloan's voice was hoarse, his fingers digging into my hips. "Come with me, Brooke."

When he thrust into me, I did.

Chapter 18

The afternoon sun was low in the sky and the shadows long when Sloan finally gave me a leg up onto Lace Ribbons. I felt both guilt and reluctance as I settled myself in the saddle. Guilt because we'd tarried longer than we probably should have. With each moment that passed, my "wedding day" was getting closer, and my masquerade would be over. So would the best chance I had of finding out what had happened to Cameron. I glanced back at the stream. In spite of that, I was reluctant to let go of this time that I'd spent together with Sloan. How would I feel when I had to leave Sloan forever?

As if he'd read my mind—which I was beginning to think he could—he laid a hand over mine. "We have to talk about us."

Panic skittered up my spine. I thought I knew what he wanted to tell me, and I didn't want to hear it yet. "First things first. We have to find out what happened to Cameron."

His hand tightened on mine before he released me. "Then we're coming back here where we can be alone. Promise me."

"All right." I managed a smile. "Although this is not the safest place to come. We nearly drowned twice by my count."

"Nonsense. You just need a little practice building up the time you can hold your breath. I'd be glad to help you."

"Oh, really? The way I recall it I nearly had to use CPR on you that last time we went under."

He was laughing as he untied Saturn.

I was finding this new playful side of Sloan delightful. Inspired by it, I called, "I'll beat you to the stables." Without waiting for him to mount up, I loosened my hold on the reins and used my heels on Lace Ribbons.

She responded beautifully, springing into a canter that took us quickly out of the trees. Then at my urging she accelerated into a full gallop. I leaned over her and said, "We have a head start, girl. Let's make the most of it."

If we'd started out together, Saturn and Sloan

would have left us in the dust, but with the handicap I'd given us, we might have a chance. "C'mon, Lacey." Air parted, then whipped past us and the ground fell away beneath us. I could hear hoofbeats now. Sloan and Saturn were gaining on us.

If I stayed on the route that Austin had chosen, there would be no contest. So instead, I bided my time and tried a surprise. When Sloan was nearly on me, I veered right and headed for a fence. He'd have to check his momentum to follow me, and that would buy me some time.

"C'mon, Lacey," I crooned to her. "Show me what you can do." I bent over her as she raced forward. The fence was only about ten yards away when I felt the saddle slip to the right. I leaned hard to my left, trying to compensate. But the horse faltered, unsettled by the shift in balance. Panicked, she reared up. Dropping the reins, I grabbed for her mane and kicked free of the stirrups. She reared up again, and when she came down this time, she bucked, lunged forward, and I hurtled over her head.

Time seemed to slow while I was airborne. My whole life didn't flash before my eyes but I did manage to conjure up an image of my first riding instructor. A tall man with the build of Ichabod Crane, his constant advice to me had been to tuck and roll. I tried, but when I rolled my head smacked hard into something. Stars exploded and the world went black.

I kept my eyes closed because the pounding behind them was more muted then. I could hear Sloan's voice. He was talking in that soft, authoritative tone that was becoming so familiar to me. The other voice belonged to James, and his tone was angry but hushed, so I couldn't make the words out. Or maybe I just didn't want to put in the effort.

Sloan had carried me to James's suite of rooms as soon as we'd arrived at the ranch. The trip back was pretty much a blur because I kept drifting in and out of consciousness. Now I wanted very much to sleep. To escape.

Cool fingers closed over my wrist. "Don't go to sleep, Cameron."

The knife-sharp pain in my head became more intense. As did the memory of my mad race across the field toward the fence, the slipping saddle and the breath-stealing impact of my body slamming into the ground. Pushing the images away, I tried to sit up and firm hands settled on my shoulders.

"Not yet."

I opened my eyes and found myself looking into Doc Carter's. He released my wrist and began to shine a small light into my eyes. "Her eyes look fine. Her pulse is steady."

"You don't have to talk about me as if I'm not in the room."

Doc Carter held up three fingers. "How many?"

"Three."

"What day of the week is it?"

"Thursday."

Doc nodded at me. "Fine. And what's your name?"

I opened my mouth and caught myself just before I said Brooke. "Cameron McKenzie."

He smiled down at me. "So far so good. It's been a long time since you were unseated by a horse, young lady."

Then abruptly, it wasn't Doc Carter's face leaning over mine. It was Sloan's.

"How do you feel?" His face was drawn with worry, and his mouth was set in a grim line.

Suddenly worried myself, I wiggled toes, fingers. "Is anything broken except my head?"

"No. I checked you out pretty thoroughly before I moved you."

"I don't see any signs of a concussion," Doc Carter said. "But I could drive her into San Diego."

"No." Sloan and I spoke in unison.

I levered myself into a sitting position and managed not to wince. "I'm not going to a hospital. I had my fill of them after my mugging." And I had less than twenty-four hours left to find out what had happened to Cameron. "I just fell off a horse. I'll live." And then I remembered. "The saddle…"

"The girth was cut," Sloan said as he took one of my hands in his. "The run created too much stress and it tore the rest of the way."

I gripped Sloan's hand tighter, but I kept my gaze on Doc Carter. "Who saddled my horse?"

His eyes widened. "I don't know."

"You were there. You and Beatrice came out of the stable with Austin and the Lintons."

Now Carter was frowning. "Beatrice, Austin and the Lintons were in the stables when I arrived. A call had come in for Austin and Elena asked me to deliver the message. The horses were already saddled when I got there."

"I'll have Gus check into it," Sloan said.

"Well." Doc Carter closed his bag. "I want you to take it easy for the next day or so. Don't go to sleep for a while."

I made the mistake of nodding and pain sliced into my head again. "Aspirin?"

He took a bottle out of his case and shook two pills into my palm. I swallowed both of them dry before he handed me a glass of water.

Doc turned toward James. "Shall I tell Beatrice to hold dinner for you?"

"No," James directed. "Tell her to go ahead and serve dinner without us. Elena will bring something up when we're ready."

None of us spoke again until Doc Carter left the room. Then Sloan looked at me. "We're going to tell James everything."

I opened my mouth, but Sloan held up a hand. "First someone shoots at you, then your saddle girth is cut. I'm putting a stop to your masquerade right now."

"No need to argue about it," James said. "I already know who she is. She's Brooke Ashby, and she's here because I sent her that letter telling her that she was adopted."

Minutes later, I was still trying to absorb what James had revealed. He'd forestalled questions, insisting that Sloan pour us each some of the brandy he kept in his desk.

I waited for Sloan to sit down beside me before I asked the question that was foremost in my mind. "Do you know what happened to Cameron?"

"Yes, I know." His face and his tone were grim. "But what I say stays in this room. Agreed?"

"All right." I nodded.

Sloan looked angry. "I'm not promising anything."

James studied him for a minute. "Her life and Cameron's life might depend on your silence."

"She's alive then?" I linked my fingers with Sloan's. "Where?"

James took a sip of his brandy. "She's safe in L.A. I've hired security for her."

"So she did run away," Sloan said. "And you knew all the while where she was."

"I knew where she was. But she didn't run away. The morning after you quarreled, she went to that spot she loves so much by the ocean. She told me that morning that she was having second thoughts about going through with the wedding." Frowning, he waved an impatient hand. "Not because she was falling for that Linton character. She wasn't. The gal was too smart for that. She was keeping tabs on him like I asked her to."

He paused to take another sip of his brandy. The light was beginning to fade outside, and Sloan reached to turn on a lamp.

"She was upset that morning," James continued. "She told me that she believed Linton was really falling for her, and that was causing her to have second thoughts about settling for a marriage of convenience. Said maybe the both of you deserved better. I've no doubt she would have come around and done the sensible thing. She always does. But while she was out there on the cliff, someone came up behind her and pushed her over."

I tightened my grip on Sloan's hand.

"Brooke figured that much out this morning," Sloan said. "She climbed down and found Cameron's locket on the ledge."

"Smart gal." He shot me an approving glance. "The ledge saved Cameron's life. But it knocked her out for a while. When she came to, it was dark. She had her cell phone in her pocket and she called me, told me what happened and drove herself back here. We sat right in this very spot and decided what to do next."

"So she drove her car back here and not the would-be killer?" I asked.

"Yes." There was a ruthless light in James's eyes now. "I wanted the bastard to worry and wonder how that car had gotten back here. And whether or not Cameron could still be alive."

"So you let us all believe that she'd gone away to think about the wedding," Sloan said.

James nodded. "Then I waited for someone to show their hand."

"And you didn't think I had a right to know where she was?" Sloan asked. His voice was soft and tight with anger.

When he answered, James's voice was tired. "Cameron didn't see who pushed her. The noise of the sea and the wind blocked any sound. I wasn't about to trust anyone." He met Sloan's eyes steadily. "You'll have to forgive the overprotectiveness of a father."

A tense silence followed.

I took a sip of my brandy to ease the tightness in my throat. "Why L.A.?"

James met my eyes, and I saw regret and something else, something that I'd seen before when he looked at me. Hunger? "She wanted to see you, to be close to you."

"She knew about me?"

"I told her that night when we were deciding what to do. I'd been thinking of getting in touch with you, but it was her idea that I send you that letter. We figured that you'd make an appearance here and that would stir things up."

"The return of the long-lost twin?" I asked around the tight ball that had formed in my throat. "How could you have been so sure I'd take the bait?"

James gave me a steady look. "You have McKenzie genes in you. I knew that curiosity would bring you here. But I wasn't expecting the memory loss story—that was a stroke of genius. I had to move up the wedding to really force the attacker's hand."

There was a knock on the door, and Sloan rose to answer it. The interruption gave me a chance to play James's words over in my mind. "You have McKenzie blood." What I'd suspected but never quite believed had turned out to be true. I was James and Elizabeth's daughter. And my sister was alive.

Elena came in pushing a cart, and for a while the only sound in the room was the clink of china and silver as she set out dinner on James's desk. When she'd lit the candles and pushed the cart out of the room, James said, "Shall we eat?"

I put my brandy snifter down. "I can't. Not until you tell me why you gave me up for adoption."

Sloan returned to his place beside me and took my hand in his. "You're going to have to explain that to me, too."

James kept his eyes steady on mine. "I gave you up for adoption because I loved your mother, and I thought it would save her life. I thought I was in love with my first wife, Sarah, too. But we met in our teens, and during the ten years we were married, we changed, grew up I guess. She wanted something besides ranch life. I wasn't surprised when she ran away. The surprise was that she chose my best friend." He nodded to Sloan. "Your father."

"That must have been hard," I said.

"I told myself that it happens. Lancelot was Arthur's best friend, and Guinevere fell for him. I hoped that they would be happy together."

"They were in love, then?" I asked.

"Why else would they have run off together?"

"You didn't try to find them?"

"Sure." James frowned. "But the P.I. I hired never found a trace."

I gripped Sloan's hand harder. Because we were

talking about his father, and it didn't sound as if James had really wanted to find them.

"I was fifty-five when I met Elizabeth Cameron, and it was love at first sight for both of us. I took one look at her and thought this was the woman I was meant to be with. It was the same for her. She'd never wanted to marry, never considered it until she met me. What we shared was a rare and special kind of love—the kind that you experience when you meet the mate that you were created for. If you haven't experienced it, you won't understand what I'm saying."

I thought I knew what he was talking about, but I didn't dare look at Sloan, didn't dare think about it.

"Elizabeth was thirty-five when we married, twenty years my junior. The one bone of contention between us was that I wanted children and she didn't. She didn't want anything else to interfere with her art. In her mind, marriage had interfered enough. But I persisted. I'm not sorry about that. In the end she gave in and agreed to give me one child."

James took another sip of brandy, then set the glass down. "From the beginning of the pregnancy, she was plagued with depression. I took her to the best doctors, and finally we ended up in a clinic in Switzerland where they supposedly had some expertise. But they could do nothing for her. When the doctor told me we were having twins, I didn't dare tell her. I know it sounds unbelievable now, but when the person you love is sick, you become desperate. Your mother's psychological condition was too delicate, too precarious. I was afraid that another baby might push her over the edge."

He drew in a breath and let it out. "That's when I made the hardest decision I've ever made. I brought you back here on a separate plane and arranged for your adoption through a private agency. I selected your parents because I recognized in your mother the same kind of dedication to work that I'd seen in Elizabeth. And I suppose that giving you to them helped me to live with the guilt I felt for pressuring Elizabeth into having you and Cameron."

Odd—there was a part of me that wanted to cry, but my eyes were as dry as dust. "Did Doc Carter know about my adoption?"

James met my eyes. "No one knew about it. I handled it myself. The first person I told about it was your sister."

"And did it work? Did bringing just one baby home help Elizabeth to get better?"

"Yes. For a while she was fine, back to her old self. She loved Cameron, and told me more than once that she was glad I'd pressured her into having a child of our own. With all the drugs in her system during delivery, she didn't remember having two babies. I thought everything was going to be fine.

Then without warning, her bouts of depression returned. This time none of the medications worked. There were times when she couldn't get out of bed. She couldn't paint. That was what destroyed her. She felt that she'd lost her art. Then she committed suicide. Carter said it was postpartum depression. They were just beginning to recognize it as a disease. But that doesn't change the fact that by pressuring Elizabeth to have a child, I killed her and lost you."

There was silence in the room. So many emotions were pouring through me, and I couldn't help feeling sorry for the man who was sitting across from me.

Finally James spoke. "Can you ever forgive me?"

I studied him for a moment. "I think you've been punished enough. You made the best decision that you could, the one that you thought was right. And I have really wonderful parents." But my hand shook as I set down my brandy glass.

Sloan rose and drew me to my feet. "She's tired. I think she's had enough for one night."

James met his eyes. "She shouldn't be alone."

"She won't be."

I followed Sloan to the door before I remembered the other question I needed to ask. I turned back to find James watching me. "My P.I. friend found papers showing that both Cameron and I were adopted. Why?"

"When I sent you the letter, I also took care to plant the other papers. Over the years, I've contributed quite a bit of money to the agency. Partly because they do good work trying to place children in the right families, but also because I thought I might need them to do me a favor someday. So they obliged me. I was afraid that if you knew I was your father and gave you away, you wouldn't come here. And I wouldn't have blamed you."

I went to him then and leaned down to kiss his cheek. "I would have come. I'm a McKenzie. I can't help being curious."

James hugged me then, tight. When he released me he said to Sloan, "You take care of her."

"I will. And we'll talk more in the morning."

Once outside James's suite, Sloan picked me up and began to carry me down the hall. "Your place or mine?"

"Mine's closer," I said.

And it was.

Chapter 19

Sloan pocketed his cell phone. The state police so far had zip. None of the tire prints they'd taken from the two SUVs on the ranch or from Austin's matched the ones they'd found on the cliff. But they'd identified the caliber of the bullet, and they were checking licenses to see who on the ranch might own a gun that would use it. First thing in the morning, they hoped to have answers.

He strode into the bathroom where Brooke lay with her eyes closed in the hot tub. Only her head was visible beneath the sea of bubbles she'd created. Once he'd undressed her and inspected the bruises himself, he'd insisted that she take a long soak to ease the stiffness she was sure to feel in the morning. She was the one who'd insisted on adding bath salts, but he'd lit the candles.

Hannibal was patrolling the edges of the tub, taking an occasional swing at a bubble or two. Whatever his original differences with Brooke, right now it looked to Sloan as if the cat were on guard duty. He knew the feeling. Three times today he'd nearly lost her.

He shifted his gaze back to Brooke. She was here. She was safe. And he was going to keep her that way. The little line on her forehead told him that she wasn't sleeping. She was thinking, worrying. Odd. He'd only known her for what? Less than forty-eight hours, and he already knew that about her.

But then from the moment he'd nearly run her down on the bluff, he'd felt on some deep, instinctive level that he'd known her forever. James had mentioned the same feeling when he'd described how he'd fallen in love with Elizabeth—meeting that one woman you're destined to be with.

It had struck Sloan then that he'd fallen in love with Brooke Ashby. Like Elizabeth, he hadn't been looking for it, hadn't wanted it really. Wasn't that why he'd agreed to go along with the proposition that Cameron and James had presented to him in Kentucky? Marriage with Cameron would have been safe. No emotional risk, no fears of abandonment where she was concerned. She'd never leave him the way his parents had because he and Cameron had both loved the ranch.

Loving Brooke was a different matter. It made him vulnerable. He didn't know how she felt about him. Oh, she wanted him, but she had her life and career in L.A. And while the chemistry between them was strong, it didn't equal love. He'd decided that he didn't want to lose her, but what did she feel? The urge to go to her now, to drag her out of that nest of bubbles and ask her was almost overpowering.

But he couldn't. If nothing else those worry lines stopped him cold. James had given her a lot to think about tonight. She'd been kind to her father, kinder than he might have been. No, he couldn't add to her burden right now. He watched the little line on her forehead deepen. He could imagine what she was feeling. Abandonment. He'd experienced that at an early age. They came from different worlds, yet they had that in common.

And he knew what he could do to make her forget about that, at least for tonight. Moving to the edge of the tub, he sat down. "Stop thinking."

Brooke opened her eyes and met his. "That's difficult advice to follow. I keep going over everything in my mind. That's what I do sometimes when I'm working on a particularly tough plot twist. I'm trying to shift things around, juxtapose them so that I can dream up story lines from all angles."

He dipped a hand beneath the bubbles to test the temperature of the water. "What particular things are you looking at?"

"The timing, for one. I think I understand why the would-be killer chose that particular day to follow Cameron out to the cliff and push her off. The two of you had had a quarrel. If her body had been found, the police would have had two theories to pursue. Suicide or murder. She either followed in her mother's footsteps or you would have been the prime suspect."

His brows shot up.

"It's always the fiancé or the husband the police suspect first. And you did have opportunity. You were at the ranch the entire day. You would have made a great scapegoat."

Leaning over, he ran a finger along her jawline. "What other angles are you looking at?"

"Motives. In all good mysteries the why always leads to the who."

"In this case, we've narrowed the field to the people who were in the barn today and could have sliced your girth."

"True. Beatrice, Marcie and Austin have alibis for the day that Cameron disappeared. That leaves Hal and Doc Carter. Unless they had accomplices. Take Hal. If the why was to make Austin the heir, it wouldn't have worked if he didn't have an air-tight alibi. So Austin and Marcie go to Vegas and Hal slips away to push Cameron off the cliff."

Sloan turned the tap on.

"What are you doing that for?"

"The water is cooling. Go ahead and tell me what your plot line is for Beatrice and Doc Carter."

She sighed. "That one is a little less feasible, but I'm thinking it might work on *Secrets*—a torrid affair between Santa Claus and the Snow Queen."

"Come again?"

After explaining her initial impressions of Doc Carter and Beatrice, Brooke went on. "In this one, the why is the same—to get rid of Cameron and make Austin the heir. I imagine that Beatrice might share Cameron's frustration and resentment that the McKenzie men are such patriarchs. If Austin inherits, she has the satisfaction of knowing that the land passes on to her progeny rather than James's."

"The only problem is that Doc Carter was a very happily married man until a year ago, and I have trouble picturing him having a torrid affair with anyone."

"Well, there is that. Not all story lines are equally good. And there's always the possibility that the would-be killer's motives had nothing to do with who inherits the ranch. Maybe it was personal. Maybe someone just wanted Cameron dead."

"Take a break. Time enough to think about it in the morning." After turning off the water, he lifted the cat off the edge of the tub, carried him through the bedroom, and put him out the door. "The state police hope to have some answers by morning," he continued as he reentered the bathroom. Sloan filled her in on what he'd learned while he sat on the edge of the tub and pulled off his boots.

"There's another plot line that I'm fooling around with, but I haven't been able to come up with anything."

"What's that?"

"Don't laugh. I can't help feeling that there's some connection between the untimely deaths of the previous mistresses of the hacienda and the attacks on Cameron and me."

"Why would you think that?" Sloan asked as he stripped off his shirt.

"Because if I were plotting this as a story line there would have to be a connection. Plus, I don't think it's a coincidence that the mistresses of this house have all...I..."

It gave Sloan a great deal of satisfaction to note the way her sentence trailed off when he stepped out of his jeans.

"You're stripping."

"James is right. You *are* a bright gal." He kept

his eyes on hers as he hooked his thumbs in the elastic waistband of his briefs and eased them slowly down over his hips. When they dropped to the floor, he stepped out of them. Her eyes had lowered to his erection, and though he hadn't thought it possible, he grew even harder.

"I want you, Brooke."

Not raising her eyes, she lifted a hand out of the water and beckoned him to join her. "Come in. The water's fine."

He lowered himself into the frothy bubbles so that he was sitting opposite her, his legs tangled with hers. "Close quarters."

"Very observant."

Sloan scooped up bubbles and tossed them at her. She grinned as she brushed them off her cheek, and he had the satisfaction of seeing that worry line fade from her forehead.

"Would you like some soap?" Without waiting for his answer, she blew a wad of bubbles into his face.

In retaliation, he lifted one of her feet and began to massage the instep.

He heard her breath shudder out. "I'm thinking of a plot line myself." He continued to massage her foot. "But I'm not sure of the technical terms. This is what you might call an opening encounter." He slipped one finger in and out between each of her toes. "Right?"

"Right." Her voice had become breathy, the way it always did when she was aroused. And her eyes—those fascinating green eyes—had darkened.

Slowly, he ran his hand up her calf and traced a pattern on the back of her knee.

She trembled.

"A complication," he said and watched her tremble again. Leaning forward, his gaze never leaving her face, he danced his fingers up her inner thigh. "The tension builds." He could feel it building within himself.

"Sloan, I—" Her voice was a whisper.

"What comes next, Brooke? Tell me." But he didn't wait for her answer before he traced one finger down the slick softness of her fold. "This?"

"Mmmmm." She arched toward where his finger lingered at the entrance to her heat.

"And then?"

"Crisis," she murmured.

He pushed his finger into her, just a little.

"More," she whispered.

"Tell me what comes next?"

"Climax."

He pushed two fingers into her. She arched upward. "Yes."

Water sloshed over the edges of the tub and two candles sputtered as Sloan moved to cover her body with his. He urged her legs apart and entered her.

"We're going to drown," she said as she wrapped her arms around him.

"Practice holding your breath," he said and took her.

In the darkness of the gardens, a shadow paced—forward and back, forward and back. She should be dead. She should be dead. She should be dead.

The chant grew louder and louder as the pacing picked up speed. Three times she'd escaped. Three times. It couldn't be tolerated. It wouldn't be tolerated.

Fury boiled up with such force that it seemed to become a separate entity in the surrounding air. The shadow stopped pacing abruptly and turned to face the hacienda.

Breathe in. Breathe out. Control. It had to be regained. It was all-important. Nothing could be accomplished without it.

She should be dead. And she would be dead. Tomorrow. Moonlight fell in a silvery blanket over the sleeping ranch and the shadow's gaze swept the gardens, the land and the hills beyond, gathering in the strength that came from knowing this would never belong to Cameron McKenzie.

When the pacing began again it was slower, more purposeful. Gradually, a plan took root and began to grow.

Chapter 20

The sky was still the color of pewter when something—a ringing sound—pulled me out of sleep. I managed to get one of my eyes open and discovered I was lying with my head on Sloan's shoulder. He stirred, removing one of the arms he'd wrapped around me, and groped on the bedside table until he located his cell. The ringing stopped.

"Yeah." There was silence for a while. A phone call at this hour couldn't be good. I opened my other eye, but when I tried to pull away, Sloan's other arm, which was still around me, tightened.

"Thanks." He ended the call and turned to me. I didn't like the frown on his face. "That was the state police. They found a vehicle whose tires match the tracks at the cliff."

"Who does it belong to?"

"Doc Carter."

I stared at him trying to process the information. Doc Carter was the last person I would have suspected of shooting down Sloan's plane. I was about to say so when Sloan continued. "The caliber of the bullet they recovered from the plane matches the Winchester rifle they found in the trunk of his car."

"But why? You don't suppose my Snow Queen–Santa Claus theory is for real?"

"They've taken him in for questioning. As soon as they get some answers, we'll know."

"It doesn't make sense."

"He had the opportunity to cut the saddle girth," Sloan pointed out.

"And he didn't have a solid alibi for the day that Cameron disappeared," I recalled. "He thought maybe playing golf."

"The state police may be able to refresh his memory," Sloan said.

But it still didn't make sense to me. Why would Doc Carter want to kill Cameron?

Reading my mind again, Sloan drew me closer and kissed my forehead. "I can't think of a reason why he'd want to harm Cameron, either, but we should have some answers soon."

Sloan's phone rang again. "It's the stables," he said as he took the call.

I could tell from the expression on his face that the news wasn't good. It just never is when someone calls you in the middle of the night. I glanced out the balcony window to see pink streaks in the lightening sky. Or at the crack of dawn.

Sloan got out of bed and walked into the bathroom to gather up his clothes. "That was Gus. He was making his morning rounds and he says there's something wrong with Saturn. He can't wake him up."

I threw back the covers. "I'll come with you."

"No." He'd already dragged on jeans when he came back to the bed. "The threat to you may be over, but we're not taking any chances. You'll stay here. Give me your cell phone."

When he handed it to me, he picked up my cell and started pressing in numbers. "I'm going to put my cell number on speed dial. If you need me, if anything at all happens, just press one."

He passed me back the phone and then met my eyes directly. "You're not to leave this room. Give me your word."

"Okay."

By the time he'd finished dressing, I'd pulled on my own jeans and a T-shirt and fastened my cell to my belt. My masquerade was about to end, and when it did, I wanted to be in my own clothes.

I followed Sloan to the door. As he stepped outside, he said, "Lock it and don't leave here until I come back."

"I gave you my word."

He leaned down to kiss me once—hard. I closed the door, locked it and then went to the window. In less than a minute, I saw him going down the path to the stable at a run. If Doc Carter confessed, this might be the last time I stood here looking out at the ranch from Cameron's point of view.

But it wasn't going to be the last night I spent with Sloan. The one thing that we hadn't done during the night was talk about what was going to happen once we figured out who was trying to kill Cameron and she was able to return. Lots of things were still up in the air. But I was not going to let Sloan Campbell walk out of my life. Walking around in my sister's clothes and living her life for a few days had at least done that much for me. I was going to fight for what I wanted.

I frowned. Right now, I needed to think. I just wasn't convinced that Doc Carter was the villain of this particular scenario. Turning around, I began to pace the length of the room. I couldn't get it out of my mind that the attempts on Cameron's life and mine were somehow connected to the deaths or disappearances of the other mistresses of the Montega Hacienda. But if I couldn't come up with a reason for Doc Carter wanting Cameron dead, how was I going to come up with one for him wanting my mother dead?

Even if he had a partner, who would it be? What was the motive? With a sigh, I sank down on the foot of the bed. I wasn't accomplishing anything except making my headache come back. Maybe the problem was that I was a writer. If this were a story line on *Secrets*, of course I'd want to connect my sister's disappearance to the other mysteries of the hacienda. But real life was never as neat as fiction.

What I needed was coffee. I frowned, realizing that I wasn't going to get any until Sloan came back. It was then that I heard Hannibal's meow. I glanced around the room, then remembered that Sloan had put him out last night.

Hannibal meowed again in a very annoyed tone and I crossed to the door and opened it.

Hannibal was there all right. So was Beatrice and she had a gun in her hand.

"I'll shoot you," she said in a voice she might use to discuss the weather.

The look in her eyes told me that she would.

She gestured with the gun to the right. "Come."

With Hannibal walking beside me, I moved down the hall.

"Where are we going?" I asked. But I knew. My body knew, too. Fear was already a hard, icy ball in my stomach. I couldn't let it spread. I needed a clear head.

"If you're hoping to be rescued, you won't be," Beatrice continued in a mild tone. "The drug I gave Saturn will keep Sloan's mind occupied for a while. I doubt he'll give you even a thought until the vet arrives and figures out what's wrong."

She'd drugged the horse. I felt a flare of anger, welcomed it. Think, I told myself. You just need a plan. What would Mallory Carstairs do in a scene like this? What would Cameron do?

"Don't think of running," Beatrice said just as that scenario flashed into my mind.

So much for Plan A, and Plan B hadn't come to me by the time we reached the door to the bell tower. I walked on past, but Beatrice said, "Stop."

Behind me, I heard her unlock the door and push it open.

"After you."

Hannibal followed me into the tower. The moment I looked at the stairs spiraling upward, a wave of dizziness hit me. The cat had no such problem. He'd already disappeared around the first curve. Feeling nauseated, I slumped against the wall for support. When I felt my cell phone press into my hip, I remembered that Sloan had programmed his number into it.

"Take a deep breath," Beatrice said.

"Give me a minute." I didn't have to fake the

fear in my voice, and I prayed she wouldn't see my hand go to my cell. In my mind, I pictured the buttons and prayed again that I was pressing number one and then Send.

The gun poked into my spine.

"I really can't do this. You know what happened the last time we were in the tower."

"Yes. You nearly fell. I was so tempted to just give you that little push that you needed. But there would have been too many witnesses."

I sagged farther against the wall. "Beatrice, I can't."

"Yes, you can." Her voice was soft and soothing just as it had been the other time, and it made my skin crawl. She didn't take my hand this time. Instead, she pressed the gun harder against my spine. "A bullet will hurt. That's what I told your mother. If you hadn't come back, we could have avoided this. Now, you'll have to go up there just like Elizabeth did."

At the mention of Elizabeth's name, my mind cleared and become suddenly calm. But I kept my steps tentative and leaned heavily against the wall as I climbed. "You killed my mother, didn't you?"

"It was so easy," Beatrice said. "She was doing so well, and then her depression came back. The doctors couldn't explain it. But I could. I'd replaced her medication with simple vitamins, and no one suspected a thing. When they tried a new drug, I just replaced that one, too. No one was the wiser. Men are such fools. Everyone accepted the fact that she climbed up here one night and followed in the footsteps of the first mistress of the hacienda."

"What actually happened?" I asked.

"She was having trouble sleeping and she would go down to the kitchen to warm milk for herself. One night I joined her and slipped a drug into the drink. Then all I had to do was to help her up the stairs just as I'm helping you."

We'd rounded the first curve of the stairs, and I could see the opening to the bell tower above me. Another wave of dizziness struck and I shoved it down. I wasn't going to think about how my mother had fallen out of the tower. Instead, I was going to keep Beatrice talking so that Sloan would know where we were.

Saturn lay on his side, his eyes open but glazed. Sloan dropped to his knees next to Gus and ran a hand down the horse's neck.

"He looks drugged."

"That would be my guess. Vet should be here at any minute. Called him before I called you."

"Good," Sloan said as he continued to frown at the horse. "Good."

For a moment they sat in silence, both trying to comfort Saturn as best they could.

"Who?" Sloan asked the question out loud, but

Gus didn't answer. He didn't have an answer himself. But he was going to find out.

When his cell rang, he lifted it automatically and put it to his ear. "Yeah?"

The voice that he heard coming through the line turned his blood to ice.

"…know what happened the last time we were in the tower."

"Yes. You nearly fell. I was so tempted to just give you that little push that you needed. But there would have been too many witnesses."

Sloan was already out of the stall and running when he yelled back to Gus. "Beatrice has got Brooke. She's going to push her out of the tower."

I drew in a deep breath as I stepped into the small space of the tower. Now that we were here, I was trapped. Any step I took brought me to the edge of the low wall. I pushed the thought out of my mind, and gazed at the landscapes my mother had painted. In the east, the sun had risen halfway on the horizon. I recalled the painting in the dining room of just this scene.

"It won't be long now." Beatrice's voice held a note of promise.

Even as a chill moved up my spine, I turned to the left and looked at the stables and the flat range beyond—another scene my mother had painted. I recalled seeing it in the main parlor.

I was not going to follow in the footsteps of the mistresses of the hacienda, I promised myself as I turned to face her. "How did you get away from the flower show on the day I disappeared?"

"I drove there early and made sure that I was seen setting up my display. Then I told the women in the booths next to mine that I had to slip away for a bit to practice my luncheon speech. It didn't take long to drive out to the cliffs, and you were there waiting for me."

"What about yesterday?"

"I went out the back of the greenhouse, walked over to Doc Carter's and borrowed his car and his rifle. He's a creature of habit just as I am, and he spends all his mornings practicing his tee shots on that green he's had landscaped into his backyard. Just as he did on the day you disappeared. I borrowed his car that day, too." She gestured with the gun. "It's time now, Cameron. Turn around."

I held up a hand. "One more question." Out of the corner of my eye, I could see Hannibal walking back and forth like a sentinel on the wall. "What happened to James's first wife?" The merest hint of surprise moved into those cold eyes.

"You know about her?" Beatrice asked.

"You killed her, too, didn't you?"

"She was weak and not worthy of being a mistress here. None of them were. Only the strong survive," Beatrice said. "Sarah was unhappy, restless, and she used to get up in the middle of the night and take walks in the gardens. So predictable. I met her there one night, offered her some sleeping pills, and then all I had to do was wait until she was drowsy. Then I was going to bring her here. She should have died here."

For the first time I heard rage in her voice, and I saw her knuckles whiten on the hand that held the gun. My throat went dry. "Where did she die?"

"In the garden. Sloan's father came along. He saw me, saw the gun. I had to shoot him. Then I shot her and buried them both near the green-house."

"And you let everyone believe that they'd run away together?"

"I made them believe it. I packed some clothes for each of them. Then I wrote the note. I'd prac-ticed her handwriting for months. Of course, it was supposed to be for a suicide note. No matter. It was so easy to kill them both. It always is."

Easy to kill people? The horror of what she was saying washed over me, but I couldn't let it affect me. Not yet. Out of the corner of my eye, I saw Sloan running up the path toward the hacienda. I had to keep her talking and focused on me. "Why, Beatrice? Why did you kill them?"

The look she gave me held the first hint of madness that I'd seen—and the second hint of rage that I'd glimpsed beneath that cold facade.

"Because I'm the mistress here. This place should have been at least half mine. James inherited only because he was a man. Our father never believed that a woman could run the place. But I can. I have. I will always be the mistress here."

"So that's why you pushed me off the cliff that day."

She blinked. "Yes." I heard true emotion in her voice. "History was repeating itself, but in reverse. James should have left half the estate to Austin. I bore my son for that very purpose, knowing that one day he would inherit and I would have what was mine. Then James decided to leave the place to you and to Sloan Campbell—a man who isn't even a McKenzie."

In a way, in spite of what she'd done, I could sympathize with the injustice that had been done to her.

Beatrice drew in a deep breath. "But you came back. You shouldn't have come back. I warned you in that phone call." She took a step toward me. "You should have taken my warning and gone away."

She was close now, so close that I could reach out and touch the gun. Her eyes were calm again, and very cold. The ice queen.

"You can go by yourself or I can shoot you," she said in that soothing voice.

* * *

Sloan was praying as he took the stairs two at a time, then raced down the corridor to the open door of the bell tower. He stopped then. He'd seen the two of them just before he'd reached the house. The image would be forever burned on his brain—Brooke standing with her back to the low wall, and Beatrice with a gun in her hand.

The sick ball of fear had settled in his stomach then. He wasn't going to reach them in time. And even if he did storm up those stairs, Beatrice would hear him coming. All she had to do was squeeze the trigger.

He took a step forward and saw the rope to the bell. Taking it into his hands, he prayed that it would work.

"I'll jump by myself." I'd said the words, but I couldn't seem to move. In a minute, she was going to pull that trigger. It was all I could think of, and yet I couldn't unfreeze.

The bell clanged—so loud that I could feel the vibrations on my skin. The noise shocked me out of my paralysis. Beatrice started, too. I prayed that my reflexes were faster as I dived at her, grabbing her gun hand with both of mine and shoving hard.

The gun went flying out of the tower. We both lost our footing and fell on the wall. For a moment we lay balanced precariously on it—teetering—I with the stones pressing into my back and Beatrice on top of me. I was sure that we were both going to go over.

Then she pulled herself off me and backed up several steps until she was against the opposite wall. I was still struggling for balance when she started toward me again. Then Hannibal leaped. He hit Beatrice midchest, and I heard her scream as she stumbled backward, hit the wall and toppled over.

Digging my fingers into the edge of the wall, I managed to get my balance. Then I had to sit down. Sloan found me on the floor of the bell tower with Hannibal on my lap when he burst through the door. He didn't say a word. He just pulled Hannibal and me onto his lap.

We sat there for a long time.

Chapter 21

When the state trooper, Lieutenant Brady, finally closed his notebook, Sloan rose. It was nearly noon, and he hadn't had a break since the police had arrived on the scene and set up shop in the main parlor. He glanced down the length of the room to where Brooke was still being questioned by a female trooper. He'd been the one who'd insisted that the police use the parlor because he hadn't wanted to let Brooke out of his sight. Evidently Hannibal felt the same way because the cat hadn't left her side since they'd come down from the bell tower.

It would be a long time before he could get the

image out of his mind of Beatrice holding that gun on her and knowing that he wasn't going to make it in time. And he didn't think he'd ever be rid of the sound of Beatrice screaming as she fell. He hadn't reached the tower yet, and for those last few endless steps, he'd thought it had been Brooke who'd fallen. Even when he'd seen her sitting there with the cat, he hadn't believed it. He'd had to touch her, hold her. And then he'd listened as she'd poured out everything Beatrice told her. When he'd learned that his father hadn't abandoned him, Sloan couldn't sort through the flood of feelings that moved through him. He'd simply held on to Brooke. It hadn't been until the troopers had finally climbed the stairs that either one of them had moved.

Since then, he hadn't had a chance to talk with her or with James for that matter. They'd all been caught up in a seemingly endless round of interrogations. As far as he knew, Austin and the Lintons were still being questioned in the kitchen wing. And he'd been told that the troopers had talked to James in his suite.

"How long before you'll be through with Ms. Ashby?" Sloan asked.

"Hard to say. We're taking her over her statement on what exactly happened in the tower in those last few minutes."

"She's told you what happened." Impatience

swirled through him. And anger. Ever since the fear and the shock and the relief had faded, a fury had been building inside of him.

"There are things that Beatrice Caulfield told her that we have to follow up on." Brady spoke in a mild tone. "We'd like to make sure Ms. Caulfield didn't have an accomplice."

Sloan frowned. "You think her son may have been in on it with her? Or Doc Carter?"

"Not necessarily. We're just trying to eliminate those possibilities." Brady's tone was mild. "There were a lot of people who might have wanted to eliminate Cameron McKenzie. It's unfortunate that no one chose to report the attack on her five weeks ago."

"Yes, it is, isn't it?" Sloan murmured.

Brady glanced at his watch. "We may be able to wrap it up in another half hour or so."

Satisfied that Brooke would be busy for a while yet, Sloan said, "I'll be back." Then he left the room and strode down the corridor to James's suite. He wanted to check on the old man, and there were things he needed to say to him.

Sloan entered the room without knocking. James was sitting in his massive chair. Only this time he wasn't behind his desk. The old man had moved the chair and angled it so that he was staring out at his domain—the stables and the land beyond.

James turned. "How is she?"

Sloan strode forward. "She's fine—or at least she will be. But it's no thanks to you. You sat there on that throne of yours, pulling strings the way you always do. Hiding Cameron away and luring into your game a daughter you'd never met. You damn near got her killed."

"Yes. Yes, I did."

Damn him. The old man's simple admission had more of his anger fading, but Sloan wasn't finished. "Why? Why couldn't you have just told the police when Cameron was attacked? Why this elaborate charade?"

James leaned forward then. "Do you think the police would have found the truth? Do you think they could have kept Cameron safe from another attack?"

Knowing what they knew now about Beatrice, Sloan had to admit he had a point.

Shaking his head, James sighed. "I decided to bring Brooke here because I thought her appearance on the scene would stir things up and bring everything to a head. I never expected that she would come here impersonating Cameron. And I never dreamed that Beatrice would... My God, I never suspected that my sister was capable of..." James raised a hand and dropped it. "She murdered three times. She murdered my wife, Sarah, and your father—a man who was my best friend. Then she murdered Elizabeth. And for what?"

Sloan narrowed his eyes. His anger still hadn't run its course, but the look in James's eyes, a mixture of shock and sorrow, had him banking it. He put out his hand and gripped James's arm. "From what Brooke has told me, she murdered three times because she felt she had a right to inherit at least half of this estate, and the only reason why she wasn't allowed to was because she wasn't a man. You might want to give that some thought before you perpetuate the problem."

James's chin lifted. "What are you saying?"

"You know exactly what I'm saying. You manipulated Cameron into marrying me in order to get half her inheritance. I don't imagine she's any happier with that than Beatrice was when she didn't inherit anything."

James rose from his chair. "If you're saying that Cameron, that a daughter of mine would turn into a crazed killer…"

Sloan's brows rose. "Don't you dare twist my words, old man. I'm not saying that at all. I'm merely saying that you'd better think long and hard about what you're doing with your kingdom. And remember, you've got a second daughter who isn't nearly as predictable as Cameron."

"True."

To Sloan's astonishment, James smiled, then

broke into a loud bellowing laugh that filled the room. He stared as James lowered himself back into his chair. When he finally stopped laughing, James said, "Cameron said much the same thing to me on the phone a few moments ago." He dug a slip of paper out of his pocket and handed it to Sloan. "She wants to talk to you."

Sloan glanced down at the paper and then back at James. "I'm not going to marry her."

Something came into James's eyes then, something Sloan couldn't quite read.

"I figured that."

A suspicion formed in the back of Sloan's mind but before he could give voice to it, James said, "Go ahead and call Cameron. If it makes you feel any better, she's already told me she's not marrying you, either. And she's in perfect agreement with you on how much blame I should be shouldering for all of this."

Reaching for his cell phone, Sloan moved through one of the open doors to the patio outside of James's suite, then punched in the number.

When she picked up the call, Cameron said, "I hear you've had a rough time."

"Rough time?" Sloan repeated. He hadn't quite put together in his mind what he wanted to say to Cameron. "I guess you could say so."

She laughed softly. "You're pissed at Dad and me both, aren't you?"

He nearly smiled then, and was surprised that he could. But then Cameron had always understood him so well. Just as he had always understood her. "To borrow a phrase from James, you're a smart gal. It was a near thing." He paused to push the memory out of his mind. "We nearly lost your sister."

"Yeah. I got that much from Dad. Believe me, we had no idea that Beatrice was the one who pushed me. My prime suspect was Austin, but I didn't think he had the guts to do it himself."

"The police are still checking to make sure he wasn't involved in some way, but I think they'll find that Beatrice was acting alone, albeit perhaps in some measure on his behalf."

"What's my sister like?"

"Like?" Sloan let his gaze move out past the gardens to the stables and the hills beyond. A series of scenes moved through his mind—nearly running her down on the bluff, kissing her in the garden, watching her stand up to James at that dinner party, finding her poking around in his refrigerator, seeing her face down Beatrice in the tower. He wondered when it was that he'd first started falling in love with her.

"Earth to Sloan," Cameron prompted.

Sloan tried to clear his mind. "Your sister, Brooke, is curious and stubborn and courageous and…amazing. And I'm in love with her, Cam."

When Cameron spoke, he could hear the smile in her voice. "I take it our engagement's off."

He smiled then. "Yeah. I'd say so. It'll piss the old man off."

"Not at all. Haven't you figured it out yet? Part of the reason he contacted Brooke was he thought the two of you might make a better match than you and I. I told him the night I left for L.A. that I was having second thoughts about marrying you. I told him that both of us deserved the chance to find what he'd found with Elizabeth."

Sloan turned and saw that James was watching him. He should have guessed it sooner. "That sly old fox."

"Oh, he's that all right, and we just continue to play into his hands. But in this case, I think he's done us both a favor. After watching my sister's soap for five weeks, I think she just might be perfect for you. You'll never be able to predict what she'll do next."

"Well, there's that." Then his expression sobered. "But that night when you left, you weren't going to go along with the old man's plans, were you? I've had some time to think about it. You were really going to call off the wedding."

Cameron laughed. "We'll never know that for sure, will we? Why don't we just say that I'm happy to have a twin who can take my place. She is going to take my place, right?"

"I haven't gotten her input on that yet."

"Want some advice from a kid sister?"

"Yeah." It was his turn to laugh now, and he felt his tension and anger melt away. "Yeah, that would be good."

When Sloan and Saturn found me, I was sitting on the bluff very close to the spot where I'd first met Sloan. He didn't say a word as he dismounted. After he'd secured the horse, he sat down next to me and merely put his arm around me. Almost at once, the thoughts that had been swirling around in my head settled, and I felt suddenly and completely at home.

"I know you needed some time to think," Sloan said. "But I couldn't give you any more."

"It's all so sad. I'm a writer. I should at least in my imagination be able to understand Beatrice's motivations, but I'm having trouble getting my mind around what she did, what she lived with all of these years."

"She did it for what we're looking at right now. But she can't have been completely sane to have murdered all of them. My father, both of James's wives." His arm tightened around me. "Then to have almost murdered you and Cameron…"

He turned to me then and tipped my face up so that I met his eyes. "I had a talk with Cameron."

My stomach knotted. I didn't want to ask the

question, but I had to know the answer. "Did you work everything out?"

"Yeah. You might say that. When do you have to go back to L.A.?"

My heart sank. Did he think that I was just going to leave, that everything that had happened between us was… Another thought occurred to me. Were he and Cameron going to go ahead with their wedding? Had he come up here to say goodbye? "I—" There was a lump in my throat I couldn't seem to get any more words around.

"I want to go with you."

I blinked and stared at him. "You want to go with me?"

"Yeah. To L.A. I've got this little plot—you'd probably call it a story line—and I thought that you might help me flesh it out and then see if it would fly on *Secrets?*"

I studied him, trying to read something in those dark gray eyes. "You have a story line for *Secrets?*"

"Yeah." Sloan tucked a piece of hair behind my ear. "It's about these twins who were separated at birth, and one of them was given up for adoption. Years later, the twin who wasn't given up for adoption disappears just before her wedding, and the other one, just learning of her sister's existence, decides to take her place."

His hand had moved to the back of my neck and

those fingers began to work their magic on me. The chill I'd experienced when he'd told me he'd worked things out with Cameron was fading as the heat spread from his touch all the way through me.

"Then there's what you call a complication." He brushed his mouth against mine, and even as he drew back, my lips parted in response.

"A complication?"

"Umm, hmm," he murmured as he leaned down to kiss me lightly again. "She finds that she's very attracted to her twin sister's fiancé."

He was trailing kisses along the side of my jaw. When he reached my ear, he said, "And another complication is that he's incredibly attracted to her. He can't be near her and not want his hands on her. Not want to be inside of her. And that's not all…."

His teeth nipped my earlobe, but then he drew away again. "The final complication is…I love you, Brooke Ashby. I'm not going to marry Cameron. She doesn't want to marry me, either."

For a moment, I didn't know what to say. My blood was pounding and there was a ringing in my ears. This was exactly the way I would have written it—if I were writing it. But this was actually happening to me—Ms. Nothing-ever-happens-to-me Brooke Ashby. Then I saw something come into his eyes. Was it fear?

"You're going to have to say something, Red."

"It's a great story line. But there are so many possible complications. There's the land and James…my father."

"Forget him. He's probably hatching some new plot even as we speak. You come by your talents naturally."

"There's my job in L.A."

"It's not a long commute."

"But—if the wedding's off—I mean—won't my father change the will? Won't you have to make new plans?"

Now it was impatience that flashed in his eyes. "I told you my plans. I'm coming to L.A. for a while. I want us to have some time together away from here. Away from all that's happened here. Gus can run things for a bit. And after James decides what to do with the ranch, we'll come up with a new plan." He tightened his hand at the back of my neck. "Haven't you ever worked with another writer?"

"Collaborated, you mean?"

"Yeah. We can collaborate. There's only one thing you have to say if you want our story line to continue. Don't make me wait any longer to hear it."

Suddenly, I couldn't wait to hear it, either. "I love you, Sloan Campbell."

When his mouth took mine, suddenly all the

complications melted away. I knew that we could work everything out. And we would work everything out—together.

Epilogue

I sat on the bed with Hannibal and watched my sister step out of her shoes and then move quickly to the sitting area of her bedroom. My sister. It had been nearly a week since she'd returned to the ranch from Los Angeles, and I was still getting to know her. Still getting used to the idea that she was my sister and that looking at her was like looking into a mirror.

Not that we'd had much chance to really talk to each other yet. The past few days had been hectic. First there'd been more visits from the police, then Beatrice's funeral and finally, my parents had surprised me by flying in from Chicago to assure themselves that I was safe and to meet James. As a result, Cameron and I hadn't been able to spend much time together. Tomorrow we had a date to go riding. Sloan had offered to let me take Saturn, and Cameron would ride Lace Ribbons.

But first we had to get through tonight. An hour ago, right after we'd had dinner, my father—I was still getting used to calling James that—had announced that he'd signed a new will that afternoon, and then he'd revealed the contents. My stomach was still churning, and I was sure that Cameron's was, too. She couldn't be happy with what her father had done.

I'd objected, but neither Sloan nor Cameron had backed me up. However, as soon as James had retired for the night, she'd asked me to come to her room for a sister-to-sister chat.

Cameron flipped on some music, and the soft strains of a Chopin étude filled the room. Then she squatted down, opened the small cabinet next to the sofa and grabbed the bag of cat tidbits. The casual way she tossed a handful of them in Hannibal's direction told me that this was part of their nightly routine. When she reached into the cabinet again, I expected her to bring out chocolate, but instead, she withdrew a crystal decanter and two glasses. "I need some brandy," she announced. "How about you?"

"That would be great." Brandy might be just

the ticket to settle the nerves that were dancing in my stomach. As she poured us generous amounts, I moved to join her in the small alcove, then took the glass she handed me. We both took a sip before Cameron settled herself in one corner of the sofa, tucked her feet under her and pointed at the other corner.

"Sit," she said. "I told Sloan I wasn't going to send you off to the carriage house until we'd hashed out this business of the will."

I found myself wanting to smile as I sat down. In the short time that I'd known Cameron, I was learning that she had a habit of ordering people around.

"You're upset with Dad because he's leaving a third of the ranch to you."

She also had a remarkable knack for cutting right to the chase. "Aren't you?" I asked. "And Sloan must be, too. I mean, he came back here to marry you and he was counting on inheriting half. Now he only gets a third. And you—" I gestured with the brandy snifter "—you were supposed to inherit half, too. It's not fair."

"Okay, let's talk about fair. In order to get half of the ranch, Sloan and I had to agree to marry and eventually produce a McKenzie heir. Don't get me wrong. I like Sloan, and there's no one I would trust more with half of this ranch, but we were never in love. If we'd gone through with the wedding, we would have had to give up what you and Sloan have found together. Would you want us to have missed out on that?"

"No. Of course not. But what about Austin? He's lost so much. Is it fair that he doesn't inherit anything?"

Cameron's eyes hardened a bit, and I could see James in her. "Austin has to get himself straightened out first. Marcie's been a good influence on him, but he was at the gambling tables in Vegas on the very day that I disappeared. We'll assure him that he has a job here and a chance to prove himself. Don't you think that's fair enough?"

I nodded. I'd had a chance to talk with both Austin and Marcie at Beatrice's funeral, and I believed that with Marcie's help, Austin had a good chance of really turning his life around. "But I still don't think the will is fair to you and Sloan."

"Would you feel better about the will if you'd been raised here?" She made a sweeping gesture with her free hand. "If all this had been a part of your life?"

I frowned as I thought about it. "I suppose."

"Then is it fair that by a twist of fate I grew up here and you were put up for adoption?"

I stared at her. "Okay, maybe you have a point there, but the fact remains that I wasn't raised here. I don't know anything about breeding or training horses or running a ranch."

"So what? Sloan tells me that you love horses, that you've always dreamed of owning one of your own. And from what I learned watching that soap you write for, you have a quick mind and a fertile imagination. I don't think it will take you long to get up to speed."

I was learning that my sister had a quick mind, too. Not to mention the fact that she would have given Pepper and me a run for our money on the debate team. I took another sip of brandy. "You've been watching *Secrets?*"

She grinned at me. "Every day for the past five weeks—ever since Dad told me about you. I insisted that we couldn't contact you personally. It had to be your decision to come to the ranch. Once he sent the anonymous letter, I made him swear that he wouldn't interfere any more than that."

I studied her. "Why not?"

For the first time, I saw temper flash into her eyes. "Because of what he did to you—putting you up for adoption. It sucks. I think he ought to be horsewhipped."

For the first time since James had revealed the contents of his will—no, for the first time since I'd learned that I had a twin sister, I felt all of my tension ease.

Cameron set her glass down, rose and began to pace back and forth in front of the sofa. "Don't get me wrong. I love Dad, but I can't understand how he could have done that. He gave you up for adoption! He kept us apart all of these years. I simply can't fathom it." She turned to me. "Leaving you a third of the ranch is the least he can do. Sloan and I told him that. We told him that if he didn't leave part of the ranch to you, he'd never see either of us again."

Shock streamed through me. I could see the truth of what she was saying in her eyes, hear it in her voice, and I couldn't even begin to name the emotions swirling through me. Words didn't have a chance of getting past the lump in my throat. Rising, I went to her, put my arms around her and held on tight. After a long moment, I pulled back. "I don't know what to say."

She took my hands and squeezed them. "Tell me that you'll stay here, be my sister and help Sloan and me run this ranch."

Suddenly, it was so simple. "Okay. Okay, I'll do that."

"Fine." Cameron swiped the heels of her hands over the dampness on her cheeks. "Now, I have two more questions."

My brows shot up. "Only two?"

She laughed as we retrieved our brandies. "Two for starters."

"Hey, Red!" We both moved toward the balcony at the sound of Sloan's voice. He was standing below us in the garden, his hands on his hips and a wide smile on his face. I was almost getting used to my heart turning over when I looked at him. Almost.

"You can't have her back yet," Cameron said.

He frowned up at Cameron. "You haven't convinced her to accept the will yet?"

She laughed. "Oh, ye of little faith. Of course, I did. And I didn't even have to pull out my best argument."

"What was it?" I asked curiously.

She made a sweeping gesture with her hand. "The fact that what this hacienda has needed all along is two mistresses. Starting with us, they're all going to lead long, happy lives."

Sloan shifted his gaze to me. "You okay?"

"Yes. I'm fine." And I knew that I was, that somehow everything was finally as it should be.

"Then why don't you stay there with your sister? Get to know one another a little better. I'll see you in the morning."

"I'd like that," I said. But I had second thoughts as soon as he turned and walked toward the carriage house.

"You can always sneak away before morning and surprise him," Cameron said, reading my mind. When he was out of sight, she drew me back into the room. "Now for my first question—what is going to happen to Mallory Carstairs when she comes out of that coma?"

I grinned at her. "She'll be suffering from temporary amnesia, and then, of course, she's going to find out that she has an identical twin sister that she was separated from at birth."

Hannibal glared at us both as we collapsed on the sofa in laughter.

* * * * *

♪ Harlequin®

A *Romance* FOR EVERY MOOD™

Discover more great romances from Harlequin® Books.

Whether you prefer romantic suspense, heartwarming or passionate novels, each and every month Harlequin has new books for you!

Use the coupon below and save $1.00 when you purchase 2 or more Harlequin® Books.

Available wherever books are sold, including most bookstores, supermarkets, drugstores and discount stores.

---✂-

$1.00 OFF the purchase of 2 or more Harlequin® series-romance books.

Coupon valid until October 24, 2011. Redeemable at participating retail outlets in the U.S. and Canada only. Limit one coupon per customer.

52610019

5 65373 00076 2   (8100)0 11763

Canadian Retailers: Harlequin Enterprises Limited will pay the face value of this coupon plus 10.25¢ if submitted by customer for this product only. Any other use constitutes fraud. Coupon is nonassignable. Void if taxed, prohibited or restricted by law. Consumer must pay any government taxes. Void if copied. Nielsen Clearing House ("NCH") customers submit coupons and proof of sales to Harlequin Enterprises Limited, P.O. Box 3000, Saint John, NB E2L 4L3, Canada. Non-NCH retailer—for reimbursement submit coupons and proof of sales directly to Harlequin Enterprises Limited, Retail Marketing Department, 225 Duncan Mill Rd., Don Mills, ON M3B 3K9, Canada.

U.S. Retailers: Harlequin Enterprises Limited will pay the face value of this coupon plus 8¢ if submitted by customer for this product only. Any other use constitutes fraud. Coupon is nonassignable. Void if taxed, prohibited or restricted by law. Consumer must pay any government taxes. Void if copied. For reimbursement submit coupons and proof of sales directly to Harlequin Enterprises Limited, P.O. Box 880478, El Paso, TX 88588-0478, U.S.A. Cash value 1/100 cents.

NYTCOUPJJ0811

New York Times and *USA TODAY* bestselling author

DIANA PALMER

The minute wild rancher Gene Nelson saw
Allison Hathoway, he wanted her. The passion between
them was explosive, but would it last? And could it be
a chance for these two wounded hearts to heal?

NELSON'S BRAND

Available in August wherever books are sold.

PLUS, ENJOY THE BONUS STORY
***LONETREE RANCHERS: COLT* BY BESTSELLING AUTHOR
KATHIE DENOSKY, INCLUDED IN THIS 2-IN-1 VOLUME!**

REQUEST YOUR FREE BOOKS!

2 FREE NOVELS
FROM THE ROMANCE COLLECTION
PLUS 2 FREE GIFTS!

YES! Please send me 2 FREE novels from the Romance Collection and my 2 FREE gifts (gifts are worth about $10). After receiving them, if I don't wish to receive any more books, I can return the shipping statement marked "cancel." If I don't cancel, I will receive 4 brand-new novels every month and be billed just $5.99 per book in the U.S. or $6.49 per book in Canada. That's a saving of at least 25% off the cover price. It's quite a bargain! Shipping and handling is just 50¢ per book in the U.S. and 75¢ per book in Canada.* I understand that accepting the 2 free books and gifts places me under no obligation to buy anything. I can always return a shipment and cancel at any time. Even if I never buy another book, the two free books and gifts are mine to keep forever.

194/394 MDN FELQ

Name	(PLEASE PRINT)	

Address	Apt. #

City	State/Prov.	Zip/Postal Code

Signature (if under 18, a parent or guardian must sign)

Mail to the **Reader Service:**
IN U.S.A.: P.O. Box 1867, Buffalo, NY 14240-1867
IN CANADA: P.O. Box 609, Fort Erie, Ontario L2A 5X3

Not valid for current subscribers to the Romance Collection
or the Romance/Suspense Collection.

Want to try two free books from another line?
Call 1-800-873-8635 or visit www.ReaderService.com.

* Terms and prices subject to change without notice. Prices do not include applicable taxes. Sales tax applicable in N.Y. Canadian residents will be charged applicable taxes. Offer not valid in Quebec. This offer is limited to one order per household. All orders subject to credit approval. Credit or debit balances in a customer's account(s) may be offset by any other outstanding balance owed by or to the customer. Please allow 4 to 6 weeks for delivery. Offer available while quantities last.

Your Privacy—The Reader Service is committed to protecting your privacy. Our Privacy Policy is available online at www.ReaderService.com or upon request from the Reader Service.

We make a portion of our mailing list available to reputable third parties that offer products we believe may interest you. If you prefer that we not exchange your name with third parties, or if you wish to clarify or modify your communication preferences, please visit us at www.ReaderService.com/consumerschoice or write to us at Reader Service Preference Service, P.O. Box 9062, Buffalo, NY 14269. Include your complete name and address.

ROM11

Harlequin®

A *Romance* FOR EVERY MOOD™

___

Experience the variety
of romances that
Harlequin has to offer...

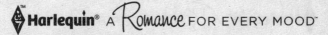